P9-BJD-889

A Map of
The Country of Lord Selkirk's Settlers
A Detailed Sketch of Colony shown below

Plan of
Red River
Colony

Kildonan
and Frog Plain
Route from
Winnipeg
Plain Ranges
Seven
Oaks
Church
School
Colony
Gardens
Fort
Douglas
Route of Grant's horsemen
Fort Gibraltar
De Meuron
Soldier
Settle-
ment
Assiniboine River
Red River

Digges Is.
Cape
Hope's Advance
LABRADOR
H
SON
BAY
BAY
JAMES
BAY
River
Fort
Albany
Moose
Factory
Rupert House
Lke Mistassini
Lake
Manooan
R. Mistassini
R. Peribonca
Lake
St John
Saguenay River
Gaspe

<< Route of Colonists from Scotland
to the Forks.
•••• Route followed by the Northwesters
from the Forks with Prisoners.
•–•– Usual Route of Brigades between
Fort William and Montreal

Lake
Nipissing
Ottawa River
Montreal
Saint Lawrence River
Quebec
e Huron

Sam'l H. Bryant

The Strange Brigade

The STRANGE BRIGADE

A Story of the Red River and the Opening of the Canadian West

by

JOHN JENNINGS

Little, Brown and Company · Boston

PRINTED IN THE UNITED STATES OF AMERICA

Foreword

IN THE FAT YEARS, WHEN THE BEAVER WERE YET PLENTIFUL IN THE northern forests, and the buffalo darkened the prairie like flies swarming on a carcass, the great fur brigades went out each spring. Those from Hudson's Bay came south, from Moose and York Factory and Fort Churchill, from Rupert's and Albany House. Those of the Northwesters and the Independent Traders flocked out from Montreal, through Michilimackinac and Grand Portage, Fort William and le Sault.

They came each year into the Pays Sauvages—the Savage Land— the great, wide wilderness of mighty mountains on the west and frozen muskeg in the north, with all uncounted lakes and streams and rivers and unbounded miles of silent forest and rolling prairie in between. North and west of Lake Superior lay the Pays d'en Haut. This was the great preserve of the fur trader, the trapper and the *voyageur;* the hunting-ground of the *Boisbrûlé*—half-civilized, half-savage who, on the prairies of Winnipeg, slaughtered the vast herds of buffalo for their meat. From the meat they made pemmican, the staple article of diet—the staff of life, it might be called—of the fur trade, for without it the winterers in the wide wilderness would starve. This pemmican the *Boisbrûlés* sold to the traders and the trappers; to the English of Hudson's Bay and to the Canadians of the North West Company alike, and so they too were dependent upon the trade.

It was not in the interest of such as these that civilization should come into the land. The man with the plough notoriously drove away the beaver and the buffalo and brought restraint to the traders' ways of dealing with the Indians. But there were rivalries among them, and it was inevitable that other farmers should come. They came not long after the beginning of the nineteenth century, when there set out from the sorrowing hills of Scotland a little band of hopeful pilgrims, bound for a bright, new, fabled Eden at the Forks of the Red River, in the heart of Assiniboia, a new—a strange brigade. . . .

—JOHN JENNINGS

Contents

PART I

The Exiles

❁❁❁

From the lone shieling in the misty island
Mountains divide us and the waste of seas;
Yet still the blood is strong,
                              The heart is Highland,
And we in dreams behold the Hebrides.
Fair these broad meads—
                    These hoary woods are grand,
But we are exiles from our Father's land.
—CANADIAN BOAT SONG, ATTRIBUTED TO JOHN GALT
                    Blackwood's Magazine, 1829

1. THE LONE SHIELING

THERE IS A SHORT CUT, UP OVER THE MOORS, FROM BERRIEDALE water to Kildonan, in Strathullie, and if a man must make the journey afoot he will do well to choose that road, for it will save him many a weary mile.

The path, for it is little more, swings under the peak of Morven and then traces a fingering way around Maiden's Pap. From there it skirts the head of Loch Scalobsdale to the burn at the far side, climbs quickly over the low divide, and then plunges down in a tortuous zigzag course into Kildonan Glen. I think it is true enough for me to say it here: If I had not chosen to go that way when I went up out of Caithness into Sutherlandshire, that weepy-wet day in April 1813, I would not be here now, telling this.

Kildonan Glen, for more than half its length, is a narrow, gloomy place, all cluttered up and down with great boulders, loose rocks and twisted, tortured looking birks and tangled heather. Kildonan Burn chuckles and shouts and leaps along close beside the path, which swings back and forth across it a dozen times or more before the valley widens; and all along its length the wind blows incessantly and the rain drives before it like the thin edge of an invisible knife. In such circumstances I think it is hardly surprising that I hurried down it with my head bent against the wind so that I could scarcely see where I was going, or that my pace quickened and my anticipation of a warming dram grew as I approached the end of the steep defile and began to draw near to Jamie Gordon's little holding.

That was hardly a place where one would expect a man in his right mind to set his hand to farming, for the Gordon croft backed up hard against the last rocky pitch of the wild gully, and it was only on the downward side that the little valley broadened and began to grow green. Indeed the pathway from over the hills and the little, brawling burn came bursting out together, like children getting out of school, around the last sharp snout of gray, outcropping rock, and then turned all at once almost guiltily sedate, as if suddenly ashamed of their recent romping, and passed quietly within an easy pebble's toss of the neat-thatched, spotlessly whitewashed little cottage and its twin byre just beyond. But it was clear from the neatness of the yard and from the lush green of the oat and barley fields below, from the fat sheep in his high pasture and the sleek cattle in his byre, and from the raft of chubby-cheeked weans in his crowded loft, that Jamie Gordon was not merely a man of sense and sobriety but one of industry and thrift as well.

I knew Jamie, of course, reasonably well, as I believe I knew nearly every tenant and crofter in those northern counties—in a nodding sort of way. He was a stocky man, thick set, with bright blue eyes and a smile of welcome for me ever on his ruddy face. I had never found him a weighty thinker or a man of more than ordinary imagination. But he was well thought of in the neighborhood and he knew the gossip that was going about, whatever it might be. More, he was thoroughly friendly toward me and if there was any possibility of a place for me between Helmsdale and Auchintoul, he was the one who could tell me of it.

As I have already said, his cottage snugged against the hill, no more than a skip and a jump from the place where both path and burn came running, in a sort of race, about the last gray shoulder of the gorge. There was a pool at that spot, a sort of sudden pausing and widening of the stream before it went on along its way, rippling and dancing across the stony bottom. It was deep enough to hold a trout or two, and there was a little fall at the head. For the moment I forgot that it was so close to his house that it was Jamie's habit to draw his water from it for both his kitchen and his kine.

Nor, really, was there any reason why I should remember so small a thing until, as I came swinging down about the way, I came close to stumbling across the child scrounched down in the middle of the path, broadside to me, reaching down the heavy, wooden bucket to fill it at the stream. At least she seemed no more than a child to me in that first glance. I had a flash of a brown calf and soft, white thigh, half exposed, thrust out from beneath a shapeless heap of brown homespun skirt for balance as she leaned over. Tawny, dark-honey-colored hair hung down upon either side of her face, and her back was toward me so that I could read nothing there. I caught myself upon an outcrop of rock and kept myself from falling. At the same time I cried out petulantly:

"In heaven's name, child, what the devil are you about? Have you no better place to fill your buckets than right here where half of Scotland must tumble over you?"

She must have been as startled as I, for she leapt around as if I had slapped her on the rump, and at the same time she let go of the bucket which went rolling and bouncing and bumping off merrily down the stream. In an instant, she flipped her skirt down self-consciously to cover her ankles, and as she turned the thick wisp of hair, wind-dragged across her cheek, scarcely served to hide the bright flush of her cheek or the angry blaze of her blue-gray eyes. Nor did the rough homespun stuff of her gown disguise the fact that there was nothing half-grown about the figure that lifted and thrust, ripe and round, against the front of her bodice.

Obviously it was my turn to be embarrassed. And she proved to me then that her wit was sharp enough.

"If I'd thought half o' Scotland'd be passin' this way," she retorted caustically, "I'd ha' seen th' road was clear. But if th' half o' Scotland gi'es nae warnin'—indeed, if he doesnae even look where he's goin'—what th' de'il can he expect but t' find th' rest o' Scotland gang about their ain business?"

The answer was so pert and ready that I could not help but grin at her sheepishly.

"I—I'm sorry!" I blurted. "I'm afraid I mistook you for a wee bairn—"

I broke off abruptly, and at the same instant I think we were both stricken with confusion. Perhaps something of my thoughts—my admiration—showed in my eyes before I could veil it. At any rate she blushed furiously, and I could feel the red creeping into my ears and spreading up over my neck and into my cheeks.

"An' ye found—?" she began, I think as much to say something as to seek an answer.

But I replied. Indeed, I doubt if I could have stopped myself.

"A wee lass," I told her, "but a grown one! Aye, and a gey, sonsie one as well!"

I don't know if she heard me—although I think she must have. Even as I spoke she clapped both hands to the sides of her face.

"Ai—th' bucket!" she cried.

It was as well she thought of it I am sure, for I will admit that I had forgotten all about it. But in that country a bucket is a bucket and not to be lightly flung into the burn! I knew that Jamie Gordon had none to spare.

"Forgive me!" I cried, and leapt past her and went scrambling off after it.

I caught up with it at a spot about fifty yards below, where the burn widened and grew more sedate as it rolled through the gentler meadows that began here. When I came up with it I plunged in and retrieved it, splashing my socks to the calves and filling my brogues with water. As I caught the bail and lifted it I filled it, and then I carried it back to her in a sort of triumph that I realize now was out of all proportion to the event.

She watched me as I came back up the path, my boots squishing water at every step, and it seemed to me that much of the hostility that she had at first shown had been rubbed away. Her look now was reproving but almost affectionately so.

"Now look at ye!" she said. "Ye've been an' got your feet all wet!"

I glanced down at my boots, for some reason feeling unaccountably guilty.

" 'Tis no matter," I replied. "At least I caught your bucket."

"If ye'd waited," she retorted matter-of-factly, "ye could ha' fished it out below, where th' burn narrows, wi'out steppin' in at all!"

That was no more than the simple truth, but the statement of it was hardly calculated to put me at my ease.

"There's small difference," I growled, " 'twixt the burn below and the glen above! They're both wet. But since I've rescued your bucket I hope you'll allow me to carry it up to the house, yonder. I take it 'tis there you're staying—at Jamie's."

She gave me an amused look, such as made me wonder what I had said now, then shrugged.

"If ye wish," she replied.

As she turned away and started up toward the cottage I was aware of my rudeness. It was as if I were angling for her to tell me first who she was, and almost guiltily I fell in behind her. She was barefoot of course, as would any Highland lass be who was at home among the heather. The only time our upland folk put on their shoes was when they went to kirk on Sunday or undertook a journey—and then they carried their boots in their hand and only put them on when the mud of the path was behind them and the cobbled pavement of the town lay before.

That way of going barefoot, I believe, was what gave to our women their characteristic proud, poised walk that went so far to show them at their best, and as I followed her I could not help but admire it. The erect way she carried herself emphasized the curve of her back and the flatness of her stomach; the thrusting lift of her firm young breasts. Yet the set of her head upon the column of her neck was graceful but unyielding.

I remembered my manners abruptly.

"My name is MacAllister," I said, "Malcolm MacAllister. I've been a schoolmaster hereabout for some time."

"Why then ye're a kenspeckle man, Mister MacAllister!" she tossed at me over her shoulder, laughing.

For some reason that irritated me.

"None so kenspeckle that I know you or you know me, Mistress—" I retorted.

She turned about to face me then, at the cottage door, and looked properly contrite.

"Forgi'e me, Mister MacAllister—" she began.

"Malcolm!" I interrupted her. "Malcolm's my name."

"Forgi'e me, Malcolm MacAllister," she replied gravely, accepting the correction without protest, but nonetheless refusing to make use of my Christian name alone as I hoped she would do. "I'd nae mind t' be rude t' ye. I'm Jean MacLean, an' aye, I'm stayin' wi' Jamie Gordon. Ye see, he's a cousin o' mine."

I gaped at her in astonishment, for surely she was young enough to be Jamie's daughter. Indeed, unless I was much mistaken she was several years younger than myself, and it would be several years yet before I would see thirty!

"A—a cousin?" I demanded.

"Aye—a cousin!" she laughed at my blank expression. "Ye ken, Malcolm MacAllister, yon was a fine braw family—th' Gordons. Jamie's father, who was th' eldest o' them, was grown an' married an' had weans by th' time my mither, who was th' babe o' them a', was born. By th' time she was grown an' marrit t' my father, Jamie himsel' was already marrit an' wi' bairns o' his ain."

I shook my head and smiled at her.

" 'Tis all very confusing," I told her, "and I'm not sure I've the right of it yet, Jeannie MacLean. But I will say the results of it could not have been better!"

She blushed prettily.

"Hish yer blether!" she scolded me, laughing, and leaned over and took the bucket from my unresisting grasp. " 'Twas a pleasure t' meet wi' ye, Malcolm MacAllister. An' now they're comin' yon, an' I maun be goin'. Guid day t' ye!"

I might have called after her, perhaps even have followed her into the cottage, but for the warning she had given me and for the grinding sound of a step on the gravel of the yard. I glanced that way and saw Jamie, thickset and smiling, coming down from the direction of the cattle byre. Close behind him was a much older man, tall and cadaverous seeming, with sad brown eyes that gave him a sort of a whipped look, and never a ghost of a smile. Yet for all his sorrowful air I thought I could see certain faint lines of resemblance between him and the girl to whom I had just been talking, and even before Jamie presented us I guessed he was her father.

"Eh, now!" Jamie cried. " 'Tis Malcolm MacAllister! Ho, Malcolm, whate'er i' th' world brings ye ower this side th' hills i' this de'il's ain weather?"

I grinned at him, for it seemed to me there was ever something heartwarming about the man.

"Hallo, Jamie!" I replied. "I'll tell you the truth of it, I've finished my teaching in Braemore and locked up the school for good and all. I'm on my way up into the glens now to see whatever else I can find. I don't suppose you know of aught hereabout?"

He shook his head.

"Now then, I wish I did!" he replied, and then noticing my glance at his companion he half turned to introduce us. "Here's Alec MacLean, that I ca' my wee-uncle since he's sae nigh my ain age. I noticed ye'd a'ready made th' acquaintance o' his lass."

I nodded.

"Aye, she was drawing water at the burn," I said, "and I came near to stumbling over her. Good day to you, Mister MacLean. You've a gey, sonsie lass yonder. She must be a pride to you."

"How d'ye do, Mister MacAllister?" the dour, dark man rumbled. "She is!"

Jamie Gordon was eyeing my soaked brogues and splashed stockings. "Did ye tumble i' th' stream instead?" he demanded.

I chuckled.

"The lass was startled and dropped her bucket in the burn," I explained. "I retrieved it."

Jamie Gordon looked at me slyly.

"I'll nae say I blame ye!" he said. "If I were yer ain age I think I'd ha' done th' same."

He turned to the older man beside him.

"Alec, ye ken th' bottle i' th' cupboard?" he said. "Will ye go fetch it now there's a guid lad—an' bring th' mugs wi' it? We maun see Malcolm, here, has a dram for th' road!"

The lean man turned without a word and ducked inside the cottage. I looked at Jamie Gordon, I must say, with eyebrows raised. I could not tell what was amiss, but clearly this was unlike him. Ordinarily he would have asked me inside. His return glance was apologetic, warning, yet he said nothing until MacLean had disappeared within.

"Puir de'il!" he sighed then. "Th' puir, puir man! Ye'll ken, Mac, if I could now I'd ask ye t' bide an' sup an' stay th' nicht if ye were minded. But wi' they amang us an' th' trouble tha've seen—" He shook his head. "I canna do it!"

"What—what's wrong?" I asked him. "Or should I say?"

He shook his head again, grimly.

" 'Tis nae secret," he replied. " 'Twas th' Clearances—th' cursed, Christ-be-damned Clearances! At least 'tis they're at th' root o' a'."

I knew what he meant, and I could understand the savagery of his curse. He referred to the policy, lately become so devastatingly prevalent among the large Highland landowners of turning out their tenants from the crofts and tiny upland farms, that they and their fathers before them had occupied and worked and made flourish, in order that the land might all be thrown together and turned back to pasture for the sheep. I could understand the reasons for it easily enough. With the new-grown mills of the British Midlands crying out for wool and more wool there was more profit to be had from sheep than from human beings. But with the poor Highland crofters, who were being left destitute by the thousands, with never a new home to which to turn, the policy was hardly a popular one.

With Jamie Gordon I cursed it, yet not I fear for any humanitarian reasons. My own quarrel with it, I must admit, sprang from more selfish motives, for as a hedgemaster—that is an itinerant schoolteacher who was dependent upon the poor folk of our farms and crofts for his livelihood—the fewer of them there were the less were my own chances of employment. The system was simple enough. Unable to afford a school of their own in the regular way of taxes and such, it was the custom of my clients to band together and pool their resources. One would provide bed and board, another a place to work. Still a third would put up a cask of ale or a gallon or two of stout, smoky usquebaugh, and the rest would scratch together a few groats and bawbees to jingle together in my pocket and help me on my way to the next place when the work was done.

Yet it seemed to me that Alec MacLean and his daughter were hardly the sort to be stricken so.

"The Clearances?" I asked.

"Aye!" he nodded. "Alec had a holdin' ower on th' Bran, near Achnasheen, in Ross. Wi' it he'd a sma' bit o' preachin'—enough so ye might say he was by way o' bein' a dominie o' th' auld kirk. But Cromarty—'twas him owned th' land—cried a' for th' Clearances, an' there was an' end t' it!"

"D'you mean Mister MacLean came out against him?" I cried.

"Aye—so!" he replied dourly. "An' ye'll mind Ross an' Cromarty's nae the man t' be told forby! Alec tried t' show him th' way o' things, but 'twas for nae more than t' anger him. Cromarty crossed was Cromarty cross. He turned Alec awa', an' when Alec lost his croft he lost his preachin'. When he lost his preachin' he lost his wife—"

"Lost her—?" I demanded, incredulous.

"Aye—'twas that killed her," he told me simply. "Ye see why I canna ask ye? God knows what's t' become o' them! Ye'll ken I canna keep them here fore'er. I've scarce room for my ain brood— Hist, now, here's Alec!"

He fell silent, and I could hear the older man's footsteps approaching. When MacLean came out he carried a squat jug and three cups. The brown liquor gurgled cheerfully as he poured. We touched glasses, and I nodded to him.

"To yourself, Mister MacLean," I said, "and to an end to your troubles!"

He flung an angry glance at Jamie.

"Ye've been talkin'!" he cried accusingly.

"So he has," I put in quickly, seeing Jamie's confusion. "But he said naught against you or any of yours. I sympathize with you, Mister MacLean, and I wish I could help. There's small enough chance of that, but I do get about, and if in my wandering I should hear of aught that I might put in your way, you may be sure I will do it!"

What else could I have said? But the truth was bitter within me. How could I, a poor hedgemaster, hope to help them? As a matter of fact, I wonder now if I would even have troubled myself to the extent of offering all I could if it had not been for the girl. She was a gey lass, and she deserved better of fate I felt. Yet, truly, there was little enough that I could do. I am afraid my feeling of sympathy for them was more personal than it was broad and human. For the rest of their kind I had little enough concern.

That was the tenor of my thought as I went on down the glen toward the village that sprawled along the banks of the river, just above the mouth of the burn.

2. THE BLOOD IS STRONG

I CAME TO KILDONAN ABOUT DUSK AND TURNED UP ALONG THE STRAGgling, cobbled road, where the houses crowded in against the river, until I could smell the warm reek of Davie Murray's tavern, which was the only public house in the town—a sort of combined waft of stale, stout beer and spitted mutton. It was almost dark by then and there were smoky, yellow shafts of light streaking out through the slanting drizzle. I was glad to feel that I had come to the end of at least one day's journey. As I turned in at the taproom door I could hear a lusty voice bawling an unfamiliar song:

> *Les Mandannes ont les tetons d'or,*
> *En roulant ma boule!*
> *Les Mandannes ont les tetons d'or,*
> *En roulant ma boule!*
> *Rouli, roulant, ma boule roulant,*
> *En roulant ma boule!*

The words made no sense to me at the time, nor much more later when I did come to be somewhat familiar with the tongue. But it was clear that someone was enjoying himself, and for all I was bemused the catchy tune and the thundering voice bellowing it out tugged at my imagination and fetched a small smile to my lips. I forgot my recent, somewhat sour moment in the glen. I thrust open the taproom door and stepped down into the long, low ceilinged room that was warm and full of ruddy, mellow light that came as much from the fire on the hearth as from the smoky tallow dips upon the tables. There was a row of local lads lined up against one wall upon the common bench with pots of ale scattered the length of the long plain table before them. I recognized most of them. There were Jock Wallace and Nigel Dean and slack-jawed Lew Mossie, of Kildonan, and Ben Drummond and Andrew Moffat and Rab Crockett, down from Borrobal. And there were Martin Mackenzie and little Hughie Munro, of Kinbrace, along with several more I did not know. I gave them good evening, which they returned to me warmly enough, and Davie Murray, behind his bar, bobbed and beamed.

"Welcome t'ye, Mister MacAllister!" he cried out. "What brings ye out t' Kildonan on a clarty night lik' this?"

" 'Tis not your famous climate, Davie," I grinned at him. "For a fact I've taught the bairns of Braemore about all I can, and now I must find a new place to set up a school. I suppose you know of naught hereabout?"

It was almost word for word what I had told Jamie Gordon, and his reaction was the same, though somewhat more jocular.

"Na!" He shook his head. "Unless ye've a mind t' be teachin' sheep! Ye might go see th' lairdie about that."

Across the room the voice boomed:

> *Les Mandannes port' pas pantalons,*
> *En roulant ma boule!*
> *C'etaient, on dit, pour convenance,*
> *En roulant ma boule—*

I glanced over at the tables that Davie usually reserved for gentry and caught sight of them both then. The singer was a thickset, barrel-bodied man with a thatch of scrubby, raven hair that came down in a widow's peak almost to the fuzzy-flat line where his bushy brows met over his nose. His eyes were bold and cold, hard and black as obsidian, while his nose was thick and a little askew. His companion was much taller, and beside him gave the impression of being extremely thin. However he was not. His body was long and his shoulders were narrow, but he broadened out at belly and hips so that he was actually almost, though not quite, stout. His face was long and thin, which only added to the general impression, and it was peppered with great freckles which were accentuated by the pallor of his skin. But the most arresting thing about him were his bright blue eyes and his hair, which was soft and silky and the color of spun red gold in the smoky light. Both men were travel-stained and damp, even as I myself. But the cut of their coats and breeks were clearly of the best. I think I must have colored a little as I bowed toward them, for even if I had said nothing to offend them myself it was obvious that here were two of the very gentry at whom Davie's remark had been aimed.

"Good evening to you, gentlemen!" I said.

The red-haired man nodded and returned the greeting affably enough. But the black-browed one—the man who had been singing —only glowered back at me belligerently. I turned back to Davie, to some extent, I am sure, irked by the fellow's sullenness.

"I'd rather eat his lairdship's mutton than try to teach it. Davie," I said, "I don't suppose you'd happen to have a rack of it on the spit yonder, in the kitchen, would you?"

Davie flung a momentary glance at the two strangers before he replied. Then he laughed.

"Awell, I've a rack o' mutton, Mister MacAllister," he replied, and winked.

"Tonight I'll ask no more of it than that then, Davie," I told him, "for I'm that famished my stomach thinks my throat's cut. Let me have it and a tall pot of ale to go with it and wash it down and some leeks to give it flavor and I'll trouble you no further with foolish questions, for I've tramped many a weary mile since forenoon."

He was away to the kitchen before I had finished speaking and I turned and peeled off my wet coat and slid in at the long table between Jock Wallace and Martin Mackenzie; and when Davie fetched in the smoking meat and the tall, cool pot of ale I ate and drank, chaffing the while with the lads and paying no further attention to the two strangers, whom I forgot entirely.

"So ye're on yer way again, Mister Mac?" Ben Drummond grinned. "Surely if ye were a bit less ha-ard now wi' yer pupils ye might linger langer i' one place?"

"Don't you believe it, Ben," I retorted. "If I'd not driven a bit of learning in at your behind not so long ago you'd have none in your head now!"

"Mister Mac's right," Hughie Munro broke in from the other end of the table. "Ye're a stupid lout, Ben Drummond!"

I never cared much for Hughie Munro. Maybe it was his small, scant size. But it always seemed to me he was sucking up to authority, trying to get on the right side of it. I spoke up sharply in Ben Drummond's defense.

"The devil he is, Hugh Munro," I retorted. "Ben's a fine head on him. But he's stubborn as can be and lazy to boot about what he takes in. It needs a stout man to convince him of anything, and I take pride to myself that I was able to teach him at all. If I'd not a bit of brawn on my bones I could never have done it! The sorry thing is that there're so few of us about—"

"Aye!" Andrew Moffat growled. He was a moody, thoughtful lad, but he made no secret of his thoughts. "Yon's th' plain truth! There's little need for any o' us hereabout. Th' gentry'd rather be rid o' us an' ha' th' land for their sheep than see us get a bit o' learnin'. It maun be a grim thing for ye, Mister Mac, tae see th' way th' land is goin'."

"Aye, grim indeed, Andrew," I replied, and I don't know why I went on to speak of what I had seen that very afternoon except that it was on my mind. "I stopped by at Jamie Gordon's croft, up the glen, coming down from Braemore—you ken where I mean. Jamie has his uncle stopping with him and his wee cousin, though God knows there's little enough room for them. The old gentleman was turned off his land on the Bran, where he'd a small piece—and that for all he was a dominie of the kirk, too."

They stared at me in astonishment.

"Ye don't mean it!" Martin Mackenzie cried.

" 'Tis the simple truth," I nodded. "Indeed, the shock of it did for Jamie's aunt. They put her in the ground and then came away to stay with Jamie for a bit, since they've no other place to go. Christ alone knows where they'll turn next. Surely, what with Jamie's own loft crowded already they can't stay there for long!"

That was the general way the talk ran during my supper, and I speak of it now only because of what happened later. It was nothing more or less than any Highland talk about any Highland table, wherever Highlandmen foregathered in those dark days. Across the way from us the two gentlemen fell quiet, listening, and I doubt if anyone but myself noticed that. For my part, I fear, I was the more outspoken because of it, prodding my comrades to speak their minds and making no secret of their and my opinions, for I felt it would do these gilded nabobs good to hear what such common folk as we were thinking and saying about them.

I finished my meal and called for another pot of ale around; and then I must needs have another with Rab Crockett and another with Jock Wallace, and then Martin Mackenzie rose and stretched and announced that it was a far, long walk back to Kinbrace, and that he'd best be going if ever he were to get there before morning. That fetched the others to their feet, and all together they said good night and trooped out. There was an emptiness in the room when they were gone, and then, to my surprise, it was the red-haired stranger, over across the way, who broke the silence. He rose and smiled through the smoky murk.

"Excuse me, sir," he apologized, "but I could not help overhearing you and your friends."

I scowled back at him hostilely, for I was sure that he meant only to take issue with some of the points we had made.

"Aye? Then I daresay you've had an earful!" I retorted.

But quite contrary to all I had expected of him he did not take offense. Instead he continued to smile pleasantly.

"Oh, quite!" he agreed. "Though I heard nothing new—that is generally speaking. It was only what Highland folk are saying among themselves the length and breadth of Scotland, and I must say they are justified. But there were certain specific things about the conversation that struck me. For instance, sir, did I not hear you say that you were a schoolmaster?"

"You did," I replied, immediately on the defensive, for it seemed to me at that point that this might be a more serious matter than I thought. "What of it?"

He ignored the curtness of my tone and the question, too.

"And this other gentleman you mentioned," he went on, "did you say that he had been serving as a dominie of the kirk?"

"Yes, I did," I told him. "I've not heard that that's an offense yet. Nor, I believe, is it unlawful for a man to speak his mind."

"Not at all!" he assured me. "I'm afraid you misunderstand me, Mister MacAllister. It just happens that I have particular reasons for my interest in those two points."

He paused, and I did not miss his use of my name.

"I'm afraid you have the advantage," I said sharply.

"Of course!" His smile never wavered although his black-browed companion began to look irritated. "Forgive me! My name is Douglas —Thomas Douglas, Earl of Selkirk. And this other gentleman," he turned and nodded toward his friend, "is Colin Robertson, lately employed by the North West Fur Company of Canada, but now a servant of the Hudson's Bay Adventurers, and my agent."

I did not bother to nod acknowledgment of that, so convinced was I that his motives were unfriendly. I did not even notice the last of what he had said. It was only quite some time afterward that the significance of that began to seep through into my consciousness.

"I'm not surprised to hear it," I said coolly. "I'd already marked you for a pair of toffs."

But he still refused to take offense.

"It is strange, is it not," he interrupted me gravely, "that just at this moment I should happen to be seeking a man of your peculiar qualifications?"

"My qualifications?" I demanded, astonished. "What—?"

He smiled again as he broke in.

"I wonder, Mister MacAllister," he said, "would you be at all interested in going to Canada?"

"I—?" I began, and then gulped as the meaning of his question struck me. "To Canada—I? In God's name, whatever for?"

He chuckled at my plainly flabbergasted look.

"We are all Scots together, Mister MacAllister," he told me. "That is at least one reason. If I could prevail upon you to join us at our table I would be glad to explain. Will you honor us?"

I stared at him, even yet more than a little suspicious.

"Why—since you ask it, my lord," I said slowly. "Yes. I'll join you."

I picked up my half-finished pot of ale and followed him across the room to the table by the fire. As we went the red-haired man signaled to Davie Murray to fetch us a fresh round of drinks.

3. THE HIGHLAND HEART

WHEN WE CAME TO THE TABLE AT THE OPPOSITE SIDE OF THE ROOM Lord Selkirk hospitably offered me the seat nearest the hearth, but Colin Robertson—he of the beetling, black brows—merely glowered up at me, as dour and hostile as myself, I daresay, though at the time I was not aware of being standoffish. His lordship waved his hand toward him.

"Mr. Robertson is of Scot's origin," he told me, "although he was born in Montreal."

"In Montreal?" I exclaimed before I thought, for that was a place that seemed to me then a long way away. "Do you say so? I thought there was an Indian look about him!"

Colin Robertson started up angrily, as if it were some deadly insult I had put upon him. But his red-haired friend waved him down into his seat again.

"Now, now, Colin!" he laughed. "There's no need to be so touchy. Mister MacAllister means you no ill, I am sure."

I thought the black-browed man would burst, but he subsided obediently enough and contented himself with glaring at me ferociously across the table.

"Perhaps I had best go back a bit, to the beginning," Lord Selkirk said to me.

"Tell it your own way," I replied.

"I will try to be brief," he promised. "A good many years ago— even before I went to the University, at Edinburgh—I foresaw what was happening in our Highlands and deplored it. This tendency to turn the land back into pasture and even into wild cover for deer-stalking is not new. I saw it happening when I was no more than a lad, and while, when I came into the title, I could put a stop to such evictions upon my own lands, I could hardly stop others from doing it."

"Why should you?" I demanded skeptically. It seemed to me hardly likely that any man fortunate enough to have inherited a title would be much concerned for others that were born to less. He shrugged and smiled a little.

"Say that I am more interested in human beings than in sheep," he replied.

"Get away from me!" I scoffed. "You're having me on!"

But he shook his head with deadly earnestness.

"I assure you, Mister MacAllister," he said, "I am not! Even then I determined to do something about it, and I did. I engaged agents and recruited a number of our evicted crofters, some five hundred of them, to put it in round numbers. I chartered vessels and I sent them over the ocean to Prince Edward's Isle, off the tip of Nova Scotia, where they settled and have prospered."

I stared at him, impressed in spite of myself, and opened my mouth to speak, but he held up his hand.

"Let me finish please, Mister MacAllister," he said. "Then you may ask questions. I made a second experiment a few years later. But that was not so successful—"

"Tha'd be Baldoon Farm, in Upper Canada?" Robertson put in.

"That was Baldoon Farm," Lord Selkirk nodded. "In that case I was ill advised. The land that we chose was swampy and ill suited to our purposes. But all of those folk that went over have since been settled upon lands of their own, so that it was not entirely a failure—"

"And now?" I prompted him, for it seemed to me that for all his talk we were yet a long way from the point.

"And now," he told me, "I have a plan to settle all of our destitute, evicted crofters upon good land in the heart of Canada; land which will be theirs and from which no ruthless landlord can expel them."

I looked at him incredulously, and I daresay I even laughed in his face.

"All?" I cried. "All of them? Come, my lord! Isn't that rather a big undertaking?"

But even my doubt did not appear to ruffle him.

"I am not out of my mind, Mister MacAllister, as I am sure you must think me," he smiled. "There are certain circumstances in connection with this of which you cannot possibly be aware."

"Truly?" I snorted. "I'm sure there are. But still I cannot conceive of a tiny island or a fair-sized farm—"

He wagged an admonishing finger at me.

"If you please, Mister MacAllister," he said. "I have not finished. I told you that you might ask questions later."

I subsided and took a pull at my ale. At least the drink was good and he was paying for it. I supposed that I owed him at least the courtesy of listening.

"As I say," he went on, "there was not much I could do at first. As a matter of fact I was born a fifth son, and it was only by misfortune that I came into my title at all. When that happened I found that a large block of my holdings consisted of stock in the Hudson's Bay Company. A few years ago I had the good fortune to marry Miss Jean Wedderburn, whose father was also a large stockholder in the Company."

I looked down at my ale and drank again, for by now I was convinced that the man was quite crazy. What possible interest could I have in such personal matters? But of course I said nothing. If he was mad, I told myself, he was harmlessly so. But his next words jolted me utterly out of my complacency.

"My wife's stock, added to my own," he said, "gave me voting control of the Company. Since King Charles, in his charter, granted all of Canada west of the Great Lakes and north of the Mississippi and Saint Lawrence watersheds, you can see what a vast territory this placed at our disposal. With such a vote, Mister MacAllister, you will understand that it was not too difficult to obtain a grant from the Company, for my purposes, for a tract comprising some hundred sixteen thousand square miles in the very heart—"

I gaped at him.

"A hundred and sixteen thous—?" I began.

"Square miles, Mister MacAllister!" he nodded. "If you stop to consider, as you undoubtedly know, that all of Scotland, both High and Lowland, amounts to little more than thirty thousand odd square miles, I am sure you will agree with me that the area is more than ample for the need!"

I did not know it, but it took no mathematical genius on my part to see that he was right about that.

"What's to prevent it from becoming another Baldoon Farm?" I demanded. "How do you know it's fit for human use?"

"All hundred and sixteen thousand square miles of it, Mister MacAllister?" he retorted, gently scornful. "Surely in such an area there are bound to be some spots that are suitable! Besides, this time I have taken care to be well informed. The actual colony will center about the Forks of the Red River, where the Assiniboine comes in from the west, just southward of the vast expanse of Lake Winnipeg. This is in the very heart of the fur country, with great, fertile, rolling prairies on the one side and a ridge of timbered hills on the other. This is the area in which the buffalo have always gathered in such immense herds every winter, so that there can be no lack of meat. The plains themselves are deep and fertile, and little more than a scratch upon them is needed to give root to seeds. For years the *Boisbrûlés*—"

"The *Boisbrûlés*?" I demanded, bewildered.

"The half-breed hunters," he explained. "For many years they have lived in the area and have hunted the buffalo that flocked there, making a business of supplying both the North West Company and the Hudson's Bay folk with winter meat and food for their fur brigades. So you see I am not proposing to send out folk into a wholly unknown wilderness."

"I've been there myself," Colin Robertson put in. "I'll tell ye 'tis a fair land."

I glanced at him.

"A far land, too, Mister Robertson," I said.

"Aye, a far land," he retorted dryly.

I looked at the red-haired milord.

"And what's the flaw in it?" I demanded. "Surely, if it's all you say it is you don't propose simply to give it away?"

"Certainly not!" Selkirk replied.

Aha, I thought. Now we come to the truth of things. But his explanation was not what I had anticipated.

"A man works best for what he has earned," he said. "For that reason I do not propose to give away the land outright. Besides, an undertaking on such a scale as this calls for a far greater outlay than any one individual can make. On that account we have stipulated a nominal sum which each settler is asked to pay for his lands and the title to them."

"So it's only a scheme of land speculation, then?" I scoffed.

"Not at all," he retorted. "The sum we ask barely covers the cost of a man's passage out—let alone passage for his bairns and all. For a matter of ten shillings an acre, a matter of five pounds total, we will give a man title to a hundred acres of the best prairie land for his very own, to have and to hold for himself and his heirs and assigns forever. The only stipulation we will make is that he settle upon it and work it, by himself or with his family; that he will build a house and plant a crop and cultivate the land; and that after raising his food crop and first withholding enough for his own subsistence he then offer the Hudson's Bay Company the first choice of it. I think nothing could be fairer than that. Why, in return for the small price he will pay us we will even transport him and his family to Canada, regardless of what it numbers; and we will feed and clothe and house him on the journey!"

I studied him skeptically. Surely, I felt, there was more that he was not telling me. As he painted the picture for me there in the murky taproom it seemed to me that the thing was far too bright and flawless to be true.

"And what do you want of me?" I demanded. "You know I am no crofter."

He nodded precise agreement.

"Exactly so!" he said. " 'Tis a natural question, Mister MacAllister, and I'd think the less of you if you did not ask it. So that I may give you an honest answer, let me first point out that such an undertaking calls for certain public services which we, the proprietors, must provide. Among the chief of these are a school and a kirk. In order to have the school we must have a schoolmaster; and to have a kirk we must have a dominie. When I heard you speak it came to me that you might be interested in the former, and at the same time it struck me that your friend who has lost his preaching would be ideal for the kirk."

"And what is this to cost us?" I demanded, thinking then that I had discovered the key to the whole business.

But he shook his head.

"Not a groat, Mister MacAllister," he replied. "As I have just explained to you we have recognized that it will be our duty to provide both. Out of the first survey we have set aside plots for both kirk and school, and we have also designated adjoining parcels of one hundred acres each as residence farms for the dominie and the schoolmaster. These are not offered for sale. They will be given in fee simple, without charge, to those who qualify for the posts. From what I heard tonight I judged that you have been at your work long enough and are well enough known among these folk, and popular with them—for I will make no secret of it, I wish to make my selection for this group from this portion of the Highlands—to be so qualified. I rather hoped the idea might appeal to you, for as you yourself have said, and as I have had good occasion to discover, there is not an overabundance of your sort scattered about!"

"Amen to that!" I told him fervently. "But if you heard that you also heard the reasons for it. Besides, it is a long way to Canada!"

He smiled faintly.

" 'Tis not so far when you are there. What I mean, Mister Mac-
Allister, is that while the distance between Sutherlandshire and Assiniboia may be great—"

"Assiniboia?" I interrupted.

"The name we have given the territory," he said. "As I was about
to point out, it may be far from here, but a man is never far away
from where he is, if I make myself clear? That depends upon a certain self-sufficiency which some have and some do not. I have an idea
that you have it, Mister MacAllister, or you would not be engaged in
your present calling. Of course, you understand, there will be a small
but steady salary connected with the post. You would not be expected
to teach for nothing!"

I grinned at him.

"Now," I said, "you begin to interest me!"

"Pah!" snorted Robertson.

But Selkirk turned on him.

"Not at all, Colin!" he exclaimed. "We must remember Mister Mac-
Allister's position. He cannot afford to be other than utterly practical!"

He turned back to me.

"As a matter of fact, Mister MacAllister," he went on, "I will need
an agent in this locality to recruit our settlers. I must have someone
who knows the people and who can talk to them without arousing
their suspicion, for I will say to you that the skepticism you have
shown tonight is nothing new to me. I fear our people are suspicious
of the hand held out to help them unless they know whose hand it is!
At least that has been my experience."

That, I will say, made me feel a little ashamed of myself.

"Then," he continued, "once the group is gathered I will need someone to take charge of them; to help them aboard ship and to go with
them to York Factory, where they will be helped by the Company's
agents to find their way up through Lake Winnipeg to the Forks. Even
once they are there I will need a personal representative to look out for
their interests. For such a man I will pay handsomely, and I think
there could be no more logical choice than the schoolmaster. Would
you accept that?"

"For how much?" I asked guardedly, yet sure that there was some
skulduggery here.

"Say, twenty guineas a month?" he suggested.

Twenty guineas a month! Name of God, that was more than I was
likely to see in a year, room and board included, at my present rate.

For twenty guineas a month I'd lead emigrants to hell, I thought. But I was careful to let no such thoughts appear in my face.

"I'll think about it," I told him.

"Of course!" he smiled. "Sleep on the matter and let me know your reactions to it in the morning."

"I will," I promised, and I tried hard to think of something that would bring out the basic flaw in his offer, for I was positive there was one. "I take it we'll have to start out entirely from scratch, so to speak. You've picked the ground from over here, of course, and we'll have to go into a howling wilderness—?"

"Not at all!" he interrupted me. "This will be the third such party to go out upon this venture, and I mean to send a new group each year. The Governor, Mister Miles MacDonnell, who has had a good deal of experience in that region, went out with the first lot. A second group, of Irish and Orkneymen, joined him at the Forks last year, so that, you see, you and your people will have only to step into an already established colony, pick your plots, and then set to work raising your houses and breaking the ground for your crops."

I stared at him, witless and wordless I have thought since, for never had I heard anything to equal this. Yet there was no doubt that he was serious about it.

"You'll consider it, Mister MacAllister?" he asked.

"Aye, I will that!" I assured him.

"Very well then, let us talk more of it in the morning," he smiled. "We can settle it then, I daresay. Oh, and by the way, do you suppose that the gentleman of whom you spoke—the one who had a preaching of his own before he was turned out of his holding—do you suppose he would be interested in assuming the kirk for us?"

"I can ask," I replied guardedly.

"I wish you would," he told me earnestly. "Whether you yourself decide to accept my offer or not I wish you would mention it to him, for I would like to talk with him."

"Aye," I promised him. "I'll speak to him."

We said good night then, and I stumbled off wearily to the room that Davie Murray had set aside for me and tumbled somewhat dazedly, I fear, into bed. Of course I would mention the matter to Alexander MacLean. I was at least a step ahead of this man, who called himself Lord Selkirk, on that score, for I thought of the MacLeans at once— or perhaps it would be more accurate to say that I had thought of Jean MacLean. Indeed, I had thought of little else since I had left the Gordon cottage in the glen, and surely, if this were all that the red-haired man promised and I accepted the proposition, I could think of no one I would rather have accompany me upon the long journey.

At the same time I could not rid myself of the feeling that somehow, someway, I had stumbled upon a sharp game. Upon the surface it seemed all right. I could find no flaws in it. Yet somewhere, I felt skeptically certain, there must be a catch in it. I argued about it with myself in the darkness. In the main, I told myself, it made little difference to me what became of the folk I would be called upon to recruit and lead to Canada. After all, it was not I who had turned them from their homes or who threatened them with eviction. If Assiniboia proved to be all that this man, Selkirk, said it was, and if they liked it, that would be all well and good. If it was not, and they did not, if they chose to pick up and go on to some other place in Canada—then, surely, that would be their affair, not mine. And even if they did make such a choice they could hardly be worse off than they were now.

On top of that, I reminded myself, I would receive a steady salary for acting as schoolmaster, and an even handsomer remuneration for acting as recruiting officer and Lord Selkirk's agent in the matter—a salary larger, steadier and certainly much handsomer than anything I had ever known before.

I think I made up my mind then. Each man's first duty, I remember thinking, is to himself. Yet oddly, when I fell asleep that was not uppermost in my mind. On the contrary, the most vivid of my restless dreams swirled about a fresh, flushed young face and a pair of blue-gray, angry eyes, half hidden by a mass of wind-whipped, dark-honey-colored hair that kept tangling about me and drawing me after her whether I willed it or no.

4. BEHOLD THE DREAM

I THINK IT SHOULD SURPRISE NO ONE THAT IN THE MORNING I SOUGHT out the red-haired man who called himself Selkirk and offered him my acceptance. He beamed broadly over his porridge, seizing my hand and clapping me upon the shoulder in congratulation. Then he turned upon Robertson who was bellowing for eggs and pork and salmon, if there were any, since that was what he had grown used to.

"Did I not tell you, Colin?" he cried. "There's never a skeptic among them once the plan's been made clear!"

I could have set him right on that score since I was more than slightly a skeptic myself. But I let it pass, having made up my mind to it, and after that we haggled a bit over the terms, closing finally upon fifty-two guineas a year for the schoolmastership, that is a guinea a week throughout the year, in addition to the twenty guineas a month that he had already offered me for serving as his agent. The steady pay for my teaching was more than I had ever before been able to anticipate, and I think it hardly extraordinary in the light of that that I should accept so willingly. There were contracts to be signed and witnessed, of course. Colin Robertson and Davie Murray served for that. And as soon as it was done I was off up the glen about my new found business. It never struck me as one whit strange that the very first place I chose to go was to Jamie Gordon's in search of the former dominie, Alexander MacLean. After all, Lord Selkirk himself had especially asked to see him.

I came to the cottage a bit before midday, and to this day I have never been able to say whether or not I was surprised or confused to find her the only one in sight. I think I can say it without boasting that I am not hard to look at in addition to my size, and I hope I will be forgiven for adding that ever in my life I have had something of a way with women. Yet at the sight of her, sitting there in the misty sunlight, on the bench by the front door, carding out the wool that Jamie kept for his own use from the shearing, the devil seemed to have got my tongue, and I bumbled and blurted and could not seem to say the right thing however hard I tried. For her part, at sight of me she blushed, but she did not seem displeased.

"Eh, now, Mister MacAllister," she greeted me, "I'd no expected t' be seein' ye sae soon again."

"Oh," I replied unthinking. "Good day to you, Mistress MacLean. 'Tis your father I came to see."

She had blushed before. She flushed now.

"Did ye so?" she retorted. "Excuse me, then! I'll see if I can find him."

Before I could protest that I would far rather sit there and talk with her until the others came in for their noonday meal she was up and away, leaving me standing on one foot first and then the other, wondering how I could have stopped her. In a few moments she was back with her father, who gave me a searching, almost suspicious glance.

"Hallo t'ye, Mister MacAllister," he greeted me. "Ye're quicker back this way than I expected ye. Is it th' weather's cleared a bit, perhaps?"

He ignored his daughter's obvious but unspoken protests and my own shaking head.

"The' lass says ye were askin' for me," he went on.

The girl turned about and stalked into the cottage, leaving me, I think, more confused than I would have been if she had stayed. For an instant I gaped after her. Then I wrenched my eyes from the door and looked at him.

"Aye, sir," I stumbled. "Aye—you mind I promised I'd speak of you if I came upon aught that might fill your need?"

He nodded sharply, and it seemed to me his scowl softened somewhat. He eyed me intently.

"So, well? Ye've heard somethin' then?" he demanded, uncertain whether to believe me or not.

"I have," I said. "I'll be honest with you and confess I scarcely know whether to believe it or not myself. But I have chanced on something that might interest you, if you'd care to hear it."

"Aye, what's it?" I could see the hope in his eyes struggling against his natural pessimism.

" 'Tis a living as a dominie," I replied, "though aye far away."

I went on to tell him, then, all that Lord Selkirk had said to me. When I was done he studied me uncertainly, I could see, half anxious to believe what I had said, and at the same time more than half doubtful.

"Can I speak wi' yon Selkirk?" he demanded.

" 'Tis why I came to see you, Mister MacLean—" I began.

He waved his hand.

"If ye please—Alec!" he growled. "I am nae used tae these 'Misters.' "

"Alec, then," I went on. "Of course you may speak with him! 'Twas himself asked me to come and talk to you to see if you'd be interested in the undertaking to that extent. There will be a meeting tonight of such threatened crofters and evicted tenants as I can gather together. 'Twill be at Davie Murray's tavern, and we'll hear there what all he has to offer. Will you come?"

"Aye," he nodded. "Aye, we'll come, an' pray t' God 'tis nae fraud."

" 'Tis not a fraud, Alec," I assured him. Yet all the way down the glen I kept wondering to myself if there was any way I could be sure about it.

In the course of the day I gathered up a number of farmers of the neighborhood: leaders, I knew, of the community, yet men who stood now threatened with eviction and the loss of their holdings because of the Clearances. I cannot say that I was proud of my work, for I was yet far from convinced that it was all aboveboard. But somehow that did not deter me to any great extent. Instead I painted the whole thing in glowing colors, and because they knew me they accepted my description without question. I could never be sure which was the more troublesome to my heart—the things I said to my old friends in my efforts to sell them this golden opportunity, or the things I did not say. At least a score of Kildonan folk, the MacLeans among them, foregathered at Davie Murray's that raw, wet night, and all because of my doing.

I will not dwell upon the details of that meeting. When they were all come together, and Lord Selkirk had stood each man his pot of ale and offered each of the ladies a pasty, he rose and spoke and described what he was about in much the same terms as he had told them to me. When he was finished Colin Robertson stood up and described the countryside about the Forks, as a man who had been there, and answered questions about it, all in a way that seemed even to me, doubtful as I was, quite honest and aboveboard. After that Lord Selkirk spoke again, showing how a man who did not feel that he could afford five guineas all in a lump might spread his payments over a term of years, and even take them out in produce; and for others who might yet be doubtful he outlined still another plan whereby a man might rent his farm for ten shillings or thereabout a year—although in that case whatever improvements he might make or any buildings he might raise would belong to the land, and Lord Selkirk was quite frank to say that he did not advise it.

When it was done even I was fairly convinced that what he outlined was an entirely altruistic venture. Yet even in spite of that somehow I could not rid myself of the feeling that somewhere in this there was fraud, and that I was a party to it. On the one hand I told myself that it made no difference. *Caveat emptor!* Let the buyer beware! But on the other hand I had a damnable conscience, and I was especially troubled that the MacLeans should have swallowed it all.

And they did, right down to the shank of the hook, if it was that. As a matter of fact there were few who shared my suspicion. More than a dozen of those who came to the meeting signed articles then and there. And when all the rest were gone Alec MacLean and Jeannie, at Lord Selkirk's special request, stayed behind. I would have left, myself, if the red-haired man had not glanced at me.

"If you please, Mister MacAllister," he said. "Will you give us the pleasure of your company? Since it was yourself that mentioned Mister MacLean, I think you should be here to second me in what I am about to say."

It was no secret, of course, that he was going to offer the post of dominie, and the lands that went with it, to the lean, dour man. I had told Alec MacLean myself that that was what he had in mind. But evidently Alec had said nothing to his daughter. She shot me a quizzical glance: half grateful, half questioning, and at that moment I felt as if I could fall through the floor.

"Will you have a small cup for the way, Mister MacLean?" Selkirk suggested.

But Alec was apparently on his best behavior.

"I thank ye, no," he replied.

His daughter's expression was one of mingled surprise and relief, and whether Lord Selkirk noticed that or not he did not press the point.

"Mister MacAllister tells me that you were dominie of the kirk over at Achnasheen," the red-haired milord went on.

"Did he now?" Alec MacLean glanced dourly in my direction. " 'Tis th' first I've heard o' anythin' sae grand as that—"

" 'Twas Jamie told me," I interrupted hastily. "You'll mind we were talking yesterday, and it was from what he said that I judged you might be interested in what his lordship had to suggest."

"Aye?" growled Alec. "Well then I maun be honest about it. I did ha' a wee, sma' bit o' a preachin' ower th' way, but 'twould nae be fair t' say 'twas as grand as a' that!"

"Well, we'll not quibble over the point," Selkirk said. "What's needed is a man, qualified by experience and inclination, to serve the place of dominie at the Forks. You've heard the outline of the thing I plan, Mister MacLean. If you'd be interested in the position I will donate the kirk and a hundred acres of good farm land for your own residence, and, of course, there will be a small salary for the preaching in the bargain. Will you take it?"

"Aye? How much?" Alec MacLean's expression was as skeptical as I am sure my own must have been.

Lord Selkirk chuckled.

"I've already promised Mister MacAllister fifty-two guineas a year —a guinea a week—to instruct the colonists according to the words of men," he said. "I could hardly offer less for God's word! Would that be satisfactory, Mister MacLean?"

As little as it might seem I knew it was a generous stipend for an unordained minister even without the addition of the land; and the farm alone must seem a princely domain to one accustomed to think of holdings in terms of five or six or rarely more than a dozen or so acres. Yet Alec MacLean managed to look duly meditative and thoughtful. He slid his eyes toward me, with something of a look of surprise. Then his glance passed on questioningly to his daughter. But there was no guile in her. She clapped her hands eagerly, as if they had fallen squarely on the pot at the foot of the rainbow.

"Eh, Father!" she cried excitedly. "D'ye mean t' tell me ye've need t' consider it? Ye're plain daft, then, for 'tis wonderful!"

She gave me a look that set my blood to pounding. Nevertheless I sought to draw back and pretend that I had had naught to do with it.

"I'd not want you to do a thing you'd no wish for," I said foolishly.

Alec MacLean smiled cryptically.

"What's tae be lost at any rate, eh?" he asked. "Yer Lordship, if ye're convinced I'm yer man—if ye'll ha'e me—?"

"You'll accept then?" Selkirk demanded.

Alec MacLean nodded.

"Aye!" he said. "I'll accept. An' if a' that ye promise is true, may th' guid Lord bless ye, an' may I serve ye well—both o' ye!"

As you may imagine, I felt no better for that. Once Alec had given his promise there was little more to be said. Colin Robertson entered their names and mine upon the rolls, and his lordship outlined my own duties to me. I was to circulate about all that part of Sutherland-shire, as well as Ross and Cromarty and Caithness, and do everything I could to recruit settlers.

"How many?" I demanded.

"As many as possible," Lord Selkirk replied. "I'll undertake to get transportation for as many as you can find."

"And how long am I to be doing this?" I said.

Selkirk glanced at Robertson.

"They should sail no later than July," the black-browed man growled, "if they're t' beat th' ice in th' Strait."

I felt something like a thud of surprise in my stomach. I had not counted upon ice—and what did he mean by "the Strait"? But out of my ignorance and inexperience I had not the courage to question them.

"And we'd best allow a month's time for the ships to rendezvous and load," Selkirk mused.

Robertson nodded wordlessly.

"Then suppose you meet Mister MacAllister here about the middle of June," Selkirk said. "That will leave you time to foregather with the settlers at Helmsdale and meet the ships I will bring up for them."

"That's all very well, Milord," I interrupted him, "but how is this to be done? I doubt I have three shillings altogether in my pocket at this moment. I cannot—"

He smiled and turned to Colin Robertson, who clearly was the bearer of the privy purse.

"Advance Mister MacAllister a month's salary, Colin," he commanded airily, "and see to it that he has fifty guineas besides to meet the expenses of his work."

"Fifty—!" I gasped.

"I can't expect you to do it for nothing or out of your own pocket, Mister MacAllister," he smiled at me.

" 'Tis damned expensive!" growled Robertson, counting out the money in good hard gold.

"Hush, Colin!" Lord Selkirk grinned. "It's more than a saying that you can't make an omelet without breaking eggs! Mister MacAllister, I'll ask you to act as my special agent, my sole agent, while you are recruiting. Once you are aboard ship with your people I'll ask you to share that leadership with Mister MacLean. Since he is the older man, and since he is to be shepherd of the flock at the Forks I think that is only fair. Mister Robertson here will be out later, by a different route. When you've reached the Forks you will turn your charges over to Governor MacDonnell, who administers the colony at the present time, and you will take your place on his council by virtue of your position as my representative. All this, of course, will be put into my written instructions to you, but I want to be understood before we close the bargain. You do agree?"

Since I had already discussed most of these points with him that morning, I could not help but feel that much of what he said now was for Alec MacLean's information. All of the ground except this matter of sharing the lead with the dominie once we were on board the ships had already been covered, and I was not so sure I cared for that. Yet it seemed to me there was no point in argument. It was still far better than anything I had ever dreamed of doing before. Who was I to complain? I nodded.

"Whatever you say, your Lordship," I told him.

So it was settled and we shook hands all about and said good night to the two gentlemen, since they would be on the road early in the morning, before I would have a chance to see them. After that I walked out with the MacLeans to the glen, as I said to show them the way, although more accurately I only wanted to be close to Jean as long as I might.

We went down over the swinging footbridge at the lower end of the village, and thence turned up into the glen. Alec MacLean walked sedately, for all I could see he was excited.

"Malcolm!" he cried, giving way to it once, "Mac! I cannae thank ye enough for puttin' me in th' way o' this! Ye'd nae notion—"

"Nay, nay!" I interrupted him. "I'd a fine notion, and I hope 'tis a favor I've done."

He shot me a questioning glance.

"What d'ye mean by that?" he demanded.

I shrugged.

" 'Tis just that Canada's a far long cry from Scotland," I replied. But he was too excited, I think, to hear that.

"Mac!" he went on, excited as a bairn with a bawbee. "Mac, d'ye believe we'll see Indians yon? Indians an' savages an' buffalo a' about?"

"Of course!" I assured him, never realizing how nearly right I was, yet not in the way that I meant it at all. In fairness to myself I should add that I was only repeating what every one of us in that day and place believed implicitly. "Surely! In Canada they're all Indians and savages."

"Mister Robertson's a Canadian an' he's nae th' one nor th' other," Jean put in.

I glanced at her, suddenly remembering what I had said to him when first we met, and all at once then understanding his furious reaction.

"So he's not!" I chuckled.

"Eh, well!" Alec MacLean sighed happily. "Surely there'll be some civilized folk there. An' o' course there'll be a' o' us. Ye think there'll be a-many willin' tae go, Mac? God knows there's need o' it!"

"Aye!" I agreed glumly. "I daresay we'll have no trouble that way."

"An' th' land, Mac!" he gabbled on in his rapture. "Who'd o' thought that ye an' I could e'er ha' sae much?"

" 'Tis a grand, mighty land, Alec," I told him.

"Aye, it is so!" he agreed. "An' there'll be room for a'."

"And to spare, I don't doubt," I grumbled.

Yet he was too wrapped up in his dream, I think, to notice my skepticism.

We were crossing the bottom field by then, the one that Jamie Gordon had put out to barley, and the lights of the cottage gleamed ahead, a thin, glowing point of spark in the darkness. Down along the burn the row of birks was a looming, black shadow, soft and fondling and a bit chastening as we walked. But as we raised the lights of the croft ahead Alec had eyes for none of that. He quickened his pace.

"I maun tell Jamie o' this if he's nae already gone t' bed," he cried, and cast a questioning glance at the two of us. "Ye'll be all right, th' pair?"

"Of course!" I assured him quickly. I noticed that Jean did not protest, and after all we were in plain sight of home.

I had not much more than spoken before he was away in the dark, leaving us to follow at our own pace. We walked a little way in silence, Jean and I, and then all at once I saw the dim oval of her face turned back toward me, looking over her shoulder.

"Why, Mac?" she asked.

"Why what?" I retorted gruffly, evading. I knew what she meant, but I would have preferred to put my own interpretation on the question.

"Why did ye do it, Malcolm?" she went on. "D'ye ken th' difference it's made t' him already? Oh, Mac, 'tis a grand thing."

"Is it?" I growled. "I wonder—"

I heard her breath catch.

"Ye wonder what?" she cried. "Malcolm—?"

I shook my head.

"Is there aught wrong with it?" I finished her thought.

"Aye!" she told me. "Aye! Is that it, Malcolm? Ye—ye've a strange way about ye."

I smiled a little thinly in the darkness, thinking that well I might.

"I don't know," I told her. "How can I know? It seems all open and aboveboard and honest as we hear it, yet—"

"Yet, somehow, it seems too good to be true," she said. "Is that it, Mac? Ye're nae sure?"

"That's it," I replied.

"Then why—?" she began.

"Jean, will you hear me?" I cried desperately, for it was clear to me by now that I could not let things go as they were. "If it were anyone else I'd not care a hang. As I heard it first it seemed to me, just as it does now to your father, that here was a thing that was too good to be true—but was! It seemed to me that here was a need for him and for me—a new way of life held out to us, and with profit to the bargain. When Lord Selkirk spoke of a dominie my first thought was of your father, whom I had just met. And so I came to him with the suggestion. Now I am not quite sure—"

That was not accurate. After all, it was Selkirk himself who had suggested that I broach the idea to Alec MacLean. Yet this was near enough. The details made little difference.

We were not far from Jamie Gordon's cottage by then, and as I talked she walked slower and slower until I came up with her and even bumped against her in the dark. As we touched she turned abruptly to face me.

"Mac—Malcolm," she cried, "d'ye mean that—"

"That it might not be all that he promised?" I interrupted her, yet full of my own thoughts. "Something like that."

She waved the idea aside impatiently.

"Oh, aye, aye, Malcolm!" she said. "I ken a' that, but as Father said, 'What's tae lose?' We've naught here. We may ha' naught yon, but how will we be worse off for that? 'Tis what ye yersel' said just th' now, that—that—that—"

"That—?" I said blankly.

"That ye'd not care if 'twas anyone else?" she went on. "That ye'd a special concern for us?"

For an instant I stared down into the misty glow of her face. Then I reached out and caught her in my arms, drawing her close to me, burying my own face in her soft hair, seeking out her lips with my own.

"Aye!" I cried. "Oh, Jean! Jean! Jean! What would it matter if all of Scotland were to find it a fraud? If you yourself were not hurt by it, 'twould mean naught to me! But here I've brought you into it! I could not bear to see you harmed and think it was my own doing!"

For an instant she clung to me, and I felt that the kiss that I gave her was well returned. I would have kissed her more, but she laughed, gay and lighthearted, with a note I had not heard in her voice before; a note of mingled relief and happiness, as if all at once a dark cloud had been brushed away from all around her and at last she could feel the warming sun and begin to live again. At the same time, though, she turned away her face and twisted her body struggling a little against me.

"No, no, Malcolm!" she protested, laughing. "No more now. There's aye much we must be sayin' tae each other yet—"

I let her go at that. But even as I did so Jamie Gordon and Alec MacLean came bursting down the path from the cottage above, and what with the moon and the stars and the fact that we had been standing clear in the open together I felt sure they must have seen us. It was too dusky for me to see if she changed color, but I could feel the hot blood mounting to my own cheeks, and I was glad that it was at least dark enough to hide that.

At sight of us they came to an abrupt, stumbling halt, just as we started guiltily apart, and for the space of a breath there was thick silence. Then it was Jamie who spoke quickly, plainly seeking to smooth an awkward moment.

"Mac?" he cried, chuckling. "Malcolm, is it ye now? Alec tells me ye've tumbled on a grand, fine solution t' their troubles."

"Perhaps," Alec's voice came grimly from behind him. "Perhaps 'twas more a solution than I was aware!"

Our folk, especially those of the Auld Kirk, are inclined to be aye strict about such matters!

I threw a glance at Jean, wondering how she would feel about all this. She'd already made it plain to me that we should take time to examine our feelings more closely, and even in my way of thinking, as anxious as I might be for her, I had to admit that one wee small kiss could scarcely make a wedding.

But again it was Jamie Gordon who broke in, and I daresay he honestly believed he was acting the part of peacemaker between us and Alec.

"Alec!" he cried. "Dinna ye be hasty, Man! For many a year now I've been acquaint wi' Malcolm, here, an' I tell ye ye couldnae wish a better son!"

I gathered then that, so far as Jamie Gordon and Alec MacLean were concerned, and no matter what Jean might feel about it, we were as good as betrothed!

5. THE MISTY ISLES

For my own part, I must say, I did not mind, though I suppose I should properly have spoken up then. A true gentleman, no doubt, would have stepped into the breach and explained that there were yet matters to be decided between us. In some way he would have given Jean an opportunity to speak for herself, and for any man of honest force it would not have been too difficult. Why I did not do so I can only lay to my own confusion of the moment and to the fact that in my own heart I only wished it so!

In the back of his throat Alec MacLean made a sort of strangled noise that might have been a snort of disgust or a growl of acceptance, and again Jamie hastened to ease the tension.

"Eh-well, now!" he cried brightly. "Here's cause for unco celebratin'! Come up th' house th' lot o' ye an' we'll take a sma', wee cup around tae success for a'—eh?"

In the face of that I felt that I could hardly say anything!

We turned back up the path and climbed to the cottage, the two older men busy with their walking in the dark, and Jean and I both occupied with our thoughts. No one said anything on the way, though it seemed to me that when we came into the warm, firelit room she looked at me curiously, strangely. Jamie fetched down the tassies from their row of hooks above the hearth, while Alec, who seemed well enough acquainted with its hiding place, dug out the tall jug; and this once, a most unusual thing there and then, a small splash of whiskey, well watered was poured for Jean. Perhaps Jamie meant it for a pledge, though I was far from sure that she accepted it that way.

Nevertheless she drank with us the toast that Jamie finally decided should be: "Success to a' that's been begun this day!" When that was done there was an instant of awkward silence. I decided that it was time for me to speak. I cleared my throat.

"Ahem!" I said. And my next words were not at all what I first meant to say. "Now, then, Gentlemen, if you'll excuse us! I'll be on my way tomorrow about this business of recruiting, so I should be getting back to bed. Before I go I'd like a word with Jean."

For an instant they looked startled. Jamie's jaw dropped and Alec scowled wonderingly, and I thought I saw a flicker of amusement in the curious depths of Jean's blue-gray eyes.

"Eh—uh—o' course!" Jamie grinned and jogged the older man's arm, at the same time tipping me a wide wise wink. "Come along, Alec! Come along t' bed, now! Can ye nae see we're ower many?"

Alec MacLean started and glowered first at me and then at his daughter.

"Dinna be long then!" he admonished us.

"We'll be no more than a moment," I told him. "I've said I must be on my way."

They gave us good night then, and when they were gone I walked to the door. Jean followed me curiously. Outside I turned to her.

"I'm sorry, Jeannie," I said. "I never meant to force you into such a position."

"Ye didn't object, Malcolm," she replied accusingly, and as full as my mind was with the idea that she might not want it so I did not see then that there was more than one way the remark might be taken.

"I know what's in my own heart, Jean," I said. "I'm not sure of what's in yours."

And this time, I think, it was she who leapt too quickly to conclusions.

"Dinna ye fash yersel' about it, Malcolm," she said lightly. " 'Twill be all right wi' me. I'll speak wi' Father about it."

I leaned over then to kiss her, but she turned her head away.

"Not now, Malcolm!" she protested.

If I had been half a man, I suppose, I would have insisted, and after that I would have thrashed the matter out with her, so that we both knew—aye, yea or nay—where we stood. But stiff-necked pride withheld me.

"I'll see you when I come back, then," I said. " 'Twill be a matter of weeks."

And without so much as good night, then, I turned away and strode off down the path, bound that if she did not want my love I would be damned if she would have my heart for a play-toy. As I turned, it seemed to me, she looked at me almost as if I had slapped her in the face. But I put that down to her own attitude. Mine, I thought, had nothing to do with it.

Nevertheless I went down the path torn between sensations of elation and grim foreboding. My heart wanted to sing that all was well. But my mind kept warning me that somehow, someway I had been something less than sparkling.

That odd mixture of feelings stayed with me throughout the following weeks, although they were always at a distance, remote but nagging, since I had little time to draw them to me and examine them closely. I worked hard in that time. Indeed, I worked like a galley slave, so that there was time for nothing else during the day, and at night I fell into bed and was content only to dream of her. Yet it was work in a popular cause and required little effort on my part, aside from the actual listing of the names and drawing of the agreements. The fever of Canada apparently bit deep, and I had little more than to mention my mission before I was besieged with almost more applications than I could write. It mattered little to me at that point whether or not the plan was all I had been told. It could even have been a pure scheme of land speculation for all I cared. It was enough for me that I was doing the job I had been set to do, and I was doing it well and beyond the possibility of any complaint by my employer.

In that time, of course, I saw nothing of either Jamie Gordon or the MacLeans, for I was too busy even to be in and out of Kildonan. My travels, of necessity afoot, since there was no other way to get there, took me the length and breadth of the Sutherland Highlands, and even all the way across to the coast on the west and north; from Portskerra to Invershin, from Lochinver to Cape Wrath and back again to Ben Hope and around to Bettyhill and thence to Loch Naver and Lairg. And everywhere I went I found five or ten or twenty new recruits for the undertaking waiting for me. They came down from the glens and over the hills to hear me talk and describe the richness and beauty and equable climate of Canada. They asked questions about the soil and the prairie and the vast lakes and the forests and the furs, and about the Indians and the buffalo, mostly about the Indians and the buffalo, of which they had evidently all heard. And where I did not know the answers myself I was quite conscienceless about making up something out of whole cloth, not neglecting, you may be sure, to make it as attractive and easy as my imagination allowed. Why I should have done that I can hardly say, unless perhaps it was to impress Jean with my prowess as a recruiter.

By the end of May I had gathered the signatures of some seven hundred recruits, and I believe honestly that I might have had double that number had I been able to travel farther and faster and had an assistant to help write down the names of all who applied. But perhaps it was as well that I did not.

It was the first day of June, I remember, when I came down again into Kildonan from a turn about Ben Clibreck, through Lairg and the Crask and Altnaharra. This was to be—and, it turned out to be, though for a different reason than I anticipated—the last of my recruiting tours. Thereafter I planned to rest in Kildonan and Helmsdale, to make arrangements there for the accommodation of all of those who would soon be coming in to join us, and to devote a little time to my own pleasure—to the courting of Jean MacLean, for instance. As I whistled my way along the highroad from Kinbrace, along the last few miles of Strathullie toward Kildonan, it seemed to me for a bit that the eternal mists were rising and the warm spring sun beginning to break through. But this may have been some hallucination in my own mind, born of my own lightness of heart, no doubt. Certainly it was not so the next day.

I reached Davie Murray's some time before dusk and turned into the taproom for a small dram before supper. To my surprise and delight I found a familiar, black-browed figure lounging there in the shadows, waiting for me.

"Mister Robertson!" I cried, delighted. "Now here's a surprise, and a pleasant one, I'll warrant! What brings you to Kildonan? News for us, I daresay, of the rendezvous?"

"Aye! Ye've guessed it," he said, offering me his hand dourly with never a smile, "an' none o' th' best, I might add!"

In spite of his glumness his grip was strong and friendly, and apparently he had lost his hostility for me as easily as he had acquired it. But I fear I took little notice of that at the moment. At his tone my heart went bucketing into my boots.

"Why?" I blurted out. "What's wrong?"

But he shook his head.

"Call yer tipple," said he. "I'll tell ye when we've wet for our whistles before us."

When Davie had fetched the tall, brimming canisters of ale, the Canadian clinked his solemnly against my own and held it up.

"Success!" he growled.

"Success!" I echoed.

We drank a good draft and as he took the mug down he wiped his mouth and belched silently, puffing his cheeks to let out the wind.

"Aaahhh!" he breathed. " 'Tis a sorry business—to drink alone! I've been three days at it, waitin' for ye to come back. Ye've done well, I hear, with yer recruitin'?"

"As well as might be in the circumstances!" I nodded proudly. "I could have gotten more given help and a way of getting around faster. As it is I've signed up seven hundred or so—"

His great jaw dropped and consternation was plain on his face.

"Seven hun—!" he began. "Lad, ye've not!"

"Certainly!" I said stiffly. "What's wrong with that? Lord Selkirk himself said—"

"Aye! Aye! Aye!" he interrupted me. "I mind what he said, 'Th' more th' merrier!' But ye see, Man, he thought then he could get all th' shippin' he wanted. 'Twould seem now that th' Northwesters have been there first an' boosted th' charter out o' all reason. Th' most he's been able to find is one vessel—"

"One vessel?" I cried. "But one ship will never take—"

"Exactly so, lad!" He nodded soberly. " 'Twill take at most a hundred. There's another vessel, the *Eddystone,* but she's supply ship for th' Company and will have only room for another score or so. D'ye follow me, then? If ye've seven hundred, as ye say, some're bound t' be disappointed. We can't take all, an' there's a surety—"

"But Lord Selkirk—" I broke in frantically.

"Oh, aye, aye!" he exclaimed. "Dinna ye blame th' good man! He went to London, an' when he found the Northwesters had been there before him and taken up all th' charters he tried Liverpool an' Bristol, aye! And Glasgow an' Edinburgh even. 'Twas th' same everywhere! They've power, I tell ye! Don't think th' shipowners themselves were not angry. Th' Northwesters had been about an' picked up every open charter about th' coast on an open contract that allows 'em t' cancel at will so long as they pay a reserve fee an' th' daily time th' ship is tied up. With yon control, then, they were able t' put up th' price o' recharter beyond all reason! Oh, aye! 'Twas clear th' dirty game they played, but there was naught he could do about it."

"Are they so strong as that, then—these Northwesters, as you call them?" I glanced at him sidewise.

"Strong?" he laughed harshly. "If any can tell ye that, Man, 'tis myself! Ye mind Lord Selkirk himself told ye that once I was one o' them? But for yon Crooked-Armed MacDonald—that salaud—! But hold, now! Ye've promised? Ye'll no funk out now?"

"I've no intention of it," I told him curtly, though I did not say why.

"Well then," he grinned at me, " 'tis as well ye were forewarned in

that case. Ye should know that where yon devil's spawn're concerned
there's naught too low—e'en murder—but they'll dip their hands in't
to block a pelt or a profit for th' Bay people. Ye'll ken, then, th' hate
that lies betwixt th' two o' 'em? 'Twas because I did not care for their
way o' dealin' that I quarreled with 'em, an' 'twas on that account I
turned t' his lordship. There's two can play at that game, but o' course
he'd ha' none o' that! All th' same 'twill be a point for ye an' me to
remember, for I misdoubt we'll ha' need o' it before we're through."

"Aye?" I said absently, for at the time I thought him a bit fuddled
and perhaps so to be humored. In a way we were both right. He could
have been soberer, and I should have paid more attention to what he
said.

"But none of that solves my problem just now," I went on. "By his
lordship's instructions I have recruited as many for this as I could, and
now you tell me that only a bare hundred or so can be taken. What
are we to do?"

"Do?" He goggled at me. "Do, lad? Why, that's your own problem!"

"My problem?" I flared at him. "Is it my problem that there are
not enough ships to carry them? I acted in good faith! Can you not see
the position it puts me in?"

"Position?" He blinked. "Why, I don't see that 'tis so sore a spot. Ye
need only explain to 'em th' trouble, and assure those that can't go
this time that next voyage—"

"Aye! Aye, next voyage!" I shouted at him. "Next voyage! But when
will that be, can you say? And how am I to tell those that cannot go
this trip that they must wait?"

"Tell 'em?" He leaned back in his seat and stretched. "I've just been
sayin' it to ye! Call 'em together in a meetin' an' explain. As for
choosin' them that shall go—draw straws for it, why not?"

But obviously it was not as simple as all that. With my recruits scattered all over the country it would take me weeks to call them all into
conclave, even if I would. And, of course, there was not such time to
be lost. In little more than a fortnight they were all to have given up
their holdings and come down, lock, stock and barrel to the rendezvous.
Clearly I could not let that happen. If six out of seven of them must
wait for another ship, I could not let them give up the homes that they
must live in meantime!

I took what seemed to me the only possible course. I called a meeting of all of those who lived near enough to Kildonan to come in, and
when they were all assembled in the village kirk, which was the only
building large enough to accommodate them all, I climbed to the pul-

pit and tried to explain the situation. I think it is evidence of my own good faith that as I told them what had happened I felt miserable and guilty and apologetic.

They heard me out without a word, and when I was done there was a long silence in the midst of which the creak of someone easing his position on one of the hard pews sounded like a clap of thunder. At last Donald Gunn, of Borrobal Parish, cleared his throat and voiced the question that was undoubtedly in all their minds.

"Aye, then, an' wha's tae go?"

"That is what we must decide this night," I replied. "The one vessel that Lord Selkirk has been able to charter can take but a hundred. More than seven hundred have applied."

There was a sort of murmurous stir among them, and it was almost as if I could feel the chill wave of hostility rolling up at me from that mass of stony faces. I had explained, but it made no difference what I said. It was clear that they held me to blame.

"And how are they that go t' be pickit?" old Donald Gunn demanded.

I shook my head.

"I'll tell you, I've not been able to decide about that," I said. "I suppose we could put everyone's name in a box and take the first hundred that were drawn—"

Again there was that murmuring stir, and a few muttered voices protested "No! No!" At the back of the room someone bawled out "Fraud!"

I held up my hand.

"I'll give you my word there's no fraud," I called out. "Those that have already paid, and who do not wish to wait for the next ship, have only to signify and their money will be refunded, their names withdrawn from the list. In the meantime—"

I only hoped it was true. After all I had no way of being certain! At one side of the room Jean MacLean rose, small and fiery. It was the first time I had seen her since that night on the path, and when I caught sight of the glint in her eye I had a presentiment of trouble abrew.

"Are ye sure, Mister MacAllister," she demanded, "that there is naught here o' cheatin'?"

I remembered what I had said to her that night. I had not hidden my fears then. Yet it seemed to me that now she was taking advantage of a moment of weakness. Perhaps I had been convinced by my own glibness.

"I have already said so, Mistress MacLean," I replied. "What have I to gain by misleading—?"

"Are ye sure, Mister MacAllister?" she persisted, and it seemed to me that she was carrying the thing to extremes.

"I am sure, Mistress MacLean!" I retorted stiffly, and so far as I was concerned at that moment I did not care. I was ready and willing to wash my hands of the whole mess—and of her, too, if this were to be the way it would be.

But she would not let me go so easily.

"Then d'ye think it fair t' make th' choice o' they that go a matter o' chance so?" she demanded.

"And why is it not?" I replied. "None would have advantage that way."

"But are there none among us but deserve some advantage then?" she cried hotly.

I scowled down at her.

"I don't follow you," I said. "Why should any be preferred?"

"Because some ha' already lost their holdin's," she retorted. "An' others ha' gi'en theirs up on th' strength o' what ye've promised. If this is a' ye say it is, then I would think 'twould be such as they that had th' preference. They that ha' yet their crofts, or can haud t' them for th' interval, should be th' ones t' wait till there's a ship t' take them."

She glanced about almost defiantly, and there was a muffled chorus of agreement.

"Very well!" I nodded, still stiffly for I was not accustomed to being faced down so in the classroom, and this it seemed to me, was not so very different. "Very well! There's justice enough in that. But how would you go about making the choice. D'you think, Mistress Mac-Lean, that you'd offend none? I'm sorry—"

"Appoint a committee," she interrupted me. "Three, or five, or seven, just so there can be no tie vote among them. Then sit down an' select th' neediest from yer list. If there be any left over let them draw, but first take they whose need is worst!"

The storm of applause that swept across the room at her suggestion made it obvious that here was the popular course, and I must say that it seemed fair. I backed down as gracefully as I could, yet I was determined that none could accuse me of favoritism.

"As you will!" I said sharply. "I will appoint Colin Robertson to sit as chairman, with John Sutherland and Donald Gunn, of Borrobal, to act as committeemen with him. The smaller we keep the group the faster it will work. I myself will sit with the committee, supplying the list of names and all the information I have at my command. But I will serve without vote, so that I may exercise no undue influence."

It seemed to me that I could not have made a more just arrangement; that I had demonstrated my own good faith—or at least signified my willingness to take the same chance as all. Yet when I went down among them people turned away from me as if I had been the veriest scamp. One would think that I had tried to sell them Ben More with the Isle of Skye thrown in, when the truth was that if I had made any such farfetched offer it would have been entirely in good faith. How could I tell, I wondered, if the project were all that it claimed to be? Was I not, I asked myself, a little resentfully, taking the same risk as all the rest?

Yet when I sought out Jean after the meeting, in the hope that I might escort her home and in the walk perhaps come to the bottom of this thing that had risen up between us, she was more than a little cool to me.

I went toward her with a smile on my lips and my hands outstretched in greeting.

"Jean, lass," I cried, "it's been longer that I thought it would, but I'm back at last—"

She stared at me coldly.

"Why good evenin' t' ye, Mister MacAllister," she replied. "I wonder that ye're back at a'."

I stopped as if she had slapped the back of her hand across my mouth.

"What? What d'you mean?" I cried.

"Mean?" She stared at me—through me. "D'ye not recall, Mister MacAllister, that ye once said t' me ye cared naught what happened tae these—these peasants?"

"Jean!" I cried. "Jean, for God's sake! It was only the thrawn truth! After yourself and your father what does it—"

"Aye! Ye see?" she replied. "It so happens I've a bit sympathy wi' a' folk in our own place. I care what happens tae them an' tae me. An' how would I know ye'd care what came t' us if ye'd nae been ta'en a bit by my ways? Ye were fine shy o' it a' when once it seemed th' matter was serious!"

"What? Eh? Oh, Jeannie, in the name of God!" I cried.

But she interrupted me sharply.

"Dinna be swearin' at me, Malcolm MacAllister!" she cried.

"Ah—women! Women—!" I wailed hopelessly. "D'you not see—?"

"Aye, put it t' women! 'Tis like a man enough tae do that!" she interrupted, turning away. "Oh, an' aye, I spoke wi' Father about ye. I told him it was naught but a bit o' twosin' i' th' moonlight that he saw—"

"Jean!" I cried. "You didn't! You—"

"Was it nae what ye wanted?" she demanded as she turned away to join her father.

"Jean, wait!" I called after her.

She half turned toward me.

"Good night t' ye, Mister MacAllister," she said flatly.

Even at that I think I would have gone after her and persisted in my argument, but at that moment Colin Robertson came up and caught me by the elbow.

"Since ye insist on it," he said, "we may as well be meetin'!"

By the time we were done all but the committee had long since gone home, and there was no hope of talking with her further.

Nor had I time thereafter to brood upon the matter. The selection of those who were to go had to be made that night if I were to take the road as promptly as possible and forestall those others who had signed, but could not be taken this time, from disposing prematurely of their present homes. We worked until dawn and even then there was no time for rest, for there were six hundred families, spread up and down the length and breadth of Sutherlandshire, that must be notified. I called in half a dozen volunteer messengers and armed each with a list and a story that they must tell and sent them forth on ponies whose hire I paid myself, out of my own pocket. When they were gone, even though I was staggering with weariness, I took the remaining names and rode out myself to spread the grim word.

I did not see Jean MacLean again after that until the rendezvous at Helmsdale, where we were to take ship for Stromness in the Orkneys. But there was many another in Strathullie and up and down the Highlands of Sutherlandshire, for that matter, who did not hesitate to tell me of the pickle I had brined. She was not alone, apparently, in holding me responsible.

It was past mid-June before I got back to Kildonan, and once I came there I had only time enough to gather my own scant belongings and say good-by to what few friends I seemed to have remaining in the neighborhood. Davie Murray, I believe, was still in my favor, and so was Jamie Gordon—though I seemed to sense some hesitancy there. After I had drunk my pint of ale with each I packed my things and hurried down to Helmsdale, where I found some hundred and thirty or so of our people already foregathered and waiting; waiting, I had begun to hope, for something like what I had been so glib as to promise them!

There were about a hundred and thirty of them, divided among twenty-seven families, with a handful of odd strays like myself to make up the balance. They were huddled all together in a single, large musty warehouse on the stone quay that stared out over the gray, restless, gale-torn sea. There they waited for the transportation that Lord Selkirk, through myself, had promised them would come up from Aberdeen. For most of them this was the first glimpse of salt water, and even so soon I was conscious of a restless sort of apprehension among them.

Nor could I much blame them for that. The sea's only promise seemed a grim one, for it was sullen and storm wracked, while the quarters into which they had been packed were cold and dank. The windowless warehouse was built of stone, and the roof, while porous enough to let the rain in at several points, was still sufficiently tight to hold all the fetid mustiness of the place. There was a thin coating of mildew over the walls, and after a day and a night blankets and portmanteaus and even the shoes on our feet began to show telltale signs of green too. Since there was but a single long room in the building it had been necessary to separate men from women and children by hanging a makeshift partition of blankets across the middle, blankets that such poor folk ill could spare.

Alec MacLean, who had been in charge of the gathering, was nowhere to be seen when I came in. Instead, to my surprise, it was a frosty Jean who greeted me.

"So, ye've come then?" she said. "We'd begun t' wonder!"

The contempt in her tone was like a stab in the belly, but I was careful not to let her see that.

"That was silly of you," I grinned. "I thought you were not speaking to me."

She tossed her head as if she cared nothing for what I might think.

"If I'd a choice I probably would not," she retorted, "but ye act for th' Earl o' Selkirk, so ye must be told."

"Eh, then," I said dryly, "you've come back to your faith in him at least!"

"I've nae choice there either," she replied. "Father's out after the others—trying to hold them together. 'Twas he told me I must tell ye as soon as ever ye came—"

I jerked up my eyes sharply and glanced around, and all at once I became aware that there was not another man in the room. The blanket partition had been looped up over the ropes that held it, and from one end of the room to the other there were none but women.

"What is this?" I demanded, alarmed. "Where are all the other men?"

"The men!" She all but spat on the word as she flung it out at me. "Where else but in th' dram shops and tipplin' halls from here half way around th' blessed bay!"

I could not help but grin, and I fear it only made her more angry.

"What's wrong with that?" I demanded, although I will say I could see the unfairness of it. It was one thing for a man to slip off to the tavern and leave his wife to scold and ruffle her feathers by her own hearth. It was another for them to take their ease in the warmth of the taproom while the womenfolk, who could not go with them, perforce huddled about a smoky peat stove in the dank chill of the ancient warehouse.

Just the same I was already beginning to learn it was no good to give a woman a strap to scourge you with, for she'd not hesitate to use it!

"What's wrong with it?" she cried indignantly. "Apart from the fact they're housin' away everything they own in their idleness an' leavin' their womenfolk to suffer the consequences, they make themselves fair game at the same time to some who'd see the whole thing fail. I tell ye they're no idle!"

I flung round at her, startled, remembering what Colin Robertson had said about agents of the North West Company, warning me to be on my guard.

"You mean they're at work already—here?" I cried.

She looked at me stonily.

"Ye were expecting it then?" she said.

I don't know why I did not notice the way she said it. I suppose I was too preoccupied with the fantastic thought. I nodded.

"Robertson warned me," I told her. But then the seeming absurdity of it struck me. "But here in Helmsdale? Oh, no lass! 'Tis too ridiculous. They'd not dare in so small a place!"

"Would they not?" She scoffed at my naïveté. "What better place could they find than such a one, where they'll find a' together? An' if 'tis not whom ye fear, then who would it be that's spreadin' amongst our lads such tales o' dreadful winters and savage beasts and murderin' red men?"

"They—?" I stared at her. "There's someone been spreading such?"

"Aye!" She nodded dourly, and her little jaw was set but her blue-gray eyes studied me intently. "So much so, ye ken, that a body canna so much as cry out in th' night o' a bad dream but th' lot o' 'em are up an' whimperin' an' millin' about like frightened kine."

"Och, you exaggerate, Jean!" I laughed.

But she did not smile in reply.

"Eh, well, so 'tis exaggerated," she retorted. "But come an' judge for yerself! Leave yer kit yon—"

"But you can't take me to such places!" I was aghast.

She snorted at my dullness.

"An' who said I would?" she replied. "Ye've said yerself 'tis a sma' place—Helmsdale. In twenty minutes I can point out to ye a' th' tipplin' houses in town. After that 'twill be yer own choice as t' how ye go about learnin' th' truth o' what I've been sayin'! Will ye come then?"

I had no quarrel with that. Indeed, I was pleased that she would walk out with me, though you may be sure she let it be understood that she meant it by no means as a favor to myself.

She was right enough about the time it took. Helmsdale is no city, although as a seaport it does have a greater proportion of dram shops and bousing kens and sailors' dives than places of like size inland. There were perhaps a half a score of such and only two or three of them could have been taken for anything else. I believe I could have found them without her, but that did not prompt me to refuse her help. Even were I so inclined this would have been rude, surely!

Slowly, and I am sure with all due solemnity on my part, I walked with her around the curve of the cove, and up around the flank of the seaward hill where the last few houses of the village straggled. As we went she pointed out to me each little public house and I nodded solemnly and made much of noting each, until finally we came to the end, well up on the rock and heather, gray and purple, windswept promontory above the village. There we halted, and she turned to face me.

"That's all there is," she told me.

I was gazing out over the white-capped sea, watching the mists swirl about the lower rocks, and I did not answer at once. When I did I fear it was not just what she expected.

"There's something grand and wild about this coast, lass," I said. "Have ever you noticed it? 'Tis ever like this, it seems. Always blustery and more often than not wet, but—"

She stamped her foot in the mud so that it splashed my stockings.

"I've not laid eyes on it before, Mister MacAllister," she said, "and

I've no time to admire the beauty o' it now! I ha' said to ye yon's all there is o' Helmsdale, an' now what d'ye propose t' do about it?"

I looked down at her and made good note of how anger and the wind had whipped the color into her cheeks.

"About Helmsdale, lass?" I said.

"Ah! Och!" she snorted furiously and turned and went striding back down the hill.

I ran and caught up with her.

"Na, na, Jean!" I said placatingly. Somehow, as angry as she was, I felt lighthearted just to be near her. "Never you mind me! I'll have a look at things, and if 'tis as you say I'm obliged to you for telling me, and I'm sure his lordship will be too. Which shop did you say your father was in?"

She glared at me as if I had suggested that Alexander MacLean was something of a toper. If it turned out that such was the case, how was I to know it?

"I don't know!" she retorted shortly.

In my preoccupation with what I planned I did not notice her distress. I passed off her curtness with a shrug.

"Well, no matter," I said. "I'll come across him no doubt. Now, here lass! Here's what I want you to do!"

I told her, then, the plan that had come into my mind as we walked, and I gave her four guineas to spend in setting up her end of it. She bridled at that, and I think her pride would have made her refuse. But I scoffed her to shame.

"Och, come now, Jean lass!" I cried. " 'Tis not just to tempt the lads back where they belong. 'Tis a thing I've had at the back of my mind for a long time. If the brig is on time, then this might be the last night for all of us in Scotland, barring of course the short whiles we'll be at the Orkneys, which is not the same at all. I think 'tis a time to be gay and merry—for auld lang syne, if you wish! Certainly 'tis no time for mournful long faces. And if it serves also to call our wandering Willies back to the fold from which they've strayed, I'm sure Lord Selkirk will agree! Will you leave that end of it to me, now, and yourself and the other good ladies tend to the rest, eh? Mind, now, what I say! It must be such as can compete with the best Helmsdale can offer, else it will all be for naught!"

She closed her mouth in the midst of a breath drawn so that she might say something, a protest I suspect, and looked at me strangely. And then as meekly as ever I think I had seen her she smiled and nodded.

"Whatever ye say, Malcolm," she said.

I waited until she was gone and then turned in at the nearest of the public houses that she had indicated. I was in luck apparently. Of the ten or a dozen dives that fronted on the little bay, only five or six seemed to be favored by our folk, or it might have been the other way round. Although Alexander MacLean was not there it was my fortune to stumble on one of the most popular. As I entered there was a sudden clap of silence in the crowded, noisy room. I recognized a number of the men of Kildonan, hugging the fireplace, and they of course knew me. The rest I did not know, but then I had seen so many faces in the course of the last few weeks that I felt I could be excused for not being sure of all the others, although those that I had signed on, I knew, recognized me.

But there were two, short, blocky, heavy-muscled fellows, whom I knew I had never laid eyes on before. Orkneymen I came to discover they were later on; lads that had been in the employ of the Hudson's Bay Company for a time, and then had been whiled away by the Northwesters and sent back home with orders to do what they could to hinder Lord Selkirk's undertaking.

There was something afoot. That much was perfectly clear to me. Such a sudden silence does not fall upon such a group unless there is a feeling of guilt in the air. But I pretended not to notice.

"Hallo, lads!" I cried. "By the Lord I've got back at last, and I tell you the last few days I wondered if I'd make it!"

There was a half murmured greeting and a stiffening which I pretended not to notice. I moved up to the small bar and pushed in between one of our lads and the burlier of the two Orkneymen, and I saw then that Jean MacLean had not exaggerated. I must be careful. But I must also move fast. The idea came to me all at once, and I was desperate enough to snatch at it.

"Who'll help me wet down?" I cried over my shoulder. "I'm thorough wet outside, but dry as dust within, and I like company when I drink. Speak up, lads! I'll buy once for all."

A half dozen voices rose, naming their preference, and I noticed that the two Orkneymen did not hang back.

"Make mine ale," I nodded to the host. But I spoke out in protest as he reached for the regular glazed noggin. I pointed to a tall pewter canister on an upper shelf. "No, no! None so sma'! I'll take that one!"

If the heavy mug had not held twice the ordinary one I think the landlord might have protested. As it was he climbed up grudgingly and fetched down the pot, filled it and handed it to me. I lifted it and turned to the Orkneyman at my elbow. No out-islander, I felt, was going to spoil my game!

"To the voyage!" I said, and drained half the mug down.

The fellow seemed somewhat disconcerted, but he followed my example. I leered at him.

"Aaaaah! That's better!" I said and wiped my mouth. "Tell me, friend, how long have you been working for the North West Company?"

He goggled at me. If he had been quick of wit he would have denied it, of course, and so hamstrung me. But he was a dull clod.

"I—unnh—hey?" was all he could say.

"Come, come!" I rapped impatiently, giving him no time to recover. "You do work for them, don't you?"

He might have taken warning from the abrupt silence that fell upon the room. But evidently he was too engrossed in what I was saying, as I had hoped he would be!

"Unnhh—yuh!" he replied.

"And weren't you sent here to tell these lads a pack of lies to scare them off?" I demanded.

He turned purple under the deep dark of his skin.

"Hey, now! Wait a minute!" he snarled.

"Weren't you?" I persisted.

"All right, if I were!" he flared. His temper was up now and fought for expression. "Eh, now, whut's yon t'ye?"

He half cocked back his fist, but I was expecting that.

"This!" I told him, and flung what was left of my beer in his face.

While he was mopping at the suds, half bending over, pawing at his eyes, I smashed him across the back of his head with the heavy pewter mug and he went down in a lump.

The other Orkneyman was on me, even as I struck, as I had expected. But because I had expected him I was able to drop low upon my knees and send him clutching and hurtling through thin air above me. It was just luck that in his fall his chin cracked against the bar and he fell with a grunt of inert unconsciousness across the body of his comrade.

I have always tried to be a peaceful, docile sort of man, and you may be sure that the sight of two such bruisers, lying slumbering at my feet was as much a surprise to me as God in heaven knows it must have been to those others in the room. There was a moment of astonished silence, then someone at the back of the crowd spoke out, half-whispering his surprise.

"Aye now! Will ye look yon!"

I glanced up, half dazed myself.

"See?" I said. "D'you see how easy 'twould be to scalp such as they? No wonder the poor devils are afraid!"

A roar of laughter greeted the remark.

"Tak' th' birks tae 'em, mon!" someone cried.

"Aye, mind ye learn 'em tha pay's and cues!" shouted another.

I was not so foolish as to take offense at their good-natured raillery. I straightened.

"I think they've learned 'em," I retorted. "Now ye and I have a thing to do, for this should be our last night on shore, and it should not be wasted. Come up, lads, and fill your mugs. Listen while I tell you, for I'll need your help in this!"

So I made allies of them that might have opposed me otherwise. I knew that I could not hope to repeat such luck in other places, but having a nucleus of my own around me now there was no need for that.

"Now, look ye, lads!" I said when they had all drawn and held glasses in their hands. "Tomorrow it should be Lord Selkirk will come with the ship from Aberdeen to carry us along the first leg of the way, as far as Stromness. There'll be work and hardship before ever we come to Canada. But mind 'twill be no harder than what you've seen before, and not you nor I have the right to let down those folk that count upon us. You've wives and kin. I've none, but I've all of yourselves, and I'll not let you cry ruin for me!"

"Hear! 'Ear!" grumbled some older man at the back of the room.

"Hear so!" I retorted, catching up his cue. "Hear what I have to tell you. I've come to this place because I felt I could count upon this particular group. I need you to help me. Now this is what must be done!"

And I told them what was in my mind. I told them that at the warehouse, where the general quarters were, that there was to be a general banquet: Roast mutton and pease and barley and oaten bannocks and as much ale as a man could tuck away. But all this, I said, was being prepared and set out by our own. It was not to be expected that such as these two clods that lay at my feet, the one across the other, could ever ask or offer anything like the same. But whether they could or no it was up to us. We could not disappoint our own.

Therefore, I said, I wanted them to walk down the main quayside street with me; to stop in each and every dram shop and public house along the way, and help me round up our people. For there were those that would rather they were not gathered up, and to whose advantage it would be if we never sailed, and of that I promised to speak to them all in detail if they would first do as I asked. After that, after we had supped on what would be provided, and after I had spoken—then they might suit themselves.

It was just luck, I suppose, that we had no more such trouble as I had encountered in the first place that I visited. It might also have been the fact that as we went from place to place our numbers grew, and the Orkneymen who had been hired by the Northwesters to smash our undertaking were too few to care to tangle with us openly. I noticed, or at least I was sure I noticed, a number of them. But by the time we had made the entire round and gathered up our own I had had a chance to count noses, and I was delighted to find that not one of all our lads was missing!

It was in the next last but one that we came upon Alec MacLean. As we came trooping in he recognized me and stood up, with his stout mug of ale in his hand, and stood weaving and blinking a little, I thought.

"Ah, now, Mister MacAllister, so ye've come at last!" he exclaimed.

"I couldn't come sooner," I replied, and looked at the half-empty tankard in his fist.

He noticed my glance and drank up hastily and then set the mug down as if he would pretend that he'd had naught to do with it. He coughed a little apologetically behind his hand.

"I was just tryin' t' convince th' lads that 'twas time t' be goin' home!" he said. "Ah, Mister MacAllister, ye've no notion th' trouble it's been t' hold 'em t' line an' make 'em realize th' ways o' th' Lord are ins—inscrubtibible, an' that God's righteous wrath will fa' on all!"

"Aye, so," I replied, "and have you described me as this 'Righteous wrath'? In any case 'tis time to be going. We're all wanted this night at the warehouse, for good reasons."

He brightened suddenly, as if all his problems were all at once solved.

"Ha' they come, then?" he cried. "Is th' ship here?"

I shook my head.

"Not yet," I told him, "but she should be by tomorrow. No, this is something else, and you must be there."

He assumed a somewhat wobbly dignity and bowed.

"Verra well, then, Mister MacAllister! Yer sairvant, sir!" he said, and followed me out with all the rest of our people at his heels.

The potlatch, a word I learned later among the Indians of the western coast, to which I invited them was the thing I had sent Jeannie back to tend. By the time we were trooping down along the quay she

had turned out the womenfolk and younkers at the damp building and
laid out the sumptuous board.

And a sumptuous board it was, too! The women, wearied of doing
naught but blowing their own and their children's noses on their aprons,
were prepared to fall in with the scheme. And when Jean showed
them the money I had given her for the purpose they grew all excited
and fell to at once. Womanlike, of course, they did not provide enough
of the cheerful cup. But that I was able to remedy by sending out a
half dozen stout and trusted lads to fetch down a brace of hogsheads
of ale—enough, I thought, to do for all.

So far as Jean was concerned, the job was well done. With what I
had provided she had rounded up the women and set some to laying
out long tables, some to fetching peat and such odd bits of wood as
they could find. Still others went with her and found the food: six good
stout legs of mutton and a dozen geese, plucked from the roasting
spits of half as many public houses that had anticipated our trade.
Pease porridge and barley broth, potatoes and kale made up the rest
of the feast, and as we approached, even before we reached the quay
where the warehouse stood, we could smell it. I noticed that the men
about and behind me perked up at the first whiff of the aroma, and I
decided that it was about true: There is no way to a man's heart but
through his belly!

For all of that we dined fine and drained the barrels, and all, I
think, even the womenfolk, enjoyed the banquet that was laid out that
night. When the eating was done we snatched off the cloth, and I
climbed up on the table. I suppose it was fortunate that I had been a
schoolmaster. I could look down at them and feel sure of myself.

"Now, then!" I told them severely. "Ye've all your bellies filled and
I'll ask you to listen to what I've to say. 'Tis little enough by way of
payment for such as you've just had. Yon's a joke of course, but lads
and lassies, and younkers all among you, mind—what you've enjoyed
here is but a taste of the plenties Lord Selkirk offers. There are some
that would say you different, but put this test to any such as may try to
turn you off: What's the advantage for him? There's advantage for you
if all I've promised comes true, and it will. Naturally there are those
would see you not settled where we're bound. 'Twould hurt their
business. But we have the right and we have the backing! Shall we cry
craven now?"

"Na! Na! Be damned t' that! Let th' de'il tak' his ain!" That was the
gist of the chorus that rose in reply, and perhaps I should not, but I
took it seriously.

"Hark ye!" I cried. "You've had my warning! Not of us, but of those that would hinder you. Mark me, pay no heed to them. If they persist—throw them in the bay—!"

Loud cheers went up.

"I see," I went on, "that you've lost none of your enthusiasm. Here is the crucial moment! See that you lose none of it now!"

They cheered me. I wondered what I had said that was so remarkable. But it is a truth that they did not show the same inclination to waver after that—not, at least, while we were in Helmsdale.

That night was a happy one; one at least in which we all were friends. The next morning dawned as a hundred others had before it—gray and wet and dismal. There were a few who felt as dismal as the day. But in the main heads were clear and hearts were lightened by the evening's celebration of the night before. I mind it was toward noon when I came out on the quay, having naught to do but sleep, and plenty of sleeping to do! There was a grim, somewhat dilapidated brig warping into the wharf a little above the warehouse as I came out, but I did not notice it. My own attention was drawn to a little knot of men at the townward side. I turned toward them.

Some of our lads were there, perhaps a baker's dozen or more. And for the other five or six, I recognized the cut of their jib. My two friends of the night before were there, but they did not see me immediately. It was clear that some very earnest discussion was going forward between them.

I wasted a few moments, trying to decide what I should do. So long as there was no actual movement among our people to go with the Northwestmen I was not sure I had a right to interfere. I watched them out of the corner of one eye, and out of the other noted that the grimy brig had sent her lines ashore and made fast. I started toward it. But at that moment two of the Northwesters turned from the little group down the quay and started back toward town with half a dozen of our fellows at their heels.

Abruptly I did an about face and bore down upon the little group, raising my voice to those who were townward bound as I went.

"Hold on, there!" I called, and the interruption, unexpected as it was, made them pause and look back.

At the sight of me walking toward them one of the two hulking chaps I had managed to stretch upon the barroom floor the night before recognized me.

"Yawn 'e iss!" he yelped.

His shoulders hunched and his head drew down, his arms spread wide and he charged toward me.

I have never claimed to be a brawler, or even skilled at self-defense, but that rush was clumsy and obvious, even to me. I was close to the wharf's edge as he came, and it was a simple matter to step aside and let him pass! It seems to me incredible as I write it now, that he could ever have thought to snatch me in so crude a trap. But apparently he did, for when he reached for me and found me not there, he went careening on, his arms waving wildly, one, two, three steps and then over the edge of the wharf and into the cold, wet water of the harbor some ten or twelve feet below.

There was scarcely a sound while it happened. Only a sort of gurgling wail from him as he went over, that was choked off abruptly as he went under. For an instant after he had disappeared there was not a sound from the little knot of astonished onlookers. Then one of the Northwestmen spoke up.

"Hi! 'E cawn't swim!" he said matter-of-factly.

"Can't he?" I said, glancing at him. "Then maybe you'd best fish him out!"

He might have argued, but at that moment there came a sudden sound of bawling and splashing from below. The one who had spoken and one other rushed forward, forgetting me for the moment and they dropped to their knees at the edge of the quay, leaning far out to look down at their sodden companion and shout down well meaning, but not very sound, advice.

Behind them I turned and went curiously to the edge. My late assailant was flapping his arms frantically and inhaling deep gulps of sea-water between yells. The same curiosity fetched the others up behind me. I touched the nearest Northwester on the shoulder.

"Can you swim?" I demanded.

"In course!" he retorted indignantly.

I tapped the other.

"And you," I said. "Can you swim too?"

"Like a ruddy duck!" he snarled.

"Ah, then!" I replied. "You'd best help your friend, for he seems to be having a little difficulty with it!"

With that I planted an open hand in the middle of each one's back and pushed.

God alone knows what prompted me to such a prank. It was foolishly easy. They had never even suspected that I would do it, and consequently they soared out, with arms flapping, like a pair of hapless gulls and dropping to join their soaking comrade. As they fell, of course, the other Northwesters in the crowd uttered a yelp and turned toward me. But the trick had taken the fancy out of my own fellows, and in less time than it takes me to tell about it all the rest of them were deposited in the bay.

"Now there!" I cried, as soon as laughter would let me. "You see, now, lads? Remember! There's the way always to do it. The bay's the place for any that would interfere!"

"I say, now!" said a voice from outside the outer fringes of our little group. "I say, now! That's not a bad idea at all, eh? Well done, Mister MacAllister. I'm proud of you."

I turned about abruptly with a little shout of surprise and welcome for the tall, red-haired newcomer.

"Lord Selkirk!" I cried. "Wherever did you drop from?"

He chuckled as he began to shake hands all around, and nodded back along the quay toward where the untidy little brig now lay moored.

"We just arrived, Mister Robertson and I, in the *Arethusa,* yon, from Aberdeen. She's to carry us to Stromness, where you'll transfer to the Company's ship, the *Prince of Wales.* As soon as we had tied up I could see that something was afoot on the quay, so I came down at once."

"But you came only in time to see the finish of it." I laughed. "Ah, my lord, if I had suspected that you'd be so prompt I'd have delayed things a bit so that you would have seen more of the fun!"

"I don't think I missed much of it," he grinned.

He turned back toward the brig and I fell in beside him.

"But this was just the climax of a number of events," I told him. "Last night, for instance, there was a considerable deal of activity. Seriously, your Lordship, the Northwesters have not been idle. Our folk have been restless and on the verge of abandoning the project."

He glanced at me quickly.

"You've not lost any?" he demanded.

I shook my head.

"Not yet," I assured him. "But yesterday it was close. Their confidence has been somewhat shaken by the stories that have been spread among them. I think it would cheer them up a good deal if you said a word to them. They're all together now."

He nodded soberly.

"Is there aught to wait on?" he asked, "any reason why we should not embark today?"

I glanced down the quay to where the little group of bedraggled

Orkneymen were dragging themselves up on shore. The scowls that they flung in our direction boded no good of this adventure.

"I'd say the sooner we sailed the better," I replied.

He followed the direction of my stare with a faint smile of understanding.

"I see what you mean!" he said. "And quite right, too. Very well. Suppose I have a word with them, and then we'll be off, eh?"

And that was the way it was. Fortunately, after the festivities of the evening before, it was still early enough in the day so that none of our people had drifted away to the town as yet—at least none that I could be sure of. When Lord Selkirk and Colin Robertson appeared among us they were at once seized by excitement and fired with enthusiasm renewed. He spoke to them, standing upon one of the rough plank tables so that all could see him.

"This is the day, my friends," he said, "that we have all so long and so tediously and so desperately awaited. There have been times, I know, when it has occurred to you to doubt—to wonder if it were true; and if it were true, whether it was worthwhile—whether it was worth all the trouble and misery and heartache that I know it must cause you. But let me reassure you. It is true and it is worthwhile. Remember that what you give up today is what would have been taken from you, without return, tomorrow. This way you will be among the advance guard of new people settling in a new world! I have seen this new world and I promise you it has many advantages that this old one of ours has not. The soil is fertile, the climate is good, the winters are cold, but the summers are warm. However, the main thing, the great thing, is that there is land enough and plenty for all—and you, being among the first to go, will have first choice!"

A cheer went up at that and he paused and smiled.

"Now then," he went on as soon as they were quiet again, "I want each family and group among you to gather up its belongings and carry them on board the brig. If any are not here now, see that they are summoned back at once, for as soon as we are all aboard, and as soon as the tide swings and begins to run out in the evening we will sail. I will go with you as far as Stromness, where the *Prince of Wales* is awaiting us, and if any of you have questions that you wish to ask I will be glad to answer them en route."

He leapt down lightly, remarkably agile for a man of his size, and it was plain that only the sight of him had done wonders toward restoring the somewhat tattered morale of our group. Between his brief talk and my own efforts of the night before, I felt that once again things were as they ought to be. I was pleased to notice, too, although I had no time then to speak to her about it, that Jean MacLean seemed to be relieved of a load of care. Nevertheless, when we cast off at last and swung down with the outrunning tide and I finally had a chance to count noses, I discovered that some half dozen of our people had listened to the ominous croakings of the Northwesters, and had slipped quietly off and left us.

The *Arethusa* belied her name, for there was nothing at all about her resembling the wood nymph, unless it was that she leaked like a fountain. She was old and grubby; she had once been a collier and the dust had been rubbed into her timbers until it was too deeply embedded ever to be cleaned away. Besides this she was small and cramped, and even though her belly bulged there was not room in her holds to accommodate such a crowd as ours in any degree of comfort. When we sailed, however, we were hardly inclined to trouble ourselves about that. What mattered a little discomfort? We were on our way at last, and at worst it was less than a hundred miles voyage to Stromness. The next evening at the latest would surely see us there, and we could bear with a little hardship to accomplish that.

But we did not reach Stromness the next evening, or even the next. In fact we were three whole days making that miserable, insignificant, eighty-five-mile journey. The gales howled and the seas hurtled down upon us, for all the world it seemed to me, as if all the Highlands had suddenly gone to sea. Our people were seasick, and I was no exception to that rule. Indeed, I think there was not one in twenty who did not think that he was about to die, and in fact rather hoped he would—the quicker the better. The ship was a shambles, and those whose sea legs kept them strong enough to clean it up were too busy, while the rest of us hardly cared.

On top of all that, it seemed to me bitter cold and wet. Scotland's winds are often raw. But the sea's blast was savage and incessant, and it lashed at us with a knifelike edge that seemed to bite deep into our flesh. Even when we were comparatively snug below we could hear it howling and tearing at the rigging until we came to hate its moaning shrill almost as much as we feared its piercing bite.

Against the wind and the seas we clawed our way northward. We bumbled up past Wick and around between Duncansby Head and the Pentland Skerries and left John o' Groat's behind. We battled our way up across Pentland Firth, past Swona and Switha and Flotta and turned around Pan Hope into the swirling currents of Scapa Flow. There, in the lee of Mainland, the fury of the wind and sea abated somewhat and we beat up through the Brinig Deeps and under Graemsay and into Hoy Sound in comparative comfort; and there, at last, we were at Stromness, a desolate place, I thought, all drab, gray granite hills with the straggling village spattered against them, and only the fine harbor in the crook of its arm to recommend it.

But it needed no more recommendation than that for us, for though the mists swirled down, soft and gray, from the island hills, casting an eerie softness over everything in sight, there was still no mistaking the shapes of the ships moored in the harbor. There were several of them, although we were only later to learn their names and each individual mission. The smart vessel, lying farthest out, toward the Hoy, was a sloop of war, H.B.M. *Brazen,* which I learned was at Lord Selkirk's request to convoy us; although we saw no other sign of it, and indeed I had almost forgotten it, we were still at war with the United States, and Yankee cruisers, when they managed to evade our blockade, were dangers to be reckoned with. Next inshore from her lay the brig *Missionary,* bound for Labrador with workers for the Moravian Missions there. Far inshore, closest of all to the jetties at the village, no doubt for convenience in loading the supplies and trade goods that she was taking on, was the small, ship-rigged *Eddystone,* the supply ship for the Hudson's Bay Company.

But these we noted only in passing, for it was but natural that all eyes aboard our grimy little brig should be drawn to the great, hulking ship that lay moored, a little aloof, as it were from these others, out in the center of the harbor. I realize now what I was not then sailor enough to recognize, that she was fat and tubby and so built as to roll and wallow in any kind of a sea; that while at a distance she looked shipshape and smart to a landsman's eye, her flaking paint and gray spotted sails, her frayed rope ends and Irish Pennants, loose blocks and insecure tackle marked her for a poor found, badly managed vessel. In fairness to Lord Selkirk, however, I think it should be added that he was as much a landsman as any of us, and he no more than we saw aught wrong with her. We swept in close under her stern and came to anchor not a cable's length away. From there we could make out clearly the scrolled lettering on her stern: *Prince of Wales.* We had guessed it, of course, but here was proof irrefutable. A cheer went up at sight of it, and it seemed to me that some of our folk glanced at me and smiled more trustingly. Several turned and plunged below to gather up their families and belongings, and I could almost feel the pulse of new life and hope that went surging through them.

I was studying the big, fat, solid-looking ship, leaning on the brig's rail and thinking that here, at last, was the real beginning of our adventures, when Jean MacLean came to stand beside me. I gave her a quick, wondering look, not yet sure that she meant peace between us.

"Well, Jean," I said quickly, to cover what might be an awkward silence. "Yonder she lies. There's the ship that will carry us to America."

She nodded very slightly, soberly, but though she was looking at the vessel, clearly her thoughts were not on it.

"Malcolm—" she began, and then paused not just sure how to say what was troubling her.

"Aye, Jean?" I prompted her.

"Malcolm!" she said again. "Can ye forgi'e me?"

"Forgive you, Jean?" I cried. "For what?"

I knew what she was talking about, of course, but I suppose it is not in human nature to let well enough alone. I wanted to hear her say it.

"I misjudged ye, Malcolm," she replied in a small voice. "I minded what ye said t' me that night on th' way home, an' when things fell out as they did I thought ye were a' fraud. Can ye—can ye owerlook my foolishness—an' excuse me?"

At that I should have been content, surely. But even so I could not seem to let it stand. At least I can offer this in my own extenuation— that I sought to ease her own sense of guilt by taking blame to myself.

"But, Jean!" I cried. "Of course 'tis all forgiven and forgotten, if you feel that there was aught to forgive and forget! But the truth is what I told you that night, I know naught of the honesty of the thing, and but for yourself and your father I care less! I've been given a task to do and I've done it to the best of my ability. I'm sorry, of course, about those others that had to be left behind."

She gave me an odd look.

"But, Malcolm," she said, "yon's th' ship, th' *Prince of Wales*, that's tae carry us t' Canada. Surely there's proof enough—"

"Aye!" I told her. "There she lies and here we are, and knowing that here is where we really start makes me the more willing to believe in the thing. But we've a far long way to go yet, Jean, and there's no way for us to be sure till we get there and see what's in store for us at the Forks of the Red."

She stared off across the gun-metal bay toward the grim, misty hills of the rocky island.

"Ye think, then, ye've fetched us a huntygowk?" she asked.

"A fool's errand?" I shrugged. "How can I tell? But if I have, Jean, then I daresay I'm as great a fool as any! All that I know is that I'd like things to be as Jamie Gordon made them. I'll make no bones of it, I love you, Jean. I'll marry you tomorrow—aye, tonight, if you'll say the word!"

She flushed. I will say that. Yet she avoided my eyes.

"Na, Malcolm!" she protested. "There maun be banns an' a', an' then we'll be at sea for aye weeks an' weeks. Ye'll be th' men tae yer hold, an' we'll be women in ours, an' what for o' a honeymoon would that be? Na, leave it now, Malcolm, an'—"

"And, perhaps, Jean?" I cried. "Perhaps when we're come to Canada—? Alec himself could say the words over us, and we'd be the first in the New World to start out the new life together?"

"Perhaps, Malcolm," she said. "Ye mind, I canna tell ye now?"

I think I might have protested that, but there came then the whispering sound of a scraping foot and I turned abruptly to find Lord Selkirk himself, who had evidently willy-nilly heard all that we said, trying to slip away.

When he realized that I had seen him he stopped and turned as red as his hair.

"Will you forgive me, Mac?" he said. "And you, Mistress MacLean? I came up for a moment to speak with you, seeing you here at the rail, and I could not help but overhear what you were saying. Believe me, I did not mean to eavesdrop!"

How much he had heard of what we had said, of course, I had no way of knowing, but naturally I put the best face on it that I could. I nodded to him.

"Good afternoon to you, Milord," I said. "I daresay that's the first time a man has offered a proposal of marriage with his employer as a witness. I hope you'll give me a good character reference!"

He chuckled, falling in with the spirit of what I said.

"Of course!" he agreed. "Mistress MacLean—"

He turned toward her, but she was already gone, hurrying down the deck with one hand over her mouth, toward the women's quarters. He looked back at me sharply, seriously.

"I—I hope you understand, Mister MacAllister," he said, "it was inadvertent!"

"I understand, your Lordship," I replied glumly.

He smiled sympathetically and put his hand on my shoulder.

"I'll do what I can," he promised me, "though from what you said she is not too sure of my own bona fides."

I glanced at him sharply.

"I'd not want you to think we've any doubts, your Lordship," I said.

"Of course not," he laughed. "But yet you have them, quite naturally. So do I! But I'll give you my word as to the honesty of my intent. None of us can be sure of what lies around the corner. But if you will accept what I've said to you at its face value, that's all I ask."

"I've no reason, aye, yea or nay, Milord, to question it," I told him. "The time to worry about such things was back in Kildonan. Now we must make the best of it—and the best will be what we make it!"

"Aaaah, brave words, Mister MacAllister!" he smiled. "I assure you that so far as I am concerned everything that can be done will be done to make them come true. I'll not pretend that the land to which you are going is not, just now, a howling wilderness. But it will not always be so. And you will be first on the ground. I hope all goes well between you and Mistress MacLean."

"Thank you, sir," I said, not altogether sure what I should say. "We'll do our best."

"I could ask no more," he chuckled. "But now, Mister MacAllister, I think we should lose no more time. Our folk are crowded and not just as happy as larks aboard the *Arethusa*. The sooner we can move them to the *Wales* the better for all. But first we must call on Captain Riker, in command there. Will you join us?"

Since he asked it I could scarcely refuse. Within a matter of minutes the longboat was out and we were dancing and dipping across the choppy harbor seas toward the tall ship.

I see no reason to go into the details of that meeting. Had there been anything extraordinary about it there might well be some reason for describing it at length, or even for some doubt or wonder on my part. But there was nothing of the sort. We climbed up the ladder to the *Prince of Wales's* deck and were greeted by Captain Riker himself, who led us below to his cabin and served us full tumblers of French brandy from his own sideboard.

In passing I was aware of a vague general air of dilapidation about the vessel, but I saw nothing that such a lubber as myself would not be like to accept. It might not be the best appointed ship afloat. But then, neither was Davie Murray's public house at Kildonan the finest in all Scotland. The comparison seemed to me apt.

Like his ship, Captain Riker was unprepossessing. He was a short, wiry, dark little man who seemed affable enough, and who certainly gave us no cause on that occasion to doubt either his ability as a seaman or his courage in the face of an emergency. He seemed no more, no less than a man who could be counted upon to do his job quietly and with at least reasonable efficiency, and I think we all accepted him as such.

He welcomed us, literally. There is no doubt in my mind but that he was glad to see us, for he had been waiting nearly a month. The ship was ready, he told us. She was watered and cleaned, and hold space had been set aside for our passengers. Let them come on board at once. There were still a few loads of supplies to take on. But that should not take long. In the meantime there was no reason that he could see why the colonists should not take advantage of the more spacious quarters on the *Wales*. After all, they would be aboard for some time—might as well get acquainted now—ha-hah! And that would give his lordship and the *Arethusa* reason enough to return. From this point on, he implied, he was quite capable of taking full charge.

I must admit that I was conscious of a slight chill at that. The Captain seemed to me a shade too cocksure and assuming, and I ventured to speak out.

"Would it be presumptuous of me," I put in generally, "to remind Captain Riker we would not presume to dispute his command of the ship, but that the passengers are to be in the charge of Mister MacLean and myself?"

Their reactions to the remark were varied and interesting. Colin Robertson smiled cryptically. Riker himself looked as shocked as if an innocuous caterpillar had turned and bitten him, and he shot me a venomous look. Alexander MacLean looked grateful, and Lord Selkirk was a little impatient.

"I'm sure Captain Riker understands the situation!" he said curtly.

Since the point was made I saw no sense in continuing the discussion. I simply bowed silent acknowledgment and let it stand at that. That very afternoon the *Arethusa* was warped in as close as possible to the *Prince of Wales* and the colonists set aboard the ship and assigned to the quarters that had been prepared for them amidships, in the upper tiers of the two main hatchways. Some ninety-seven of us were crowded into the *Wales*, and I daresay there would have been room for all but for the stores and trade goods that we were carrying out for the Hudson's Bay Company and which had been stowed in the lower holds. Those colonists that were left over, numbering a score or so, were set over on board the *Eddystone*, the regular supply ship.

In the excitement of the moment it did not occur to any of us to question that, and even if we had thought of it I think we would have dismissed it as a quibble. What difference could it make? At the same time, coming as we did from the cramped and grimy holds of the tiny *Arethusa,* we scarcely were critical of our new quarters. Nor had we much opportunity to look more closely into our situation. Lord Selkirk had evidently come prepared to give us a rousing sendoff, for that evening he brought off from the brig vast quantities of ale and brandy, roasts and all manner of delectable foods, such as were fit to grace his own board, and thereupon he bade us sit down to such a banquet as few of us had ever been privileged to see. There were toasts and speeches, fine prophecies and an abundance of optimistic enthusiasm. Whether it was that or the wine I could not say, but I know that that night, at least, everyone inside the ship and out, everyone on our side, at any rate, was a prince of fine fellows, and we loved him dearly. It was well past midnight when the last of us stumbled off to our blankets and Lord Selkirk and Colin Robertson returned to the *Arethusa.*

When we awoke the next morning and soaked the cobwebs from our eyes in a bucket of cold sea water it was to find them gone already, back again to Aberdeen and Scotland, where there was yet much work to be done. From that point on we were on our own.

6. THE WASTE OF SEAS

IT MAY BE THAT LORD SELKIRK'S VISIT TO STROMNESS STIRRED CAPTAIN Riker to unwonted action. It was my impression that it would be several days yet before the last lot of supplies were brought on board and stowed. But evidently I was mistaken there, for that very afternoon they were lightered out to us and by night they were under battened hatches and we were ready for sea.

Even in so brief a time, however, there was opportunity to gather some inkling of what lay ahead. I was cold in the 'tween decks that first night aboard the *Prince of Wales*. It was true that there was more room than aboard the brig, but by the same token our body warmth did not help to temper the chill and there were more drafts. I judged from the restlessness of the twisted sleepers around me, whenever I awoke enough to open one eye, that my companions felt the same. I noticed, too, that the great, cavernous space was clammy as a tomb and fetid with the stench of the bilge, far more so than the grubby little *Arethusa's* malodorous mid-section. The brig, at least, was occasionally aired. But to judge from her musty aroma such a fate had never befallen the *Wales*. Lying in harbor, as we were, in comparative shelter, with the air mild if wet, there was no reason why the 'tween deck's ports should be kept tightly triced up. But when I attempted to open some of them the following day I found that they had been spiked and barred solidly, so that short of using a hammer and crowbar they could not possibly be opened. I made up my mind to speak of it to the captain, but in the press of other events I forgot it until some time after we had gotten to sea. By that time Captain Riker had excellent reason to reject the idea, since in such weather as we were having by then the ports could not have been opened in any case.

The happenings that drove the thought from my mind, however, were not insignificant. In the first place, as soon as I awoke and joined some of our other passengers on deck I noticed that a good half of them were hacking and coughing and snuffling already, and I feared that by the next day there would be more of them. I spoke of it to Alexander MacLean.

"Aye, I've noticed," he replied dourly. "I tell ye 'twas bitter th' night. Did ye no notice it, Mac?"

"I did so!" I assured him. "But what can we do about it?"

He pondered the problem for a moment and scratched his cheek.

"Aweel!" he growled at last, and paused to hock and spit over the side. "Aweel, I mind there was a sailor lad i' th' brig was saying t' me that oft'times tha'd light coal braziers i' th' 'tween decks t' tak' th' chill off—that's o' course i' guid weather."

We tried that after we had breakfasted on vissid, treacly porridge and oaten bannocks, burnt on the outside and doughy in the middle. I supposed later that my mouth was still thick from the night before, for at that meal I noticed nothing peculiar about the water that was served out to us from the scuttle butt.

As soon as we had done eating we bargained with a bumboatman to go ashore and fetch us out a dozen sacks of sea coal and ten or twelve large, flat stones. While he was about that we scoured about among our own and our companions' belongings until we found two large, round-bellied iron kettles and a pair of middle sized gridirons. These we commandeered, and when our bumboatman returned from the town we propped the kettles up upon the stones, so that they would not set fire to the deck, placed the gridirons inside the kettles, to allow for some draft, and in a few moments had a warming fire going merrily in each.

But we congratulated ourselves upon our success rather too soon, for our kindling burned quickly away and our coals sank down into a smoking, smoldering heap. In the confined space of the 'tween decks, with all the ports shut, even though we kept the hatches open, we soon found ourselves gasping and choking and coughing with the smoke, and wondering if the cure were not worse than the disease. Certainly our improvised braziers did not give out enough heat to compensate for the discomfort they caused, and to top it all Captain Riker, seeing the smoke rising from the hold and fearing for a moment that his ship was on fire, came tumbling down in a flurry of panic to investigate. When he found what we were about he became furious and ordered us to fling our burners overboard, and never again, under any circumstances, to dare to light another aboard his

ship. He had no intention, he muttered as he climbed back on deck, of
seeing it burned out from under him by a pack of blethering idiots!

Somewhat crestfallen at the results of our experiment, we traded
our sea coal to the cook for extra rations of tea for all, and then, for
warmth, sent our bumboat friend ashore again for a dozen casks of
brandy. With that, at least, we felt, if we were to freeze to death we
would not feel it so much!

It was well past midday by then, and so again we broke our fast
on soggy bannocks and hardtack, washed down with tea that tasted
suspiciously like dishwater. In the circumstances it is not surprising
that I sought out the water butt after the meal was done to wash the
taste out of my mouth. Clearly if this was a fair sample of the food
we were to be served throughout the voyage we would hardly live
like kings! And since this was just the start of the voyage it seemed to
me logical that we could expect to fare worse before we were done.

To my surprise the water was not much better. I drew off my
allotted cupful and lifted it to my lips. I had drained off half of it
before I noticed anything wrong with it. Then I took the cup down
and sniffed. The water had tasted brackish, stale. And when I smelled
it there was a definitely stagnant odor. I glanced at the sailor who stood
constantly on guard by the spigot.

"I thought this was fresh water!" I said.

"Sure it is!" he grinned. "Ivery one o' th' butts has ben filled since
we ben here, s'welp me!"

"Were they scrubbed?" I demanded.

He looked at me in surprise.

"Scrubbed?" he cried. "Lumme, no! We never worshes 'em out!
Where's th' need—specially w'en they already've got some worter left
in 'em?"

"Do you mean to say that you didn't pour off the old water first?"
In my incredulity I may have spoken more sharply than I intended,
for he turned sulky.

"Wot for?" he growled. "An' make just that much more work fer
ourselves? Be blowed! I should think not!"

I could not tell, of course. I supposed that it was all right since it
was what they were accustomed to. It did not seem to have harmed
them. Still I must say that it did not make the water taste any better.

Nor did Jeannie MacLean think highly of it when I chanced to
mention it to her that evening. I came upon her after supper, when
the day was just in the gloaming, at the edge of the dusk. The last
load from the lighters had been swung aboard and the hatches were

battened down, for the night, we thought. At least we had no way of knowing that it was to be for any longer. Most of the rest of the ship's company, officers, seamen and passengers alike, were below. But I had come up for a turn in the air and there she was, leaning upon the rail and staring somberly at the rocky, bleak mass of the island. It came to me that here was as good an opportunity as I could ask to press my advantage. She was obviously glum, and if I could cheer her a little wouldn't that be proof of my concern for her? All that day, I had felt, she had been avoiding me, although I thought I could understand why.

"Come, lass, why so grim?" I asked cheerfully as I took my place beside her. "Are you not pleased that we're away at last?"

She flung me a startled glance, for she had evidently not heard me approach, and I could hear her breath catch in her throat. Then she turned away and would have gone if I had not caught her hand.

"Don't go, Jean!" I begged.

She swung back then, and even in the dusk I could see that she was flushed and embarrassed.

"Malcolm, he—he heard—?" She could scarcely whisper it.

"Aye, he heard, Jean," I told her. "But what of that? 'Tis naught shameful for a man to say he loves you, and if he chanced to be where he could overhear it—why, then, 'twas he who should not have been there!"

"But, Mac," she cried, "th' other! Th' other things ye said! He must ha' heard that, too. Oh, I tell ye, I could fair die!"

"Nonsense!" I scoffed. "You know it's an old saying that eaves-droppers never hear good of themselves. Besides, Jean, he did not mind. He's quite aware of all our doubts and fears, and I think he felt better for hearing them expressed. It gave him a chance to assure me of his own good intentions. D'you know, Lass, since I talked with him here on board I've had a good deal more confidence in what he's promised. It might not be all just as he hopes, but at least I have the feeling that he is sincere."

She looked at me again with that same curious stare that she had given me the day before.

"An' were ye no sure before, Mac?" she asked quietly.

I shook my head.

"I'll confess it to you now," I replied. "I was not!"

"Then, I'm glad it happened so." She looked down at the deck first and then swung to gaze out again at the rocky island.

I had a feeling that this was not exactly the way I had planned things. I laughed and sought to swing the conversation in the way of more congenial things.

"Well, at least, we know there are none to hear us now, Jean," I said. "We can pick up where we left off! You mind what I said yesterday?"

But she shook her head almost violently.

"Please! Not th' now, Malcolm!" she told me. " 'Tis a thing t' be thinkin' about in happier times. Here's na th' time nor th' place for such."

I stared at her.

"Good God, Jean!" I cried. "You are glum! What's wrong? Are you homesick?"

"No, no, Malcolm," she said. " 'Tis no that. 'Tis only, I suppose, that I've a sort of an ill feelin' about this voyage—"

"Why? Why on earth—?" I began.

But she put her hand on my arm, interrupting me.

"Nay, 'tis naught that yerself or Lord Selkirk or my father could help," she assured me. "I daresay 'twill be all right once we're there. But these ships, Malcolm! First yon smelly little brig—an' now this! 'Tis no just what I was expectin', I suppose."

I laughed a little grimly.

"No more was I, Jean," I told her. "In fact at this point I don't know just what I did expect. But now we're here I imagine this is about what we'd find in any vessel—uncomfortable, cramped quarters, bad food, stinking water! These sailors, I find, are a race apart from the rest of us. This is the way they do things, and I guess we'll just have to put up with it so long as we're aboard."

"Aye, I expect so," she replied, "but I'll no pretend I like it!"

I thought she'd be amused and a little shaken out of her glumness by my story of the water casks and my conversation with the sailor-guard at midday, and I told it to her meaning only for that reason. But she did not laugh. On the contrary, her eyes began to shine angrily and her jaw set.

"And ye said naught o' this t' anyone, Malcolm MacAllister?" she demanded as I brought the tale to a rather faltering end.

"To what purpose?" I demanded. "For God's sake, Jean, 'tis the way they've always done and they're not likely to change their ways for me now. It seems to have done them no harm!"

"Dinna ye swear at me, Malcolm MacAllister!" she cried.

"I'm not swearing at you!" I said, desperately confused now by this bit of feminine logic.

"Dinna take th' name o' th' Lord in vain, then!" she retorted.

"Aaahh—!" I began disgustedly.

"As for this matter o' th' water, that ye seem t' think so funny," she went on, "I'll tell ye 'tis no joke t' me! An' if ye're afraid t' speak wi' th' Captain yersel', Man—then I'm no! I'll see him mysel' th' mornin' an' he'll hear frae th' women aboard what we think o' it! In th' meantime, Malcolm MacAllister, I'll gi'e ye good night, an' may ye sleep well wi' th' memory o' what ye ha' done!"

The memory of what I had done, indeed! I must say I had no answer to that, and I stared after her through the gloom as she turned about on her heel and strode off stiffly toward the hatchway that led down into the women's quarters. For a long time after she was gone I stood and stared down at the dark waters, wondering how in the name of God a man was ever to guess what a woman might say or do next.

In a way I did have the last laugh, however, for Jean MacLean never did have an opportunity to speak to Captain Riker about the water. We were all tucked sound asleep in our musty blankets below decks at three o'clock the next morning, when the tide turned and the *Prince of Wales* dredged up her anchor and shook out her sails. When we came on deck the following dawn we were already well away and standing farther out to sea.

There is a monotony in a long sea voyage that dulls the senses and is particularly paralyzing to the imagination. One day slips into the next and the next with such incredible similarity that while time drags heavily, plodding by, once it has slipped past it seems hardly any time at all. It is soporific; it is hypnotic. But it is also irritating. Tempers flare and petty jealousies become molten hate, churning in a man's belly, and there is no doubt that much happened during the time of our crossing that was of significance later.

We met with miserable weather from the very start. Day after day immense mountains of water thundered down upon us, and day after day we were kept battened under hatches with only the same air we had already drawn a thousand times to keep breath in our bodies. There was no hot food, of course. In such seas it was impossible to keep a fire in the galley, and we had only raw potatoes and salt junk and hardtack to eat and cold, noxious water to drink.

Small wonder, I think, that under such circumstances many of our people began to fall ill almost immediately. Either the very young or the very old to begin with. We blamed the cold, the wet, the raw food. Some thought it simply seasickness, and God knows the seas were rough enough to account for it. The important thing at this time was that we lost none by it, and looking back I suppose that this was because this first bout of coughs and colds and fevers and chills, of vomiting and diarrheas, was not the same thing that struck us later. Whatever it was even Mister LaSerre, the surgeon whom Lord Selkirk had engaged himself, was at a loss to name it.

In consequence of this it seems hardly astonishing that there began to be distinct mutterings among both the crew and the steerage passengers against the Captain and officers. It was rumored through the ship that they fared better than the rest of us; that a makeshift galley had been rigged in the after cabin, and that there was no dousing that fire. Who started it I cannot say, but there were even darker hints spread among us by someone based on the fact that the women's cabin lay aft of our own, between ourselves and the wardroom. A bulkhead partition had been raised between us, and when the hatches were battened we were unable to check the stories. I am sure most did not believe the scurrilities, yet I fear there were some who did.

As we rounded the tip of Greenland and bore up for Cape Chidley, at the entrance to Hudson Strait, oddly enough, the battering storms eased off and the seas quieted enough at least to permit us to come out on deck for a few hours each day. The weather seemed a little warmer, and the winds that came down out of Baffin Bay less gusty and savage, though I daresay it was just that we happened to strike it so. There the fog, which up to now had not troubled us, began to send down long, wispy gray fingers, trailing across our course and growing thicker and thicker, until more often than not we were alone in a misty, gray world of our own—alone, that is, except for one or another great snow-white and green-glass floating mountain of ice, off to one side or the other.

Two days after we had altered our course to the northeast the sloop *Brazen* ran in close and spoke to us.

"I'm off!" her commander called. "You'll be all right from here on. No Yankees in these waters. Good luck!"

And that was the last we saw of him. That night the fog closed down again and we saw no more of any vessel for a full week, though the occasional creak of rigging, or ghostly sound of men's voices drifting through the gray clouds told us that some vessel was off there, somewhere. When a clear day came again not only did we find the *Brazen* gone, but the brig *Missionary* was also missing. Whether she had struck a berg and foundered, or whether she had hauled off upon a different course, we could not know, but we hoped it was the latter.

A few days later the fog closed in again and somewhere between that place and Cape Chidley we lost touch with the *Eddystone*. Captain Riker, however, seemed unconcerned.

"She's either gone on ahead, or she's dropped behind and will come up with us presently," he said. "Captain Gault is an old 'un on this run. Ye need have no fear for him."

Of course, it was not for Captain Gault that we felt any apprehension. But I thought it unnecessary to point this out to Captain Riker.

We were in Hudson Strait, running north and east with the rocky, barren, sparse-grown lump of Ungava rising against the horizon to the south and the icy steppe of Baffin Island only a thin, blue line in the north, when the terrible blow fell.

Until then, as I have said, we had lost none of our people. True, many of those who had been stricken earlier in the voyage remained ill. But many had recovered entirely, and it seemed to us that those who were still sick were winning back slowly. Then all at once it came, striking with the sudden viciousness of a wounded snake, as we were plodding hopefully along, just above Cape Hope's Advance. Hugh MacDonald, a carpenter, and not an old man compared to many among us, had taken the first illness when we were no more than a week out. He had come through that, but he had been slow to recover, and he was yet feeble when we came to Hudson Strait. All the same we had definitely thought him well on the mend by that time, and out of reach of danger.

It was Alexander MacLean who found me on deck and asked me quietly to find Mister LaSerre and fetch him to the men's cabin. He looked white and strained, for all he was outwardly calm, and I knew something was the matter.

"Surely!" I told him. "What's wrong?"

"Hhusshhh!" He laid a bony finger to his lips. " 'Tis Hugh MacDonald. All at once he's taken bad. I am afraid for him. But mind ye, say naught to anyone until the surgeon's had a look at him!"

I promised him and he was off in the instant. Five minutes later Mister LaSerre and I came down the ladder and found him standing by MacDonald's hammock, helplessly wringing his hands and bathing the sick man's head with putrid water.

There was no question but that MacDonald was a sick man. Indeed, he was quite out of his head and raving. LaSerre stepped to the side of the hammock and felt his brow, which was burning with fever and took his pulse. That is easier to tell about than it was to do, for MacDonald was thrashing about and seemed possessed of the strength of ten devils. Alexander MacLean and myself had to hold him. When he was done Mister LaSerre stepped back and mopped nervously at his brow. MacLean and I let go, and contented ourselves with keeping MacDonald in his hammock.

"What d'ye make o' it, Doctor?" MacLean asked anxiously. "What is it, could ye say?"

LaSerre shook his head.

"I can't venture an opinion," he said. "The man's too violent now for a diagnosis, though it appears like a virulent form of the prison fever. If we could calm him enough so I could dare to bleed him it might help. MacAllister, he keeps moaning for water. Suppose you give him a pannikin and see if it doesn't quiet him a bit—eh?"

I went to the scuttle and fetched back a mug of the noxious stuff and held it to MacDonald's lips. The sick man sucked at it greedily, gulping it down, and I will admit that it did seem effective for a moment. LaSerre nodded and glanced at me popeyed. He was a dark, stout, pompous little man, not strictly a settler but a Company man loaned to Lord Selkirk for the purpose, until we could obtain a surgeon of our own.

"That does it!" he nodded. "I'll go and fetch my gear, and we'll see if bleeding doesn't do the trick."

He was gone, up the ladder, before we could cry out to him, and he had no more than disappeared through the hatch opening to the deck than MacDonald groaned aloud, doubled up with belly cramps, bewrayed himself enormously and died—as quickly as that!

It was a horrible thing, but I suppose I have become hardened to the contemplation of it. That may make me seem callous, but when I say that this was just the beginning of it I think I may be understood. We buried Hugh MacDonald in the sea overside, in a canvas shroud with a cannon ball sewed in at his feet to carry him down. And we had hardly done with that before we had three more down with the same violent fever. Two of them were men and one was a woman, and the men died before we had come up as far as Digges Island. The woman recovered. But by that time there were a score more down and coming down, in various stages of attack, and the whole ship was in a panic. Folk who had been comrades before the epidemic would not approach one another, even in the name of mercy, save in a few of the most diligent cases. The sailors, in an effort to check the spread of the disease, built hurried barricades at break of poop and fo'c'sle and rigged a catwalk between the masts, high above our heads, so that they might pass from one end of the ship to the other without being contaminated by us. They even turned the swivels down into the waist of the ship, so that they bore upon us, and threatened to shoot if we made any attempt to break out of our well, either forward or aft.

I was pleased to see that Jean did not shirk the chore of tending to the sick. Indeed, her example kept me at work! I might well have wished us both elsewhere, but since obviously we could not fly from it we might as well do what we could to check its spread and bring what relief we could to the stricken. Curiously enough, although we were not alone of course, we who were most among the sick, day in and day out, were for some strange reason never touched by the fever, and it may be that Jean unwittingly touched upon its real cause when she came to me one noontime, where I was talking to Mister LaSerre on deck.

"Have ye found the cause o' it yet?" she demanded.

I glanced at LaSerre and he shook his head.

"That's straight to the point, Mistress MacLean," he said, "and I must be as frank with you. The answer is no! 'Tis a mysterious business—a dreadful, mysterious business!"

"Perhaps so," she replied grimly, "but I'll ask ye, Mister LaSerre, have ye noticed two things?"

"What's that?" the surgeon asked.

"Have ye observed," she said earnestly, "that o' they that have died o' this thing, what e'er it is, all but one have been teetotalers, an' that not a one o' them would drink tea?"

Mister LaSerre looked surprised.

"That's so!" he exclaimed. "I hadn't thought of that. But what—?"

"Have ye noticed, Mister LaSerre," she interrupted him, "that there's fewer women than men sick o' it? An' ye know yersel' there's three times th' tea drunk in th' women's quarters that there is in th' men's. In fact there's those o' us will drink naught else—an' we're th' ones that aren't affected!"

LaSerre knit his brows and nodded, scratching his chin.

"As for th' men," Jean went on, " 'tis th' tipplers amongst them that seem no t' be touched. 'Tis well known, for instance, that Malcolm, here, always laces his water generous wi' brandy."

I turned as red in the wattles as a bubblyjock.

"I can't stomach the water else!" I explained lamely.

LaSerre chuckled.

"Aye! 'Tis foul enough, I'll warrant!" he agreed, and looked back at Jean. "And so you think it might be something in the water, Mistress MacLean? That's as good a theory as any I have been able to suggest. But what of the crew, eh? They drink it, and there's not a one of them affected. How d'ye explain that, eh?"

" 'Tis simple!" retorted Jean firmly. "Whatever it is, they're used to it."

"Immune by cause of use?" Mister LaSerre stroked his chin and pursed his lips. "Aye! Aye! 'Tis possible!"

We were coming round the edge of Digges Island at the time, swinging into the sweep of Hudson Bay, and I am afraid that LaSerre saw what she was driving at before I did.

"But we must act quickly if we're to do anything about it," he said, "before we're out of reach. Come!"

He turned about and Jean and I trotted after him to the break of the poop, where he spread his legs and cupped his hands about his mouth and called up over the barricade.

"Captain Riker!"

A startled seaman looked over the heavy planks and swung the swivel in our direction.

"Hold your fire, my good man!" LaSerre told him pompously. "We don't mean to expose ourselves to your contamination! Let me speak with the Captain, if you please!"

Riker's face appeared.

"What d'ye want?" he demanded, holding a handkerchief soaked in vinegar to his nose, a sovereign preventive of the plague, as everyone knows.

"Good day to you, Captain!" LaSerre greeted him affably. "I've come to tell you that we think it may be the water that's causing us trouble—"

"Th' water?" Riker barked. "What's wrong with it? My sailors drink it! I drink it!"

"Aye, but you're used to it," LaSerre replied. "And besides, Captain, 'tis well known the devil won't claim his own! We want you to put in at the nearest river, so that we can clean out a few butts and obtain a fresh supply. I'll make a wager with you, you'll find we have no more outbreaks of this after that."

Captain Riker looked sullen.

"There's no river near enough!" he growled.

LaSerre flung out an arm and pointed toward the blue, barren coast that lay off to the south and east.

"Yonder lies Ungava," he retorted. "I'll warrant if we sail along the coast we'll not go many leagues without finding a stream!"

But Riker was angry, and in his anger stubborn.

"There's naught wrong with the water," he barked. "And we've no time to lose on foolish whims. We'll not stop till I reach a place where I can set ye all ashore, and good riddance it will be!"

Perhaps I should have noted that little speech more closely than I did. As it was I fear I was too agitated. But clearly there was no sense in arguing. Captain Riker had made up his mind. We turned away, and as we did so LaSerre shrugged and offered Jean a small crumb of comfort.

" 'Twas the best I could do—you saw that," he said. "But frankly, Madam, I would not be too distressed. I am afraid it was but a lean possibility, at best. Truly, between us, I doubt if the water has anything to do with it!"

Nevertheless, from that day we drank either hot tea or water laced, half and half, with brandy—all hands, and it is a curious thing that all the way across the Bay we had not another new case!

We were five more days crossing the reach of Hudson Bay; five days that would have been pleasant and promising, but for the fact that near half our number were writhing with the fever below. For they were fine days at last, typical of the middle of the brief northern summer; bright and hot and with only enough wind stirring to drive us on our way. But in spite of them we were impatient to reach land, for hardly a day passed but what we turned one or more of our stricken dead over the rail. And you may be sure that the Captain was anxious to be shut of us—even more anxious for that event than I realized, as I discovered to my distress!

The day came at last when the lookout on the foremast cried out "Land, ho-o-o-o!" As if pulled by magical strings all those of us who could boiled up out of our hatchways and stood leaning over the bulwarks staring ahead. And presently it came up over the horizon, so that we could see it; first no more than a faint, blue line, like a rim of haze that lay upon the water, then gradually it took shape and became a long, low-lying coastline, sparsely dotted with shaggy evergreens that stood out against the gray of the shoreward rocks. In between were patches of lighter green, from a distance seemingly inviting meadows of grassy sward, though later, on closer inspection I found them to be quaggy, deluding patches of muskeg and tundra.

It was shortly past midday when we swung in around a low point, into a wide, shallow bay at the mouth of a broad river, and there we cheered to hear the anchor chain rattle out and the blocks creak as the wind was spilled from the sails. There was a stone fort at one side of the river, and a larger, log structure opposite, and both of them hunkered low under a flagstaff at whose peak fluttered a British Jack in the upper corner of a red field, across the bottom of which were sprawled the giant letters H.B.C.

A boat was swung out and the Captain dropped into it, but I noticed that no ladder was swung out for the passengers as yet.

"What the devil?" I muttered petulantly. "Is he going to hold us on board indefinitely? Isn't he going to set us on shore?"

Mister LaSerre, who looked curiously pale and strained, glanced toward me strangely.

"Here?" he demanded.

"Why of course!" I retorted. "Where else? We've arrived, haven't we?"

I think he might have said something more in reply, but at that moment he wavered and nearly fell, only saving himself by clutching at the bulwark. All around him men drew back, but I had forgotten the fever in my excitement of the moment. I sprang forward and held him up, letting him lean upon me.

"What's wrong?" I said. "What ails you?"

He gave me an apologetic glance.

"I—uh—it will pass!" he said. " 'Tis just an experiment I have been trying on myself. I've had naught but water to drink for the last three days, and I must say it leaves me queasy!"

"You fool!" I cried. "Now 'twill be you, and we've need of you! Here. You'd best let me help you below!"

I took him down and rolled him into his hammock and fetched him an enormous dollop of brandy which seemed to help him, for his color returned and with it, I thought, some of his strength.

But I could not bide below while there was excitement such as that above. I went back to find that my companions had hauled out most of their gear and piled it ready for landing close by the gangway.

It was perhaps an hour and a half before Captain Riker came back on board. As he clambered up the side he threw a wry look at the pile of baggage and then glanced at the huddled passengers with what seemed to me almost a sneer.

"All right!" he barked. "Now get that trash overboard and ashore and take these cattle with it! I want th' ship cleared within th' hour!"

"Aye! Ye can no be too quick about it fer us!" growled someone in the crowd, and we all felt better for one of us, at least having spoken his mind.

I was surprised at the despatch with which it was done. It was with almost guilty haste, it seemed to me, yet it never occurred to me that there was anything wrong. First the baggage was taken on shore and piled at the end of the wharf. Then the passengers were crowded into the ship's boats and rowed to the landing. Our sick were placed in an empty boat and towed ashore, where we were forced to lift them out ourselves.

All through the operation it seemed strange that no one from the fort above came down to greet us. But I guessed that Captain Riker must have spread the word among the people there about our epidemic, for I could see an occasional figure standing on the ramparts, watching. But they made no effort to come down to welcome us or offer any help. Ah well, I thought, that was a bridge we would cross later. Just now I was too excited merely to be on shore and in Canada to worry much about it.

When the last of the boats was emptied and had returned to the *Prince of Wales*, they were swung aboard, and faintly over the still water we could hear the clank of the capstan pawls as the sailors walked round and round, heaving in the anchor. Presently the great hook came up, all dripping and covered with mud from the bottom of the river. On the wide yards the gray sails shook out and bellied and filled, and the ship swung and moved, heading out the way she had come, gathering speed.

There were a few who watched her go with tears in their eyes, reluctant, now that the moment had come, to sever this final tie. But as for me I turned my back upon her and set my face toward the fort.

"York!" I cried out. "York Factory at last—!"

From his pallet on the ground, where we had laid him, Peter LaSerre looked up, lifted his head.

"York?" he gasped. "Did you say 'York Factory'?"

"Of course!" I am afraid I glanced at him almost impatiently. "Why not? Isn't that where we're bound—first, anyway?"

He groaned.

"But—but, man! This is not York!"

I flung about to stare at him, open-mouthed, and I could feel the color drain from my face. Unlike the rest of us, he had been out before. He could speak with authority.

"Not—" I gulped. "Not—York, ye say? Then, where—?"

"I—I thought you knew," he said faintly. "This is Fort Churchill. York Factory lies yet another two hundred miles or so to the south!"

PART II

Lodging in the Wilderness

✱✱

> Oh, that I had in the wilderness
> a lodging place of wayfaring men. . . .
> —JEREMIAH, IX. 2

1. CHURCHILL

If THE GROUND HAD SUDDENLY OPENED BENEATH MY FEET AND LEFT me to drop into a black, bottomless pit, I could not have been more shocked or plunged more deeply in despair. I sank down upon a nearby pile of baggage and took my face in my hands. At one side of me Peter LaSerre looked as if it were his fault and the thought might kill him. Alexander MacLean, on the other side, had a gone look, as if he had just been punched in the stomach. Around us the rest of our people stood and stared at us, dully, as if they had heard all right, but were unable to believe what they had heard.

"That's it!" I groaned. "We need no more than that to put a cap to our troubles! Where's the sense of going further?"

"For shame, Malcolm MacAllister!" The sharp, vibrant rebuke in her voice, even more than what she said, snatched me back to reality. I looked up at Jean MacLean who stood with her feet planted firmly before me, her fists on her hips, her small chin thrust out belligerently, her eyes blazing.

A little irritably I wondered vaguely why she should pick on me.

"We can't walk two hundred miles," I protested wearily, "not like this!"

I waved my hand around the gaping circle of emaciated, tattered figures, pointing out the helpless sick, the huge mountain of baggage that seemed to have grown even greater since Peter LaSerre had spoken.

"That's plain enough," she retorted. "But it must be just as plain t' ye that we can no just sit here!"

"What do you propose?" I demanded caustically.

"Propose?" She tossed her head. "Ye ask me then? Since ye do I'll gi'e ye my answer! 'Tis plain they've no mind up yonder t' come down and welcome us. Th' Lord knows what yon fushionless flesher has

said t' 'em, but whate'er 'twas 'tis clear that we must mak' th' first
move. An' if all o' ye are too weak in th' knees t' face 'em, then by
th' grace, I'll do 't myself!"

She turned about abruptly and stalked off, up the path toward the
log palisade that stood up stark and lonely above the weedy river's
edge. A little shamefacedly I fear I threw a glance at her father, and
Alexander MacLean's return look was sheepish. Without a further
word I rose, and together we followed her.

We walked up the path, Jean first and then her father and I following last, and so far as she was concerned we might as well not have
been there. On either hand the cattails thinned and gave way to a
slight, rising, stony ground, green with sparse grass and thin moss
and spotted with rocks. And then the log walls of the fort loomed
close enough so that we could make out the interstices between the
joints.

We had seen from below a few figures standing against the skyline,
on a parapet behind the tops of the logs, no doubt. As we drew near
all but one of these dropped back from view, and the only one who
remained raised his musket.

"*Assez!*" he called. "Sto-op! Stan' w'ere you are!"

I pushed on past Jean.

"What the devil is wrong with you?" I demanded. "Are we lepers?
We are from Lord Selkirk—the Hudson's Bay Company—"

"Lee-pair?" The man seemed startled, and fastened on the one
thing that seemed familiar. "The Co-mpany? Pardon! Stan' w'ere
you are!"

He ducked down, and the three of us stood fidgeting. Presently
another head rose above the tops of the logs.

"Hallo down there," it said.

"Who the devil are you?" I demanded.

"Who are you?" was the reply.

"We are the settlers sent out by Lord Selkirk," I told him, "bound
for Red River. You've no right—"

"What? Hey?" he demanded. "This is Company—"

"Aye! So are we!" I yelled. "If—"

"Wait!" Jean interrupted me. "There's no need for fightin'! We've
no come th' voyage we have for that. Aye, we've sick! Hae ye none
yoursel's?"

"But ye're infectious!" he called. "Ye'll give plague to all."

"The devil we will!" I yelled back at him. "We've spread it to none yet, even aboard ship. Those that have taken it have not done so by contagion."

"How then?" he demanded.

"By the water, I think," I replied. "Those that have taken it have all depended on it. Those of us—the three you see, for instance—that have gone all through it and not been touched, have taken naught but tea or brandy. There have none sickened but took water plain."

"A likely story—" he began.

"Likely enough!" I was amazed at Jeannie MacLean's sudden fury. "Likely enough to cost a good deal of trouble at Fort Churchill!"

"What is it ye want, Ma'am?" The man on the wall was suddenly meek.

"Let us in and we'll talk about that!" she shouted up at him, and to my surprise he turned his head and said something to someone down below him, and in the next moment the ponderous log gates of the fort began to swing back.

I remember now that I was conscious at that moment of a curious, shuddery sense of apprehension, totally unfounded, as if once we had passed in to that log stockade we would not soon again be likely to return. It was foolish, I own, but I recall how I looked around me at the slate-blue sky and the brassy sun that was yet far above the horizon, although it was well past four in the afternoon. That was a thing I had to get used to—the long days and short nights of the arctic summer, and the short days and long nights of winter. We were not far, I suddenly realized, from the northern circle.

But then I had no time to see more. The gates stood open and we moved forward, the three of us, Jeannie for an instant moving in close to me almost as if she too were apprehensive of what awaited us and looked to me for protection. I think it was that which put a little metal in my own spine. At least I took the lead.

As we walked the mosquitoes and black flies swarmed about us in clouds, so that we had constantly to keep waving and whacking and batting at them. I don't know why I hadn't noticed them before—too much preoccupied with our troubles, I suppose. But it was clear that they were going to be a major problem.

Inside the gate we found ourselves in a bare, packed earth compound, dry now but obviously not so long since a sea of mud, for it was pocked and pitted with foot marks, and cracked where it had baked in the hot, midday sun. What we had taken for a fort, I saw then, was not so much that as a log enclosure, encircling a number of buildings. On our left was a long log house—flat roofed, so that it did not show above the wall. Beyond it were a series of much smaller, one room log huts. To the right was a row of such long structures, and I guessed at once they were most likely warehouses for the storage of furs for shipping and inbound goods for trading, as well as for supplies and stores of food and the like for the traders themselves. The main building of the post stood directly in front of us, at the far side of the enclosure. It was an enormous log house, with wings on either side and a curious seeming, almost effete hip roof. There was a walkway and railing along the ridgepole, obviously a lookout station, and it was here that the flagpole rose against the northern sky and proudly bore the Company flag.

There were people inside the enclosure: folk who gaped at us curiously. A few were fair, blond or brown or red-haired, blue and gray eyed. But most ran the gamut from slightly copper tinted, little more than a glow on the skin, to deep mahogany, all with black, inquisitive eyes. Their dress ranged from what one would see in any Scottish city —strangely incongruous here—to easier, more natural fringed buckskins, smoked and stained by countless campfires, or fur lined capotes that looked warm and comfortable. Here was a new world, colorful and fascinating, but I could do no more than glance at them then for as we entered the gates a tall man, lean and sallow and stooped, with the expression of one who is continually annoyed by such frivolous interruptions, came forward.

I recognized the man who had talked at us—that is the right word —from the parapet.

"I'm a busy man," he growled, "and can spare ye little time. Who are ye, an' what d'ye want? Who sent ye?"

I swallowed.

"Lord Selkirk—" I began.

"Who? Lord Selkirk?" he barked. "Who's he? Ah never heard o' him."

I don't know what I would have said to that, but Jeannie saved me the trouble.

"Lord Selkirk controls th' stock o' th' Hudson's Bay Company, as ye well know!" she cut in. "If so be ye're no acquaint wi' it, ye soon enough will be, for there are near four score o' us left to send back th' word t' him o' th' way we ha' been welcomed. I daresay ye'll be hearin' from his lordship when he learns o' it!"

The gaunt man was clearly irritated, yet I noticed that he was less truculent when he spoke.

"I dinna ken what ye mean," he said. "What—?"

"Perhaps," I cut in, "it would help if we introduced ourselves. This is Mistress MacLean and her father Alexander MacLean, lately of Kildonan Parish. Mister MacLean is to be dominie—"

"My own name is Auld," he interrupted me sourly. "I'm chief factor here."

"And mine is MacAllister," I retorted, "schoolmaster to the settlement, and with Mister MacLean, here, in charge of this group of settlers."

"An' ye might add, Malcolm," Jean put in, "that ye're th' personal representative here o' Lord Selkirk!"

"E'en so, I canna see—" Mister Auld growled, and I could almost see his hackles beginning to rise again.

"If you'll have the patience to hear us out, sir," I cut in hastily, "you'll soon be better informed."

"Aye, then?" he glowered at me sullenly.

"There were about a hundred of us all told," I replied, "that set out from Stromness in the *Wales*. Lord Selkirk himself sent us, recruits for his Red River Colony, to be landed at York Factory—"

"York?" he fairly bleated. "Then why th' de'il did ye no go there? Dinna ye ken this is no York? This is Fort Churchill."

"If ye'd keep a still tongue in yer head an' hark while th' man speaks, Mister Auld," Jeannie burst in, "ye'd find out how it happened. We've no seen either York or Churchill before, or any other part o' this Godforsaken land, so we'd no way o' knowin' that yon clarty rogue, Riker, was no settin' us down at th' right spot."

"He was only anxious to be rid of us," I explained.

His face slewed around toward me sharply.

"Why, then?" he demanded. "Would ye say?"

"Why—why—for the fever among us!" I retorted. "Why else? The cowardly dog was frightened—"

"Ah, come, come, Mister MacAllister!" he interrupted me. "I wouldna say that. To me 'tis natural he should ca' canny. If th' fever is catchin' I'd not want ye mysel', for th' sake o' th' others that must live here."

"But, I tell you Man, it is not!" I shouted.

"Na, how d'ye know that?" he asked blandly. "Are ye a doctor, too, Man?"

"No, but Mister LaSerre is!" I replied triumphantly.

"Peter LaSerre?" He pricked up his ears. "Where is he?"

"Unfortunately," I admitted before I realized how damaging the thing sounded, "he is down at the landing, sick himself. He came down with it only this morning."

He spread his hands and smiled unctuously.

"There! Ye see?" he crowed. "E'en yer own sawbones comes t' it! Then how d'ye think Captain Riker sh'ld no be afeared o' ye? Or I mesel', for that matter?"

I raised my eyes and shook my fists at the heavens helplessly.

"Ah, God!" I cried.

But Jeannie MacLean was more practical. She fixed the factor with a look I recognized.

"But ye forget one thing, Mister Auld," she snapped. "We're nigh a hundred o' yer own folk, an' ye'll no be wantin' all o' that blood on yer hands—say naught o' what Milord Selkirk may say!"

He cocked an eye at her.

"Aye! It may be ye're right, Ma'am," he said. "What's t' be done? There's th' question!"

He ran his bony fingers along his jaw, from one ear to the other and wagged his head from side to side, the while he glowered at me speculatively.

"I'll tell ye," he said presently. "Ye can see that I canna run th' risk o' takin' ye in here. But there's a place upriver a piece, about fifteen mile, I'd call it. Colony Creek is th' name o' it. Th' folk from Churchill retreated there when th' French came in '82, an' th' old cabins're still standin'. With a bit o' fixin' they'll do for ye nicely. Ye can stay there as long as need be—till th' fever runs its course, or till yer sick are strong enough t' travel—then we'll see what's next t' be done, hey?"

"What about our baggage?" I demanded. "We can't carry it that distance. And what about our sick now? Half of us can't walk at all! And how about food? It seems to me it's not so simple—"

"Na, na, Mister MacAllister!" he interrupted me. "Dinna ye fash yersel' o' that. I'll send down boats t' carry yer baggage an' they that're too weak t' make it afoot, an' for th' rest o' ye, I'll gi'e ye a guide overland."

"That's very handsome of you, Mister Auld," I said dryly. "But you'll be aware that it solves only half of our problem."

"Eh, how's that?" he demanded, affronted.

"Our people must have food as well if they are to survive," I replied.

"Aye! Aye!" He scowled and calculated rapidly. "I see what ye mean! Aweel, we're no overstocked ourselves, but there's na help

for 't. I'll ha'e t' be rationin' ye out o' our stores. O' course ye'll understand that I canna be lettin' ye ha'e these things free. They'll ha'e t' be
charged t' th' Company, though I daresay yer Lord Selkirk'll ha'e no
objection t' that?"

"Not at all, I'm sure," I told him. "He has no thought of profit in
this undertaking."

"In that case," the factor rubbed his hands together unctuously. "In
that case I might let ye have a sack o' pease an' a sack o' onions an' a
sack o' potatoes and six sacks o' pemmican each week. In th' bargain
I'll gi'e ye a chest o' tea an' a bushel o' salt each month if need be, an'
I'll ha'e one o' they lads show ye th' way o' making spruce beer. 'Tis
a sovereign remedy against th' scurvy! Ye can live high off th' hog wi'
all that, I'm thinkin'."

"Perhaps," I said. "I know little of such things. What—"

"There's no perhaps about it," he interrupted me. "Ye say there are
four score o' ye? Then, what I've named t' ye allows for a little more
than a pound an' a half o' mixed rations a day for each, an' a pound o'
pemmican alone is enough for a man workin'."

"I can hardly dispute with you," I retorted. "But what is this pemmican you mention? I never heard of it."

He chuckled dourly, his sallow face breaking out of its dolorous cast
for the first time since we began talking.

"Pemmican, eh?" he said. "Ye've a treat in store for ye. Pemmican's
th' mainstay and staple o' our diet here i' th' north country. 'Tis made
by th' *Boisbrûlés,* th' half-breed hunters o' th' very part o' th' country
ye're bound for, out o' buffalo meat an' fat pounded together wi'
sugar an' summerberries added. They put it up in hundred pound
sacks, an' 'twill keep forever, so they say."

We were to hear a good deal more about that particular article of
diet before we were through. Indeed, it was destined to be a serious
cause of difficulty for us. But naturally we had no reason to suspect
that, and in our innocence we were inclined to be naive about it.

"Buffalo meat!" Jean exclaimed as if it had not occurred to her
before that we would actually eat it.

"It sounds quite palatable," I remarked.

"Palatable?" He shot me a wry glance. "Och! I'd no go so far as a'
that! But, fush na, ye'll soon be the judges o' that for yersel's. Now if
ye're t' be making yer camp while 'tis yet light, ye'd best be gettin' on.
I'll send th' lads down wi' th' boats an' th' rations, an' when ye get
t' th' creek they'll show ye how t' make yer pemmican up into a

rubiboo or a rasho. Mind ye, parcel it out wi' care an' ye'll find it adequate. If ye'll send down a couple o' lads each week t' th' Fort I'll see 'tis renewed for ye, as we've agreed!"

The solution was not entirely to my liking. I felt that there was no reason, really, why we should not have been allowed to remain at Churchill itself for the time being. But apparently Mister Auld felt that there was danger of contamination, and I was hardly in a position to quarrel with him. I had a sense of vulnerability and a fear lest if I angered him he might loose his wrath on the entire group. But Jeannie MacLean had not seemed hampered by any such considerations. I had the feeling that she had shown herself in a better light than I, and the knowledge of it piqued me and drove me into an attitude of reserve toward her which might at first glance seem rather complicated, but which in reality was quite simple. After all, no man likes to feel inferior to any woman, no matter how much he admires her.

If it had been only this once I don't suppose it would have been so bad. But from the time we had gone aboard the *Prince of Wales,* and now throughout that miserable winter, she showed an amazing capacity for leadership; an ability to reach out and take charge, to cheer and rally us all, when even Alexander MacLean and I were fairly ready to give up in despair and call it quits. Mind, I do not say that this was an ability that she should have kept hidden—from me or from the rest of us. I acknowledge it freely that more than once in the course of that bitter season her courage and good cheer and firm hand led us through the grimmest trials when the faith and hope of the rest would have failed. All that I say is that I should have matched her in those qualities, and not being able to I felt that any suit I might have pressed would have been incongruous—like the jackass that looks longingly at the mare, you might say. It is done, but it is not gracefully done!

Perhaps I was wrong to take that attitude. But the fact remains, I did. The time that I had so hopefully anticipated when we left Scotland turned out to be one of false expectation; of much cry and little wool. By the time it was done I had made up my mind that I must redeem myself, at least in my own eyes if not in hers, before I could dare to venture to speak to her again of what was closest to my heart. I felt miserable, humbled, bitter, and I am afraid I was hardly good company. Naturally I could not speak until I felt myself upon an equal footing.

In the meantime we remained at Colony Creek. John Auld was

right in one thing, at least—the creek was located just about fifteen miles from Fort Churchill. Apart from that things were hardly as he had described them.

About as much as could be said in its favor was that there was an abundance of good water and that the country that lay behind it, reaching down to the mouth of the creek and spreading a sheltering arm around the tiny group of cabins, was far more thickly wooded than the country near the fort. All in front and on one side, across the river and down toward the river mouth, to be sure, was soggy, barren muskeg, rank with swamp grass and the home of millions of mosquitoes. But back of it the tall, dark spruce and cedars crowded down over the swampy, rocky land; in places high and overgrown with vines and briers, in other spots thrusting up out of a mossy, inviting looking carpet that in reality only concealed a miry bog in which a man might sink to his middle if he ventured to step upon it. But at least here were trees, not just swamp and rock and thin grass and muskeg.

The cabins that Mister Auld had told us about were there. But I doubt if he had seen them for a long time. The walls were standing about a rank, overgrown clearing. But in the main the ridgepoles were broken and the roofs caved in, and where they were not they sagged wearily in the middle, like the backbone of a tired old horse. The clearing itself was abandoned to rabbits and rats and porcupines, and had grown seedy with weeds and berry brambles and was threaded with the beaten paths of wild things. As we came into it a trio of bears scrambled out of the patch where they had been scooping down berries and disappeared into the woods. Inside the cabins themselves we had to chop down the pale grass, and even those whose roofs were yet standing were musty and stinking of neglect.

In the weeks that followed we managed to repair them enough to make them liveable, so that before the month was out we had a half a score of stout log buildings in which to shelter. Some we set aside for the sick. Some we reserved for the healthy. But nothing seemed to go exactly as we dared to hope. Indeed, more of our people died after we had arrived than we had lost in the course of the entire crossing. Mister LaSerre was one of the first to go, leaving us without medical assistance of any kind, other than our own common sense and the little experience we had gained during the epidemic. I don't know how it happened that Jean or I or Alexander MacLean escaped being stricken by this mysterious plague. But we did. And there was always a little group of hardy souls that stood through it with us. At least, I think it proof of our theories that the water on shipboard was in some way to blame, or that some other condition of the vessel was the cause, for once we were clear of her we had no new cases, though our losses were heavy from those who fetched it on shore.

Somehow, however, we managed to cope with the fireweed and briers and rank grass, and to cut ourselves a supply of firewood. We found that bears and deer and grouse and caribou were plentiful, and there were fish in abundance in the river: trout and salmon and sturgeon and some fish with great ugly jaws and needle sharp teeth that the Indians called muskallonge, but which the men at the fort said were a sort of a pike. There was also another, smaller species of pike that was called dory, and a fine kind of whitefish as well as a slender, silvery-gray fish with blue speckles along its sides that were popularly known as *poisson bleu,* but which seemed to me to be a kind of a grayling. There were also red deer, or *biche,* and white bears and white partridges, or ptarmigan, which were very fine eating but not so plentiful as other kinds.

I daresay we shot more than we should have, but it seemed to us that there was no harm in that, for we ate all we killed; the mess of pemmican that Mr. Auld had allotted us might very well be sustaining but it was hardly delicious. I saw no reason why there should be any objection in any case. In that apparently, however, I was in error, although Mister Auld was too devious a person to say anything directly. He merely bided his time and awaited his opportunity to take action.

It was some time, however, before it came, and I daresay that had it not been for the fever and the resultant weakened condition of our people we might have avoided it entirely. But for that difficulty I think we might have been able to patch up our miserable resources and make the long trek overland to York Factory. But as it was we had no chance for that. At the outset we could hardly abandon our sick to the mercies of such hostile attendants; and when at last all who were going to recover had done so and there was no more fever among us our convalescents were too weak to undertake the journey and we could only wait and hope that they would regain their strength before the snows came.

Vain hope! It was already almost the middle of August when we reached Churchill, and the northern summers are short. It was mid-September before we had buried the last of our dead and shaken off the fever entirely. It was the end of the first week in October before I felt that those of us who remained were fit to travel; that we had the strength to undertake such a journey, and by then I had the sinking,

sickening conviction that it was too late. Despite the fact that it appeared to be a late fall in that part of the world, still it would take us
at least three weeks, perhaps more, since the way lay through two
hundred miles of rough, boggy forest and tangled muskeg, and we had
not only our women and children to consider but would have to transport all our baggage as well. A few of the more impetuous among us
cried out that we should pick up and go and never count the risk. I
temporized and found one excuse and then another for delay, and I
suppose it was good fortune as much as anything, though it hardly
seemed so at the time, that brought bitter cold and a powdery fall of
snow in the second week in October.

Even the most stubborn diehard then saw the danger that would attend such a foolhardy attempt, and a meeting that night put it to a
vote. Reluctantly it was decided that, since we had food and shelter
such as they were, we had better stay where we were for the winter,
and I was chosen to go into Fort Churchill and tell Mister Auld.

It was a fifteen-mile journey, and as I have said it was cold—bitter
cold, and there was a light powder of snow over everything, hiding
the bog holes and making even the barren muskeg a thing of beauty.
I went with one of the Chippewayan guides that Auld had assigned to
us—to show us how to prepare our pemmican and how to repair our
cabins and, in general, how to manage to exist in this bleak, wild land.
He was a rather short, blocky man with gnarled, bandy legs and a
great barrel of a body, quite dark to my way of thinking, indeed, almost the color of old mahogany. He went by the name of Yellow
Knife, though whether that was his own or that of the people of his
tribe I never knew. At any rate he was an incredibly skillful hunter,
and in those months that we stayed at Colony Creek we learned much
from him.

On this particular day he was especially in form, for the mottled-
brown ptarmigan had not yet put on their winter coat of white, and
they were not difficult to see against the snow. We must have killed a
score of them as we plodded the distance to Fort Churchill. It seemed
to me that they might make a tasty offering for Mister Auld; something to put him in a receptive frame of mind for what I had to say. It
appeared that I misjudged him—in what way will be apparent!

We came into the stockaded compound, and while Yellow Knife
went to see if there might not be a drink of trade whiskey available
for him somewhere about, I stepped into the Company store with my
birds and sought out the chief factor at his cubby of an office at the
rear.

I held up the birds as I entered, silently offering them. He looked up.

"Eh, oh 'tis yerself, Mister MacAllister!" he said. "Sit down. What ha' ye yon?"

"Ptarmigan," I said. "Yellow Knife and I knocked 'em over as we came in from the Creek. I thought you might like them."

"Eh, now, ptarmigan?" he muttered as he took them. "Thank ye, thank ye, Mister MacAllister! Ha' ye been gettin' a-many o' these?"

"Why," I replied, a little disconcerted at his dourness, "yes, a few. Between these and the other game we've been able to eke out our rations nicely."

"So? So, an' ha' ye?" he growled. "Now who would ha' thought o' that? Well, well! An' what's on yer mind, Mister MacAllister?"

I took the place he offered and then told him of the decision we had made. He listened looking darker and darker, and when I had done pointing out to him the need of it he fixed me with a sour eye.

"An' I daresay ye'll want me t' continue yer rations?" he demanded.

"How else are we to live?" I asked him, I thought reasonably enough.

But he only snorted.

"And we'll need clothing," I went on, more than a little piqued at his attitude. "We must have furs and the like, for the things we brought with us are not suited to such a winter as you have here."

He glowered at me, and for a moment he seemed on the point of flat refusal. Then he caught his chin in his fist and turned to stare at his cluttered desk upon which he had carelessly tossed the birds I had brought him. Then, finally, he turned to me.

"Aweel!" he sighed, "if so it maun be, so it maun! Fetch in yer guns tomorra for th' gunsmith t' tak' a look at. They maun be i' th' best o' shape if they're t' shoot at a'. We canna afford for ye t' be shootin' through yon forests improperly—"

"We're not shooting improperly!" I assured him. "Our folk are all experienced hunters from the Highlands."

"Aye, aye, I ken th' sort!" he retorted dryly. "Ye maun fetch 'em along a' th' same. An' when ye do I'll mak' shift t' see that ye're issued furs an' th' like an' point blankets t' keep ye through th' winter."

It seemed to me no more than a service he was somewhat dourly offering us, and so I saw no need to quarrel with him. Whatever his means of giving it, I thought, the gift was the same. When we came down the next day we had all the muskets in the colony piled in the York boat—for the furs and blankets, together with the week's rations,

would be more easily transported so. When we arrived at the rickety
landing at the lower fort we found a crew of Orkney lads, dull fellows,
waiting to assist us with the task of unloading, and so busy were we
with the accomplishment of that and with the replacement of our cargo
of firearms with bales of furs and bags of pemmican and other stores,
that we did not notice that once the guns were unloaded the Orkneymen merely disappeared with them, bearing them up to the fort. Only
when our regular rations and supplies were all on board and we were
ready to return did we notice that the guns were gone. I took a number
of the men with me—not more than eight or nine, for that was sufficient to carry the arms—and went up to the stockade. To my astonishment in the center of the parade, beside a heated forge, I found the
fort's gunsmith seated. On one side of him was a pile of muskets,
clearly our own, still in the condition in which we had fetched them.
On the other side of him, however, was another stack of guns—equally
clearly ours, and just as high—each weapon with the lock removed.

"What in God's name is the meaning of this?" I demanded. "What
are you doing to our guns?"

The locksmith made me no reply, but only gave me a sour, half-guilty
look, and then glanced at Mister Auld whom I had not seen standing
nearby.

I turned upon Auld.

"What is the meaning of this?" I cried. "There is no need to take
them apart!"

"Eh, no?" He grinned at me triumphantly. "Say ye so? But ha' ye
considered what will happen t' us a' if a company o' immigrants is
permitted t' come in an' play havoc wi' th' Company's game? Na, na,
Mister MacAllister, I canna ha' ye killin' an' slaughterin' ower th'
countryside t' yer heart's content. Ye ha' yer shelter an' ye ha' yer
furs t' warm ye through th' winter. Ye e'en ha' a' th' rations ye need
t' feed ye. Further than that I canna go! Ye'll get yer guns back, a' o'
ye. But I'll just be haudin' t' th' locks so ye canna be shootin' till 'tis
springtime an' ye can aye be goin' on yer way!"

"But!" I stared at him aghast.

"An' let us ha' no quarrelin' about it, else I might change my mind,"
he growled at me. "Ye'll ken well I've spoke ye fair. I can aye feed ye
an' clothe ye from th' stores, for yon I can charge t' th' account. But
th' game ye kill I canna so, an' so I maun be takin' th' step. Ye canna
kill th' Company's game! I maun see t' that!"

2. THE SAVAGE LAND

How could I quarrel with him about that—he who had all the force and power in that place? Yet I must say that when my people came to meet me as I returned with all those lockless guns they hardly saw it in that light. I was glad for a bit that the guns could not shoot, else I am not sure if I would have escaped with my own life. Even Jean MacLean was outspoken in her contempt for me.

This, I think, cut me deeper than any of the rest, for she, I felt, should have been able to see the helplessness of my position if no one else could. But she called me coward and would not speak to me for weeks although I alone sought out Yellow Knife and got him to show me how to catch fish through the ice and how to take musquash and beaver in pole pens and how to snare rabbits and knock the feeding grouse out of the thick spruces with a stick. We did not want for game entirely during that winter, though I must say that there were times when it was scarce!

I have no mind to dwell upon it, however. There were days when we were hungry; and days and nights when we were cold—bitterly, unbearably cold. At the time I thought that I had never known such cold before, and hoped that I never would again. We lost, I think without actually counting, about a dozen more of our people from consumption. It may be that they were already touched by the lung fever. But it might also be that it was the very freezing of their vitals that brought it on them. In any case they went. I will say no more of that.

My own worst affliction was hardly as drastic, though I think that there were times when it loomed as large in my eyes. I was troubled throughout the season with a flux, and this may have affected my mind to some extent, for I began to have a feeling almost of antagonism for Jean MacLean. I know that it was not from any feeling toward her—that she was less desirable in my eyes, let us say. On the contrary! From that point of view I found my bowels even more violently wrought!

But it was in my mind that I was most drastically troubled. Twice now, the first time aboard the ship, and again as soon as we had come ashore, I had watched her assert a leadership over all that it was clearly beyond my own power to bring forth. And now, as the late autumn deepened and the white snow deepened with it, drifting high against the eaves of our huddled cabins, I watched her call again upon that hidden source of strength, and this time maintain it for a far longer period. Through those long, grim months, when the sky was drab and the world outside was white with whirling snow, we were scarcely a cheerful lot. Our inclination was more to turn and snap and snarl at anyone who ventured a suggestion for our own good.

But Jeannie could do it. She could take the whole lot of us and lift up our spirits in a way that I could not. Nor could her father—the dominie, the appointed leader of the flock! It was not that I was jealous of her for that, or that I resented her ability. It seemed to me, and it still does, that the more of us there were who could have that influence upon our people the better it would be for them.

My feeling—and I honestly believe it, though I suppose there are some who will doubt me—was one of lost stature. It seemed to me that I had failed; that I had fallen down before her, and that before I could ever speak to her of my feeling for her I must prove to her my worthiness to speak. I must show her that I was not the namby-pamby, weak-kneed creature that she must believe me. I may have been wrong in that attitude, but it is nonetheless true that I felt it, and it may have made me somewhat cooler toward her; more distant than I would otherwise have been. And if I were to regain this commanding position it could not be at her expense. That was definitely a part of my feeling. If I were to do it, it must be at the right moment; at a time when she herself had signified her own sense of helplessness and I could step in without detracting either from her prestige or from her own sense of leadership. To do either would be utterly fatal it seemed to me.

As I have said, I do not wish to dwell upon that dreadful season, it has no real place in this story, other than as a chronicle of passing events. Of those who died how can I say more than may they rest in peace? Of those who lived how can I say other than that for some it might have been better had they died? The winter came and then the snow. The river froze and it was hard to get fish. Our diet narrowed and became largely a matter of pease and pemmican, and sometimes not even that when the drifts were too deep for our ration parties to beat their way overland to Fort Churchill.

Christmas was hardly a festive holiday at Colony Creek. It came and went, and I think the less said of it the better. January dragged by; then February and then March, and thanks to Yellow Knife, who had taught us to make spruce beer, none of us at least contracted scurvy. It was thanks to his help too that we began to be fairly proficient with snare and deadfall and found ourselves able to bring in a respectable amount of small game to add to our grim, monotonous diet. We were poaching, of course, but I saw no alternative.

However the association with the barrel-bodied little red man proved valuable to us in another way; in a way that I am sure none of us ever suspected. It happened that I was out with him one day, a dark, twilit day, with a slaty, overcast sky and a knifelike wind that seemed to freeze the very breath in our throats. Yet for all that it seemed to me as fine as the brightest summer day, for we had been running our trap line and found that we had been fortunate enough to catch half a score of hares and rabbits in our snares. In addition, as we turned homeward, we had the luck to stumble upon a huge covey of spruce grouse, sheltering in a thicket of drooping firs and the stupid birds had permitted us to beat down at least a dozen of them with sticks before they finally took fright and thundered away. I daresay that it was on this account that I must have seemed to him less dour and more talkative than usual, for he himself introduced the subject.

"How long you'm stay in cabin by creek?" he asked blandly.

I looked at him, surprised as much by the fact that he spoke at all as by what he said.

"Why, till summertime, I suppose," I told him. "At least that's what we planned."

"Then you go York Factory?" he persisted.

I nodded.

"Is there anything wrong with that?"

"Uumm! Plenty wrong!" he replied. "Him scheme no good. You wan' go York Factory maybeso better you go now."

"Now?" I yelped astonished. "But, it will be six weeks, maybe two months, before the snow is gone and the ice is out!"

"That so," he grunted. "But all same him no good. W'en ice all go river him hard to cross. Many river between here an' York. W'en snow all go too, groun' she be all sof' an' wet. You see! Mud to you'm belly!" He patted his stomach earnestly to show me just how deep it would be. "Come soon summertam these Bois fort she's be all full wit' mouche an' moustique. How you call—moskeet? Dam' moustique she come so t'ick you can no see sun. These mouche—these midge—these black fly she's drive even Injun mad. She's get in 'air, in nose, in mout'. She's clamb up sleeve an' creep up pants. She's crawl down neck. She's eat 'em up 'live goddam I tell you! If you wait summer, I tal you, you not get York Factory. You wan' go, better you go now! Now she's col' but you get there, dam'."

"Perhaps!" I nodded glumly. When he explained it I could see the sense in what he said, but I wondered if the others would agree.

When we got back to Colony Creek that night I mentioned his suggestion, and the howl of protest and indignation and derision that greeted me drowned out the reasons I was trying to give for such a move. Even Jean MacLean, I could see, was staring at me as if I were suddenly gone daft.

I might have been angry, or at least resentful, I suppose, had I not recalled my own first, instinctive reaction. When Yellow Knife first spoke I was shocked and startled nearly out of my snowshoes. But the more I thought about it the more sense it made. I remembered how unbearable the mosquitoes and black flies had been around Churchill the previous summer, when we had first landed. If they were that bad there, at a site selected for its slight elevation and exposure to the breeze which kept them off a little, how much worse would they be in the dank shelter of the strong woods?

What he had said about the rivers, too, was indisputably true. They were easier to cross when they were solidly frozen over. And the mud! What difference, I wondered, would it make to slog through stinking mud up to our middles or plough through snow of the same depth? Indeed, if we could contrive to get sledges and snowshoes for us all, the late winter season would actually be an advantage to us for it would be much easier to carry our supplies and baggage on sledges than on our backs.

I waited until the first blast of their scorn had passed, and when I could make myself heard again I began very quietly and plainly and simply to explain all these points. They listened to me then, a little inclined to scoff at first, but finally, as the truth of what I was telling them began to be borne in upon them, they were swept by a sort of baffled anger which they directed at me, as if they felt that somehow at bottom I had misled them. Poor old Catherine Campbell, widowed since we landed and without kin now in all the world, had some of it in her voice as she cried out, interrupting me.

"Where's th' guid o' it a', Malcolm MacAllister? Ha ye no done enough o' harm t' us? Why d'ye no go yer way an' leave us here t' die i' this Godforsaken wilderness ye've fetched us inta?"

I stared at her in astonishment, for such an outburst was certainly the last thing I had expected.

"Surely," I protested, "you don't think that I—"

"Aye an' why should we no?" It was Ian Bruce who spoke from the shadows in the corner. Only two months since his pretty daughter Janey had died of the lung fever, and I could hardly blame him for being bitter. "Ha' ye no misled us fra th' start? Ha ye no fed us on nobut lies an' fau'se hope sin' th' verra beginnin'? An' now ye winna leave us be t' die i' peace our own way but maun blether us t' go wi' ye inta worse!"

Beyond the smoky fire I thought I saw Jean MacLean give me a curious, quizzical look, and for some reason it angered me. In spite of all my efforts to restrain myself I could bear this no longer. I lashed out at them all.

"No, you fools!" I cried. "I did not and I will not! I have urged you and begged you and nursed you along, all for your own sakes, and when things have not gone as any of us hoped they would I've stood by you. Now I'll be damned if I'll change now. I've urged this thing on you because I feel that 'tis the best thing that we all can do. I still believe that. And I think that if you'll just think about it for a bit you'll see it the same way—"

But another voice came at me out of the shadows.

"Aye, so? An' supposin' a' that's true," it said, "where's th' differ-ence? Ye say yersel' th' whole thing depends on sledges an' snowshoes. D'ye think yon de'il Auld'll be gi'in' 'em t' us?"

I had not anticipated the objection, and but for my own exasperation I might have been taken aback by it. But this time I surprised even myself with my reply.

"What's to lose by asking?" I demanded. "Mister Auld can do no more than refuse. And if he does that, I say, this thing is too important to us to let it drop there. I am sure I can persuade Yellow Knife and his people to help us—to teach us to make snowshoes and sledges for ourselves. Maybe it would do Mister Auld good to know that we are not entirely dependent upon his bounty!"

That pleased them, and a fluttering murmur of approval went around the gloom of the room. Curiously, knowing that they had a higher opinion of me raised my spirits too.

"Very well, then!" I went on. "Let us leave it this way—that I will go to Fort Churchill tomorrow and see what Auld will do. If he will spare us the means to travel and the rations we should have then we will plan for the journey. If he is opposed, then I will return and we will decide upon our next move."

I did not wait to hear whether or not they approved of that, but turned away and flung out the door and was halfway to the cabin that I shared with half a dozen other lonely bachelors before I heard the crunch of running steps in the snow behind me. When I turned there was Jeannie coming toward me with a light in her eyes and a smile on her lips such as I had not seen there since those first days in Kildonan Glen.

"Mac!" she cried. "Malcolm! Wait, will ye?"

I stopped and watched her approach, still breathing heavily from my angry outburst, and she came up to me with eyes shining.

"Mac, I didna ken ye felt so!" she told me.

I was suddenly surprised myself to contemplate it. I had told her only the truth when we had left Scotland. I did not care a whit then what we found so long as I was paid and no harm came to her or her father. Now, here I was as concerned as any of them!

"No more did I," I said shortly.

She smiled a little.

"Maybe ye're comin' around t' think less o' yersel' an' more o' others, Malcolm?" she suggested.

"Bah!" I snorted, perhaps in my very embarrassment scornful of the suggestion. "I'm as anxious to get on with it as anyone, that's all!"

For an instant she looked as if I had slapped her in the face. Then she smiled again, lightly, wisely.

"Aye?" she said. "We're a' anxious t' be awa', but I think Malcolm, if ye'll look at it, yon's no th' reason ye spoke as ye did tonight."

She may have been right. I was hardly in a mood to consider it then, for there was something else that seemed to me, just at that moment, to loom far larger on our small horizons.

"Well, then," I said, "suppose 'tis so, Jean? Does that mean you've wiped away your feeling against me? Are we to be friends again?"

"I've ne'er meant t' be aught else, Malcolm," she replied, and she looked at me quizzically. It did not occur to me then that what she said could be taken two ways.

I felt my heart leap happily within me.

"Then, Jean," I cried, "can we go on from where we were? Can we think—and talk of us?"

I would have reached for her, despite the bitter, chilling cold of the compound. My heart made me warm enough. But she put her hands upon my arms.

"Not now, Malcolm," she told me. "Not now, can ye understand? Now there's much t' be doin'—too much for us t' let oursel's be distracted. When we've come out o' this—when we've come t' safety an' th' colony at th' Forks, there'll be th' time t' turn our minds t' this!"

"You'll not say me nay then, Jean?" I begged.

"I'll no say ye aye or nay now, Malcolm!" she smiled, and with that I had to be satisfied.

I found Mister Auld the next morning in the snug counting room at the back of the Company store.

"May I have a word with you, Mister Auld?" I asked.

"Aye, say on!" he growled, not even looking up.

I told him what was in our minds.

"I ha' been wonderin'," he spoke up at me dryly, and infuriatingly, "when ye would become aware o' that."

"Perhaps if you'd been more willing to help the strangers within your gates, Mister Auld," I flared, "it would not have taken so long. I shall see that Lord Selkirk and the rest of the Directors are not left in ignorance of your indifference."

It would appear that he was vulnerable at some points, at least. That shot struck home.

"Na, na, Man! Surely ye misjudge me," he cried. "Did I no tak' ye in an' gi'e ye rations an' show ye a place t' live th' whiles yer folk owercam' th' fever? Ye ken I ha' a mickle o' folk here in Churchill that I'm answerable for. I couldna do more for ye! Now, how d'ye estimate yer needs? I'll see what we can do."

That was far more concession than I had dared to expect, but apparently the one thing he feared in this world was the ire of his Directors. I started to list our needs, even adding to them a little just to drive the iron home.

"We will need six full weeks' rations," I began.

"Aye!" He nodded, agreeing so docilely that I wondered if I had underestimated the time it would take.

"Then we must have at least five dozen pairs of snowshoes and a score of sledges to carry our supplies and baggage and such of our women and children and old people as cannot manage on foot," I said.

He looked pained, but sighed and nodded again.

"We'll be hard put t' it t' find ye so many," he replied.

"Nonetheless," I retorted, "we must have them."

"Ye shall!" He beamed at me, much as to say that surely by now I would agree that he was not such a bad fellow at heart.

But I had had too many dealings with him to be deflected.

"And of course we'll need dogs for the sledges—"

"Eh, Man?" His bellow interrupted me, and the way his face reddened and his jowls quivered told me plainly that now I had asked too much. "Eh, Man? Would ye rob us? Na, na! Racquets an' sledges we can make more o'. An' if ye leave us short o' rations there's game for th' huntin' an' fish for th' catchin'. But dogs now, Mister Mac-Allister, we canna replace them th' winter! I'm sorra, Man, but beasties I canna gi'e ye."

"But, great God, Man!" I had no intention of giving up without a fight. "How are we to draw the sledges without dogs?"

He wagged a stubby finger under my nose.

"Na, na!" he cried. "Ye maun be yer own dogs for that, Man. I'm sorra, but—"

"Sorry?" I blazed. "Sorry, be damned! What good are sledges without—"

He relaxed a little and even seemed to smile.

"Na, na!" He held up his hand and repeated his cry. "Ye maun be yer own dogs. Man, 'twillna be th' first time 'tas been done. Th' Indians ha' a way o' 't. Aye, an' we ha' done it oursel's when th' food was gone an' 'twas needfu' t' eat th' teams. Ye send a few o' yer men ahead on racquets t' break out th' track. Then yer sledges will draw easy after. Yer womenfolk can follow after th' sledges where they'll find a fair trod trail. I'm sorra, Man, but there's th' best I can do."

I saw that we would get no dogs from him, and so I shifted my ground a little.

"One other thing," I said.

He raised his eyebrows.

"Aye?"

"You must return the locks you took from our muskets," I told him.

"Ye shall ha' 'em," he nodded.

I will say that for once, at least, Mister Auld was as good as his word. I returned home immediately, of course, to Colony Creek and told my companions the results of my interview. They were jubilant, excited as schoolchildren; they crowded around me slapping my back and congratulating me, as pleased, I think, that at last we were doing something, as they were at the actual prospect of the journey. It is true that a night's sleep on the matter had convinced the most stubborn of them that it was the best thing to do. But not even the most sanguine of us ever dreamt that it would be easy. The fact that we would have no dogs to drag the sledges gave some pause. But in the main the acceptance of the plan was enthusiastic, and even those who were yet reluctant felt that there was nothing else to be done. For myself, my own best reward was the light of approval in Jean MacLean's eyes.

From that moment, of course, there was no time for either thought or discussion of personal problems. The very next morning the racquets, the sledges, the provisions, the locks—all that Auld had promised arrived, and there was work and to spare for all.

During that fortnight that remained of our stay at Colony Creek I never knew that it was possible for a man to do so many things and be in so many different places at the same time. At least so it seemed to me. I checked in our rations and saw them safe stowed ready for the journey in a locked cabin that I set aside for the purpose. To this same cabin I had each family bring every possession that they felt absolutely must go with us overland. Much, of course, had to be discarded, for we could not draw everything with us on the sledges. Some of this could be disposed of entirely, and was turned over to Yellow Knife and his people, who were only too delighted to have it—worthless as most of it was. But there yet remained a mountain of gear: household goods, heirlooms and family possessions—which I had boxed and baled and deposited at Fort Churchill with instructions to Mister Auld to forward it to the Red River, via York Factory, by the very first supply ship to pass that way.

Much of all this was a heartbreaking business, you may be sure, for I think all of us have some worthless mementoes and trinkets with which we are loathe to part. But in this case, clearly, they could not be taken. Our very lives depended upon our mobility, and every extra ounce would retard us. One thing that happened, however, in connection with this process of selection was amusing.

I had done with most of the group and was coming close to the end of the line when I came to Robin Gunn, a short, hairy, thick built man in his mid-thirties. He was a stolid man, you would think to look at him, without an ounce of sentiment in him, yet there he stood with a little bundle of belongings done up in an old shawl between his feet, while underneath his arm, hugged close and loving, and almost twice as bulky as his bundle, he carried a well-worn, well-blown set of bagpipes.

I had known Rab Gunn for a piper of course, long since, for many a long evening in the course of that dismal journey and the winter at Colony Creek he had cheered us and kept up our spirits with his skirling and his reels. Still the pipes were heavy. I smiled and shook my head.

"Ah no, Rab," I told him. "You'll have no need of those for a bit. Send 'em around with the rest of the gear."

But he clutched the instrument tighter and glowered at me.

"Send me trews if ye will, Mister MacAllister," he replied. "But dinna ask me t' part wi' ma pipes. I'll carry 'em mesel' gin ye'll let me tak' 'em."

"I'm sorry, Rab," I told him. "We'll need every strong back at the sleds—for a turn at least. You'll have to send 'em."

" 'Twas in ma mind, Mister MacAllister," he persisted, "that I micht march at th' head o' ye an' pipe ye th' way. 'Twould be an aye cheerin' thing tae th' folk."

The picture rose before my mind's eye of a man in kilts on snow-shoes and the rest of him swathed in the deerskin capote of the Chippewayans, that we had all adopted, with his hood drawn up over his head and his face ringed with frost-rimed fur, his cheeks bulging and eyes popping as he piped us all through the snowy, frozen forest, through cold that set the trees to bursting with reports like pistol shots and that fairly froze the breath in his bag. I could not repress a smile at the picture. Yet at the same time I wondered if there were not something in the idea. The one small homely touch; the wild, eerie skirling music might be just the thing that was needed to lend heart to our people and lift them along the way.

"All right then, Rab," I nodded. "Pipe us along if you will, but take care not to scare all the game away!"

3. PIPER IN THE SNOW

I LAUGHED NO LONGER, HOWEVER, WHEN AT LAST WE WERE LINED UP and ready for the start. Yellow Knife and half a dozen of his swarthy compatriots had agreed to accompany us as guides and hunters, partly, I think, because of the generous presents we had given them from our discarded gear, but more because of the rum that I promised them when we came safe to York Factory. They, with an equal number of our own best woodsmen—and some of us had grown quite proficient in the course of the winter—were to take an hour's start of the rest of us; the theory being that they would break out the trail for those who followed, and at the same time be far enough ahead so that the game would not be frightened away by the approach of the rest of us. At midday they were to halt and wait for the main party, and after a brief rest and a cup of tea then we would all push on together to the night's camp which we hoped to reach about an hour before sundown.

That was the general order of our march. But it was not that which I found sobering. The specific line of the main party claimed my closer attention. In the lead, following in the tracks of the advanced group, so that there was a clear trail to smooth their way, were the sledges. These, in their turn, we believed, would leave an even yet smoother track for the women and children who would bring up in the rear. In between the sledges and the women marched Rab Gunn and his pipes.

He made as strange a figure there as I had anticipated, wrapped in his furs and with his breath rising like a cloud about his hooded head, and the wild music wailing out amid the silent forest. But he was right, too, for the familiar sound struck courage into the hearts of the rest of us as we struggled forward, and gave a lightness to our burdens that they would not otherwise have had.

We left Colony Creek without regret toward the end of the third week in April; the guides and hunters departed before daybreak, and the rest of us an hour after, just as the gray ghosts of dawn were slipping down among the firs and spruces. We moved in single file, that being easier for the sledges, and so, perforce, for the rest who followed. For a time I fetched up in the rear in order to count the stragglers as much as to help them, and to determine whether or not we had set too strong a pace, and from there I could hear the ghostly wail of the pipes and count the cadences of its beat. Even there, so far behind, I could see the way it affected the rhythm of the march, and I was glad that I had told Rab that he might bring his pipes.

Our route lay along the height of land, between the sluggish streams that flowed westward across the limitless Caribou Barrens into the Churchill River and those that fell down to the east, through the sparse, swampy forests, to Hudson's Bay. On our right as we marched, skirting the fringe of the woods, lay the vast muskeg, frozen solid now and windswept, piled deep with drifting snow. There lay the haunt of the great caribou and of the wolves that hunted them. On the other side, to our left, lay the woodsy thickets, the tall stands of spruce and fir and hemlock and cedar, patched and slashed by clumps of tangled swamp alder and gray birch and willows and beech and chokecherry and moose maple. Here were abundant varieties of smaller game: hares and rabbits, chattering squirrels, the white partridge, and spruce grouse, foxes, beaver, martins, musquash, otter and a dozen others. There were larger beasts, too, of course: moose, which is the huge, splay-horned deer of this northern part of America, and *biche,* or elk, which is more like our European stag. And there were wolves and white bear. In that long journey we caught at least a glimpse of them all.

Struggling along at the tail end of the line that first morning, I could not help but wonder if I had done the right thing to insist upon the march. I suppose such doubts assail every person in a position of responsibility, and for once I was conscious of a sense of concern for the welfare of these, my charges. Come what may, I knew, I must stand by the results. I kept telling myself that I was honestly and morally certain that this was the right course. Yet the thought kept occurring to me, What if I were wrong? What if I had miscalculated?

The answers, of course, could only be learned by trying. In the meantime, I am free to admit, I was as taut as a fiddlestring. We had not been gone an hour on the road when Jean MacLean dropped back beside me. She smiled at me half apologetically in greeting, and I could see that something had occurred to trouble her, but my own tension was such, I daresay, that I spoke more sharply than I needed to.

"What is it now?" I demanded.

She looked as if she had expected better of me than that, yet she kept her temper.

"Th' widow MacVeagh has a bad foot," she told me. "She ought not t' be tryin' t' walk in these things."

She glanced down at her own snowshoes significantly.

"Are you sure?" I said gruffly.

At that she flared.

"O' course I'm sure, Malcolm MacAllister," she retorted. "If ye'd eyes in yer head t' look ye could see for yerself! Watch how she drags! Quite apart from decent humanity ye'll ken well that if she's allowed t' go like that she'll be a delay an' a hindrance t' th' lot o' us."

I caught my tongue in my teeth, biting back a hot retort, for even in resentment I knew well enough that she was jabbing at me, prodding me to help one whom she thought needed helping.

"I'm sorry, Jean," I managed. " 'Tis just I'm overwrought, I fear. We must have as little delay about this as possible if we're to get through."

"I can be seein' that as well as yerself," she replied, a bit sharply it seemed to me. "But here's a thing that can't be avoided."

"Aye!" I sighed. "You're probably right! Well, let's have a look!"

"If ye can persuade her!" she said dryly.

I passed up the word, and our little column halted and I went forward and argued with the widow MacVeagh. The old girl was as stubborn as an old bull, and I think she would have refused to let me look if I had not threatened to call up reinforcements and have her boots pulled off by force. She gave in then grudgingly, and I found that she had developed a most painful carbuncle between the toes. Quite obviously she should not be trying to make her way across two hundred miles of snowy waste on snowshoes. Fortunately eight months of trying to fill Peter LaSerre's boots had given me some small practical experience in such matters, and I lanced the boil and dressed it as well as I could and ordered her to a permanent place among the sleds, distributing the load of one among several of the others. After that she seemed to get along happily enough.

But the event had caused us considerable delay already, to say nothing of a tautening of my own belly nerves. As a result of it we were late at the rendezvous with our hunters. Until we came up with them I had no way of knowing what success they might have had, and when midday passed and we had not overhauled them I was on edge with anxiety, and I daresay tempery to boot.

It was almost mid-afternoon before we found them, waiting for us with fires built and kettles put on to boil and succulent strips of venison set to roast on willow withes over the hot coals. They had found good hunting—so much I was relieved to learn. Among them they had killed and dressed out, which was important, forty-seven ptarmigan, eighty-four spruce grouse, seventeen geese and nine red deer—enough to supply us all for more than one day of comfortable eating. But the fact that we were late indicated that I had overestimated badly the possible length of our day's march. So long as the game held out and the hunting was good, to be sure, it made little difference. But what if the game disappeared, as it mysteriously does in spots? What if we were forced to depend entirely on our rations? Obviously, in such a case we would either have to increase our rate of march or reduce our consumption of food, and neither, I felt, would be easy!

I made no mention of these things at the time, however, but ate the belated meal in sober silence. As I had originally planned it the midday halt would be long enough to allow a rest. But now it seemed to me we were so far behind our schedule, and the day was so far advanced, that we could not afford to take the time. As soon as we were done eating I pressed forward, driving them on with every means that I could imagine; by taunts, recrimination and pleading, and I was glad then that I had allowed Rab Gunn to bring his pipes, for the skirling ring of them through the crackling woods did much to lift our pace. Nevertheless, for all his playing and for all the lashing of my tongue, for all the driving I could do, I do not think we came more than seven or eight miles that day, little more than half the distance I had hoped we might cover.

We camped that night in the shelter of a spruce thicket, and the way of it is worth telling. We followed the Indians' example, for obviously they being old hands at travel in this barren wilderness knew the best ways. As soon as we had located our site we broke up into a number of small groups, each one of which was allotted three sledges. A wide semicircle was then scooped out in the snow with our snowshoes, the shovelings being piled to the windward and the sledges were set on top of the heap to act as a windbreak. A roaring fire was then built on the downwind side of each half-circle, and as soon as each group had cooked and eaten its rations its members then crawled into their blankets and settled for the night, their feet bunched close together toward the fire, their heads fanned out in a half-circle toward the shelter of the high-piled snow.

Such an arrangement, sleeping under the stars in weather far below zero, was hardly as comfortable as if we were snug at home in a deep feather bed. Still it was far more snug than I had anticipated, and I will admit that I for one slept soundly despite the cold and the hardness of the ground. Somehow, it is a curious thing, but if a man's feet are warm so is the rest of him like to be.

We were up again at daybreak and driving forward with all the speed that I could whip into my companions' heels. We did somewhat better that day, I think, and the next. But on the fourth day out it snowed a blinding blizzard and we dared not move. Perforce we stayed where we were and kept our fires piled high with stout spruce logs, and only on the sixth day were we able to resume our journey.

That, with minor variations, was the general tenor of our march for close to two full months, and I must say that in that time I came to be a most unpopular man, for I was ever at them, ever snarling at their heels, like a driving dog. I mind it was at the end of the first week that Jean MacLean came to me with trouble in her eyes.

"Don't ye think, Malcolm," she said, "ye could take it a mite slower?"

I glanced at her. We had met and we had talked throughout that time, but only of inconsequential matters. I wanted now to cry out to her for the help and ease that only she could give me. But I had already learned the uselessness of that.

"I wish we could, Jean," I told her. "But we've got to drive it!"

And I tried to explain. When I was done she nodded, only half convinced.

"Aye, well, ye're th' leader, Malcolm," she said. "We'll do aye as ye say!"

I was surprised. So she had noticed that. Alec MacLean might be the shepherd of his flock, the dominie, but when he came up against a situation calling for decision he was hardly to be depended upon. He might quote the Word of God, but he could not command it. It was I who drove our people on; I, in spite of my skepticism—with Jean behind me, and I suppose that does do things to a man!

By the end of our first fortnight on the trail we had developed several cases of snowshoe fever, which is a painful swelling of the ankles and lower legs, brought on by the unaccustomed use of the racquets, and from that day we were never wholly clear of it. At the worst of it nearly half of our people, including myself, suffered the shooting, agonizing pains of the malady. Yet obviously only a few of the oldest and feeblest could be given places in the sleds. The rest of us must struggle along as best we could, only halting at night to rub our bloody feet and legs with snow and wrap them in the warmest dressings we could find.

Throughout the journey the temperature remained well below freezing, which I daresay was a good thing for otherwise we would have had to add to our troubles rotting ice and maybe a wetting in one of the many small rivers that we had to cross. As it was I do not think I would care to make the journey again! Fortunately our game supply remained plentiful, and I think that had we had time to pause and try it in the many small lakes that we passed we would have found an almost equally abundant supply of fish through the ice.

Not all of the game that came to us, however, was small or friendly. We were aroused once in the middle of the night by an unwelcome visitor. I remember only too well that I was awakened that night suddenly and from a sound sleep by the scream of a frightened woman.

How I came there I do not know, but I opened my eyes all at once to find myself standing a good twenty feet from the bachelors' fire with my musket in my hands. Except for my bare hands and bare feet I was fully dressed, for that was the way we slept those cold nights, and though I did not notice it at the time the snow crust cut my bare shanks and the wet palms of my hands froze to the icy barrel of my gun.

For an instant I was confused, looking this way and that, and then I saw a great gray form moving vaguely in the blackness off to my left, close by the side of one of the sleeping pits. As I caught sight of it the woman screamed again and the ghostly form moved forward. I flung up my musket and fired, even then not at all sure what it was that I was shooting at.

Almost simultaneously with the crack of my gun I could hear the solid smack of the lead upon flesh. The thing turned and lunged toward me, rushing forward with incredible swiftness in the blackness of the night.

Even then I did not know what it was. I knew only that it loomed head and shoulders above me, tall as I was; that it was snarling savagely; that it was obviously wounded and dangerous and that I had fired the one shot that I had in my gun. I wrenched aside and at the same time tried to reverse my musket and take it by the muzzle, clubbing it, but my hands froze to the barrel and in my struggle to win free my foot slipped and I went down upon my face.

The great gray thing, whatever it was, was almost upon me when, praise the good God, three more shots rang out in the dark and I could hear the beast grunt as the bullets smashed home. In the next instant pain stabbed at my two feet and at my legs, and then the beast whatever it was went plunging across me headlong and buried its snout in the snow beyond.

I was still struggling to rise when Yellow Knife and two of his hunters, Running Otter and Fat Beaver, came up with smoking guns and brands snatched from their own fire. The entire camp was awake by now, as may be imagined, and when the Indians held their torches up they showed a great white bear that I think must have measured at least eight feet from the end of his snout to the tip of his stubby tail. When I looked at the enormous paws with the long, sickle-shaped claws (paws that when hefted the next morning scaled more than forty pounds each), and at the dripping jaws with teeth as long as a man's thumb and sharp as a driven stake, I hardly know how to say how glad I was that those bandy-legged Indians happened to be near!

I dug myself painfully out of the snow and limped through the little crowd that had gathered about where the beast had skidded. That was well beyond where I had lain, and I thrust my way through them and stared down at the huddled heap. Oddly it was not until Jean MacLean cried out that I realized that there was anything wrong with me.

"Mac—Malcolm!" she called suddenly. "Ye, ye're hurt! What's happened t' ye?"

"I—" I said dully, and looked down.

It was true enough. In his dying plunge the bear, falling across my legs, had made one last desperate swipe of his paw and raked me from calf to heel so that the flesh lay open and all around where I stood the snow slopped in a pool of red. But I will confess it, I did not feel it yet.

"I—?" I said again. "He must have clawed me—"

I started to reach down, to feel gingerly of the lacerated areas, only to find that my hands were still frozen to the icy musket. Unthinking I wrenched one free, leaving tatters of my sweating palm hanging to the barrel and my hand sore and raw and giving me only such pain as a slash to the quick in that place can do.

Yellow Knife stepped forward and reached out a mitted hand.

"Now maybe," he grunted, "you 'member not touch cold gun with bare 'an' in wintertam, eh?"

There was no denying the sense of that, but I could only stare at him dully and surrender my weapon. Jean MacLean and Catherine Gunn came and took me, each by an elbow, and led me to their own fireside and sat me down upon a pile of furs and tended to my cuts and bruises, soaking them in warm water, washing them and then binding them up.

Fortunately for me there were no tendons torn, no muscles slashed.

The damage was gory but looked worse than it actually was. As they worked over my legs, though, I could see that Jean was close to tears. I tried to comfort her.

"Eh, now!" I growled. "There's small damage done! There's naught t' fear o'—ouch! such as this! I'll be all right in the morning. I'm—I'm obliged to you, Jeannie, Catherine—"

"But ye'll ne'er be able t' walk like this!" Jean protested.

"I can walk," I told her grimly. I was damned if I would ride! "I can walk as well as the next one!"

"But, but Malcolm, ye must not!" she cried. "Ye must take yer turn i' th' sleds, for one day anyway!"

"Th' sleds," I said, "are full. I'll not ride in them. I can't. There're others need 'em worse than I. And besides—"

"But—" she began.

The pain made me impatient.

"God damn it!" I swore.

"Ye cursed, Malcolm!" she cried reprovingly.

"So I cursed!" I retorted. "I'll not ride your bloody damned sleds! Wrap up the damned cuts and let's have it over with. I tell you I can't ride, and there's an end to it!"

I could see her lips tighten, and after that she worked on my shanks in silence, but I could see plainly enough that the remark had annoyed her. I would have bitten off my tongue to be able to take it back, but once words are out they're said!

I did not ride, that much is a fact. And after that night we did not exchange much more than a word until we came to York. I suppose I should have apologized for my sorry behavior, and I will admit that there were moments when I hobbled along in my snowshoes that I found the pain in my legs all but unbearable. So far as I was concerned I think it was just as well that two days after this event we crossed the Nelson, well up above the mouth of the Weir, on ice that was clearly rotting fast. After that three days more of struggle through the softly dripping woods, down the peninsula of Marth, brought us to the banks of the Hayes, where the palisaded log fence and stout whitewashed buildings of York Factory ranged neatly in their wide clearing.

Ninety-seven of us had set out from Stromness in the *Prince of Wales*. There were only fifty-one of us left alive when at last we came to York.

4. *HOMMES DU NORD*

We found Mister Cook, who was chief factor at York, a very different sort of a man from Mister Auld. Where Auld was grim, taciturn, suspicious, Mister Cook was affable, even garrulous at times, and ever disposed to accept a newcomer at face value, leaving it to the future to prove him wrong if it must. Mister Auld was lean and sallow. Mister Cook was short, rotund and red-faced. Factor Auld was dour. Factor Cook was full of cheer. When we reached Fort Churchill Mister Auld had left us strictly alone until we had forced ourselves on his attention. When we came to York Factory Mister Cook did not ignore us. He did not even content himself with sending one or another of his dozens of underlings to greet us. The occasion was unusual enough —and so was his own curiosity—that he came down himself from the broad puncheon veranda of the Company store to welcome us.

Our arrival was heralded first by the barking of the dogs: thousands of them, it seemed to me, clustered about the inland side of the enclosure, toward the open clearings where the post gardens were laid out in the summertime. A few swart, stocky men in blanket coats were drawing wood from the long cordwood pile against the far fringe of woods, and several others were at work in the open canoe sheds, repairing the long bark craft for use as soon as the river was open. When the dogs began to bark they all looked up and one or two stopped their work and scurried toward the post's main building. The others, too, left what they were doing and came forward to see what manner of incredible, gaunt folk were these that came stalking and stumbling out of the forest. Their dark faces showed clearly their incredulity and amazement. Quite obviously they did not understand at first whence we had come. Then, when at last we did manage to cut through their strange, to us at least, French Canadian patois and made ourselves comprehensible, they could not believe us.

"Impossible!" they cried. Such a starveling band as ours, inexperienced and burdened with women and children too, could not possibly have traversed the distance that lay between York and Churchill. And yet there was ample evidence to bear out our story. Yellow Knife and his companions were plainly Chippewayan, and the furs that we wore were of the northern cut. If this were not enough our obviously fatigued and tattered condition surely testified to the weary miles we had covered.

In all the hurly-burly of our arrival no one noticed the rotund little man with the rosy, Saint Nick's face, and close trimmed white beard until he spoke.

"Ye've had the devil's own journey if ye've come all the way from Churchill," he said. "An' from th' look o' ye I'd say ye'd agree to that!"

At the sound of his voice both Alec MacLean and I, who were in the lead, turned toward him. Clearly, by his dress and his demeanor, he was someone in authority, though I hardly thought him more than a clerk at first, so friendly and self-effacing was he. He saw the question in our eyes and hastened, smilingly, to make himself known.

"My name's Cook," said he. "William Cook, gentleman, chief factor here. And yourselves—?"

Alec MacLean was awkward, unsure of how he should meet the other's friendliness. I stepped into the instant of abrupt silence.

"MacAllister, Mister Cook," I said, accepting his proffered hand. "Malcolm MacAllister is my name. I'm assistant to Mister MacLean, here, and personal agent for Lord Selkirk. We came out in the *Prince of Wales* last year and were set ashore at Fort Churchill by mistake. I can't tell you how fine it is to see York Factory at last!"

He looked surprised and somehow relieved.

"Eh?" he cried. "The folk from the *Wales?* Damn my eyes! We wondered if ye'd be along last fall, and when ye did not come we worried for ye. Riker said ye'd asked to go ashore there—"

"Captain Riker set us ashore and sailed away before we knew where we were," I told him.

"Aye, an' there're no so many o' us as there were because o' 't," Alec MacLean put in dourly. "There were amony o' us died because o' him, good God gi'e rest t' their souls!"

"Mister MacLean is to be dominie of the Red River Parish," I put in quickly.

Mister Cook looked at him with interest and then glanced back at me.

"So?" he said. "But yourself, Man! Ye look as if ye'd tangled with a bear!"

"You never made a better guess, sir!" I told him, grinning in spite of my pain. "But I think there are others as bad off."

He looked back along our ragamuffin line.

"O' course! O' course!" he cried. "I forget my manners in my curiosity! Forgive me, and come in! We'll find ye a shakedown somewhere, and by th' look o' ye 'tis needed. Ye know, we've a score or so of others belongin' t' your party—came out in the *Eddystone* and waited for ye. Ho, Marcel! Gagnon! Coeurbois! Laurent! Th' rest o' ye! Bear a hand here with yon sledges. Come in, gentlemen—and ladies! Let us try t' make ye comfortable for a change!"

So we came to York Factory and found friends, and certainly every possible comfort that that wild northland could afford, awaiting us. I think I could not speak too highly of the way we were received and made to feel at home—or at least a part of the community. We were given quarters among our friends of the *Eddystone,* not in the main section of buildings, but in a snug log warehouse that overlooked the river, and those of us that were suffering from snowshoe fever and worse were given a chance to overcome the trouble. We had good food and good beds, and above all we were made to feel welcome; as if we were not a burden, and I think that this more than anything else was food to our spirit.

Only once did Mister Cook offer to dictate our future plan of action. And that I believe was entirely sincere. He drew me aside after supper one evening: supper that was rationed out to all hands around alike.

"I'm sorry," he said, "I cannot talk to your dominie and make sense o' it. I daresay he's all well enough as a parson. But he's vague when it comes t' sayin' what's t' be done next. Perhaps ye can tell me, Mister MacAllister. What is it ye have in mind? Ye're welcome t' stay here as long as need be, but I must know yer intentions so that I may lay my own plans."

I decided that the best course here was utter frankness.

"I'll tell you the truth, Mister Cook," I said. "It may be that Mister MacLean is vague about our plans because none of us have been able to think much beyond this point. We've all been too worn down. What would you advise?"

He tugged at his beard and grinned at me, ruddy cheeked, through the white cloud of his whiskers.

"Ye pose me a question!" he replied. "I'd hoped ye'd thought it out yerselves, but I can understand why ye have not. Well-l-l, now—"

He paused to ponder the situation a moment, rubbed his hand over his eyes and pulled his nose.

"Well, now!" he said again, "I'll tell ye. There'll be a brigade goin' up t' th' Forks about midsummer, after th' supply vessels from home have arrived. I daresay there'll be others for th' settlements comin' in with 'em. Why don't ye wait for them? I've a notion that just now the more there are o' ye th' better, d'ye understand me?"

"You sound as though you anticipated trouble," I said.

"Don't ye then yerself," he demanded, "after Miles MacDonnell's order?"

I could understand his reference to Governor MacDonnell, for it was to him that Lord Selkirk had ordered us to report when we arrived at the Red River. But his reference to an order of the Governor meant less than nothing to me.

"I don't understand," I said. "What do you mean? What order?"

"Ye've not heard then?" he demanded.

I shook my head.

"We've had little chance to hear anything at Churchill."

He gave me a quizzical smile.

" 'Twas a proclamation he issued last winter," he said. "I think myself 'twas ill-advised, but that's neither here nor there. The thing's done an' th' Northwesters an' th' *Boisbrûlés* are up in arms."

"Why?" I cut in impatiently. "What was this proclamation? And who are these *Boisbrûlés,* and why should they be up in arms?"

"Gently! Gently!" He held up his hand, laughing and interrupting me. "Let me take them one at a time. I can see there's much t' be explained t' ye, an' if ye'll be patient with me I'll try to put it so ye'll understand. In th' first place there was this order—this proclamation o' th' Governor—forbiddin' th' makin' or th' exportin' out of Assiniboia—that is out o' th' lands granted t' Lord Selkirk—o' pemmican, pretty near all o' which is made by the *Boisbrûlés,* th' métis, the half-breed hunters on th' Red an' th' upper Assiniboine. At th' same time he forbade anyone engaged in th' fur trade from huntin' within th' same territory."

"How could there be any objection to that?" I broke in. "The land has been granted to Lord Selkirk, and Mister MacDonnell is his governor. Surely there is no question of his right—"

"O' right—no," Cook shrugged, "at least I don't think so, though th' Northwesters're inclined t' dispute th' matter. Ye see, 'tis not altogether a question o' that. 'Tis rather a thing that bears on th' very existence o' those folk."

"I don't quite see——" I began.

"Ye will," he broke in. "By now I've no doubt ye've seen enough o' pemmican t' be aware o' its importance t' us in th' trade. Ye'll know that 'tis th' staple an' mainstay o' life in this north country all through th' winter months, which is a good two thirds o' th' year. Even when game's plentiful, as it has been this year, pemmican makes up about half our food. An' when th' winter is hard an' game scarce we live on it entirely. Without pemmican or somethin' like it th' fur trade could hardly exist, for th' *voyageurs* o' th' brigades, th' hunters themselves, have no time t' stop t' hunt or fish for their own. They often eat naught else for weeks at a time. An' th' savages are sometimes so improvident that th' winter catches 'em with only th' pemmican they can get from th' traders for food."

He paused and stared at me.

"I begin to understand," I said.

"Aye!" he replied dryly. "Th' Northwesters're no different from th' rest o' us. They're mortal just th' same. An' now Miles MacDonnell's moved t' cut 'em off from th' main source o' their food supply! D'ye wonder they're angry?"

"But——" I said.

"But that's not all," he interrupted me. "Ye mind, I told ye that th' métis—th' *Boisbrûlés,* th' half-breed hunters—have made a business o' slaughterin' th' buffalo that run in vast herds upon th' prairies between th' Red an' th' Assiniboine an' o' makin' pemmican from th' meat an' sellin' it both t' ourselves an' t' th' Northwesters. Now, as ye see, by a stroke o' his pen Governor MacDonnell has cut off their very means o' livin'."

"But why?" I managed to get the query in this time. "Why on earth did he do such a thing?"

The grizzled factor shrugged.

"Miles is a fool!" he said hotly. "There was no need for it. Hunting has been poor in the neighborhood o' th' Forks, an' upstream at Fort Daer, at th' mouth o' th' Pembina. Th' answer is that th' settlers have frightened th' animals off a bit. But Miles noticed th' shortage an' thought it was general. He said in his proclamation that 'twas done t' conserve th' game supply for th' settlers."

"That would be reasonable enough if they are really short," I put in.

"Aye," he agreed darkly. "If game were scarce, so 'twould be. But, d'ye see, there are some that say there's no shortage save in th' very neighborhood o' th' colony itself. They say 'twas done for another reason, out o' MacDonnell's dislike for th' Northwesters an' th' *Bois-brûlés*."

"These half-breeds—" I said.

"Don't underrate 'em!" he cut in. "They're a new race, bastards, t' be sure. Th' sons an' daughters o' winterin' whites—traders, trappers, factors—an' th' Indian women they've taken t' comfort 'em in their exile." He paused and flushed a little shamefacedly. "I must admit t' ye that I've a Cree woman o' my own. 'Tis th' custom hereabout. But ye must not think 'em inferior, for they've th' good an' bad traits o' both races, an' a few o' their own beside. They're handsome an' intelligent, an' they're volatile. They've th' Indian's capacity for resentment an' th' white man's will t' carry through. An', my friend, there's none know all this better than th' Northwesters: that miserable pack o' Montreal peddlers that'll stick at nothin' t' gain a trade advantage o' th' Company! Unless I miss my guess th' Northwesters're already at work on th' *Boisbrûlés,* an' if that's th' case I think ye'll see why I fear trouble."

I nodded. I daresay it may seem that I have reported all of this talk at much greater length than was necessary. But I have done so deliberately, for it seems to me that here for the first time I began to get some inkling of what lay in store for us. I thought of Jeannie—and of the other women and children as well, of course, though I must admit that my concern was primarily for her—and glanced at him.

"Is it safe then, do you think?" I asked.

"Who can tell ye that?" he retorted. " 'Tis as safe there as anywhere, I daresay. All th' same I advise ye t' travel in as large a group as possible. 'Twill be th' time when th' brigades are movin' on th' lakes an' rivers, an' if it should happen that ye fell in with one o' th' Northwesters' outfits it might save ye some rough goin' t' outnumber 'em!"

So we waited at York Factory for the arrival of the ships from Scotland, for it appeared that they always sailed either from the Orkneys or the Hebrides. Spring went and summer came. The ice left the Hayes and the Nelson, and the fur brigades from the Assiniboine and the Saskatchewan, from God's Lake and the English River and Athabasca came in. In a way, I suppose, the gathering that we saw there was similar to that of the Northwesters at Fort William, on Lake Superior, save that the furs that our traders baled were for shipment direct to London instead of Montreal. There was a difference, too, in that none of those who came in to us were wintering partners in the Company; none of the directing partners came out from London. In the case of the Northwesters the bigwigs of the association came out

from Montreal in their long canoes, with pomp and trapping, to meet
the winterers—actual, stockholding members of the business, at Fort
William. But in our case the men who attended the rendezvous at York
Factory were but white clerks and voyaging hunters, plus a strong
strain of Orkneymen, who seemed to predominate in the Company's
employ.

At York there was a celebration, approaching on a smaller scale
that of Fort William. In our eyes it was colorful and wicked, though
there was none of the riotous *boisson* that was our rivals' annual
attraction. Men who spend all but a few weeks in the deep woods with
no companions but Indians, and who scarcely hear English spoken
from one year's end to the other, may surely be forgiven a few days of
carousal and tippling when at last they do reach comparative civilization. The swart voyageurs strutted, swaggered, talked loud and large
and rolled their dark eyes longingly at our prettiest girls. But I think
the purse-lipped disapproval of our staid older women, together with
the Company's well-known discipline, had a chastening effect and put
something of a quietus on things.

But none of this concerned me greatly. Jean was amused but otherwise displayed no particular interest, and I felt that there was no need
for alarm for her. Nor for myself in that quarter, I might add. I was
yet conscious of a twinge of pain in my legs as a result of my encounter
with the great bear, and for a time just after our arrival I had been
too weak and fine drawn to do much more than lie in my bunk and
let the others wait upon me. But by this time I was fairly recovered
and well on the road to regaining my strength.

As soon as I was able to be up and around, of course, I made it a
point to waylay Jean and apologize to her for my gruffness that cold
wild night.

"Will you forgive me for it, Jean?" I asked. "The pain was bitter
hard to bear, yet I felt—I knew there were other, older folk that
couldn't come through unless they rode the sleds. So long as I could
walk I thought their need was greater than mine. I'd no mind to fly
out at you."

She gave me a curious, speculative sort of look, and though she did
not smile her eyes were soft, with a light of sympathy, and not at all
stern.

"I understand, Malcolm," she assured me. "I dinna hold yer words
again' ye."

At that point we were interrupted by the arrival of a pack of young
folk on the veranda of the post, and there was no time or chance to

say more. It was not much, but such as it was—in her look as much as her words, I read some hope, and I made up my mind to press the matter farther as soon as the opportunity arose.

But such moments were few and far between, and I was careful to watch for a time when we would not be interrupted again. Accordingly I passed over several moments when I might have spoken, and I truly believe that my silence then whetted her interest.

In the meantime we were not idle. As the ice in the river broke up and the buds burst into leaf upon the trees suddenly as they do in this wild northland, with scarce any transition from the season of snow to that of sun and summer, there was plenty to keep us occupied. Because we did not wish to draw too heavily upon the resources of York Factory, which were so generously offered, Alec MacLean and I maintained a constant schedule of hunting and fishing parties that went out daily to supplement our staple supplies with fresh fish and meat. At the same time we bribed some of the Indian women about the post to show our womenfolk the proper ways of dressing out deerskins and moose and bear and caribou hides, as well as more delicate furs, so that we had leather and soft rawhide, and the like, with which to patch and replenish our tattered clothing.

Still, as the geese and ducks flew south, and as my legs healed, I will admit that I gave more thought to the matter of mending my fences with Jean. The moment I waited for came at last, I felt, on a day late in June; a day when our hunting parties were out and our fishermen were hand-lining in the estuary for sturgeon—a less exciting sport than angling for trout or grayling, but much more rewarding for such a large group as ours.

By that time the major chores of rehabilitating ourselves for the move south had been accomplished, and there was little left for us to do except see to our daily needs and our personal chores; I, who had neglected my own washing and sewing sadly, decided that here was a moment in which it should be done. I gathered up all the things I had stuffed into odd corners of my baggage and carried them down to the river, where I washed and dried them on the rocks in the sun. When that was done I dumped them all, willy-nilly, back into the box and started up toward the bachelors' loft. It was on the veranda of the Company store that I saw her. She smiled, and my heart bumped.

"Good day t'ye, Malcolm," she cried. "What's that ye have yon?" For some reason I was embarrassed.

" 'Tis my wash," I said stiffly. "It has to be done sometime."

"Let me see how ye've done," she demanded, and before I could stop her she was pawing over the bits of ragged ends of underdrawers and the like until I was red in the face, though she paid no heed to that.

She held up two undershirts and several handkerchiefs that I will admit had now because of their age assumed a color that was rather that of an old mop than of fresh, new linen.

"Fie on ye, Malcolm MacAllister!" she cried. "D'ye call these clean?"

"They're none so new as they were," I retorted defensively. "Of course they're clean. They've been soaped and rinsed in the river!"

But she was not even listening to me. She dug on through the box, dragging out yet more sorry looking garments.

"Will ye look now?" she cried. "Here's buttons ye need on yon shirt! Here's a hole in yer breeks!"

"I've meant to fix them," I said gruffly, "but I've not had time."

That, of course, was patently silly, for after we had reached York I had been days on my backside with nothing whatever to do.

"Will ye bring 'em t' me, Malcolm?" She glanced up at me earnestly. "I'm no th' best seamstress or washwoman about, but I think I can put 'em t' rights for ye!"

I smiled at her a little shamefacedly then, abashed that I had been so graceless.

"I daresay I could do it for myself if I weren't so lazy," I told her.

"Lazy?" She smiled at me cryptically. "I'd not noticed that. Gi'e 'em t' me. I'll tend t' 'em properly."

Obviously she did not intend to take no for an answer. I handed her the box, at the same time seeking to make a joke of it and somehow hold on to this moment.

"All right," I said. "Lord knows I'd be glad of a button or two that would stay put, or a pair of breeks that would not let the wind blow in upon me every time I turned my back!"

"I'll see what I can do, Malcolm," she smiled and half turned away with the box toward her own quarters, but I stopped her.

"Thank you, Jean," I told her. "I appreciate it. But there's little time left to work on them today. I don't know about yourself, but I've grown a bit tired of sturgeon and spring deer, and it was in my mind to take a light canoe and go up the river a piece to see if I could locate a few trout. Would you care to go along?"

It was not much to offer, to ask a lass to go out fishing. But from the way her eyes lighted at the invitation it was clear that even so small a break away from the monotony of the post was welcome.

"Would ye take me, Malcolm?" she cried.

"Of course!" I nodded. "That's why I asked you!"

She was away and scurrying off to the women's loft before I had finished. As she went she called back to me, over her shoulder.

"Wait, now, till I put this away! I'll borrow Father's gear. He'll no mind!"

I went up and fetched down my own tackle, for odd as it may seem to some, next to our guns, our rods and our lines were among our most prized possessions, and we never went anywhere but we took them along. When I came back Jean was waiting at the landing, and I got down a canoe and helped her into it. She rigged our lines as I paddled, and about a mile or so up the Hayes we came to a place where a black creek, its waters dark from the alder swamps through which it flowed, came twisting and surging in from the south.

Here we found the trout I sought: great, hungry, fat-bodied fellows that ran on the average from two and a half to four pounds. I was surprised to see how expertly Jean went after them; I gathered, since I think she must have taken two to my one, that she had had the benefit of expert advice from her father, in Scotland. At the same time I was pleased, for it seemed to me that it meant that if all went as I hoped it would mean that there would be more in life for her than just sewing and cooking and spinning out flax and childbearing. There would be some things like this that we could also enjoy together.

But I held my tongue for the moment at least, until we had finished our fishing and taken down our tackle and turned our canoe back downstream again toward the river and the post. Then I could restrain myself no longer.

"Jean," I said carefully so as not to offend her, "we've come through a braw, hard winter and over the grim way from Churchill to here, and I think I've shown you something of what's in me. Couldn't we —now—? I mean couldn't we talk of it?"

She paused in her paddling and looked around at me.

"Not yet, Mac," she told me, not unkindly. "We've a far, long way t' be goin' yet, an' ye mind, ye promised."

"Aye, but Jean," I cried. "The worst is all behind us now! There's no reason—"

"Yon's as we hope, at least," she replied dryly, "but we've over a thousan' miles yet t' be voyagin', an' ye'll ken well enough a' that can yet be happenin' in that time. Na, Mac, we'll ha'e other things to be thinkin' about for a while yet. When we've come safe at last t' th' Forks, as I told ye—"

"But, Jean—" I started to protest.

She looked around at me again reproachfully.

"More, ye promised, mind, Mac?" she reminded me. "Dinna spoil it!"

After that, it seemed to me, there was nothing I could say and so I fell silent and I daresay a little sullen. Neither of us spoke again until we had come to the landing and taken up our catch. At the entrance to her own quarters she stopped and faced me.

"Dinna be angry, Malcolm," she pleaded. " 'Tis just that there's yet too much ahead o' us a' for me t' think o' this as I should. It's been a fine day, an' I thank ye for it."

With that she was gone, and I noticed that although I went out again to the same place and each time returned with a good string she would not go with me. On the other hand, perhaps to make up for it, it seemed to me that more and more often, at public gatherings and when we were all together, she made it almost a point to seek me out and stay close beside me.

It was toward the end of the third week in July that the two Company supply vessels came in sight, picking their way cautiously in through the shallows at the mouth of the Nelson. At this point I do not know who sighted them first, but there was not a man among us who needed to be told that here again were our long-familiar *Prince of Wales* and her consort the *Eddystone*.

Word of their arrival spread like wildfire, and long before they had come to anchor, I think every man, woman and child in York— red, white and mixed—had gone down to the landing place to watch them come ashore, for to most of these folk the coming of the supply ships annually was the greatest event of the year. There were some of us, however, drawn up in a little knot by the landing stage, who waited in grim silence.

But when the first longboats drew in alongside the crude log wharf, to our surprise and chagrin it was not Captain Riker who stepped ashore from the *Wales's* boat, but a complete and chill-faced stranger, a man with white hair, tall and suave, yet with pale, hard eyes. As he stepped ashore he announced himself to all and sundry, in a flat, be-damned-to-ye tone of voice, as Captain Riker's successor, Captain Knight. Captain Riker, he said blandly, was no longer in command of the *Prince of Wales*. Indeed, Captain Riker was no longer with the Company. And I for one, lacked interest to ask him why or what had become of that evil man.

One thing, however, the *Wales* and the *Eddystone* brought out to us, this time all in excellent health, was sorely needed reinforcement for our little group. In the two ships some hundred and twenty-five new colonists made the passage out from Scotland and brought our total number, who would make the journey up from York to Lake Winnipeg and the Forks of the Red, to something just over two hundred. These, of course, were exclusively settlers, and did not count voyageurs, hunters, traders, trappers and bourgeois, outnumbering us more than six to one, who were also waiting to make the annual journey south and west and eastward into the wild, fur lands.

The arrival of the ships was the signal to end the carouse and turn to business. The ships warped into the wharf and some of the voyageurs swung to the work of unloading them. Others got down the canoes from the sheds and fell to patching and readying them for the next leg of the journey, and I must admit that as the day drew near for us to leave I felt a certain pang of regret at the need to say good by to Factor Cook and his open-handed hospitality, despite the eagerness with which I looked forward to our arrival at the Forks.

We left York Factory on the last day of July, and how shall I describe our going? After our snowshoe trek across the frozen, leafless barren from Churchill I think no mode of travel would have astonished me. Moreover, during the spring and early summer I had watched enough of the brigades arrive to realize forcibly that journeys of any great distance in this northern world were made primarily by water, and the vehicle by which men traveled was the canoe.

In so far as York Factory was concerned, the canoe was a birch-bark craft, cunningly contrived by the Indians entirely of forest products. Not a nail, not a ringbolt, not an ounce of manufactured pitch went into it, and at this post, far to the north of the regular routes, there were four separate and distinct types. They were types, however, only in size, for they were all of the same shape, with high, curving ends and low gunnels amidships. The largest at York, and rather a rarity there, being used only for heavy cargoes upon wide, open waters, was the *canot bâtard:* the bastard canoe—which seemed to me an enormous craft for one so fragile. It measured thirty to thirty-two feet in length and was capable of carrying two tons in addition to its crew of ten.

These, however, were considered unwieldy and incapable of carrying sufficient load in proportion to their size, so that they were not used much in the far north. We were told that in the Great Lakes' service, between the Northwest depot at Fort William and Montreal, there was an even larger type in regular use: the *canot du maître,* or master canoe, measuring thirty-five to forty feet in length and capable of carrying three to four tons of cargo in addition to its crew of fourteen and two to four passengers. This, I admit I took with a grain of salt, considering it of a piece with the tall tales of the voyageurs, who delighted in a heavy-handed waggery toward us, until I saw the canoe for myself, some time later.

The type of craft most in use by the Company, and that which came most often down with the brigades from the outlying forts and factories, was the *canot du nord*, or north canoe. This was some twenty-five feet in length by four or five feet broad, and it carried, in addition to its crew of eight paddlers, a ton or a ton and a half of cargo and three or four passengers.

In addition to these there were the *demi-canot*, or half canoe, which might be twenty feet long and carried a crew of four to six, and the light canoe which ran from ten to fifteen feet long and was generally used by the Indians to transport themselves and their families.

North canoes were assigned to us for the long, incredible journey inland to the Forks of the Red. Somehow it had not impressed me before what a vast distance that would be, but now it was brought home to me. Of course I had looked at the charts before and realized that it would be no mere afternoon walk. And Jean had more than hinted at it. But now that the thing was imminent I stopped to measure it off against the scale, and found that, without taking into consideration all the bends and turnings of the river, all the long portages between lakes and streams and around falls and rapids, without measuring the convolutions of lake shore that must be followed up Lake Winnipeg, it came to nearly seven hundred miles. Truly, I thought, this was a land of enormous distances!

And yet that glance at the map, that moment of calculation, gave me no more than a hint of what lay ahead. I think no larger brigade was ever seen north of Lake Superior. In all we were more than a hundred and twenty canoes. Seventy of these, both freight and passenger, carried the colonists and the annual shipment of trade goods and provisions for the Red River. Thirty were for the Assiniboine brigade, and twenty or so for English River. In numbers we were a small army: more than nine hundred and fifty voyageurs—swarthy men, half-French, half-Indian in most cases, and flamboyantly gay; some two hundred of us settlers; and more than eighty bourgeois, or wintering traders, guides and interpreters.

As much as possible the men of our contingent were spread among the crews, both in order to reduce the deadweight load of the passengers and so that they might learn the tricks of voyaging: of wielding a paddle and packing over a carry; for many of the canoes were to be left at the Forks for our own use. Since I was unattached myself

I was one of these, and as Lord Selkirk's personal agent I was given a place in the lead canoe—seventh paddle, as I recall it, just in front of the steersman in the stern, where if I missed a stroke or faltered in the cadence, I could do little harm.

At the same time Jean MacLean and her father were placed in the second canoe in line, where when I had time to glance back I could see her, but with little opportunity to speak.

William Cook himself came down to the landing in the Hayes River estuary to wish us Godspeed, and twenty minutes later we, in the lead canoe, passed around the islands above Ten Shilling Creek and plunged into the wilderness once more.

I would hardly have believed it possible that the little spot of civilization at York Factory, which had been our world for so many weeks, could have so little effect beyond the close encircling rim of its own forest. Yet it was true that we were no more than around the bend before we were in a world as primitive as ever God had made it in the beginning. The green walls of the forest closed in upon us, and the river became a silver ribbon: sometimes placid and quiet, sometimes roaring and turbulent, but ever present, growling, muttering, whispering, chattering, thundering. It was our highway, and even on the portages we were never very far from it.

Day after livelong day—forty strokes a minute, hours without end, until my back and shoulders ached—we paddled. And where we were not paddling, it seemed to me, we were bucking the rapids, poling and tracking our long craft up wherever it was possible to do so without unloading them, or landing and carrying the canoes and lading all around a falls or rapid on our backs. I was amazed at the immense weight that some of our voyageurs took pride in carrying. Our cargo was so packed as to make a number of standard-sized bundles of ninety pounds, and most of the time I found it as much as I could do to stagger across the portage around a rapid or a fall or from one small lake to another with just one such package. Yet the average load per man was three, and more than once I saw individuals among them pile up as many as six and seven upon their load and carry them across the portage without turning a hair. He among them, apparently, who could show himself the most powerful and at the same time the most willing beast of burden gained a feather for his cap, and they vied with one another for that honor, as they did for honors at paddling or dancing a jig or eating or drinking. They were all tests of endurance so far as these simple, uncomplicated fellows were concerned.

For myself, although I took part in none of the contests of strength or endurance, yet by the end of each day I was sore and weary and exhausted and only too happy to fall into my blankets and leave matters of romance to others if they persisted in pursuing them. In such circumstances I think it is scarcely extraordinary that I saw little of Jean, even though we were in adjacent canoes, save to say "Good morning" to her at breakfast and "Good night" to her at supper. Certainly I could no more have prodded myself to make love in what seemed to me a state of living exhaustion than I could have flown, and I would certainly have flown if I could!

Our route, without pausing for the interminable business of describing each fall and carry and tracking place, lay up the Hayes to the mouth of God's River, where the brigades for God's Lake and the English River left us. We ourselves continued on up the Hayes for nearly two hundred miles, passing through Oxford Lake and stopping at Oxford House for a regale, and then on through Molson Lake and across to Jack River, which is a part of the Nelson River system, and so down to Norway House, near the upper end of Lake Winnipeg. There we had another regale, or *boisson* as they call it, little more than a plain drunken frolic for the voyageurs, whose whole aim in life seemed to be little else. Then we were off again, through the flat, reedy gullet of Playgreen Lake, by which the waters of Winnipeg empty into the Nelson's roaring channel, and out into the broad expanse of Winnipeg itself, rough and shallow and storm-tossed, ringed with rank stands of grassy reeds and wild rice, water, often as much as a mile and a half through what appears to be the green shore.

There was a stiffening here among the men, a sudden tension which even I, dull as my senses had become through fatigue, could perceive. When I spoke of it to Pierre Labadie, the steersman of our lead canoe, a great garrulous man with the nickname of "Bo-bo-bo" because he talked so much and was such a hand at a song, he merely looked serious and nodded.

"It is becaus' 'ere is the *pays des hommes*—of the Northwesters, M'sieu," he told me, "an' at this tam' of year it is possible that we meet some of them. The brigade for Athabasca pass 'ere about now. So, too, does this of Saskatchewan. Below, farther to the south, 'oo can say w'ich we meet?"

"Pooh!" I snorted. "Don't tell me you're afraid. Surely we outnumber any brigade that we are likely to meet!"

The way he sat up stiffly against his thwart and refused to smile made it plain enough that I was joking about a thing that lay close to his own honor and that of every voyageur in the employ of the Company.

"You do not unnerstan', M'sieu," he told me soberly. "It is not that I or my comrades would not wish to fight. You 'ave seen we do this gladly! But now we 'ave the women an' the children with us. We 'ave the *salop* settlair—if you will forgive the saying. We do not know 'ow you will fight, but we do know that three bull in the big 'erd that run away 'ave not the much chance to stop the stampage!"

It was crudely put, but I got the gist.

"I don't think you need worry Labadie," I said sternly, not a little piqued at the slur. "You'll find us ready enough to fight for our own, you or anyone else."

"Ouai, M'sieu!" Labadie replied dutifully, and that was as much as was said aloud, though I noticed a difference in the stiffening attitude of our canoemen after that. It was as if they were carrying a chip on their shoulders and were even looking for the Athabasca brigade, which seemed most likely to cross our path.

But the Northwest Athabascans did not come in sight. We coasted south up the eastern shore of Lake Winnipeg, through the shallow water, slamming across the open bays where the surf pounded in upon the bowmen, and hugging the grassy points, never venturing out into the open lake. We may have crossed them, but if so we did not know it; and every day that passed seemed to fill our own canoemen with greater defiance and courage.

Perhaps I should have been warned by their attitude. Not that our own folk were cowards, but the reputation of these Northwestmen—a reputation largely built up by themselves—was such that it bred defiance among our own people. Laboriously we reached the mouth of the Berens River without conflict. That was on the first of September, and it seemed to me that Pierre Labadie breathed a sigh of relief at that point.

"You think we have passed them, Labadie?" I asked.

"We have passed the Athabasca brigade, M'sieu," he replied. "They are the worst of the lot. I think they have swung across the lake at the narrows and gone up the western side, pray God, M'sieu, that this is so!"

"And you think, then, that we are free of danger?" I demanded.

He glowered at me.

"Danger, M'sieu?" he retorted. "We have hardly been in that! But we have been in danger of a fight. If you mean that, yes M'sieu. I think that that has passed, unless we meet with other brigades of Northwesters above."

"Labadie!" I scoffed. "You jump at your own shadow. Surely no one would dare pick a fight with such a group as us!"

"Perhaps so, M'sieu," he replied harshly, but he offered no opinion beyond that.

Apparently we were both right to a degree. We coasted Grassy Bay and Pigeon Point and flung into the narrows, all the long parade of us. No soul passed us there save for a Cree canoe heading north. We passed Punk Island and the Block and Manigotan and the long, reedy shores below. Overhead the ducks and geese flew northward, and once or twice we were able to catch swans floating on the long inlets where the rivers came in. But well down on the far side of Traverse Bay, on an island where we had drawn up along the sandy beach for the night, something of what Pierre Labadie had been dreading happened.

We had cut across the mouth of the treacherous bay, where the Winnipeg River falls into the lake, bucking the wind and the waves, and on an island, southward of the river, had found a long, driftwood covered beach of gray sand. There we stopped, only too happy to pause and dry out our clothes and the canoe loads, when another long train of canoes appeared from the direction of the river mouth, falling down out of Rainy Lake and Lac des Bois. We watched them as they drew near and stood silent as they drove upon the beach.

They were Northwesters, as we had surmised, thirty or forty canoes of them, no doubt coming up from their annual rendezvous at Fort William, on Lake Superior, and outbound for their posts in the *pays d'en haut*. The fact that they had turned this way seemed to indicate that those posts were on the upper Assiniboine and the Red, where according to our law and to the proclamation of Governor MacDonnell they had no right to be. Yet we could understand that they must be allowed to close up such sites as they had claimed. We were not disposed to be unreasonable about that.

I must say that I watched them come ashore with considerable curiosity. I had heard so much of these fellows that now I found myself face to face with them I could not help but study them with some care. They seemed to me a swaggering lot. They beached their canoes and the bowman in each leapt ashore and steadied the craft for the others who followed. Our own men, I noticed, were gathering in little knots, sullen and watchful, and though I felt little doubt how any brawl might come out, since we outnumbered them more than two to one, still I hoped to avert any open clash for the sake of the women and children who were with us. I passed the word among the more reliable of our settlers, and after that we passed from group to group of our canoemen, whispering:

"Gently! Gently, *mes enfants!* We seek no trouble. Remember, a truly brave man waits to fight when the women are not at hand!"

I was pleased that the thought had occurred to me, for I think there is little doubt that had it not our beach camp would quickly have become a brawling, battling shambles. I believe the newcomers must have seen what we were about, for as they stepped ashore they preened and strutted so blatantly that if the situation had not really been so tense it would actually have been laughable. There is no question but that they were a colorful lot. In dress they were not greatly different from our own canoemen. But they had added just a touch of dash and swagger here and there that bespoke their pride. There were bright ribbons on their shoulders and scarlet garters held their leggings close about their calves. Their moccasins were bright beaded and they wore long, varicolored tassels in their caps and bright feathers in their hair. For the most they were dark-skinned, swarthy as our own men, French and Indian, though here and there was a blue-eyed blond. None apparently could speak English—or would in our presence, if one excepted the bourgeois and the interpreters. These men needed no guides. But all seemed to have one thing in common: a magnificent, barrel-chested, powerful physique, and now as they came ashore they sought to show it to the best advantage. They flexed their muscles ostentatiously. They strutted up and down the beach in front of their canoes, lifting their feet ridiculously high and planting them again with the widespread care of a buffalo bull stalking a rutting cow.

"Nous sommes hommes du nord!" They proclaimed proudly, childishly, blatantly.

For some reason that seemed to be the supreme insult, and I could sense the stir among our own men: almost a surge to meet these arrogant, sneering fellows. Yet the word that we had spread was effective, and the clash did not come. Fortunately, when the tension reached its peak, it seemed to me, the bourgeois and passengers began to step on shore, and theirs was a quieting influence.

First ashore was a remarkable figure. I stood somewhat above him, at the point where the beach met the low-cut bank behind; he was yet tall to me. I judged him to be at least six feet four, yet he had none of the lean asceticism usually connected with such height. He was florid in complexion, with a flowing, golden mane of hair that swept down about his shoulders and was obviously well tended. He was broad-shouldered and broad-bellied, thick-legged and jovial. On his head he wore an enormous, beaver top hat and on his feet were immaculately shined Hessian boots. Between, his coat was bright red and obviously a uniform, though spotted and unbuttoned. His breeches were tight, white and skin-fitting and marked with the remnants of a dozen feasts. He stepped from his canoe and turned toward me where I was standing with Alec MacLean and Charles Belly, the leader of the Assiniboine brigade.

"Hallo, Messieurs! Hallo, Charles!" he cried. "Belly, ye've the manners of an Englishman," and it was only much later that I learned that when a Northwester spoke of an "Englishman" he meant an employee of the Bay Company. "Gentlemen, my name is Cameron, Duncan Cameron, Captain o' th' Voyageur Corps an' commander o' this district. Ye'll forgive my fellows, I hope, but we are 'Men o' th' North' an' somethin' inclined t' boast about it."

It was clearly a challenge flung recklessly at our feet, inviting us to trouble if we wanted it. I looked at Alec MacLean, but he did what I daresay I should myself have done in the circumstances.

"I'm pleased t' make yer acquaintance, Captain," he said. "We've womenfolk with us and seek no argument, so I hope yer men will start none. My name's MacLean—Alexander MacLean, lately appointed dominie to Lord Selkirk's colony at th' Red River, an' all those ye see o' us here are bound there. Here's my assistant, th' schoolmaster, Mister MacAllister. I tak' it ye've already made th' acquaintance o' Mister Belly."

The hulking blond man acknowledged the introduction with a courtly bow, and I noticed that while we had been talking a number of others of his company had come up behind him. He turned toward them and beckoned them forward. A tall, thin-faced, reedlike wisp of a man, sallow and shifty-eyed with black hair that grew low on his forehead was first. So interested was I in him that I did not notice that Jean MacLean had joined us, nor, I think, did any of the others.

"I give ye Alexander MacDonnell, gentlemen," said Cameron. "Mister MacDonnell will be in charge o' our post at Fort Qu'Appelle, some distance above th' Forks."

I inclined my head.

"Mister MacDonnell?" I said. "This is likely to be confusin'. Are you related to our own governor: Miles MacDonnell?"

"Coosin!" he growled, and that was all the acknowledgment he made of the meeting.

"An' then, gentlemen," Cameron went on, "I'd make ye acquainted with some o' yer other neighbors—Cuthbert Grant, here, an' Bostonnais Pangman."

He swiveled slightly to one side and waved a hand toward two men that came up behind him. The first was a slim, swart, handsome man with an intelligent, mobile face, a tapering body and bright white teeth, black eyes and black hair. His comrade was a stocky, blocky, square-built, Indian-looking fellow with an even darker complexion. How little did I guess, as I nodded my acknowledgment to them, how much more closely and with what bitterness I was to come to know these two in the months to come!

But now another man had joined the group; a man as tall as Cameron himself and equally broad across the shoulders. Where the florid, blond man was a little on the stout side, however, the newcomer showed no hint of fat or flabbiness. His waist was slim and his legs tapered with the fine proportions of a Praxitelean statue. His face was clear-cut and a little on the square side, with a wide slash of mouth that seemed to have an habitual curve of good humor at the corners. His nose was straight and his eyes level and bluer than the lake we had just crossed, while his hair flamed like the glow of the sunset. I noticed he wore, like Cuthbert Grant and Bostonnais Pangman, Indian leggings—pants, without a seat and only a broad loincloth dangling fore and aft to cover his intimates. Not to put too fine a point upon it—like his comrades', his arse hung out with painful immodesty.

But Duncan Cameron seemed not to notice anything out of the way about that, I suppose because it was quite customary in that savage land and no one expected anything else.

"An' this, Gentlemen," said Cameron, "is Andy Ross—Andrew, th' gentlemen for th' Forks. Mister Ross will be actin' as bourgeois at Fort Alexandria, near th' head o' th' Assiniboine, Messieurs."

I nodded, as I had to the rest, and I noticed that Alec MacLean did the same. But, as I have mentioned, neither he nor I realized that Jean had come up to stand near us. But Andrew Ross was aware of it, no question of that. He goggled past us, over our shoulders at her and weaved a little unsteadily on his feet, for he still seemed half full of the powerful trade rum that was served up to the voyageurs at Fort au Bas de la Rivière. Rather tipsily he bowed.

"Yer servant, Madam!" he hiccupped, and then he blinked owlishly around at the rest of us.

"Je suis un homme du nord!" he boasted, and then flushed as red as any bashful boy and turned as silent.

I think I must have blushed myself for his costume, and that of his companions, to say nothing of his half-recovered state of celebration. But I was startled by Jean's presence. As for Jean, I don't believe she even noticed how he was dressed. I watched her with a bucketing heart, for she looked at him gravely, and her eyes were fastened on his face in a gaze of sudden awaking.

"Mister Ross," she breathed. "I—it is a pleasure, truly."

5. ASSINIBOIA

THE SOUND OF HER VOICE, I THINK, AROUSED US. I SAW ALEC MACLEAN half turn toward her in a gesture of embarrassment and then check himself. I myself stiffened. I saw the ghost of a smile flit across Cuthbert Grant's swart, handsome features, and his bold eyes raked appraisingly over her. Then Duncan Cameron had swung back toward us and was speaking again, rapidly, as if to gloss over an awkward instant.

He bowed toward Jean.

"Forgive me, Ma'am!" he said. "I did not see ye come up."

Alec MacLean suddenly remembered himself.

"Gentlemen, my daughter Jean," he said shortly.

Duncan Cameron smiled cryptically as if to himself.

"Gentlemen, and Ma'am," he said, and glanced at Jean who was not looking at him; who, indeed, seemed unaware of his very existence. The only person there, so far as she was concerned, seemed to be the red-haired giant. " 'Tis a pleasure t' meet ye, but th' night's fast closin' in on us. If ye'll forgive me I'll see camp made and dinner set t' cook, an' after that would ye now—I wonder, could I persuade ye t' sit down with us an' take a bit pot luck?"

I do not know why I felt so, but I will confess it was a great relief to me to see Alec MacLean shake his head with grave dignity.

"Our thanks t' ye, Mister Cameron," he replied, "but we've our ain kettles on an' th' parritch maun no be wasted."

Duncan Cameron bowed suavely, never hinting by so much as the flick of an eyelash that he guessed at the real reason for Alec's refusal.

"As ye will," he said, and I gathered that he was almost equally glad for the excuse not to be too cordial. After all, it must have been something of a shock to him to find himself suddenly come up with such a large contingent of reinforcements for the enemy! "I understand. Some other time, eh?"

He turned about and with a change of tone that was as startling as it was abrupt, bellowed in the very faces of the men he had just presented to us.

"*Eh, bien! Au travail, salops!* Enough o' gowkin'! Get t' yer duties."

As they scattered he turned back again to us and bowed ostentatiously to Jean.

"*Au 'voir, Ma'm'selle,*" he said, and I was not myself sufficiently acquainted with French to realize the familiarity he was taking.

We watched them go, scattering and strutting, down through the dusk along the gray beach toward where their canoemen had brought their long craft ashore and begun the work of making camp. From that angle the open seats of their breeches were even more painfully apparent, but they seemed quite unconcerned and unconscious of them. Alexander MacLean gave his daughter a scandalized glance.

"Turn awa', child!" he commanded her gruffly, and at the sound of his voice she seemed to come to herself with a start. She flung a quick, embarrassed look first at him and then at me, and then without a word she turned away herself toward our own fires. All at once, for no reason at all that I could give then, I felt indignant and irritated, furious at the North West Company and everyone connected with it, especially Andrew Ross.

In the circumstances, perhaps, it is as well that they did not molest us again that night, probably because Duncan Cameron ordered it so. At least, in retrospect, that seems the most logical reason for their leaving us alone. Although I was not aware of it at the time, I was presently to realize the fact that this opencountenanced, blond hulk, who seemed so affable and hearty and who styled himself a Captain in the Voyageur Corps—a regiment which I presently learned had been some time since disbanded—was in reality a most devious fellow, and such an order would be quite in keeping with his character and later actions.

At the time, however, when I had opportunity to give it more than a passing thought, I attributed it to a long day at the paddles. The poor devils, I thought, were probably thoroughly fagged, for the Northwesters were noted for the tremendous length of their day's marches. At that moment I would not have been surprised to learn that they had even come all the way from Rat Portage, where the Lac des Bois falls into the Winnipeg—a distance I now realize would have been quite impossible, but which in my then ignorance of the country I believed might be done. Actually, I learned later, they had come no farther than from Bas de la Rivière, no more than five or six leagues distant, where the Northwesters were accustomed to pause and provision their brigades for the journey ahead. Since it was the last chance for a rousing carouse, apparently, the men had taken full advantage of it, and this fact alone accounted for their late start. Had it been otherwise, had they embarked as early as they ordinarily did when on the march, they would undoubtedly have passed on before us, and our meeting would have been postponed for a few days—not, I daresay, that this would have mattered much since it was inevitable that we should fall in with them sooner or later. But at least we might have been spared an awkward convoy, for from then on until we came to the Forks they matched their pace to ours and marched with us.

The night, as I say, passed without further interruption. We ate our supper and tumbled wearily into our blankets, for if the Northwestmen had not come so far that day, we had. It seemed to me that there was a good deal of shouting and horseplay from the camp down the beach, although this may have been because of my own stiff disapproval, which left me prepared to find fault with anything they did. Then the next thing I knew the shouts of the Northwest voyageurs became the stentorian bellows of our own canoe foremen, thundering out the reveille, *"Au canot! Au canot! On y mouche la bas!"*

As I rolled out of my blankets and crept from under the overturned canoe that served us as a tent by night, and rubbed the sleep from my eyes in the blackness of the pre-dawn dark, it seemed to me that our canoemen were overdoing this more than a little. So far there was not even a faint streak of silver showing in the east to separate the serried tops of the spruces from the blackness of the sky. Never before had they called us out before it was at least light enough to see one's hand before one's face. But this time, in the ragged gloom, it seemed to me that I could understand. Far down the beach the Northwesters' campfires were already alight, and the same cry of awaking was also going up. Clearly our own lads were not to be left behind.

That dawning was devoted to eating a swift breakfast and packing the canoes; to making an early start. There was no visiting; nothing but intense rivalry, as if a race had been declared and each group was determined to win it.

Our camp had been made on the lee shore of Isle à la Biche—which is to say Red Deer Island—just off the tip of Traverse Point, on the southwest side of the bay. Between it and the mainland is a narrow strait with a sandy bottom and so shallow that we were obliged to stand out of the canoes in the water to lighten the load and track them through by hand. This was a somewhat ticklish task as any strain placed upon them, especially if the water was at all rough, might result in slamming the bottom of the craft against one of the hard-packed ridges of sand and bursting open its seams. As it was, even though the weather was quite calm and the day fine, we scraped two of the canoes so that we must needs pause and gum them when we came to the other side—much to the outspoken derision of the Northwesters, which it may be assumed did the tempers of our own lads no good. Why the Northwest brigade did not go on—for they could easily have out-distanced us—I do not know, but they appeared to be in no hurry, and while we dawdled on the beach they lay around, heckling our fellows and in general making nuisances of themselves. When we finally did get underway once more, coasting southward under sail along a rocky lee shore, the wind being fairly strong at the north-northwest, they kept pace with us, at first shouting frequent taunts and offering to race. But when they found that we were not disposed to notice them they gave over and fell silent.

By midday the wind had increased so much and the seas along the rocky shore were so large that we were obliged to stay out in the lake and satisfy our hunger with a handful of pemmican for each. By sunset, however, we reached the Point of the Grand Marais and, rounding under its shelter, were able to bring our canoes ashore on the broad beach that separates the Big Swamp from the lake. That evening there was no tendency to visit. Even the Northwesters were wearied from their battle with the wind, and all hands in both camps were early in bed. In the morning, though the wind had fallen, the surf along the beach and the swells that ran in the shallow lake beyond were such that our guides did not think it wise to push on since it would involve a traverse across the lower end of the lake to the mouth of the Red River, which would expose us to the full sweep of the wind should it rise again. Apparently the Northwestmen felt the same, for they too remained in camp and the day was devoted to lazing in the sun and drying our loads, repairing our canoes and hunting in the broad reaches of the swamp behind the beach, where we killed quantities of ducks and other wild waterfowl, so that we had enough to give us all a grand, succulent feast that night.

I must say, however, that I was a little apprehensive of that brief pause, for knowing the temper of our fellows and seeing the swagger of the Northwesters, it seemed to me that a day of idleness in such close proximity might easily result in an unwanted clash. I mentioned the thought to Alec MacLean and Charles Belly, who agreed with me that for the sake of our womenfolk and children no such thing

could be allowed to happen. Accordingly the strict order was spread—
no visiting in the Northwesters' camp. Apparently their own leaders
had something of the same idea, for I noticed that throughout the
day they gave us a wide berth.

We had visitors after supper, however, when the meal was done
and the beach was a blue haze from the smoke of the inevitable pipes
of the voyageurs and the big fires burned bright against the blue-
black backdrop of the broad lake. In the mild, summer comfort of the
evening a number of us had gathered about our central fire, a sort of a
drawing together of folk who now were long old friends for the simple
purpose of breaking the monotony. As I recall there were Alec Mac-
Lean and Jean, of course, and Charles Belly and his dark, rather
handsome interpreter, Michel Cadotte. In addition we had been joined
by the fire by the Bannermans: quiet, sober George of Kildonan, and
his two rollicking, good-humored cousins, Hugh and Alex from
Dackalury. Their two sonsie sisters, Elizabeth and Mary, were there,
and so too, I think, were most of the younger Sutherlands—a half
a dozen of them altogether, all good young folk and gay and
cheerful and willing. To top the list was Rab Gunn and his pipes to give
us a reel or two. A few of our voyageurs stood and lolled around
at the edge of the circle of light cast by the fire, listening to the wild
wailing of the music, and no one saw the Northwesters approach
until just when Robin was fairly warmed up and had finished us a
fine strathspey, full of grand slow dignity, and the voice spoke out
of the darkness behind him.

"Ah, now! 'Tis 'Moonlight on th' Green.' Man, 'tis many a year since
I've heard it so well piped!"

Our heads turned, startled for an instant out of our voices, and
saw the hulking blond figure of Duncan Cameron looming up out
of the darkness. He still wore his scarlet coat and his almost too ingra-
tiating smirk of gallantry. Behind him I could see other shadowy
figures, who as they came forward assumed the shapes of Alexander
MacDonnell, who seemed to hang as close at Cameron's elbow as
his shadow at his heels, Andrew Ross and Cuthbert Grant, the latter
looking a little cynically amused while Ross appeared incredulous.
Both of them, I noticed with considerable relief, for the moment at
least, had discarded their Indian breeches for something more suitable.

"Surely it was not music?" said Cuthbert Grant dryly. "For a moment, there, I thought it was a windigo in distress!"

I was startled at the clear, carefully trained way in which he spoke,
and I realized all at once that it was the first time I had heard his

voice. But that was not the end of my surprise, for Andrew Ross turned almost savagely upon the darker, slighter man.

"*Ta gueule,* Grant!" he growled. "I daresay yer father'd ha' recognized it, if th' rest o' ye did not!"

It was only then that I realized that here, in Cuthbert Grant, must be one of those very *Boisbrûlés* that William Cook had warned me about, and I remember that I was surprised because despite the grizzled factor's warning I had not anticipated anything as suave and evidently well educated as this. I don't know what devil prompted me, but I picked up the cudgels in his defense. Something told me that Ross himself had never been out of Canada.

"And are you so familiar with the piper's music yourself, Mister Ross?" I demanded.

There was a moment's surprised silence during which Cuthbert Grant looked first startled and then craftily cynical at my abrupt interference. Cautiously his puzzled eyes turned from me to Ross and back again, and then swung a little aside to study Jean MacLean where she sat with her feet tucked up beneath her by the fire. Duncan Cameron smiled a little, almost happily. But Andrew Ross turned a cold, ice-blue stare upon me.

"I havena had th' pleasure o' much o' it, I admit," he said flatly, "since my people were already in th' land when I was born. But what I ha' heard I ha' liked."

He looked toward Jean.

"May I sit down by ye, Ma'am?" he asked without the least further notice of me, and Jean, of course, being asked so directly could hardly do other than flush and move over slightly to make room for him.

"Please do," she murmured, though I am not aware that they spoke another word to one another throughout the evening.

My own nose, I daresay, was somewhat out of joint. For all the exchange was inconclusive I could not help but feel that I had come off second best, and I too fell silent. The others of Andrew Ross's companions, without by your leave, moved up and sat down among us, and Duncan Cameron at once called jovially for a rollicking pibroch, which Rab Gunn gave after a little urging, and after that he warmed up and there were more songs and reels and flings, and once even some of the Sutherlands and Bannermans paired off for a round of dances, but the soft sand made that too difficult, and presently Rab Gunn ran out of wind and had to give over his piping for a blow, and while we sat silent then Duncan Cameron began telling us stories of the country to which we were going.

Come to think of it, now that I look back upon it, they were not very pleasant stories, most of them, though the talk started innocuously enough.

"Aye," he said in response to an inquiry put to him by one of the Sutherland girls, " 'tis a wide country, far flung, like th' sea in a good many ways, full o' strange creatures with strange ways. There's bitter cold an' brutal starvation, aye, an' brutal folk for neighbors, too, as I daresay ye'll find out for yerselves soon enough. O' course, they're not so bad as they once were—th' Indians, I mean. Th' time was, not so long ago, when they were as thick as fleas on a dog. But a few years since they were carried off in great numbers by the lung fever, which is very prevalent thereabout, and which attacks whites as well as th' savages."

That was a shot sent home in the dark, although he did not know it, for both the Bannermans and the Sutherlands had lost several of their old folk at Colony Creek by that miserable disease.

"As for those Indians that remain," he went on, "ye'll have but little trouble wi' th' Saulteurs or Ojibways that will be t' th' east o' ye. They're a murderin', cutthroat crew, fond o' debauch an' rape, but harmless enough unless they're drunk, an' then ye must be on yer guard against 'em. Th' Assiniboines—th' Stone Indians, some call 'em —that live on th' other side, are more warlike an' more dangerous. I heard there was some talk o' a risin' amongst 'em earlier in th' summer, just before I went down t' Fort William, but whether or not they've taken th' warpath I've yet t' learn. O' course, if they have, then ye must be on yer guard, for they're a vicious cruel lot that will stake a man out an' drive th' buffalo over him as soon as look at him. For th' women," he glanced significantly across the fire at the wide-eyed Bannerman girls, " 'tis worse for them!"

I cannot give the whole of his discourse, for in his own words it was too long. But he cited cases of murder and rape and starvation and death by disease that, so he told us at least, had fallen beneath his own observation. He spoke of the fires that raged across the plains each spring and autumn and did untold damage, destroying the pasture for the elk and buffalo and exposing all who may be in the region to starvation in the coming season for that reason.

As we listened the flames of the fire grew low and died, and finally Mister Cameron, having amused himself sufficiently, rose and stretched and yawned.

"Well, lads!" he said, "we must t' our blankets if we're t' make an early start in th' mornin'. Ye know how severe th' passage can be!"

He paused and looked around at the rest of us.

"I must give ye good night for us all, for a most pleasant an' un-usual evenin' on th' march," he told us. "I only hope, ladies an' gentle-men, that ye meet with no trouble either on th' way or at th' Forks!"

I glanced up at him, suddenly finding my tongue again.

"Thank you, Mister Cameron," I said. "We anticipate no trouble, unless it be not of our making."

He bowed, but his smile showed clearly that he understood me. Then with a nod to his companions to follow him he turned and went off into the night.

After that I was not sure. I thought perhaps the hint that I more than suspected him and his friends, might prod them to some action, and in my then reckless mood I did not seem to care. If trouble were coming, so I felt, then let it be now as well as later.

But curiously nothing at all of the sort happened. In the morning we were up with the first faint dawn and found it a perfect day for making the traverse, about six leagues, across to the middle mouth of the Red River, by which we were to enter the stream. Here we found an excellent camping site amid low willows and high grass, with hard-packed sand to offer at least a clean if somewhat hard bedding ground, and an abundance of ducks and wildfowl once more. The next day we were away early again and found the way winding up the broad, gently flowing river between low banks, thick with reeds and bogs, past the mouth of Rivière aux Morts, until in about six leagues we came to the Sault à la Biche, or Elk Rapids, the first and only rapids that we encountered in this stream. There we camped for the night.

In all this way, and even to the end of that journey, I must admit, neither Duncan Cameron nor any of his companions, ever so much as hinted at hostility. They were affable. They were as courteous as anyone could expect in this backwoods corner of the world. And though they kept pace with us throughout, they yet kept their distance. Indeed, their behavior, from beginning to end, rather eased my own mind and that of most of my companions and left us with the feeling that these Northwesters were not such a bad lot as they had been painted after all which, I suppose, was exactly the effect that the crafty Duncan Cameron sought to achieve.

At the dawning of our third day out from the Grand Marais we embarked again for the last time. The rapids, we found, were little more than swift, sleek currents, sliding down over a series of stratified rocks, over which the task of tracking our canoes was comparatively simple. Above them we came again into deep, slow moving water where we passed between low, marshy banks on the east, and somewhat higher banks, clothed in willows on the west. Behind the trees, through occasional openings, we could see lovely, lush, verdant plains, stretching away in undulating waves like those of the sea, as far as the eye could reach.

Shortly after noon the character of the country changed slightly. The banks on the east grew higher and rose toward wooded hills behind, while on the other hand we passed an opening in the bank that revealed a grassy meadow surrounding a low, marshy tarn, known as the Frog Pond. Here we saw our first human habitations: a group of tall, conical Indian tepees, the camp of a band of Assiniboines, we learned, who had come down to trade for the summer. Beyond this the bank rose again and we rounded two or three brush covered points with tall, thin trees growing behind, and then all at once came upon the first of the row of hewn log and sod houses of Seven Oaks and Colony Gardens which marked the beginning of the Red River Settlement.

The sudden apparition came as a surprise to us, for we were under the impression that we had yet some distance to go before we came to the settlement. At the same time the appearance of such a vast fleet of canoes upon the river must have startled the few colonists who chanced to be working on that side of the houses equally. As we rounded the bend there was a woman leaning over a huge washtub at the rear of one of the cabins. Two clearings beyond a man and a boy were chopping firewood. Down among the willows, on the river bank, two young boys with crooked poles were fishing. While yet another hundred yards or so farther along two men were replacing the sod roof of one of the cabins with one of hand-split shakes.

None of them noticed us as we first swept around the bend. Then all at once the small boys fishing caught sight of us. Who they thought we were, or what we were about, God only knows. But in a panicked haste they dropped their poles and went scrambling and screaming up the bank. Above them first the woman at the tub, then the man and boy with the axes, and last the two men on the cabin roof, heard them and paused in their work, turning to look and learn the cause of the commotion. At sight of us they stood, as if spellbound, for an instant. Then the woman and the man with the ax turned and scurried around the cabins and disappeared from view. The two men on the roof also shinned down to the ground and disappeared, and for a moment only the one boy woodchopper remained, gaping at us. Then, one by one, people began to appear from around the houses and crowd along the bank: men, women and children—many of them carrying muskets, I noticed, and all of them strangely silent.

We were nearly halfway up the straight stretch where we had first come upon them by that time, moving upward swiftly, yet not a sound did they make. They simply stood and stared, unsure, I realize now, what such a huge collection of canoes could mean. Tentatively I raised my hand and waved to them, and in the canoes that followed others did the same. For an instant there was no response, then one by one, slowly at first, a hand here and there went up and acknowledged the salute. Then faster and faster their arms rose and they began to jump and cheer and slap one another on the back. Here and there I saw a woman turn to the man beside her and bury her face in his shoulder, and all at once a half dozen men and boys broke away and went racing up along the bank, carrying the word of our coming, I imagined.

Then, the river took a sudden sweep to eastward, looping through the wooded country and for the moment leaving the little clustered row of cabins behind us. For almost a mile it seemed to bear directly away from the settlement. Then in a great oxbow it doubled back upon itself and drove a like distance almost due west. Once again the banks upon our right opened up and showed evidences of clearing and of new buildings going up. Then abruptly once more the river swung to the northward and flowed again in a straight sweep.

A mile away, it must have been, we could see the wide-mouthed opening where the river Assiniboine fell down into the Red, and upon the point of land above it were the cluster of stockaded buildings and red beaver ensign of the North West Company's Fort Gibraltar. Nearer at hand, however, and of much greater interest to us at the moment, was a building far more pretentious than any we had seen in the settlement below, nestled at the bend on the banks. There were a number of outbuildings scattered around it, and at one end it bore evidence of the beginning of a rough stockade. Over all, upon a flagpole raised above the main house, floated the flag of the Hudson's Bay Company, and at the head of a path that led down to the wide landing below a little group of men was just starting down to welcome us. This was Fort Douglas and the Forks at last.

PART III
Tread of Pioneers

✥✥

I hear the tread of pioneers,
  Of nations yet to be;
The first low wash of waves where soon
  Shall roll a human sea.
          —JOHN GREENLEAF WHITTIER
                    "The Seer"

1. THE FORKS

W̲E̲ ̲S̲L̲I̲P̲P̲E̲D̲ ̲I̲N̲ ̲B̲E̲S̲I̲D̲E̲ ̲T̲H̲E̲ ̲C̲R̲U̲D̲E̲ ̲L̲A̲N̲D̲I̲N̲G̲ ̲P̲L̲A̲T̲F̲O̲R̲M̲ ̲O̲F̲ ̲R̲O̲U̲G̲H̲-hewn logs, and since mine was the lead canoe it happened that I was the first to step ashore. From force of habit I turned about at once and knelt to hold the craft steady for the others. As I did so the first of the Northwesters' canoes went past and slid on up the turgid river. Amidships the red coated hulk and glowing flowing mane showed clearly, despite the distance between us, where Duncan Cameron lolled in magnificent idleness and left the menial work of paddling to his voyageurs.

He was watching us with evident curiosity, and as I glanced up in his direction he raised his hand in a languid wave of farewell. Quite without any thought whatever I returned it, but even as I did so a harsh voice behind me dashed itself like a bucket of icy water against the back of my neck.

"I see ye're none too choice o' th' company ye keep, whoe'er ye are!" it said.

I forgot the canoe and rose, turning, to find myself face to face with a thickset man, square-hewn as one of the logs of the landing on which we stood, and giving a feeling of immense strength and power, though he could not have been within a head as tall as myself. His hair was grizzled-sandy, his face broad and square and at present brick-red with fury. His jaw jutted and his thin-lipped mouth was compressed in an angry, twisted line.

Clearly he was the man I had noticed at the top of the path, starting down to meet us. Behind him were a number of other men of various sizes and shapes and assorted complexions; I saw that none of them were smiling either. I had a fair notion who he might be, but I had no mind to let him or them browbeat me.

"My name is Malcolm MacAllister," I said curtly, "and I've been sent out by Lord Selkirk to act as his personal representative and to teach school at this place. As for waving a salute of farewell to a man that's kept pace with us for five days, since we left Traverse Bay, it seems no more to me than mere, decent courtesy! Who are you, sir?"

One bushy eyebrow shot up toward the hairy forest above, and while he looked surprised his scowl deepened. He seemed to ignore my question entirely.

"Ho, MacAllister? Aye!" he cried. "We've had despatches about ye an' yer people. But we looked for ye a twelvemonth since. What kept ye?"

"Fever," I said briefly. "Fever and a rascally captain who set us ashore at Churchill just to be rid of us. We spent the winter there and came on over the snow to York in the spring."

He merely glanced at me without commenting on that and then looked away toward the river where the Northwest canoes were breaking away from our own and passing on upstream by ones and twos now.

"He kept pace wi' ye, did he? From Isle à la Biche?" His stare was speculative. "Who did ye say it was had charge o' 'em?"

"I didn't say," I retorted, "but if you're interested his name is Cameron, Duncan Cameron."

"Duncan Cameron?" he exclaimed, and his face looked even grimmer.

"Aye, you know him?" I replied.

"I know no good o' him," the dour man answered, then added as if by way of afterthought: "I'm Miles MacDonnell, governor here."

"I thought so." I took pains to be just as dryly unimpressed with him as he obviously was with me. I had seen his kind before. In fact, in school they are one of the commoner kind. "By the way, you've a cousin with the Northwesters yonder, did you know? Alexander Mac-Donnell is bound up to Fort Qu'Appelle."

He turned livid at the information, uttered a blistering curse and spat sourly into the river alongside.

" 'Fore God, yon bodes naught but evil for us!" he retorted. "I declare t' ye Mister MacAllister, 'tis poor tidin's an' worse luck ye bring t' us, I fear!"

I gathered that there was little love lost in the MacDonnell clan.

A number of the other canoes had swung into the landing by now and had discharged their passengers before passing on to the strip of gravelly shingle to beach and unload. Alexander MacLean, Jean, Charles Belly, John and Catherine MacPherson and Donald Sutherland

and Robin Gunn, of the pipes, had already clambered out upon the
landing stage and more were coming every moment.

I ignored his none too complimentary appraisal and tried to present
those who had stepped ashore.

"Aye! Aye!" He nodded and shook two or three by the hand almost
reluctantly; then turned toward the men who had followed him down.
"Here's John MacLeod, Factor for th' Bay Company here, an' James
MacIntosh an' Archibald Currie, clerks—they're th' Company folk wi'
us. Yon's John MacKay, boatbuilder, an' Magnus Isbister, farmer—
both o' th' council—an' Pat Corcoran, one o' our carpenters."

They stepped forward, as they were presented to us and gave us an
abashed sort of a bob of the head. I had not time to note the outstand-
ing characteristics of each, but so far as I could see none of them was
over thirty. MacLeod was fairly tall and well formed, with brown hair
and level gray eyes and a look of keen intelligence about him. Both
MacIntosh and Currie were short and chunky; Currie with sandy hair
and a ruddy, good-natured face, and MacIntosh dark-eyed and dark-
haired and dark-visaged, though both wore the easy cloak of com-
petence. MacKay was short and thin and wiry, almost colorless. Isbister
was a black Orkneyman. And Corcoran, there was no mistaking him,
had Ireland stamped upon his face and the smell of the bogs still upon
him.

But, there was little time now for more than this quick, superficial
glance. We came to know all of them better—and, so far as I was
concerned, very much better—before we were done. But just then
the landing was becoming almost precariously crowded. Governor
MacDonnell took note of the fact, and his remark upon it, I felt, was
sensible.

"Here, now!" he said. "We canna all be meetin' here. We'll be
tumblin' all o' us into th' river if we try. Come, lads, we'll step aloft
an' all meet more formally on th' green above. Mister MacAllister,
will ye take some o' yer lads an' direct yer folk, as they come on shore
t' follow up yon path? When they come t' th' top o' th' bank they'll
no can miss th' gatherin' o' us before th' house. Mister MacLean,
Ma'am, ladies, will ye do me th' honor t' walk up with me? Th' others
can follow."

And so they withdrew and for the next half hour or more, I cannot
remember exactly the time it took, I found myself busied with helping
our people ashore, men, women and children, and sending them on
as rapidly as possible toward the little group of buildings on the
bluff, trusting to our voyageurs to draw the canoes up on the narrow

shore and unload our baggage and supplies and carry them up to us.

When the last canoe had set its human freight upon the hewn planks I showed them the way the others had gone and walked up with them along the wide path that angled sharply from the landing to the top of the flat bluff, through a tangle of willow and alder growth, spotted here and there with taller, thick-boled elms and aspens. There were a dozen or more of them, and at this point I do not remember who all of them were. But one was young Angus Sutherland, of Auchraich Parish, bright and eager; another was Christie Mathieson, gay and pretty and obviously much stricken with Angus. And there was old Elizabeth Sutherland, of course, who was Angus's mother and who was stout and sturdy and untiring, both in body and in mind, a tower of strength to all of us despite her sixty years. Beside these there was sour, dour, young George Campbell and his pretty but petulant wife Helen, both of whom had done nothing but growl and complain since we were beached at Fort Churchill; I think I was not alone in having marked them down as malcontents and troublemakers long since.

"Is it far?" asked young Sutherland eagerly. "We don't want to miss anythin'!"

"No, we mustn't miss anything!" Christie echoed him.

"I couldn't say," I smiled at them, "but I doubt it's a great way."

"Na, na, 'tis na far, I'll warrant," Elizabeth Sutherland put in stoutly, "an' we'll be yon a lang time—a lang time, I hope!"

But the young folk were in no mood to wait for the rest of us. They raced ahead, up the steep path.

"You'd think they'd put steps here!" Helen Campbell complained.

"Was it a marble staircase ye were accustomed to, then, back in Archwigle Parish?" Elizabeth Sutherland asked flatly. "If so be, 'tis pity ye e'er cam' away!"

"I'm wonderin' if that's no th' truth!" put in George Campbell darkly, slapping futilely at the clouds of mosquitoes that I must confess came joyfully to meet us. There was no spark of humor in the man. "Did e'er ye see such outsize bloodsuckers? Did ye no know about them either, Mister MacAllister, when ye were tellin' us yer pretty tales?"

I was already hot, and now I turned red and angry and spoke out without thinking, for I never liked the man.

"I'll remind you, Mister Campbell," I said, "that 'twas not any tales of mine that lured you into this business. You came of your own free and eager will, by special arrangement between yourself and Lord Selkirk."

"Aye! An' mark me," he retorted, "his lordship will hear how his own special representative has behaved toward us all!"

"If you've aught of complaint—" I began.

But Elizabeth Sutherland laid a restraining hand upon my arm and cut in.

"Och!" she cried. "An' when ye're tellin' his lordship about it, Geordie lad, ye maun be sure t' tell him how th' wicked Mister Mac-Allister had th' special winged beasties fetched in alone for yer ain torment. Ye maun be sure an' say that, Geordie, sae that Lord Selkirk'll know exactly what yer plaint is worth!"

I gave her a thankful glance and she drooped one eyelid at me with a small grin. It was hardly subtle, but at least we heard no more from the Campbells during that brief climb.

When we came to the top we found ourselves, all at once, come into an entirely different land. There was the fringe of trees, to be sure, along the top of the bank. The fringe widened a bit downstream and filled the little dell, and then wound off along a tiny stream, west and a little south, until it thinned and grew sparse and finally disappeared altogether in the waving grasses of the prairie. There were other fingers of trees that grew out in feathery clumps and nubbles from the crest of the bank; in the main the land that lay before us was a rolling, undulating sea of grass that stretched away for mile upon endless mile, until far in the distance it met another hazy, almost smoke blue rim of trees, like those behind us, marching away into the empty prairies, and marking, I supposed, the course of the Assiniboine.

But this was only a part of the difference. As we stepped over the crest a fresh breeze, that came warm but steadily out of the west, caressed our sweaty faces and drove the swarming clouds of mosquitoes down again to the humid shelter of the bank. To left and right, as we passed between them the central buildings of the post—the little fort with its two small swivel guns and the factor's store, the smithy and the governor's house, a single story though it was—took on a more substantial air and seemed larger than when seen from below. I noticed now that there was even a small watchtower on the tiny fort. The green that lay before us, crowded now with our own folk as well as with those who were already settled here, was broad, spacious, level, well fenced, and *green*. Down along the river bank the cabins and squared log houses, whose backs had seemed so nondescript and woebegone from the river, presented neat, well-tended fronts upon a broad-beaten lane that could hardly be called a road, but which was certainly more than a mere track; while across the way each settler's acres of corn,

wheat, oats, and potatoes and other vegetables stretched out in carefully plotted, almost geometric lines. It was all neat and sturdy and
clearly well cared for, even if, quite obviously, only hard, back-break-
ing labor had made it so.

From the green even the bastions and buildings of Fort Gibraltar,
plainly visible at a distance over the plains, seemed small and harmless and hardly significant rather than looming large and forbidding
as they had from the river below.

I do not know whether Miles MacDonnell had prepared a speech
of welcome for us, and taken advantage of our delay in landing and
gathering on the green to rush in and get it, or not. Nor, as a matter
of fact, do I much care. It may well have been a rehearsed address. As
I recall it was full of sonorous phrases:

"—happy indeed to welcome you to our little colony—and delighted
to receive new blood and both those tender and warlike reinforcements
which we have so long needed and looked forward to. . . . You are
a sight to gladden our eyes; a breath of the moist, cool winds of
home. . . ."

And so on and so forth. I admit that in my curiosity, in the study of
my new neighbors and in the study of these surroundings to which we
had come from such a distance, I scarcely heard him. Presently, however, he entered upon general directions: where we should camp and
what we should do until such time as we were able to select our lots
and build upon them. At that point I forgot all else and paid close
attention.

"Th' newcomers amongst us, as well as th' Bay people an' th'
voyageurs, will pitch their tents northward o' th' fort an' southward
o' th' first lot, on th' tongue o' th' river. Ye'll find sawpits at th' end,
an' stacked lumber close by. But th' ground's cleared and is level and
it's suitable till we can choose yer lots and move ye to 'em. Ye'll find
water handy, an' ye're welcome t' make use o' th' facilities o' th' fort
until ye're settled, which ye'll find adequate if no' luxurious. As for
th' lots o' yer choice, I must tell ye that all o' them nearest t' th' fort,
in Colony Gardens an' Seven Oaks, are bespoke by them that came
before ye. However, ye'll find plenty as good, an' perhaps some better,
awaitin' yer pick in th' districts farther t' th' north, but touchin' on th'
rest, in what Lord Selkirk has already named Kildonan an' Frog Plain.
That's all. Good luck t' ye, an' again—welcome in th' name o' us all!"

That was as much as he had to say, and I think for most of us it
was enough. Already our canoemen had begun to carry up our gear,
and we were anxious to be off and raising our camp for the night, for

the sun was far down and it would soon be dark. We scattered and sought out our sites, laying our camp in surprisingly straight lines considering all the confusion, and when night fell we were all safe, tucked away under some sort of shelter and snug in our blankets: the bachelors encamped together at one end of the line; the unmarried women without families to bed at the farther side; and all of the married groups and children in between. I remember I fell asleep with the sound of the peeper frogs in my ears and the soft wind of the moonlit prairies blowing across me.

That wind, I must say, turned bitter cold by morning. But the day's sun warmed it as soon as it rose. I recall that from force of habit I got up with the dawn, and curiosity drew me out to look at the sawpits and stacks of lumber that Miles MacDonnell had mentioned. They were important later, in a way that I did not anticipate. Then I was only curious to see what building materials they had on hand and how they were produced.

The pits themselves were wide and deep enough so that a man could stand down in them and have room to drag down the heavy saws. There was a log across them with a platform, open in the center, run out to them. In some the sawing logs were still standing, as they were when we had surprised the sawyers with our arrival. These ran out along the opening and rested on the crossbeam log. Then a man standing on the platform above dragged the heavy cutting saw up, while another— assuredly on the dirty end of the task—drew the whip down, bowing his head so that the falling dust did not drop in his eyes. When the crossbar was reached the foreman above called a halt and moved the log forward, and by this means boards and squared logs and even planking were ripped out of the raw lumber that crews of the settlers brought from across the river. The stacks, were simply piles of these green-sawed boards laid crisscross in great rows, ready for whatever use might be made of them. In one corner I found a place where colonists, grown expert with experience, had rived out shakes from larger logs floated down the river from someplace, then unknown, far above. Clearly we had a good supply; a better supply of sawed lumber than I had anticipated. Yet we would need more before all of us were housed.

The breakfast gong, sounded at the cook tent nearest the governor's house, roused me from my survey, and it is from that moment that I count the beginning of a week of almost feverish activity. I was hungry. Of a sudden I realized it, for I had eaten but little during the day before. Yet when I reached the tent I found a score of our

companions of the voyage already before me, ready I guessed to take
advantage of the principle of "first come, first served."

My heart sank a little at that, for the MacLeans, father and daughter,
were next behind me, and I could see that the most avid of our settlers,
including somehow George Campbell and his wife, were ahead of us.
I was thinking of the choice of lots, of course, when I turned to Jean
and greeted her.

"Good morning," I said. "I see, like myself, you slept too long and
too well!"

She cast an almost unseeing glance at the river, and then looked
back at me.

"Did you see Mister Ross before he went on?" she asked.

I gaped at her.

"Ross?" I replied. "No, why?"

She did not answer that directly.

"I suppose they've already gone to the upper forts," she said.

"Oh, I don't know," I retorted absently. "I suppose so. What difference does it make?"

She glanced off across the prairie, and she might have flushed, but
under her sunburn and in my indifference I did not see it.

"None, I suppose," she replied.

What reply I would have made to that I do not know, but at that
moment I came up to the cauldrons and extended my mess kit for the
parritch and salt and boiled pemmican that were issued to us.

My own thoughts were full of the lots that we might find ourselves
left to draw, and I use that as an excuse for not answering. But somehow I found myself uneasy because of it.

Yet there was a surprise in store for us. Despite the early hour
Miles MacDonnell was already out before us and had a low table set
up before his own residence. There were maps and plans spread out
upon it, but though we lined up as quickly as we finished our meal
he would hear none until the last of us was finished. Then to my surprise he called out:

"Mister Alexander MacLean an' Mister Malcolm MacAllister, are
they here?"

The dour man and I glanced at one another astonishedly.

"We're here," I said.

"Will ye step forward then?" he asked.

We did so and he pointed with a pencil at his plan.

"Ye see here," he said, "numbers three and number four ha' been
set aside by his lordship: Number four t' be th' kirk an' th' manse,

for ye, Mister MacLean; number three for yerself, Mister MacAllister, for a schoolhouse an' th' residence o' th' schoolmaster."

I gaped, for the lots to which he pointed were in Colony Gardens, close to the fort itself.

"Are you sure?" I could not help blurting.

He did not even smile.

"Certain!" he assured me. "They're choice lots for th' sites. As ye see they're separated by Parsonage Creek, from which ye can get yer water. Th' land beyond is no so good—that is t' say 'twill bear no strong wheat fields or grand crops. But ye can raise all that ye need on it for a livin', an' ye'll ha' water beside t' put on it."

He turned to Pat Corcoran, who stood close at his elbow.

"Ye're th' man, Pat," he said, "t' show 'em th' where o' it. Will ye help 'em t' lay out th' dwellin's, an' after that we'll set a crew to 'em. They're th' first t' be done."

"Aye, sor!" said Corcoran. "I'll be glad to."

I must say that I followed Pat Corcoran in something of a daze, and I am sure that Alec MacLean and Jean did much the same, for none of us spoke a word until we had come to the spot. It was a wooded hollow, with a number of large trees on either side of a tiny rivulet, yet above and below the banks were level and well suited to building. Across the lane the little brook wound in an S course, so that while directly across from the schoolhouse there were open meadows, there were few scattered woods opposite the place where the parsonage would be; and in the middle of where the schoolhouse fields would be there was a deep twist of trees. But below the main track both sites had been cleared, and even the foundations had been laid, for a combined school and residence on the side nearest the fort; and on the other side for a kirk on the upper, or western side of the road, and for a residence for the dominie and his family toward the river.

Pat Corcoran glanced aside at MacLean.

"An' what d'ye think o' that, yer Reverence?" he asked.

Jean answered for her father.

"Oh, 'tis perfect!" she cried excitedly. "And d'ye mean 'tis all for us?"

"For why else would I be showin' it t' ye?" the Irishman demanded.

Alec MacLean nodded, yet scarce able to speak, and glanced at me.

"D'ye like it, Malcolm?" he finally managed.

"What better?" I cried. "Why leave it to me? You know yourself you're as pleased as Punch!"

"Bejasus then, beggin' yer Reverence's pardon!" The Irishman grinned. "We'll have min at work on 'em before th' day is out. Now, shall we be plannin' 'em?"

That was the beginning of a week that was utterly without parallel in my life. On the basis of the foundations already laid there was little enough planning for us to be done, save in our own arrangement of the interior. My own place, as I have indicated, was to be a combination dwelling and schoolhouse, calling for a building some twenty by fifty feet, with a face toward the south for the best possible light, and a flat roof, called by Pat a "single gable" because it was higher toward the south and pitched at an angle of twenty degrees toward the north to allow for drainage. There were to be two doors and a large window with board shutters on the south. One door would lead into my own living quarters, a space twenty feet square at the eastern end of the building. The other would open to a spacious schoolroom, which would occupy all the rest of the building. Besides the large window on the south, there would be windows at either end of the building, and two additional windows on the north side—all without glass, of course, for we had nothing of that sort, but they would let in light and air and in bad weather could be closed and barred by heavy wooden shutters.

Within, a door would lead through the partition from my own room into the classroom, to a slightly raised dais on which would be my schoolmaster's desk. Below and directly in front of the desk would be the rows of wooden benches for the students, ending in a single, long bench that stretched from wall to wall across the western end. They had not, as yet, Pat told me confidentially, discovered a bed of slate in the neighborhood. But the word had been sent out and every trader and trapper in the Hudson's Bay Company was on the lookout for one from which a slab large enough to serve as a blackboard could be brought! Indeed, our only problem seemed to be one of heating the classroom and making a heating-cooking place for me. There were no stoves in that wilderness, of course, and so the only solution was an open fireplace. But how was it to be done without building two separate chimneys?—the most difficult part of the work apparently—and where were we to put them anyhow? We finally settled the matter by deciding that it would be simpler to build an inside chimney, leaving merely a hole in the roof for the present, and placing the fireplaces back to back: the one in the schoolroom to face out from the northeast corner, while that in my own room would occupy the northwest corner. In this way a single chimney with a double flue would do for both, and there would be no need to leave a hole in the wall for future building.

It seemed to me that I had never presided over such a princely establishment, and it is small wonder that as we crossed the tiny dividing creek, from the schoolhouse lot to that of the parsonage, I felt as if I were walking on air. But what followed made me even more lightheaded and giddy, for it meant that I would be living within sight and sound—within almost whispering distance—of Jean Mac-Lean.

I believe I have said that there were two crude foundations already laid down on the parsonage lot. That designed for the kirk itself was fifty feet square and far too large for a house, at least in that place; and, praise to my god of good fortune, it lay upon the far side of the road from the schoolhouse! As a result the manse, the parsonage itself, could only be on the same side as myself, and was of exactly the same dimensions. I think Alexander MacLean would have built the kirk first. I knew exactly how he felt, for to me the important part of my own dwelling was the schoolroom. But in this Pat Corcoran overruled him.

"Th' schoolmaster, God bless him!" he said, "may live an' teach in th' same house. But ye, yer Reverence, ye must sure now be havin' a place fer yer family—an' a mighty pretty one it is, too, ye may be sure! After we've done buildin' that, then we can be puttin' up th' House o' God with proper, lovin' care."

I could see that Alec MacLean would have argued with him about that; perhaps even sought to find out what gave him such a philosophy. So I dared to speak up.

"Mister Corcoran's right," I said. "You must be housed first, and after that—"

"Sure, an' after that," Corcoran interrupted me, "we can all be turnin' to an' helpin' ye wid th' other!"

So we prevailed, and I flatter myself that Jean gave me a shy glance of thanks for my interference. The parsonage we planned, on the same twenty by fifty scale as my own combination, was different in that it allowed for a bedroom at each end, about twenty by fifteen, and a central living area twenty feet square. In this case there would be but the one door to the outside, in the very center; directly across from it would be the one wide and tall, cooking and heating fireplace—large enough, according to our plans, to accommodate a full-length stick of cordwood.

All this, I thought, would be sufficient for the day, though it was not yet past mid-morning, and there were other houses to be considered. But to my astonishment Pat Corcoran returned to the fort with the word that all had been decided and by noon there were a score of husky workers busy upon each building, while others came and went with heavy, ox-drawn sledges of lumber from the reserve piles that I had noticed that morning. We both protested, for Alec felt as I did that this was our work. But our new friends only laughed at us.

"Ha' done!" they said. "We'll do these first, for they're laid out. When we get them raised ye can do yer own inside: th' floorin' an' th' partitionin', an' lend a hand if ye will wi' th' raisin' o' th' other houses. But now we've these."

There was no arguing with that. It was on Thursday that we laid the plans. By Saturday, with so many hands to help, the thick, squared log walls were up and the frames of the roofs were laid. On that day the rough skin and sod covering was applied, so that our homes, bare-floored and all unfinished as they were within, yet became shelter to us; we had a place to live and sleep while we finished the details ourselves.

On that day, too, an inspiration came to Alec MacLean, and with it he went straight to the governor.

" 'Tis a long time," he said, "since yer own folk an' those that came wi' me ha' heard an honest gospel sermon. Wi' yer permission, then, let us waste no more time, but gi'e me leave t' ha'e services upon th' green th' morn."

Governor MacDonnell, I believe, was a decently religious man, although, like most of us I fear, had not much missed what he had not had. He gave his permission, little dreaming that there might be any difficulty about it, and accordingly the notices were posted prominently on the board that stood outside the fort gate.

Who carried the word I do not know, but to the astonishment of us all, when the moment of assembly came upon the green grass of the common, there were visitors among us; visitors from the North West Company's forts. Duncan Cameron was one, resplendent but spotty in his brilliant red coat and conspicuous with his tossing mane of gold-blond hair. Andrew Ross was another, looking quite enormous in his buckskins, I thought, but a little abashed. The third was the handsome but shifty-seeming Cuthbert Grant.

There were some Indians, too: stolid, blanket-swathed men and buxom, greasy women from the camp at the Frog Pond, as well as several I did not recognize; they seemed quiet, dignified men and their quick, black eyes were observant and intelligent.

When he came out of the front door of the residency, stepping with a degree of pomp and pride, it seemed to me, that was hardly in keeping with the occasion, and caught sight of them, I thought Governor MacDonnell was going to have a fit upon the spot.

"Stop!" he shouted. "Nae more o' these proceedings until they that dinna belong here gang awa'!"

For once, it seemed to me, Alexander MacLean vindicated all the hope I had placed in him. He turned to the irate governor, and the clash was like iron upon iron.

"I'm sorra, Mister MacDonnell," he said harshly. "I ha' not yet a kirk, but here is th' whole wide world one kirk! Am I t' deny a man th' Word o' God because his kirk is different from yours an' mine? Excuse me, sir! I care no what ye may think, but my preachin' is open to a' who come, an' if I can make one honest Christian o' one who doubted before, yon's as much as I'll ask!"

I think Miles MacDonnell must have been flabbergasted at being so addressed. At least he made no reply, but turned about upon his heel and went straight back into the governor's house. Nor did he come out again so long as the service on the green continued. I think, perhaps, that was the beginning of a hostility between him and Alec MacLean, a hostility that lived faintly from then until the time he was gone from us. But Alec MacLean preached his sermon and held his services in the face of secular objection as he saw fit, and for that I was proud of him.

The sermon ended and the service was over and I could see no hitch in it. At the end Duncan Cameron bowed low over Jean MacLean's hand and paused with a brief comment for Alec. Then he mounted his horse and rode home. The other Northwesters most decorously followed his example, and I daresay I was a bit piqued that none of them so much as nodded to me.

But that was on Sunday. By Monday I had forgotten it. Both Alec MacLean and myself were busied then with the interiors of our new homes, laying down the puncheon floors, raising partitions, hanging cabinets and building furniture and necessaries: woodsheds and cold rooms behind the houses, and indispensable outbuildings down toward the river bank, while the building crews went on to the lower lots and started work on the homes of the other settlers. Tuesday was the same thing; there was a world of work to be done and keep us occupied. Wednesday, I recall, in the afternoon, I was in the front yard, which I had not yet attempted to clear up, working upon the frame of a bunk bed that I meant to set up in my living quarters, when I heard a step upon the gravel of the roadway. I looked up and to my astonishment found myself looking into the level, ice-blue eyes of Andrew Ross.

For some reason my belly wound into a tight knot, and I felt the hackles on the back of my neck rise.

"What do you want?" I demanded.

He stared at me with a look of startled surprise for an instant, and then his face settled into a hostile mask.

"I'm looking for Mister MacLean," he said then.

"You'll find him at the next lot, just past the creek," I told him. "But are you sure you did not mean 'Mistress'?"

He made no answer to that, but glared at me coldly.

"Th' word I've to carry," he said, "is mainly for th' MacLeans. But ye're included, so I may as well pass th' message on t' ye now. Mister Cameron wishes me t' say that there's t' be a send-off party for th' Assiniboine brigades at Fort Gibraltar this next Saturday night. He hopes that ye'll all come t' it."

I straightened.

"A send-off?" I said. "Does that mean that you'll be going?"

"Sunday or Monday at dawn," he replied.

"I'll be there, then," I told him, "with pleasure!"

Just what we expected of such a frontier affair I sometimes wonder, now that it is done and past. Duncan Cameron had the effrontery to send an invitation direct to Governor MacDonnell, and very nearly caused that gentleman a stroke. Naturally, under the circumstances, the governor would not go. But it did not occur to him to forbid others of the colony to attend. As a result quite a number of us went, out of curiosity, if nothing more.

I walked over with the MacLeans myself, but I noticed that there were quite a number of other settlers on the road. And I noticed, too, that all I saw were newcomers; those who had come up with us from York Factory. Although Duncan Cameron's invitation had been general, the old-timers seemed to shun it. That made me wonder. But George Campbell and his luscious wife did not seem to worry. Nor, apparently, did a number of others.

We found Fort Gibraltar a stronger place than we had imagined it, even after seeing it from the river. There was a strong, star-shaped stockade all around it, and a revetment, dug in a most military manner; the only entrances were through the mainland gate upon which the tracks from our own camp and the road down the Assiniboine converged, and from the water gate that led down to the landing. There was no guard at the gate, though I noticed that the stockade

could be closed in case of necessity, and inside there was a wide compound with a number of neat log buildings arranged in an open square
around it.

The largest of these buildings did double duty as the residence of
the factor and the main Company store and counting room, and it
was here that we found the bright-maned Duncan Cameron, still
resplendent in his scarlet coat and blotched breeches; I wondered,
I remember at the time, whether he did not sleep in them! He was
supervising the task of clearing back the long counter and stowing
away the trade goods, setting up the casks of high wine and rum on
trestles in the corner and testing out the slippery edge of cracked corn
meal upon the well-worn puncheons of the floor. He greeted us with
hearty courtesy.

"Well, now!" he cried. "Here's Mister and Mistress MacLean an'
Mister MacAllister, say naught o' George Campbell an' his lovely wife!
I declare t' ye, gentlemen an' ladies, I fair wondered if ye'd join us.
Here! Let me show ye my own quarters, where th' ladies may leave
their wraps, an' ye, gentlemen, will join me in a cup o' choice brandy!"

He turned to a swart half-breed who was supervising the spreading
of the corn meal on the floor.

"Take charge o' this, Alcide," he commanded, "an' see that all is
ready when th' *boisson* begins. This way, Messieurs, ladies!"

He led us through a caged door first, past the counting rooms, and
then by a passage into the part of the building with the luxurious
apartments set aside for himself.

I could not but gasp as we came into them. Even in Scotland I had
never seen such luxury. There was a vast living room that must have
measured a good fifty by seventy feet, larger by far than the kirk we
planned for the little colony just below. His own bedrooms and rooms
for occasional guests lay off at one end, and the kitchens were at the
other. In the bedrooms the huge, four-poster beds—not bunks—were
covered with bearskin robes, and the chairs scattered around the living
room, mostly in a semicircle before the immense fireplace, were up-
holstered in the skins of the red deer. There was an immense plank
table at the kitchen end of the room; this was obviously the dining
area, for there were wooden chairs ranged about it and glasses and
decanters of amber liquor set out upon it now, and the door to the
great kitchen was close by.

He flung open the door to one of the guest bedrooms with a fine
flourish.

"There ye are, ladies!" he cried. "Go in an' make yerselves at home.

Throw yer wraps on th' bed, an' help yerselves t' th' commode if ye need to. 'Tis all there for yer own use."

He turned back to us, the gentlemen, before either they or we could show our embarrassment.

"Now, Messieurs," he said, "what's it t' be—brandy or choice whiskey? I tell ye, I've just heard th' most choice yarn o' one o' our lads an' a Saulteur woman—"

And he launched into a tale of a trader who had coveted an Ojibway girl and insisted upon having her until her husband in a fit of drunken jealousy threw her upon the floor and thrust a burning brand into her parts.

Such cruelty, I came to find, was by no means extraordinary. But at the moment it turned my stomach. Duncan Cameron cast a cynical eye upon me.

"And yours, Mister MacAllister?" he asked.

"Brandy," I said. "And, if you please, make it double."

He chuckled.

"Ye're a connoisseur, I see!" he remarked.

I tossed the drink off, and I must admit I felt none of it, though I knew it was smuggled and of the best.

"Have I e'er told ye o' th' windigo?" he demanded, leering in my direction. " 'Tis an Indian myth, an' not altogether such a legend as it may seem. Ye may o' heard that th' windigo is a cannibal spirit that descends upon a savage tribe an' lives upon human flesh until th' tribe is wiped away? 'Tis a gruesome thing if ye believe it. But I tell ye that there are cases o' traders that ha' lived an' waxed fat in a period o' starvin' by a judicious use o' th' legend—not only our own, Mister MacAllister, but those o' yer own Company as well! I see ye're not acquainted wi' th' possibilities o' starvation in this land!"

I saw that the ladies had come out of the bedroom to join us, and green as I must have been I changed the subject.

"You invited us to a dance, Mister Cameron," I said.

"Why, so I did!" he replied, with an unctuous smile. "I daresay 'twill be the first in th' northland that can boast of white ladies attending!"

The outer door of his quarters opened and a blustering crew came through. The tall, red-haired Andrew Ross was among the first, and appeared almost sober. But Alexander MacDonnell and Cuthbert Grant and Peter Pangman, called Bostonnais, had clearly started early.

"Where are they? Where're th' girls?" they cried. "We've started out yon wi' th' dancin' an' there's no sense in dawdlin'!"

"Gentlemen!" Cameron cried easily. "Surely ye'll take a cup with us? Th' ladies will be out at once!"

My stomach growled, yet I saw no reasonable way of objecting. Drinks were poured for the newcomers and ourselves but they did not seem to break down the air of tension that surrounded us. Duncan Cameron seemed even gayer than ever. He caught sight of our ladies all at once.

"Lads," he cried, "now, mind yer manners! Ladies! What will ye have? A glass o' Madeira, perhaps? Or better? Name it an' it will be yours!"

I was interested to note that Jean accepted a glass of sack while Mistress Campbell bawled for a cup of rum.

It seemed to me, all at once that the room—that spacious room—was crowded, and Duncan Cameron seemed to catch the thought.

"Shall we join the party, Messieurs, 'Dames?" he called.

I must say that what followed was hardly what a schoolmaster would approve. Call me prissy if you will, but I will confess that I was shocked at what we found in the main hall. The voyageurs were there in all their finery, with ribbons at their knees and shoulders and feathers in their hair, swaggering and boasting according to the amount of rum they had taken.

"Je suis un homme du nord!"

It was as if they sought to provoke a fight.

The rest of us harkened to the fiddles and to the pipes, Rab Gunn had refused to come. At the outset a number of us did a fancy fling, myself pairing off with Betsy Bannerman, since Jean MacLean seemed preoccupied with her father and the big, red-headed Andy Ross. After that there was a regular reel, in which all took part: swarthy breed and fat, gay squaw, while stolid, moccasined, mahogany-colored Indians sat about the walls and drank themselves into a stupor or worse as the evening progressed.

Prodded somewhat by the excellent brandy, I must admit, I found myself slipping some small bit into the spirit of the thing. My partner was a pretty Indian child, Qua-na-Shee-tits, so she told me she was called, a Saulteur from somewhere upriver. There was no question of her femininity. Under her close fitting, almost thin as paper, fine deerskin dress, I could see plainly were breasts as malleable and ductile as any white girl's. In a way I was intrigued, but I was also embarrassed.

The dance grew warmer and wilder, the Indians and voyageurs drunker. Our decorous dances gave way to wild jigs and stomps by the canoemen, while Indians reeled blindly about the room or were sick in the corner. The women, Indian and métis alike, were brazenly wanton and seductive, even to the point of outspoken lechery. To cradle a white hunter or bourgeois between their thighs was apparently deemed honorable and exciting beyond anything their own men might offer, and for a mug of high wine—pure alcohol mixed with water and flavored to taste with a little cayenne—a man might have anything he asked. Qua-na-Shee-tits, my prurient partner of the comparatively sedate reel, left me in no doubt about that. Even when I tried to flee to the comparative safety of our own women she followed me among them, rubbing her belly against me suggestively, trying to hang herself about my neck, and slobbering drunkenly upon my shirt so that she made a disgusting spectacle, not only of herself but of me as well.

Nor was the brawling and drinking and lechery by any means confined to the savage and lower elements. Duncan Cameron quite obviously was having a fine, high time, though I must say that not once during all that evening did the vast quantity of liquor that he consumed show itself in his gait or make itself apparent in his speech. I think the man must have had beer barrels for legs, and certainly his flowing, golden mane made him a much sought after prize among the dusky maidens who attended the party. At intervals he would disappear into his own rear quarters with one or another, quite obviously to try them out. He seemed to be indefatigable as well as hollow!

His capacity, however, was not shared by those closest around him. Alexander MacDonnell withdrew early and I saw him stretched out, flat on his back on one of the counters that had been shoved back against the wall, snoring away rhythmically and almost loudly enough to drown out the music. Cuthbert Grant was reeling and maudlin, making ineffectual attempts to maneuver Jean MacLean out of the room, into Duncan Cameron's quarters. The enormous, red-haired Andrew Ross was almost as tipsy, I thought, though I was thankful for his presence for between us we managed to forestall the most determined efforts of the *Boisbrûlé*. Even some of our own folk seemed to be having a merry time, in particular George Campbell and his lushly busty wife, who seemed to have forgotten anything she might ever have been taught of modesty.

But I could see that Jean and her father, to say naught of most of the rest of our party, were growing apprehensive and wondering how they might break away without giving offense. That question was fortunately solved for them in quick fashion when a brawl broke out among some Indians near the front door, and one of them apparently casting some slurring remark upon another's squaw was promptly and literally hacked to pieces before our eyes!

Duncan Cameron instantly dashed toward the spot, scattering red men and white before him, this way and that like straws in the wind, though as far as I could see that was all the punishment that anyone ever received for the deed. By the time he got there, of course, the Indian was dead. The doors were opened and the corpse was flung unfeelingly into the yard. A few old women of the tribe, professional mourners I was told, all very drunk, went out to sit beside the body and pour dust on their heads and give way to the ghastly, wailing chant for the dead. But beyond them none seemed to care, or even to be aware of what had happened. Duncan Cameron returned and the doors were closed again; the dance seemed about to be resumed when Alec MacLean stepped forward and held up his hand.

"We've had enough o' this!" he cried. "We'll be sayin' good night, an' may ye enjoy yersel's!"

In the astounded hush that followed the announcement one might have thought it a sudden, almost insulting decision. A few of us went quickly and quietly to fetch our ladies' wraps, ignoring the dozen or so couples in various stages of amorous drunkenness that had taken refuge in Cameron's quarters. I wondered if he knew that they were there but felt it none of my business to inform him. When we returned the doors were opened quietly and we passed out all together, to the accompaniment of the drunken jibes and jeers of the fine *hommes du nord*.

Duncan Cameron followed us, and for a moment, after the doors closed out the racket of the *boisson,* we stood in the lemon-pale moonlight and listened politely while he, a little unsteadily, tried to explain —not apologize. In the background the wailing chant of the mourning women was a weird accompaniment.

"I told ye 'twas a rough country t' which ye were comin'," he said. "I hope no worse comes t' ye. Thank ye for comin', all o' ye. An' come again—often. Mister MacLean, I liked yer sermon. I'll be over again t' hear ye."

And all the time there was a dead man lying just where they had flung him, not a half a dozen feet from the steps down into the compound.

Jean was silent all the way home, and I was jumpy and nervous until Monday morning, when I heard that the Northwest brigades had departed for Fort Qu'Appelle and Alexandria. Our own, of course, under Mister Belly, bound for Brandon House, had gone on long since.

2. THE HANDS OF ESAU

I LOOKED FORWARD TO AN INTERVAL OF PEACE AFTER THAT. THE ASSINI-
boine brigades were gone—and with them Andrew Ross, I take shame
to say it, though I felt him a fly in my ointment of content. But to my
dismay and impotent anger Cuthbert Grant remained. It was his duty
evidently—somehow he had arranged it—to act as a liaison officer
between Fort Gibraltar and Fort Qu'Appelle, Alexander MacDonnell's
headquarters in the heart of the *Boisbrûlé* country. He came over to
announce his presence and the fact that the western crews had gone;
there was no hint of embarrassment or apology in his manner.

Nor did Duncan Cameron's attentions cease. Hardly a day passed
that he did not walk over with his shotgun under his arm, smiling,
bowing, admiring this child, that girl, or the roof of a new house.
Miles MacDonnell noticed it and quarreled with Alec MacLean about
it. They argued back and forth, and in the end MacDonnell persuaded
MacLean to allow him to take his case directly to the people. Alec
allowed Miles to preach the sermon, and for a text the governor took
the twenty-second verse of the twenty-seventh chapter of the book of
Genesis: "The voice is Jacob's voice, but the hands are the hands of
Esau." And he warned us that though we might be deaf and blind as
Abraham, we should not be wholly without perception.

"Beware," he said, "the hands of Esau!"

And he looked directly at Cameron as he said it, so that there could
be no mistaking his meaning.

But the tawny-maned Northwester was either obtuse or indifferent.
His visits continued, and in desperation Governor MacDonnell finally
sent him a formal letter:

DISTRICT OF ASSINIBOIA

To MR. DUNCAN CAMERON,
  ACTING FOR THE NORTH WEST COMPANY
    AT THE FORKS OF THE RED RIVER:

Take notice, that by the authority and on behalf of your landlord, the Right Honourable Thomas Earl of Selkirk, I do hereby
warn you, and your associates of the North West Company, to
quit the post and premises you now occupy at the Forks of the
Red River, within six calendar months from the date hereof.

Given under my hand at Red River Settlement this 21st day
of October, 1814.

MILES MACDONNELL

But the result of that gesture was no more than a loud bray of derision from Duncan Cameron and a renewed invitation to various
selected colonists to take dinner with him.

Both the MacLeans and myself were included in this summons,
but both of us deemed it wise to reject it because of the almost apoplectic tension that was mounting in Miles MacDonnell. Some of our
folk, however, were not so squeamish. They told the governor in no
uncertain terms that he might have the regulation of the colony in
his care, but that he could not and would not regulate their private
lives. Thereupon they attended Duncan Cameron's dinner party and
returned to spread the tale that the great flaxen-haired man had been
conciliatory and gracious, a charming host who served them good
food and fine wine—better things by far than any we were accustomed
to at Fort Douglas, and who allowed no such shenanigans as marred
his last party to upset this. As I heard them I must admit to a certain
sense of regret that I had not gone, and I had a suspicion that both
MacLeans felt much the same. After all a steady diet of pease, porridge and pemmican does grow exceeding dull in time.

That at least was the result of the report upon me—a result that
was bad enough, I now realize. And the effects upon the colony in
general proved even more serious ultimately. For the moment, however,
we were all of us far too busy finishing off our houses and setting in
our winter's supplies to be much concerned with the problem. Since
I was no great hand as a cook myself I made an arrangement with
Jeannie and Alec MacLean whereby he and I would hunt together while
she would put up—smoke, pickle or preserve—all that we brought in.
At this we did reasonably well, bringing home a considerable amount of
small game, mainly rabbits, although we did manage in that time to

bag three red deer as well. Birds: ducks and geese and prairie chickens, were plentiful; and it was merely a matter of how many a man could hit with one shot. Curiously enough there were no pigeons during the fall, although they came over in the spring in such numbers as to blot out the sky and make the day seem overcast. When the annual northward flights began we found that an almost sure way of obtaining a full bag of the birds was to set up a long ladder against a tree at dusk. The pigeons coming in to roost found this a most convenient stopping place, and before dark every rung would be pack-jammed with them. Just before it became too dark to see, a man with a fowling piece could stand beneath the ladder and, sighting up along it, blast a month's dinners from the rungs with a single shot! At the same time there were catfish and sturgeon of immense size in the river, as well as pike, piccanon, brim, pois d'oile, male achegan, lacaishe and such.

It was in this pursuit that Alec and I went out one morning and spent most of the day across the river, in the brushy, thickety country, hunting deer. On that particular day, however, we had no luck. Apparently there were too many of us out in the chase, and the animals in the neighborhood had grown wary. When we returned toward dusk, we were surprised to find that Jean was entertaining company. Cuthbert Grant had walked over from Fort Gibraltar and finding her engrossed in the work of preserving venison had undertaken to show her some of the Indian methods in use among his own people—a friendly gesture, and a valuable lesson, since she was far from expert yet. At the same time, however, it was nothing more, I felt, than an excuse to insinuate himself into her good graces.

I am afraid that I was more brusque than I had any right to be when we returned to the cabin and I first saw him there.

"What the devil do you want?" I demanded, for some reason very angry that he should be there at all.

"Want?" he blinked at me blandly out of eyes as bright and immobile as a snake's. "Excuse me, Mister MacAllister, I do not understand—"

"You understand all right—" I said.

But Jean MacLean interrupted me.

"Please, Malcolm! Mister Grant has been showing me how to make jerky and pemmican, and how to smoke and bone a goose."

The half-breed spread his hands and flashed his teeth in a mirthless smile.

"It is not much," he said. "Some of our women could do it better, for I am not too familiar with that end of it. Among us, you know,

they call a man 'berdash'—a little queer—if he seems too interested
in such things."

He looked at Jean.

"Perhaps," he said, "if I bring one of the women over they will be
able to show you ways that I cannot."

"Oh, would you?" she cried. Clearly he had put himself out to be
agreeable to her, for until then she had not been favorably impressed
by him.

"I would be glad to," he replied. "If you will give her a small glass
of rum—"

"Oh, no!" said Jean. "I couldn't do that!"

"Well then, one of the hides," he grinned. "That will satisfy her."

He meant of course that the woman would be able to trade the skin
for rum at Fort Gibraltar, though he did not say it.

"Surely, I'd not want her to work for nothing!" I thought Jean was
a bit sharp about that.

But Cuthbert Grant pretended to ignore it. He glanced at Alec
MacLean and then at me.

"What I came over for, really," he said, "was to ask you gentlemen
if you would hunt with me? I think you have not had the luck you
should, and perhaps I may be able to show you a trick or two. The
buffalo are not far away, and a week or two of hunting should find
you all the game you need to carry you through the winter. If I
may—"

I must admit that I still had reservations, but Alec forestalled me.

"Would ye?" he asked. "I'm obliged t' ye, Mister Grant, an' I'm
sure Mister MacAllister is likewise. We're ready whene'er ye gi'e th'
word."

"At daybreak tomorrow?" said Grant.

"At daybreak, we'll be ready!" The dour preacher was as near to
enthusiasm as I think I had ever seen him.

It was only common sense, of course. Clearly the man knew his
ground and could show us the game that we ourselves had failed to
find. His offer was not to be refused. Yet I must admit I was not too
happy about it, though I refrained from quibbling.

"An' now," Alec MacLean went on, " 'tis so near suppertime perhaps ye'll stay an' take pot luck wi' us?"

"I'd be happy to," the half-breed shot me a glance of triumph, "if
Mistress MacLean will have me."

"O' course!" Jean cried out of a heart that was almost as big as she
was. "I'd hear o' naught else!"

And so he stayed to supper, and I must admit he was a most decorous guest. More so, I daresay, than many of his fellows would have been. His flashing smile and his cheerful good humor on that occasion, I am afraid put my own sullen manner completely to shame, and he talked frankly and easily of his people and their problems.

"You must not despise the métis," he said once. (He seemed to prefer to call them by that name.) "We are honest folk like yourselves, and have only the misfortune to have been born on the wrong side of the blanket, and that is no fault of ours!"

I had to admit that was the truth. Three times during the evening he quoted from the Bible, and twice from Shakespeare, and once he came up with an obscure passage from Harrington, proving I think that he was better educated than I, for all his rough surroundings and exterior. When he left I think I almost liked him despite my misgivings, though Jean could hardly be aware of that. Quite obviously she had entirely revised her opinion, and the door had scarcely closed behind him before she turned on me.

"Ye—ye beast, Malcolm MacAllister!" she shouted.

I stared at her in astonishment for I was not conscious of having done anything wrong. At the same time I felt a curiously sinking sensation in the pit of my belly. Ever since we came to the Forks I had been watching and waiting for an opportunity to speak again of the thing that was closest to my heart. But now it looked as if I had waited too long.

"Me?" I stated. "What have I done? Don't tell me, Jean—"

"Aye, ye!" she interrupted me fiercely. "Ye deliberately called attention t' th' poor man's mixed blood an' th' chance o' his birth, e'en though ye know well 'twas as much th' fault o' our own folk as his that it should be so. Ye treated him like dirt underneath yer feet. Yet he showed himself t' be a better gentleman than yerself. If ye think I'd e'er marry wi' such a narrow, sma'-minded bigot—"

"Wait! Wait now, Jean, for God's sake!" I cried, confused by her tirade. "In the first place I don't care a damn what his breed might be."

"What do ye care, then?" she demanded belligerently.

Could I tell her that I was jealous? Hardly!

"You know why I care, Jean," I replied, holding myself in check and, I daresay, restrained as well by Alec's presence. "I care because I'm fond of you. I care because I don't want to see you made sport of."

"Then ye'd best show better faith in me an' my judgment," she flared, "if ye care as much as ye say."

"Please, Jean," I managed to break in. "Here's no time to go into it.

We'll talk of it more when we've had time to cool a bit. For now let it go at good night, eh? And good night to you, Alec. I'll see you in the morning."

I did not wait to hear what she might say to that but flung out hurriedly into the night and crossed to my own cabin, barred the door and went to bed. But I must admit I did not sleep much.

Cuthbert Grant arrived before daybreak the next day at the MacLean cabin, bringing with him a sober, efficient Qua-na-Shee-tits, who set to work at once to show Jean all the ways in which food might be preserved in that wilderness. Grant told Jean that we would be gone several days, and after he had installed the Indian wench in the MacLean cabin he took Alec and myself back upriver in his long canoe to the mouth of the River La Sale, where he showed us buffalo in such vast herds that we sometimes missed our aim because we were uncertain at which to shoot.

We killed twenty-seven of the huge beasts, after which he took us across the river to the hills and showed us where to find *biche* and bear, who were scratching about in the wooded country in search of winter quarters. Within the week we were back with a canoe load, high piled, of fresh meat.

By way of variety he then showed us some ponds down and across the river, where the wildfowl flocked so thick that a man had only to pull the trigger to knock down all he could eat in a day. These we carried home again, where Jean and Qua-na-Shee-tits boned and smoked them. In fact, while we were busy at our hunting the two girls were even busier at home. They put up pickled fish and jellied venison, made pemmican and salted bear hams, pressed goose and duck and prairie fowl, and when there was no more of this to occupy them they picked quantities of summerberries and wild rice and made jelly of the first and sacked the latter in rawhide bags.

It might seem on the face of it that all this was very pleasant and innocuous; that all of the differences between us had been forgotten, and that the hatchet had been fully buried. But that was the deceptive thing about it. To begin with the situation was not without embarrassment. Qua-na-Shee-tits would have remained in my cabin if I had let her, and in fact if I had not been already so much in love with Jean I am not at all sure I would have refused her, for as I have hinted, apart from her pruriency, she was rather temptingly attractive, and I was a lone bachelor. As it was, I thought at one point that I might have to flee to the woods in desperation to escape her brazenly open advances.

But that was really only the smallest part of my trouble: the mosquito that sings in a man's ear, so to speak, after he has lain down to sleep. I suppose I was jealous. Certainly I was piqued at Jean's cordiality toward the black-eyed *Boisbrûlé* who had befriended us. And what was even worse I was confused by my own liking for the fellow, for there can be no denying that when he wanted to put himself out Cuthbert Grant could be as easy and charming and as hail-fellow as anyone could wish.

Yet fundamentally Jean was right. I distrusted him vaguely; and by the same token I resented him. For months I had been trying to drop my heart at Jean's feet, perhaps not as avidly as I might have done, but that was out of consideration for her. But each time I had spoken she had put me off, saying that it was not the proper moment; that when we were at the Forks there would be time to speak of it. Now that we were come to the settlement, it seemed to me, she was no more anxious to hear what I had to say or to give me an answer than she had been before, and in my resentment I was inclined to blame those most constantly present—in this case Cuthbert Grant—forgetting, perhaps, some other things that had not long since happened.

In any case I scented danger, and I made up my mind to speak before it was too late. The moment came after we had visited the duck ponds across the river, when, for a time, Cuthbert Grant and Qua-na-Shee-tits deemed it wise to go back to the Northwesters' fort on the Assiniboine for a day or two. I watched them go with mingled reluctance and relief, and when evening came and Jean went down to the creek to fill her water buckets I was there with my own. It was not the best time I could hope for, but I felt it would have to do.

"Why, Jean!" I said, falsely excited. "This is like old times, meeting at the burn."

She glanced at me frostily.

"Did ye no' expect it?" she asked.

That rocked me back upon my heels.

"Why, aye!" I said, desperately seeking a way to explain the thing that was troubling me yet hardly succeeding. "Of course I expected it. 'Tis why I am here now! Jean, we've reached the Forks. We're settled in. You told me that when we'd done that—?"

She stared off into the shadows of the rim of trees along the brook.

"Aye, so!" she replied. "So, I did, Malcolm. I—I think I'd an idea then what I might say. Now, I'm no' sae sure."

I stared at her unbelieving.

"What?" I said. "For God's sake Jean, what've I done?"

"Dinna sweer!" she reproved me. "Mister Grant ne'er sweers."

"That—!" I began furiously.

"Aye!" she nodded. "Yon's th' way ye've been e'er since we've come tae th' Forks! Ye've lookit down yer long nose at th' folk here—at least a' but th' one, t' hear her tell it!"

"What d'you mean?" I demanded.

"I hear th' Indian lassies're no so hard t' take," she retorted.

"Qua-na-Shee-tits?" I cried. "Jean, you can't believe—?"

"She's aye fond o' ye!" she retorted, and picked up her buckets and stalked back up the pathway toward the parsonage.

"Jean!" I called after her. "Jean, you've not let yourself be dazzled by a pair of black Indian eyes, have you?"

But the words were no more out than I realized I had said the wrong thing!

Alec and Cuthbert Grant and I went off again the next day to the Shoal Lakes for more waterfowl, although I was not a little reluctant and sour about it. I daresay I was more outspoken than I should have been.

"For God's sake!" I said. "Haven't we enough, for our use at least? Why must we keep up this farce? What's in your mind, Mister Grant?"

He looked at me, startled at first I think, and then blandly amused, as I had reason to remember him later.

"In my mind, Mister MacAllister?" he demanded suavely. "Only what I know, sir: that there's never enough! You'd best take what you can get while you can get it, for tomorrow it might not be there!"

Of course I did not want to press the obvious reply to that, although it seemed to me open enough. At the same time, without the passage between us things might have run a different course.

We came back to the settlement at the Forks a few days later to find Qua-na-Shee-tits already gone and Jean MacLean wearing a hangdog air. At the cabin door Miles MacDonnell was waiting for our appearance.

"What is this!" MacDonnell cried. "D'ye go over t' th' enemy altogether? I've warned ye these folk are no' t' be trusted. Must ye be hit i' th' heads t' see th' truth o' it?"

He swung sharply to Cuthbert Grant, not waiting for an answer from us.

"Get ye gone!" he cried. "Ye know th' de'il's get ye are! Get out! I'll ha' nae Nor'westers here!"

I will say for Grant that he kept his temper well. He turned to Jean stiffly, ignoring me, whom he clearly held responsible.

"Forgive me," he said, "for having been born as I was! Your servant, Ma'am!"

He bowed and swung on his heel and strode away, and I must say that in spite of his obvious misconception I was entirely in sympathy with him at the moment. But there was no arguing with Governor MacDonnell, and no more with Jeannie.

She turned upon me when the governor had left.

"Ye did this!" she cried.

"For God's sake, what, Jean?" I cried, flabbergasted.

"Ye put th' governor up t' it!" she retorted. "For shame, Malcolm MacAllister!"

Nor would any amount of argument on my part convince her that it was not so. In vain I quarreled with her. She would not listen.

In November came another invitation to dine at Fort Gibraltar, and although we did not consult one another in the matter, the situation being somewhat strained between us at the moment, I think that they as much as I decided to accept mainly because of Governor MacDonnell's unnecessarily peremptory behavior that evening. We did not intend to be bullied and we wanted him to know it.

The occasion appeared to be the celebration of Duncan Cameron's birthday, and I must say that I for one accepted with some doubt. I walked over alone, of course, since Jean had been cool to me since the events I have described, while she and her father followed in the dusk. But I might have saved myself the worry for the affair proved to be quite harmless. It was gay but decorous, and only Cuthbert Grant brought a jarring note. He, I thought, partook a bit too freely of the cheering goblet, and in the course of the evening, revealed himself in a completely different role from that I had come to expect of him.

It might have been the fact that he was on his own home grounds that encouraged him. At any rate he seemed to me far more the man that I had originally judged him. He positively strutted, and was brash and bold. Toward me his attitude was close to insolent, though that did not trouble me nearly so much as the fact that his attentions to Jean were blatant and obvious and much too easy and familiar. Why she did not notice it herself, I cannot guess, unless perhaps she felt abashed at the way he had been treated and was trying to make amends, in which case her eagerness might have blinded her. As we walked home late in the evening, for some reason, I suddenly remembered the text of Governor MacDonnell's sermon but I said nothing, deeming the thing over and done with. There was no use, I thought, in scratching at the wound.

But I was mistaken, apparently, in assuming that that was the end of it. On the contrary it was no more than the beginning of a situation that I watched develop with increasing apprehension. Three nights after the dinner party at Fort Gibraltar I stepped across the little creek that ran between my own schoolhouse and the parsonage for the purely social purpose of paying a friendly call upon my neighbors. To my surprise, as I opened the door and stepped into the central living-dining room-kitchen, just then warm and cozy with a huge fire blazing on the wide hearth, I saw that they already had a visitor; as he turned around at the sound of my entrance and I was able to see his face, I was still more amazed to recognize Cuthbert Grant.

"You?" I said, startled, I fear, out of all habit of ordinary courtesy. "What the devil are you doing here?"

He grinned at me insolently, his white teeth flashing brightly in his swarthy face in the firelight.

"Paying my respects to Mistress MacLean," he retorted almost tauntingly. "Is aught wrong with that?"

"Wrong—I—no, I suppose not." I was confused. "Only you remember what Governor MacDonnell had to say last time you met here. What if he should happen by?"

Cuthbert Grant laughed aloud.

"Don't worry about me!" he cried. "I'm not afraid of old Frozen-face. For that matter he'll never know I'm here."

I glanced at Alec MacLean, but his own eyes slid away toward the fire uneasily, and I guessed that he was as troubled as I but did not know what to do about it. I decided that it was hardly my place to speak up in another man's house about such a thing, which I suppose was a mistake.

"I—I didn't hear you come in," I said, feeling that I ought to make some attempt at conversation.

He smiled cryptically.

"No," he replied. "I didn't make any noise."

And I remembered then how, when we were hunting he could glide like a soundless shadow through the leaf-strewn woods or over the dry prairies or through the tall reeds at the river's edge as if he were no more than a smoky wraith that never touched so much as a twig or a blade of grass. For some reason the thought was chilling, sobering.

That night he stayed until near midnight, and then vanished as silently as he had come, into the shadows along the riverbank. But two nights later he came back again and made himself comfortable beside the MacLeans' fire. The next morning I spoke of it to Alec.

"I don't like it," I said.

"No more do I," he replied. "But what's a man t' do? I ken th' lass. She's headstrong, an' she's a notion that th' governor's discriminatin' against th' man. If I forbid her t' see him she'll be turnin' that same resentment against mysel' d'ye follow me?"

That might be all very well for his way of reasoning, but it was far from satisfying to me. I took matters in my own hands and made my own remonstrance to Jean, though much good it did. So far as I could see it only aligned me further with the forces that she seemed to feel were persecuting Grant merely because he happened to be illegitimate and of mixed blood.

"You might at least have a thought for yourself!" I cried finally in desperation.

But her reply was frosty as the December wind that whipped at us.

"I don't see what business it is of yours, Mister MacAllister! I'll remind ye that I'm capable o' handlin' my own affairs by now!"

So I said no more, even though between then and Christmas, it seemed to me, he was at their house nearly every night.

Such was the state of affairs at the year's end, when once again a little note of invitation was carried across to us from Fort Gibraltar, asking us to attend the New Year's celebration there. So far as I was concerned this one-sided entertainment was becoming monotonous, and I think I might have refused. But the MacLeans were going, and I was reluctant somehow to let Jean go without me. Moreover the invitation was general and for some reason Governor MacDonnell seemed disposed to let the spirit of the season guide him. I daresay he thought that a show of neighborliness might soften the hostility between the two camps, momentarily at least, though he would not go so far as to attend the Northwesters' gathering himself.

I remember that it was a crisp, clear night, bitterly cold, but so dry that we hardly noticed the temperature as we trod across the creaking snow to the other fort. To our surprise almost the first person we saw on entering the storeside door of the main building was Andrew Ross. I happened to see him first.

"Hullo!" I cried, even cheerfully, for somehow I seemed to like the rangy, red-headed man for all he was a Northwester. "How the devil did you get here?"

At the sound of my words Jean turned and I heard her gasp.

"Andy!"

For a moment I wondered if she would not go into his arms—or at least he take her in them. But apparently I started at shadows, for he smiled down at her cheerfully while she gazed up at him almost breathlessly, but neither one moved toward the other.

"What *are* you doing here?" she managed finally.

"It gets pretty grim upriver about this time o' year, Ma'am," he said.

"Stop calling me 'Ma'am,' " she cried. "My name's Jean."

"It gets kind o' lonesome up there around Alexandria, Jean," he tried again, "along about th' middle o' winter. I just thought I'd come down an' tie on a little celebration for a change."

She looked as if he had slapped her in the face.

"I hope you enjoy yourself!" she said stiffly.

"I plan to," he told her bluntly, with a curious, studying smile. But he offered no further explanation. "I must go back tomorrow."

"On New Year's Day?" Jean cried out in spite of herself.

He sighed in mock self-pity.

"Aye, on New Year's Day, there's th' way 'tis in our service!" he smiled. "Yer Bay folk have it easy that one day at least!"

But if he implied that Hudson's Bay people suffered from the results of too much celebration while Northwesters did not, I think he shot arrows at the moon, for that evening's jollity was hardly less wild than on our first visit to Gibraltar. The details of it are unimportant, except that Cuthbert Grant became somewhat disgusting in his persistence while Andrew Ross, though it seemed to me that he had equally as much to drink never seemed so much as to stagger or turn a hair under the effects of the raw liquor. Forewarned by our previous experience we left shortly after the crack of midnight, after we had sung "Auld Lang Syne" and joined hands around and sipped a glass on it which I think we, on our side of the fence at least, were honest enough to mean sincerely.

Reluctantly, I must admit that both the food and the wines that they served to us were far superior to any we ever tasted at our own establishment. But that, of course, was not the fault of the Company, which was every bit as generous as our rivals. It was simply that our own routes of supply were so much longer and more complicated that such things were apt to be spread rather thin by the time they reached us.

When the New Year's toast was drunk and a momentary truce, at least, had been declared by each of us, we took our leave. It was luck, I suppose, that Cuthbert Grant had stumbled off somewhere by himself, so that he was not present at the moment. I wondered a little when Andy Ross insisted on accompanying us, to guard, he said, against the dangers o' th' way.

" 'Tis only a mile or so, Ross. There's no need for it," I said.

"Noneth'less!" he growled.

And nothing else would satisfy him. He got his capote and snow-shoes while Jean and I waited and Alec MacLean went on ahead to stir up the fires and see if there was aught in the house to offer him for a nightcap. When he came back I thought he seemed extraordinarily cheerful, and while Jean was seeking her wrap he looked at me and smiled grimly.

"We'll not be troubled now," he said. "But I feel the need of a breath of air. I'll walk with ye."

I shot him a puzzled look.

"What's got into you?" I demanded. "You're very mysterious to-night."

But at that moment Jean reappeared and even if he would there was no chance to explain. I think we were halfway to Fort Douglas before he spoke up and gave us a hint of what was in his mind. I think he expected me to walk on ahead and leave him and Jean to follow, but even if I had not felt about her as I did I would hardly have done that! When he saw that I meant to walk with them all the way to her father's house he flung me an impatient look and then scratched at the back of his neck.

"I hear ye've been seein' a good deal o' Cuthbert Grant o' late," he said.

Jean stopped in her tracks and stared at him in the white moon-light in a way that made me glad I had not said it.

"Yes, we have," she said—and I noticed the "we." If it included me, I thought, I ought to speak up. But I could not be sure. "Is there any reason why we should not?"

He stared at her, studying her almost carefully as if he were wonder-ing how he might go about convincing her of what he was thinking.

"Ye'll be angry with me," he said finally, "but yes, there is."

"What?" she demanded defiantly.

He scratched at his neck again.

"Ye know," he said, "I'm not a man t' be tellin' tales out o' school. But, well—I want ye t' be on guard against th' slippery devil."

Jean laughed aloud and scornfully.

"I suppose you're going to warn me against Mac, here, too?" she demanded.

He gave me a sidelong glance and his face, in the moonlight, was immobile as if it were frozen.

"No-o-o," he said presently. "No, at least Mac, out o' his regard for ye, would offer ye no slight. From what little I know o' Mister Mac-Allister, though we may be in opposite camps, he's an honorable man, an' he's fond o' ye, an' I'd ne'er warn ye beware o' him. But—"

"But what, Mister Ross?" she demanded mockingly.

I was still staring at him in surprise when he gave me yet another.

"But, I'll tell ye, Mistress MacLean," he said abruptly, as if he had suddenly made up his mind to a thing he was not sure that he should say. "As I've said to ye, Fort Alexandria is a lonely post. I've had time aplenty to think this last fall and winter while I've been there. I've had such time before, but I'd never a reason to apply it so. Now I have been thinking, and wondering—"

"And wondering what, Andy?" she asked him.

"I've been wondering," he said, "about the right o' this whole quarrel. There's a thing called loyalty, an' it's what we've had drilled into us from th' day we first sign indentures with th' Company; I know 'tis th' same with th' Bay People. 'Tis a good enough thing, in th' main. But lately I've been wondering. Never before have I questioned th' right o' th' Nor' West Company, or th' way things were. But now, is it right t' sit by an' watch things done that're wrong—that ye know are wrong —as between people—for th' sake of th' business—be it th' North-westers or the Hudson's Bay Company. D'ye see what I'm drivin' at?"

"I—I don't exactly, Andy," Jean replied. "Do you mean that for the purposes of the North West Company Mister Grant has some—some design on me?"

His face was grim.

"I can't tell ye what Cuthbert Grant's intentions toward ye are," he told her, "except t' say that I know his usual aims toward women, an' they're not pretty. But I can tell ye that neither he nor Duncan Cameron mean well to th' lot o' ye, an' either one o' 'em'll see one single person among ye shamed an' destroyed in order t' be rid o' ye all!"

We were come to the crossing of the creek by then, and Jean halted and turned to face him.

"Andy! Andy Ross!" she cried. "You mean—?"

"Believe it or not as ye will!" He stared down at her soberly. "But remember what I'm tellin' ye, an' if anythin' goes amiss in th' spring, remember I'm at Alexandria. If ye can get a message t' me I'll do any-thin' I can t' help!"

"Do you know of anything particular that's—" I started to say.

But Jean apparently did not hear me. She broke in, interrupting. "Andy, ye're joking!" she protested.

"I am not joking, Jean," he told her grimly.

He turned abruptly to me.

"An' ye, MacAllister," he said, "ye keep yer eyes wide, too. I must be goin' now, for 'tis not wise for me to be too long away from the fort. Good-by, an' good luck!"

He put his hand momentarily on Jean's arm and gave it a little admonishing shake. Then quickly he swung away and was gone in the darkness.

Jean stared after him, as if she could look through the night.

"Good—goodness, Malcolm!" she said at length. "D'ye think he was serious?"

"He didn't sound to me as though he were making a joke of it," I replied.

"Pooh!" she cried, and I suppose I should have recognized it for whistling in the dark. "He starts at shadows!"

I remembered the way Cuthbert Grant had of coming and going silently, like a shadow.

"Maybe," I said soberly.

Whether he was unduly concerned or not, however, the first week of the year was not gone entirely before Cuthbert Grant came slipping down once more like a dusky, silent wraith, through the fringe of woods between the cabins and the river. It happened that I had just stepped across to fetch in the MacLeans' night's supply of wood, Alec having been laid in his bed for a day or two by a pleuritic attack. It was not serious, but I had offered to take over his chores for him until he was able to be up and around again, and just as Cuthbert Grant came sliding in I was out by the woodpile at the back of the cabin.

He startled me, for I did not hear him at first, and only became aware of his approach when I caught sight of his dark shadow looming against the white of the snow. I came erect so suddenly that I surprised a fleeting expression of utter malevolence just slipping from his eyes and mouth. In the next instant he was smiling unctuously.

"Hullo!" I said, none too cordially I fear. "So it's you again?"

His smile grew a little more wooden, more fixed.

"Yes," he said simply. "Is there a reason why it should not be?"

I decided that it was time something was done about this.

"Aye!" I told him. "There is. In the first place Alec is ill and wants no visitors—"

He looked at me resentfully, sobering.

"Ye're visiting," he pointed out.

"No I'm not," I replied. "I'm doing Alec's work for him, since it has to be done. 'Tis a load off his mind and only neighborly."

Grant grinned almost triumphantly.

"Then I'll just give ye a hand," he said.

"No you won't," I said. "Look here, Grant, doesn't it occur to you that coming here like this, after the governor has warned you away, puts the MacLeans in an awkward position? Of course they don't want to forbid you to come over. They're fine, hospitable folk, and that's why I'm speaking out now about something that you probably think is none of my business. If you can't see it then somebody must point it out to you. Think naught of any possible danger to yourself. We'll lay that aside for the moment. How do you think it would look for Alec and Mistress Jean if it became known that you were visiting their house in the night, sneaking in like an attainted thief?"

There was no effort now on his part to disguise the hatred in his eyes.

"Why, ye meddling fool!" he cried. "What the devil is it to you, anyway."

"I've told you that," I said calmly, though I am afraid my answer was not entirely accurate. "They have to live here—in this settlement, remember, and 'tis not a large world. The good opinion of their neighbors is precious."

He swung away from me suddenly.

"Let's see what the MacLeans have to say about this!" he cried, and he started to pass around me on my left.

Instinctively I put out my hand and caught his sleeve.

"I wouldn't trouble," I said.

But my touch seemed to pour fuel on the fire of his wrath, and he spun about sharply.

"Take your hand off me!" he raged, and at the same time his arm jerked back from the bright voyageur's sash that he wore, and in the dying flicker of dusk I caught the wicked flash of the knife in his hand.

As I stood my left side was exposed to him, and but for a lucky chance he might have buried the blade in my heart before I could cry out. But it happened that I stood as he had surprised me in the act of picking up wood from the woodpile. I had a stout billet in my right hand at the moment, and when he jerked away from me so savagely I instinctively swung it up and across toward him, half expecting some sort of violence.

It was just luck that the weight of the billet parried the knife, for I have never claimed any skill either as a swordsman or at play with a quarterstaff. The razor-edged blade, deflected by the wood, slipped across and down, slashed at a corner of my heavy capote, slicing a gash in it that was more than a foot long, but fortunately never touching me. Grant, swung off balance by the very savage force of his wild thrust, half spun back toward the woodpile, and at the same time, spurred I daresay by the desperation of my need to defend myself, I swung my clumsy cudgel back again and caught him squarely on the point of his elbow.

It did not seem to me that it was a particularly powerful blow, but to my astonishment I heard the bones of his arm crack, and the knife went spinning through the air to land against the woodpile and then drop into the snow. Grant yelped in pain and then leapt to scramble for the knife in the snow. But I had the advantage of knowing exactly where it had fallen, and I jumped in between him and the pile of wood and kicked the weapon out of the way. At the same time I held up my own billet threateningly.

"Back!" I grunted. "Get back, Grant, or by God I'll beat your brains out in the snow."

He crouched in front of me, and I even think that in his rage and pain he would have come at me unarmed as he was, had not Jean's voice at that moment suddenly cut through the gathering dusk.

"Malcolm, what is it?"

I know that I had no idea that she had come out to find out what was delaying me, and I think Grant was equally ignorant, for only complete surprise could have checked him. For an instant we remained poised there, face to face. Then Jean spoke again.

"What? Malcolm! Put that stick down!"

It was well intended, of course, but I was hardly either in a mood or in a position to obey.

"Stay where you are, Jean!" I snapped, and then to the half-poised métis, "You too, Grant!"

Having made sure of that for a moment, I edged back along the woodpile until I came to the place where I had kicked the heavy knife off into the snow. Without taking my eyes from Grant I bent down and fumbled in the icy stuff until I found it. I straightened and stuck the weapon in my belt.

"I'll keep this," I said. "Now, Grant, you'd better go."

Mystified, Jean watched us.

"What—what's happening here?" she demanded.

Cuthbert Grant straightened slowly, clutching his elbow and looking almost green with pain. Swiftly I told her what had occurred. When I was done she glanced at the half-breed reproachfully.

"I think 'twould be best if ye follow Mister MacAllister's advice, Mister Grant," she said. "I'm sorry."

He glared at her and spat out something in the French-Indian patois of his people which I did not understand, though I guessed it was not complimentary. Angrily I rapped with my billet on the woodpile.

"Good night to you, Mister Grant!" I said sharply.

He turned bitter eyes upon me then for just an instant, and then all at once turned about on his heel and, still clutching at his elbow, plunged straight down over the bank and disappeared in the gloom.

When he was gone I turned around to face Jean.

"I'm sorry!" I said. "I'd no notion he'd be like that. I'm afraid I've made you no friends this night."

Her eyes rested for a moment on my slashed coat before she looked up again, very white and shaken and deadly serious.

"Are—are ye hurt?" she asked.

I laughed and shook my head.

"He missed me," I said, and then thought it best for her peace of mind to make light of it, at least until she had time to regain her composure. "His aim was poor and the light none too good. Tomorrow I'll sew it up and it will all be forgotten."

But she shook her head.

"He won't forget," she said.

I am afraid I thought as much myself, though I would not admit it to her. I sent her back into the house and fetched in a heaping arm-load of logs to keep the fire going through the night. After that we ate, and when supper was done she insisted on sewing my blanket coat before I went back to my own cabin. While she worked, Alec MacLean, whom I had thought asleep, and whose room was at that end of their cabin nearest the woodpile, called me in to him.

"How are you, Alec?" I said as I entered, grinning at him so that he might not suspect that anything had been amiss.

But he did not smile back.

"I thought I heard scufflin' a bit ago," he told me. "What was it?"

"Just a varmint," I said, using a word that I had heard some of our Bay Company hunters apply to timber wolves and other pests of the forest, and thinking to reassure him.

But he did not smile. Instead he fixed me with a stern eye.

"A two-legged one?" he demanded.

Seeing that he must have overheard more than I thought, I saw nothing for it but to nod and tell him what had happened.

"I don't like it," he said when I was done.

"No more do I," I replied. "But there didn't seem much else for me to do."

He nodded.

"He'll be back, unless I'm sair wrang," he said. "Ye'll be aye wise t' ca' canny, Malcolm."

"Don't worry about me," I said. "I'll keep my eyes open. 'Tis Jean I don't want to see hurt by it."

That, however, was one worry that we might have spared ourselves. I kept my promise to Alec MacLean, but cautious and vigilant though I was I could not even find a trace of his having come skulking about the cabins, and it was many a week before we saw him again.

When I stop to consider it now I find that hardly surprising, though it puzzled me at the time. For a little I wondered if I had frightened him away, but common sense told me that I was hardly awe-inspiring. Next, I recall, I asked myself if his better nature could have prevailed, and rejected the thought even more promptly. From what little I knew of him I guessed that his was not a forgiving nature.

Since it was neither of these, then, I lay his absence to a combination of other circumstances. First there was his elbow, which—whether I had broken it, as I suspected, or not—must certainly have been too sore to risk in another rough and tumble fight for some time. Then there was the light, powdery snow that sifted almost nightly through the woods behind our cabins, and laid a fine, unbroken mantle of white all about us. Obviously it would be impossible for him to approach under such conditions without leaving a clearly legible trail. Then, when the elbow might have healed and he might have summoned up his courage for a try at us regardless of the snow that would leave telltale tracks, the winter closed in upon us in earnest, crashing down out of the west, roaring in from the open prairies on the wings of a bitter wind, lashing us with blizzards that piled the heavy snows in immense drifts all about our cabins and sent the temperature tumbling to such vicious depths that only a fool would leave the warmth of his fireside, let alone step out of doors if he could help it.

And it seemed there were no more fools at Fort Gibraltar than there were at Fort Douglas. We saw no more of our neighbors from the North West Company's post so long as that bitter season persisted. Indeed, we saw little of one another even, for when the gales howled and the battering windstorms picked up the prairie snow and drove it through the air with the cutting bite of countless icy knives, school was

out of the question and church was no attraction. My own longest
excursions were across the creek to the parsonage to see how the Mac-
Leans were doing, or around to the woodpile or the necessary house,
close by, which was literally snowed under so that I had to dig a vent-
hole up through the snow for air. Most folk, I think, did not go even
that far; and as for going down to the river or up to the fort or out to
the wintry fields, it was difficult and even foolhardy. Those of us who
had any livestock at all, there were a few horses and cattle that had
been brought in before our own arrival, could only try to keep them
snug and secure in the log sheds that passed for barns, heaping the snow
up over the roofs and under the eaves, and leaving as small a blowhole
for air as possible to keep them from freezing while a narrow corridor
between snow walls that towered above our heads was the only way to
the door. There we sought to keep them alive and fat on such meager
supplies of prairie hay as we had been able to cut and store during the
previous summer. Grain was too scarce and too precious to be wasted
on animals.

Such was our first winter on the Red River, and it was one that I
learned later was considered by the Indians and fur hunters and the
Boisbrûlés at Fort Qu'Appelle as an unusually open one since the season
of the deep snows did not arrive until the middle of January and then
did not last much beyond three months. Those of us, however, who
found ourselves so circumscribed for the first time, in our tiny quarters,
thought it anything but short. But there is an end to everything, and
I can recall with what delight I went out to the woodpile one evening,
not long after the middle of April, to find the air grown suddenly,
astonishingly warm and a light, drizzle falling. The snow had already
begun to melt from the roof of my cabin and that of the parsonage,
across the creek, which I could see, thrusting black and peaked, a
dark corner amid the surrounding snow. Doubtless the rapid melting
was helped by the warmth of the fire inside the building, for long icicles
were forming from the eaves. From the direction of the river I could
hear the groaning thunder of the ice, not yet ready to break up, as it
strained against the waters that flowed beneath it and presently began
to trickle down over its surface. It froze again before morning, of
course, and it was yet long before we began to see the ground break
through its pock-marked mantle. We watched the river rise with apprehension and then breathed a sigh of relief as the ice at last broke up and
the threatening waters began to fall. Then, finally, we heard the geese
go honking northward, high overhead, and after them the clattering,

raucous ducks in mighty flocks, leaving many a meal of fresh fowl on our tables as they passed.

And at last, one day—almost overnight, it seemed—we looked out once more upon the prairies, bright clothed in the fresh green of new grass; at the trees along the riverbank, swelling with buds; at the first, young spring flowers that sprang up out of the moist earth, and I admit that something stirred within me that had nothing to do with grim thoughts of death. At the same time, however, I could not help but think how carefully a man might move over that soft earth, so that he neither left tracks nor made a sound as he passed. Thinking of that I resumed my vigilance.

For the first time in nearly four months that Sunday Alec MacLean was able to throw open the doors of the little church and hold services. As the hour drew near I could see that the fact that he had not been able to act in his official capacity during the winter was troubling him, and when he mounted the pulpit to give his sermon he took as his text: "Man does not live by bread alone." And when he was done he made two announcements; pronouncements, perhaps would be a better word. First, he would demand of the governor, looking directly at Miles MacDonnell, that a committee be appointed whose duty it would be to see that at least footpaths were dug and kept open, the following winter, that would run the length of the village. Second, he would call upon the same source for a crew to help him knock out a portion of the church wall and replace it with a wide fireplace and chimney. When that was done he would ask the same men, or another group if necessary, to go with him to the woods for a supply of firewood, with which to keep the church fires burning throughout the winter; for, he pointed out, if folk were to freeze and shiver in the House of the Lord they were not like to have much interest in religion, which seemed to me a sound and sensible point of view.

All this was important, to be sure, but it was not the most exciting, nor even that which held the deepest interest of most of our people unfortunately. The big item of speculation among them was Duncan Cameron, and I must admit I was more than a little intrigued myself. It was more than six months now since our own Governor MacDonnell had issued his ultimatum to the Northwesters, demanding that they abandon Fort Gibraltar. But as far as any of us knew our neighbors had made no move to comply. Now speculation ran rife: would the great, tawny man come to our service, as he had always done since we came there? Or would conscience keep him away? (If he did not come, I told myself, it might be because Cuthbert Grant had told him of our encounter, turning him against us, though as soon as it occurred to me I branded the idea as ridiculous!)

Of course he came, splendid as usual in his stained red coat and long fop's sword, his grimy stock and dirty-white breeches; and with all his former strut and assurance. There was never a word about the governor's edict until MacDonnell himself elbowed his way furiously out the church door and strode straight to Cameron and confronted him with it. The big man stared down at the square-built governor as if he had been mortally offended.

"Really, now, Mister MacDonnell!" he cried. "If ye truly expect us t' vacate, ye must give us time t' make th' move! Th' ice has only just gone out, I'd remind ye!"

The argument was not altogether pertinent, but it was a sample of the man's shrewdness. There was just enough reason in it to be difficult for Miles MacDonnell to answer.

"Well, what d'ye expect t' do about it?" MacDonnell demanded.

"Do?" Butter wouldn't melt in Duncan Cameron's mouth. "Why, Mister MacDonnell, ye must recognize that I am no more than an employee. I can do only what my directors order me t' do, an' until I hear from them, certainly, I can do nothing!"

He ignored Governor MacDonnell's apoplectic rage and stared around at the little crowd that streamed out of the church.

"In th' meantime," he said in a loud voice, " 'twas in my mind t' give out a blanket invitation t' yer folk t' come an' join with us next Wednesday evening at a buffalo roast in honor o' th' coming of spring. Our hunters have fetched in several animals, which will be spitted whole, and we've broken out a couple of barrels of potatoes, an' some other good things that I understand have been scanty among ye. Ye'll come, I trust—all o' ye—an' yerself, especially, Governor?"

Miles MacDonnell ignored him and spun about on his heel to shout at all of us within earshot.

"Don't go!" he bellowed. "Don't a one o' ye dare go!"

But he might as well have saved his breath for whistling down the wind. Wild horses would not have kept most of our people from such a feast as Cameron described after such a winter as they had been through. For myself, it seemed to me that the best way to find out what Cuthbert Grant was about was to go straight to his own camp!

Perhaps it was Governor MacDonnell's rage that made Duncan Cameron smile cryptically. He glanced about.

"On Wednesday then, gentlemen—and ladies?" he beamed. "We'll promise ye a rare fling, an' perhaps when ye see how we Northmen manage hereabout ye'll be inclined to agree 'tis not ourselves should go!"

I wondered a little at that, whether the hair on Esau's hands was not beginning to show. But I said nothing at the time.

3. *BOISBRÛLÉ*

A̲L̲L̲ ̲T̲H̲R̲O̲U̲G̲H̲ ̲T̲H̲A̲T̲ ̲W̲I̲N̲T̲E̲R̲ ̲I̲ ̲C̲O̲U̲L̲D̲ ̲S̲E̲N̲S̲E̲ ̲J̲E̲A̲N̲'̲S̲ ̲H̲O̲S̲T̲I̲L̲I̲T̲Y̲ ̲T̲O̲ ̲M̲E̲, even in spite of what I took to be Andy Ross's confirmation of my mistrust of Cuthbert Grant. Because of it I had stood back. Let her come to the decision, not be forced by me, was something of my attitude. In a way I hoped that what he had said would do something to point the way, that is, the way that honest men thought. But the half-breed seemed to have caught her imagination and she insisted upon going. Since she was bound on it Alec must go too. And so long as they both went nothing in the world could keep me away. I remembered Andy Ross's words at Christmas time and it came to me that by playing Duncan Cameron's game now we might learn more than if we quibbled. I was right, it proved, far beyond my own conjecture.

The occasion was quite different from most we had attended at Fort Gibraltar in previous months. In the first place, as a picnic supper it was held early, while there was yet light; and the pits were dug for roasting the buffalo and cooking the rest of the meal, and the split-pine puncheons that made up the trestle tables were set up, all outside the fort's walls. The gates remained open, so that anyone who was so inclined, and there were many, might pass through into the compound and store and help themselves from the casks set up there on saw-horses. But I noticed, too, that a sort of a platform had been built close by the gate, and it looked to me as if we were to hear a general harangue.

In that I was not wrong. Only at a distance did I catch sight of Cuthbert Grant, and when our eyes met he left me in no doubt of the enmity he felt for me. At the same time, once or twice, without his being aware of it, I intercepted his glance at Jean—although he did not speak to her, and what I saw left me with an uncomfortable feeling. I could see what Andy Ross had meant now.

When the first convivial preliminaries were over the cooks beat upon pans and summoned us to supper, and only then did I notice that there seemed to be an unusual number of Indians about. Some of them, I learned had come down from the west. The others from up the river, and all, so far as I could see, were being encouraged to drink heavily, which was not a good thing. As nearly as I could tell, they were all Saulteurs, though to my relief Qua-na-Shee-tits did not seem to be among them. One of the Northwesters to whom I talked, perhaps a little indiscreet in his cups, told me that Grant had spent most of the latter part of the winter at Fort Qu'Appelle, and that the girl had gone with him, but that she had been so badly burned about the face and belly by a jealous buck, who in a drunken fit had knocked her across an open fire, that she could not come down.

But these were, so far, no more than stray bits of information that reached my ears. The supper, I will say, was excellent. And this, as I learned, was for a very special reason. The Northmen had put them-selves out to serve us such a feast as we had scarcely known since we arrived in the country. There was barbecued buffalo, cut into steaks, and roast of *biche* and duck and goose. There were potatoes and pease porridge, and succulent young wild greens, cut from the marshes that bordered the river. It was too early for fresh berries, but there were the dried variety, soaked and stewed; and there was as much good wine and rum as anyone of us cared to drink. When it was done, and we were presumed to be gorged to repletion and in a humor to listen, Duncan Cameron mounted the platform that had been raised near the gate and held up his hands.

"My friends!" he cried, and there was a gradual, dying hush as faces turned toward him. "My friends! Ye have come through a hard winter. Yet, truly, there has been naught unusual about it for this part o' th' world. I have watched ye, an' I have sympathized with ye, knowin' th' spirit in which ye came out an' th' hardships which ye have faced without havin' been warned o' 'em. I count ye my friends, each an' every one o' ye!"

He smiled around at us by the light of the flaring torches.

"Now, gentlemen an' ladies!" I squirmed a little, irritated at his repetition of the words in that order. "Ye have been nigh a year among us, more than a year, if ye count from th' time ye came ashore at York an' Churchill. Ye are fitted now t' judge between th' way ye are provided for by the Bay Company an' what ye might expect o' th' Northwesters; between th' lands ye have been granted and the houses ye've been assigned and th' rations that have been allotted ye, and th' good things we are prepared t' give."

There was an uneasy murmur at that. But Cameron held up his hands again.

"Na, na, dinna misunderstand me!" he cried in a brassy attempt to recapture a broad Scots accent that he had long since lost. "I'll say naught wrong o' them save that their ways an' ours are different. I'll admit that what ye've been served here, tonight an' other nights, is party fare an' not t' be compared with th' ordinary. But, mark ye, my friends, will aught that they have offered ye compare with what th' North West Company is prepared t' give—free an' gratis? We will grant, in fee simple, for no more consideration than th' acceptance o' our offer, two hundred acres o' good farm land in Upper Canada an' a full year's provisions, t' each an' every person who will give up his holdin's on th' Red River an' consent t' move east. Furthermore, th' North West Company will agree t' transport all o' ye who will so consent, without th' cost o' a penny t' ye! Ye'll be moved, bag an' baggage from this place t' th' eastern lands o' yer choice, quickly an' in comfort an' without harm or danger t' ye or yours! An' I might add yon's a consideration, for I'll tell ye there is talk this spring o' unrest among th' Crees an' th' Saulteurs, an' both this fort an' yer own are in sore danger o' attack by th' redskins who, I think I've no need t' tell ye, have small regard for women or children.

"Now, I hope ye understand what I am sayin' t' ye: if ye'll but let the North West Company, instead o' th' Bay Company, look after yer interests we'll see that ye profit by it. We'll give ye security for all, where there'll be naught but trouble for those that choose th' other course! Now there's an end o' serious talk. Think o' what I've said. Sleep on it if ye like. Then come an' see me in th' mornin' or when ye're ready, but here's th' time for merrymakin'—enjoy yerselves!"

But to my astonishment Alexander MacLean, beside me, leapt to his feet and called out to him as he was about to turn and step down from the platform. This lean dominie never ceased to surprise me. At one moment he seemed meek and almost woefully lacking in moral conviction; in the next he would be full of fury, showing more strength than any of us. He seemed a bundle of contradictions.

"A moment, Mister Cameron!" he bawled. "How can we know that what ye offer is genuine?"

I could see his point; so, I am sure, could others. But Duncan Cameron held the whip hand. He looked down blandly at the lean preacher.

"Ye have my assurance, Mister MacLean," he said, and his voice was mild but had in it a quality of challenge.

"Aye, but—" Alec began.

"D'ye need better?" Cameron interrupted him, and his voice rose a little, sharply. "Have I ever given ye cause t' doubt me?"

He had us there, no question about it. We, Alec and Jean and a few others, including myself, might have our personal reservations. But we had nothing to prove our fears—only the word of a man who was still a Northwester himself and the cut of whose jaw seemed cleaner to us than Cameron's—while to the majority of our people Duncan Cameron was a restrained and kindly man. He was the one who had acted the good neighbor to us, despite all provocation by our own governor. He had turned the other cheek and come to our church and entertained us at his board, though not once had our own leaders returned the hospitality or even gestured at it. How could they believe otherwise than that here was an honest man, greathearted and without guile, who sought only to help us?

Alec MacLean, prudently, sat down.

As he did so George Campbell leapt to his feet and threw us a sour glance.

"I vote we accept Mister Cameron's offer without further discussin'!" he cried.

But Duncan Cameron, to me at least, gave clear proof of his devious nature. He beamed down at Campbell appreciatively, but at the same time he held up his hand in protest.

"No!" he called. "Let us speak no more o' 't now. I'll ask that ye consider it carefully, not allowin' yerselves t' be carried away by th' heat o' argument. Let common sense rule! Meanwhile let us have a good time."

Common sense may have had a good time that night, though I would say that it would be more accurate to suggest that it was abandoned to all debauch. But some of us slipped away from the party early when it became clear how things were going. Back at the MacLean cabin I glowered.

"What do you make of that?" I demanded.

"It can't be genuine!" Alec MacLean said.

"That's what I think," I replied. "But even if it is we've already pledged our words here. We're honor bound, and I for one would not have it otherwise. But I tell you, Alec, I'm feared for what some of these other poor sheep might do. They're in a mood to follow the first

wether that rings a bell under their noses. I'm going to see the governor in the morning and tell him about this."

"I'll go wi' ye, Malcolm!" Alec MacLean said.

But when we called upon Governor MacDonnell the next day we
found that he had gone upriver with several north canoes to Fort Daer,
at the mouth of the Pembina, for fresh buffalo, and that he would not
be back for a week or ten days.

That was on Thursday. On Thursday evening I stepped from the
door of my cabin, on my way to the woodpile, and noticed that the
ax which I had set carelessly on the step, leaning against the side of
the building, had slipped off onto the ground. I bent down to pick it up,
and but for that small accident must certainly have been transfixed by
the arrow which came whirring through the door.

That, at least, is as nearly as I can guess at it. The arrow must have
been in the air as I leaned down, and sailed silently over my head and
in through the door to plunk into the side of the cabin across from
the opening. I did not hear it, and apparently in the dusk, whoever
shot must have assumed that he had hit me, for evidently he mounted
his horse quickly and rode away; the arrow came from the direction
of the prairie where a man on foot would surely have been noticed
before he could get out of sight.

I replaced the ax and went on to the woodpile and got an armload
of wood, and it was only when I returned that I found the arrow
sticking in the far wall of the cabin, opposite the door. By that time,
of course, he was gone, and obviously whoever had fired the shot had
been lying especially in wait for me.

There was only one answer to that. I plucked the arrow from the
wall and went across to Alec MacLean's where I showed them both
the shaft and told the story. Alec stared at it.

"That's a Cree arrow," he said. "I've noticed 'em."

"I don't know his ancestry," I retorted, "but I know as well as we
are standing here who shot it!"

He stared at me.

"Are ye sure?" he demanded.

"Of course I'm sure," I told him testily, "and the real reason why
I've come over here is to warn you. Be on your guard. You can be
sure I will be!"

But that was only the start of things. That night and Friday and
Friday night a score of our horses and cattle were killed—killed in
the fields by the very same kind of arrow that had been shot at
me!

"Crees!" cried our people. " 'Tis just as Mister Cameron warned us, the Indians are on the warpath."

In vain did we argue that their fears were groundless; that a delegation of the savages, including Tabashaw and Sesai and Aceguamanche and Le Pendu were all at Fort Gibraltar, getting riotously drunk on the Northwesters' high wine every night and remaining so until long after noon every day. They would not listen to us. And when the four chiefs themselves came over on Saturday to visit us, clothed in bright blankets, incredible dignity and even more unbelievable fumes, the rest of our people locked themselves in their houses and barred their shutters and prepared for attack, and only Alec MacLean and Mister MacDonald, our Acting Governor in Miles MacDonnell's absence, and myself were at hand to meet them.

They sat down, as we invited them, on the floor, in a semicircle before the big fire at the Post, and Aceguamanche produced from under his blanket the long, feather-decorated, pipestone pipe of peace that was ceremonial among them. With much care he filled it, took four long puffs, blowing the smoke to north, south, east and west, and then passed the pipe to me. I followed his example and passed the pipe along. When each one of us had smoked he spoke.

"Cameron Bourgeois, the chief of the Northwesters," he said carefully, "is not to be trusted. For this full moon we have been at Fort Gibraltar, and each day he has given us liquor and urged us to rise against the white men who have dared to put cabins on the Red. We have refused."

"Then you did not shoot our cows and our horses yesterday?" MacLean demanded.

The old chief looked at him blankly. From his eyes you could not tell whether he knew of it or not, but I was ready to swear that he had no hand in it.

"You have lost some?" he asked.

Alec nodded. Aceguamanche shook his head.

"It was not our people!" he stated flatly, and then I was sure, for even in such a short time I had learned that it was not the habit of Indians to lie directly. If they wished to deceive you they would look for some roundabout means. "I think it must have been the *Boisbrûlés*. Cameron Bourgeois has been talking to them, too, and there are some evil men among them!"

"Is this why you have come to see us?" Mister MacDonald asked.

The chief bowed gravely.

"This is why we have come," he said. "We want you to know that

Cameron Bourgeois has asked us to attack you, but we have refused. Now there is no more rum we will not stay longer and listen to his arguments. We will go, but we wish to smoke with you the pipe of peace and if we could fight with the Northwestmen we would join you, but we are not strong enough. We want you to know that we, the Crees and the Saulteurs both, like to see all white men come into our country, for it means rum and much trade for our people. When good white men come to stay it is better. There is not so much war. But Cameron Bourgeois is an evil man, and he would send white man to fight against white man or red man to fight against all, and we want you to send him away and bring other men to rule the North West Company here, where the rum is given to us!"

His argument showed clearly his utter confusion of the functions of Northwesters and Company men. But it showed, too, much of what had been happening in Fort Gibraltar. When they were gone MacDonald looked round at us.

"Trouble!" he said. " 'Tis comin', mark me an' prepare yerselves!"

Yet we decided that there could be no open argument or discussion of the matter until Governor MacDonnell returned. We crossed our fingers, you might say, and hoped for the best.

But on Sunday, the very following day two things happened: seemingly unrelated events, and yet, I am sure, bound up together. In the early morning I happened to see as I stepped out to my necessary house, a Northwest half-canoe pass swiftly upstream toward Fort Gibraltar.

Since it was early and the time of their passing indicated that they had paddled all night and therefore must be carrying despatches, I guessed that they must bear letters for Duncan Cameron. But even so, I gave it little thought beyond the reflection that they must be urgent. Then, that afternoon, even as usual Cameron himself came to church with us. But this time he seemed strained, curt. His nod and good day to the rest of us was perfunctory. But I noticed that he drew George Campbell aside, after the service was done, though what passed between them I do not know.

On Tuesday we drew our rations for the month; and that midday we went up for them, every man in the colony fetching his own means of transportation and his card to show that he was entitled to what he drew. Archibald MacDonald was in charge of the apportionment, and few of us noticed when George Campbell stepped up to him and handed him a folded paper. MacDonald, busy at the moment, thrust it in his pocket, and George Campbell stepped back into line and save for one or two—I was not one, I must confess—no one noticed the occurrence.

But an hour later, when George Campbell and a score of men—all from our own colony—surged forward, and demanded the keys to the storehouse, where the spare gunpowder and guns were kept, we remembered it. Slowly Archibald MacDonald reached into his pocket and brought out the paper. He unfolded it and began to read aloud:

SIR:

As your field pieces have already been employed to disturb the peace of His Majesty's loyal subjects in the quarter, and even to stop up the King's Highway, I have authorized the settlers to take possession of them and bring them over here, not with a view to making any hostile use of them but merely to put them out of harm's way. Therefore I expect that you will not be so wanting to yourselves as to attempt any useless resistance, as no one wishes you, or any of your people, any harm.

I am Sir
Your very obedient servant,
D. CAMERON

Capt. Voyageur Corps,
Commanding Officer,
Red River

"What—" I began.

But as I spoke Alan Laughlin, a great hulk of a fellow, who, I realize now, had been stationed there for the express purpose of silencing me if necessary, turned and crashed his fist against my jaw.

When I woke the thing was done. The warehouse had been broken open by our own people, and the guns and all of the powder and shot that they could find had been carried away. Duncan Cameron had evidently been hiding close at hand with men to assist George Campbell if necessary, for the stuff was hardly loaded on the carts when he and his force appeared.

"Well done, my hearty fellows!" he said, and that is a matter of record.

We were fortunate in one respect, however, we still had a small stock of powder hidden away at the factor's house. And there were additional supplies in the fort's magazine, and the two small swivels which they were unable to take. Such shot as we had was no more than was necessary for our muskets. But there was a variety of old scrap: chains, bolts, nuts, iron bars and rusty nails with which the guns could be loaded. Mister MacDonald and I, consulting on the situation, felt that if it came to a real battle we could give a good account of ourselves. We promptly buried the guns in an accessible place, and what powder and shot we could find we hid.

But Duncan Cameron's stroke, I think, worked against him for the moment. It was meant, of course, for a show of force. But it turned out to be only a show of force intended, and our people were not the sort to react kindly to such pressure if it could be helped. The delay that resulted was a blessed one for us.

But it was only a small delay. As soon as Governor MacDonnell returned, Captain Cameron, as he called himself, who had mounted the seized guns on the walls of Fort Gibraltar, sent down a demand for the arrest and surrender of our governor, claiming that he had a warrant for such action, and that it had been issued by the Canadian government.

Even in that, it seemed to me, the deviousness of the man was apparent. He did not show us his alleged warrant, and how were we to prove whether he did or did not have it? We argued. Governor MacDonnell called a general meeting of all of the settlers at the church, and the session was long and quarrelsome. MacDonnell, of course, was flatly against any surrender.

"If th' popinjay wants war," he growled, "let him have it. He can't whip us if we hang t'gether!"

But the other element, spearheaded by George Campbell, dissented.

"What have we had," they said, "of the fine things that were promised us by Lord Selkirk? Naught but hardship, as ye well know! This land is not fit for human habitation. There is nothing here but hard labor and a worse living than we had in the old country!"

I reminded them that they had no living in the old country; that they were being evicted, willy-nilly, while here they at least had land of their own, to make of what they could.

"Aye!" George Campbell retorted. "But th' Nor' West Company offers us more an' better land, an' nigher, too, t' civilization."

I could not deny that. I could argue whether or not the land that they offered was any better than this, which I knew—and they did too—was as fine as any to be found.

"I for one," I ended my argument, "will not be forced out by a group that seeks control of this place for its own selfish purpose! Let any that agree with me stand over this way!"

It was a pitiful showing that responded to my plea. The MacLeans and Rab Gunn, the piper, and forty or fifty others joined me. The rest—some hundred and fifty of them—harkened to George Campbell and his blandishments, and signed the petition which he brought, addressed to Duncan Cameron, placing themselves at the mercy of the Northwesters.

Miles MacDonnell watched and listened, after that first blast of defiance, without saying anything until the thing was done and the majority were gone.

"Let 'em go," he said then. "We're better off without that kind! I thank ye for yer support, Mister MacAllister an' Mister MacLean an' all th' rest o' ye!"

But it was not as simple as that. Alec hoped that would be an end of it, but Duncan Cameron was not content. He insisted that Miles MacDonnell be arrested and taken to Montreal for trial. George Campbell and a score of others of his ilk had already abandoned their cabins in the colony and gone to Fort Gibraltar to live until such time as the North West Company's brigade would evacuate them. Toward midweek I stepped out of my cabin about dusk and went to the wood-pile to replenish my day's supply, as was my custom. As was my custom, too, since the episode of the arrow, I went armed, with my musket under my elbow. I was just loading the long logs in my arm, when through the gloom I saw a figure skulking near the rear of the MacLean cabin. In the gloaming it was impossible to identify the man for certain, although I was sure it was Cuthbert Grant, and I dropped my wood and flung up my gun and sent a shot of warning clattering through the trees after him.

In that light, of course, I did not hit him. But the prowler quickly sped away. The next morning Duncan Cameron and a full hundred men, George Campbell was one of them, fetched over field pieces and disposed them so as to batter down the walls of the governor's house. They did not fire, but Cameron sent in an ultimatum: Either Miles MacDonnell must surrender himself or he, the military commandant of the district, as he still claimed himself to be, would batter down the post. Further, if there was resistance he would destroy the entire settlement.

There were those among us who would have fought as long as we were able: notably MacIntosh, Currie, MacDonald, John MacKay, Magnus Isbister and Alec MacLean and myself. But Miles MacDonnell came forward.

"We'll ha' but bloodshed if we do," he said. "For th' sake o' ye who remain I'll gi'e myself up if Mister Cameron'll pledge his word t' a fair shake an' an honest trial."

"You cannot!" I cried. "Mister MacDonnell, you must not!"

He swung his head around toward me ponderously.

"I thank ye, Mister MacAllister," he said, "for that expression o' yer confidence. But 'twill be better so. I'll be back, mark me! In th' meantime ye ha' but t' maintain things here in th' best order possible."

Archibald MacDonald elected to go with him, since he felt it his responsibility, so that I found myself appointed governor pro tem. The two men walked out and surrendered themselves, after receiving Duncan Cameron's assurance that they would be treated as gentlemen. Yet notwithstanding his pledged word the big, florid man had them at once clapped in irons, with both arm and leg manacles, so that they were scarcely able to walk, and it was with bitter, helpless fury that we saw them the next day, when the Northwest canoes came down to take on board all those that had agreed to go, flung incontinently across the packs in the middle of one of the boats.

One hundred and forty of our people left us at that time, placing their faith in Duncan Cameron's promise, though I never heard that any but a few—who were rewarded for their treachery—ever got all that they were offered. Some forty odd of us remained in the grim, echoing, ghostly village.

I tell all this primarily as a matter of history, as may have been observed, so that the ultimate thread of our story may be followed. But a far more personal theme underlies it. It was late May or early June when this happened, and the brigades had come down from Fort Qu'Appelle, bringing with them Alexander MacDonnell, who took Duncan Cameron's place at Fort Gibraltar, as well as an unknown number of his *Boisbrûlé* henchmen. But there was as yet no sign of the Alexandria brigade and Andy Ross. I recall that I spoke of it to Jean MacLean and her father.

"Where are they?" I said. "If he had been here, at least things might have been done differently."

Jean shrugged.

"Mister Ross is a Northwester, isn't he?" she said bitterly.

I stared at her, perhaps with too much of a lift to my heart.

"Aye," I said. "He is. But I think him an honest one, and I still feel that if he had been here things might have been done differently!"

"He'll be along in a day 'r two," her father put in. "But I can't see that it makes any difference now."

"Just the same," I told him, "if I knew where to find Aceguamanche or one of his Indians I'd send him a message. I don't like the look of things!"

"If Aceguamanche could get up th' Assiniboine," MacLean pointed out dourly, "Ross could get down."

Which was no doubt perfectly true. But Andy Ross did not arrive in a day or two, and my grim fears proved well grounded. Nor were our Indian friends anywhere to be found.

But there was work, and plenty of it, to be done by those settlers that remained. We had not only our own fields to prepare and seed, but also those of all who had gone. Their cabins might stand empty, but there was a supply of seed for all and their fields stood ready. No more than a score of men remained among us. All the rest were women and children. And it was up to the men to sow down the prepared acres.

We did it, starting down at Frog Plain, and working up the long rows of the lots, marching in line, each man with a sack of wheat slung at his belly. I don't know why, but during this process we were not molested. The seed was planted and harrowed in, although later events proved to us clearly that Alexander MacDonnell did not mean to leave us in peace. Twice we found our fence rows broken down in the night and fields trampled. But fortunately nothing had been planted there.

I suppose our enemies were biding their time, waiting until the seeding was done, figuring that then their destruction would be the more disheartening to us. At any rate, that was the pattern they followed. They must have been watching us, and known when the work was done. For we had no more than sown our last handful and gone to bed than the troubles began. When we rose in the morning we found that more than a score of our fences had been laid flat, our stock scattered, and horses ridden over the newly planted fields. We repaired the damage, raked the ground with brush drags and patiently went out to find our wandering cattle. The next night the same thing happened at other places. We posted guards. But there were not enough of us to watch them all, and they broke in where we could not see, striking swiftly and suddenly and then disappearing into the night. Once we caught a glimpse of gray, ghostly, phantom riders and sent a fusillade of shots after them. But I do not think we hit any.

The beginning of the end came when the parsonage and schoolhouse lots were broken into and trampled. I must say that I had been expecting it, for with their crooked line of trees running through them they were the easiest for marauders to attack. Alec and I were out working on them, the morning after it had happened, when we heard a woman scream from the direction of the houses. We dropped our hoes and ran, looking to the priming of our muskets as we went and not caring that we ourselves were trampling the new seeded ground, each of us, I know, obsessed with the notion that it could only have been Jean who had cried out. There were no other women near enough for us to hear.

I was younger and had longer legs and was the faster runner so that I was the first to arrive. I met Jean flying from the cabin, already halfway past the church, sobbing as she stumbled toward us. She saw me coming and swerved toward me, half in hysterics and with tears streaming down her face, and flung herself into my protecting arms and clung to me, and for one long, sweet moment I held her to me, trying to comfort her.

She had been badly frightened. There was no question about it. Her father came up and looked slightly embarrassed to find me kissing her hair. But it was no time for embarrassment. Between us we gradually managed to reassure her, though at first all she could manage, between great gulping sobs, were the two words, repeated over and over:

"Cuthbert Grant—Cuthbert Grant!"

"What! Where is he? What did he do?" I demanded furiously.

"He—he—he's gone now," she sobbed. "I—I threw boiling lye at him!"

Gradually, as we calmed her, we drew the story from her. Grant had slipped up behind the cabin, obviously knowing that Alec and I were at work in the fields. Fortunately Jeannie had been out in the front yard, trying out lye from wood ashes in a large kettle from which to make soap. The first she had known of his presence was when he slipped up behind her, on his silent Indian feet, and seized her in his arms.

Jean had a long, iron ladle in her hand, with which she had been stirring the messy, bubbling mixture, and instinctively she turned and flung the contents of it at his face. Unfortunately it did not catch him full on, but spattered his cheek and neck. The sudden, unexpected pain forced him to duck and turn away for an instant, and then her screams for us warned him that help was not far away. He turned and fled, and of course he was well beyond our reach by the time we got there. But I believe that had I been able to find him then I would have shot him like the beast he was!

We called an immediate meeting of the colonists, of course. Clearly the Northwesters were growing overbold, and were massing for an attack. Several of their brigades had come into Fort Gibraltar, Mouse River and Portage la Prairie and Sand Lake. But we heard nothing of the Alexandria brigade. We decided that it was time for us to take all such steps as we might. Our womenfolk and children and the stock that could be accommodated and everything else that seemed essential to be preserved and that could be moved were sent up to the fort, and all the men were turned to and set to work, ditching and building bastions and racing to complete the hitherto unnecessary palisades. The two tiny, rusty swivel guns were dug out and set up in the smithy, where there seemed to be more possible ammunition than any other place. Kegs of rusted nails and nuts and bolts were placed handy, and old links of trace chains were cut up to make a deadly load. From that place, too, we had a clearer field of fire than from the little fort, if it came to that, and we could cover both the prairie approaches and the path that led up from the landing and passed between the store and the governor's house. A *guetteur*—or lookout—was, of course, stationed in the watchtower, and each man among us was assigned his proper turn.

Nothing further happened that day, and at least we were able to put ourselves in some sort of position for defense. That night, however, the lookout rang us out with the alarm bell, saying that he had thought he detected gray shadows prowling near the edge of the trees, over toward the parsonage. I remember that we laughed at him, it was Pat Corcoran, and told him that he saw a windigo. But half an hour later a glow showed dim, and then brighter, and then became towering, licking flames, rising from the church, the parsonage and the schoolhouse.

I would have sallied out, I think, even singlehanded, to seek out the devils of hell that would have done such a thing. But fortunately cooler heads than mine prevailed. As Alec MacLean said grimly, obviously there was nothing we could do then to check the fires. It was quite evident that they had been well and deliberately set in several places, so that no stick of the places we had called home would remain, and by now they were all a mass of flames, spectacular, though I must say to me a sorry sight. By that one stroke I lost all that I had except the clothes I stood in and the musket in my hands: books that I had treasured carefully and brought across the snow from Churchill —books that were little enough in themselves but in this place were irreplaceable; and, of course, there was everything else I owned.

The MacLeans, to be sure, were in the same case, and as I looked at him that night, by the reflected glow of the flames, I think that I was even more sorry for Alec than I was for Jean. Jean's life lay ahead. The loss of material possessions now, while undoubtedly it hurt, would pass and other possessions would take their place. But Alec looked as if all his hopes and all his will to build a new life in this new land were going up in that smoke! He stood upon the watchtower, with the little group of us that gathered there, and though he spoke to restrain me from any rash sally, yet I could see the pain and despair that was written plain upon his face.

But he was right. There was not a thing that we could do, and Doctor White, the surgeon who had replaced Peter LaSerre, pointed out that we were not strong enough to divide our forces, and if we all went who would be left to defend our helpless ones: the women and the children and the old folk? In fact, he pointed out, that was probably exactly what our opponents wanted. Once we rushed out the way would be clear for them to step in and seize our base. We must not allow ourselves to be so trapped!

He was right, of course. So was Alec. But I can remember sitting all through that night, watching first the flaring flames and then the dying glow of the embers through the trees. When daylight came a half dozen of us, well armed and ready to shoot at anything that moved, went out to see what could be saved. But everything was gone. I think the marauders had even broken in first and carried away every-thing noninflammable that might have been salvaged afterward. All of the fences toward Frog Plain—well out of gunshot from the fort —had been laid flat, and the fields themselves were crisscrossed with tracks, this way and that and back again. Almost worst of all, Hector MacEachern's bull, the only one in the colony, had been slaughtered and quartered in its pasture and the entrails strewn around upon the ground to show what had happened. As a gesture of defiance by the raiders the animal's pizzle had been cut off and flung into the road-way, not far from the fort, at a spot where they knew we would find it!

As we were about these investigations the alarm bell at the fort began to toll, and we turned about and hastened back. When we approached a few scattered riders broke from the cover of the trees not far from the yet unfinished palisade and went pelting off in the direction of Fort Gibraltar. But though we flung a few shots after them they were running too fast and lying too low along their mounts' necks for our ragged volley to have any effect. When we reached the fort we found that James White, the surgeon, in passing in front of the governor's house, had been fired upon, while John Bourke, the storekeeper, going out of the back of the store to the necessary house to relieve himself, had only ducked into the little building in time to miss a bullet in the head. Indeed, so close was that shot that he had heard the whine of the bullet before he heard the crack of the musket, and although we, at a distance, had not heard the shots there was a bullet hole in the logs of the governor's residence and an ugly splinter torn from the lintel of the necessary to prove their story.

One thing, at least, seemed obvious from this: That the enemy was growing bolder and whipping himself up to an attack that would be open. We took steps accordingly. The women and children were sent into the stockaded portion of the fort, and warned that they must, under no circumstances, show themselves. Those of us who had been told off as gun crews—myself included—were sent to the smithy, where a swivel was mounted to point either way and loaded to the muzzle with deadly, jagged scrap. The watch was doubled, and musketmen were placed about in spots where it seemed they might do the most damage with the least exposure to themselves.

Our guess proved correct. It was not yet noon when the lookout sang down to us that a body of horsemen, some seventy or eighty strong, were marching out from Fort Gibraltar. A group on foot numbering twenty or thirty followed. They came down toward us, and then when they were yet a quarter of a mile away the men on foot scattered and went down into the trees along the river. The horsemen, who seemed to be all Brûlés, turned out toward the prairies and made a wide circle and disappeared at length amid the upper brush along Parsonage Creek.

Apparently they hoped by this to create some kind of a diversion, for the first volley that they fired came from the men afoot, from the direction of the river. But on that side, at least, our palisade had been completed, and the shots smacked harmlessly into the logs. Our men in that corner, of course, returned the fire, but since they could not see what they were shooting at amid the trees I doubt if anyone was hit. At almost the same time—an instant or two afterward, as if to catch us off our balance—the horsemen, who had tethered their mounts in the woods along the creek burst forth and attempted to charge.

I do not think they knew we had the swivels, and if we had waited I daresay we might have done some damage among them. But we were not soldiers, and we had not been trained for this sort of thing. I think that the guns were pointed a little high, but their thunder and the ugly whining scream of our improvised langrage did as much as an actual hit would have accomplished. The men before us went down on their bellies first, and then on all fours turned about and went scrambling and zigzagging back to the shelter of the trees.

The sound of our small cannon, too, apparently gave pause to our attackers along the river. They took shelter behind logs and tree trunks and sent several scattered volleys in our direction. We answered in kind, of course, but it is hard to hit anything if you don't know what you are shooting at or where it is! I have heard it said since, and I think it is probably true, that we did not even so much as pink one of them. When they found that we were ready and willing to fight, they drew off and went back to their own fort. But counting noses afterwards we found that four lucky shots found lodging among us. Daniel Lillie had a bullet in the shoulder. Lucas Bethune's scalp had been burned, fortunately not deeply. Joseph Muir's arm had been torn from wrist to elbow. And Warren Tate had been shot through the left side of his chest. He died, but only later that night after surgeon White had made a heroic effort to save him.

That was a gloomy afternoon and evening, I think I hardly need say. When the *Boisbrûlés,* for from their horses and their way of fighting I am sure it was they, had withdrawn we moved into the palisaded part of the fort and set up our swivels on the roof of the building, where they could cover every quarter. Yet here was a dreadful thing. No one said it in so many words, but the thought, I think, was uppermost in all our minds—we could not hold out indefinitely. For myself, I was quite willing now, even almost bitterly anxious, to stay and fling my little vengeance against those who had wronged me. That, of course, was the personal side. But there were all the others to consider—especially Jean and her father, whom I had urged to come out into all this. It was bad enough that they should lose all that they had worked for and managed to save and scratch and scrape together. But now they stood in danger of their very lives. So did all of these people—it hit me suddenly; and I had persuaded most of them to join us. Their lives, their hearts, to them, to someone, were as precious and cherished as were Jean's and Alec's to me. Yet here I was responsible for all this mess!

There was no time during the afternoon for anything but defense, and we made our dispositions as best we could. But after supper there was a general meeting which I could not attend since mine was the watch from six to midnight. Jean brought my supper up to me in the tower: half a pound of pemmican, a canister of tea and a buffalo steak broiled. I don't think I even remembered to thank her, though it was in my heart.

"Where the devil is Ross?" I growled petulantly. "I can't believe that he's in on this thing!"

"He's a Northwester isn't he?" she retorted stiffly.

"Yes, but still he wouldn't lend himself to this," I retorted. "I think he'd do something to stop it!"

She turned to me abruptly, with eyes wide, and I had the feeling that she was going to say something that she did not. Then she turned away, almost bitterly, and stared out across the plain to where we could see the lights of Fort Gibraltar.

"I—I don't know!" she said. "Have they moved? Have you seen anything?"

I shook my head. I was hungry and the buffalo steak tasted fine.

"No," I told her. "I don't think they'll do anything now for a while. They're probably all getting decently drunk. It's a custom of the country!"

She swung toward me sharply.

"Malcolm!" she cried. "It's not the country. You know that. He—"

When she stopped I did not pick up her thought. I had other things on my mind.

"What's going on down below?" I demanded between bites.

She did not answer at once, but seemed to be fighting something within herself. She drew a long breath.

"They're going to quit, to give it up," she told me. "If they can get out."

"Sensible!" I mumbled through the steak. "We can't go on like this. There aren't enough of us to fight the whole North West Company. And they seem determined to be rid of us. We'll just have to pull back until Lord Selkirk can get enough people out here to stand against 'em."

"You—you're not taking their part?" she cried.

"Certainly not!" I retorted. "It's just that in the circumstances I don't see what else we can do. Those chaps aren't fooling, and with our little handful, soon or late, they'll wipe us out. With the traders—the Company men, now—Currie and Isbister and MacIntosh, it's different. They don't mind that sort of competition. It's just when they think that there's something here that may destroy their trade completely—like us, people with ploughs, folk with homes to make and lots to fence off, one from the other—that they are roused and start to fight."

"But they can't—they can't always, do you think, Malcolm?" she cried.

"No, of course they can't!" I replied. "They can't hold out always against people that are going to keep on coming in spite of them. They can't hold a country like this forever wild and deny people—not only little people like you and me, but people who make up the nations of the world—the right of entry. Sooner or later we'll win. But in the meantime we'll have our setbacks and our defeats and we'll have to take 'em."

I don't know why I said that. The thought must have been boiling around inside of me, although I hadn't put it in words, even to myself, before then.

She stared at me in the moonglow.

"Ye've changed, Malcolm!" she said softly.

"Have I then?" I demanded gruffly, embarrassed.

"Aye, so!" she replied. "Ye were not like this before. I mind ye told me that ye doubted th' thing could be done. Ye e'en wondered if Lord Selkirk were sincere, an' as for th' folk that came out wi' us, ye said 'twas their own risk!"

"Well, there's no need to rub it in," I growled.

"I'm not rubbing it in, Malcolm!" I thought she smiled slightly, though in that faint light there was no way of telling. "I'm only re-markin' on it—that 'tis curious, I mean."

"Is it?" I said. "I'm not so sure. I got them into it, not half sure then that 'twas all aboveboard, and not so much caring. 'Twas my own doing! But now we're here and there are those among us are more than half convinced 'twas all a hoax. I'll tell you Jean, I've turned about and seen it as it is—an honest effort on Lord Selkirk's part to help such folk as we. And if we will not stand by and help him when the battle grows rough, then how is he ever to succeed?"

She looked confused.

"But ye just said that we should all be goin'!" she protested.

"Aye!" I nodded. "Is that strange? I said that you should. But I'm trying to tell you, too, that some one of us should stay and look after Lord Selkirk's interests. Someone must remain to keep the claims of all in force legally and hold them until reinforcements can come out from Lord Selkirk, and those of our own people who're willing to can come back. Since I'm responsible I think I should be the one to stay. I'll not shirk it."

In the half-dark I could not read her expression.

"But, Malcolm," she protested. "What good will that do?"

"Who can tell?" I demanded petulantly. I could not tell her that I scarcely knew myself. " 'Tis just that I think I should."

She looked at me soberly.

"Is that what ye'd like me to tell 'em below?" she asked.

"If you wish!" I shrugged. " 'Tis what I mean to do!"

She turned away and went to the top of the ladder, where it led down to the lower level. There she paused and turned to look back at me through the night.

"I—I wish ye'd let me see this part o' ye before, Malcolm," she said. "It might ha' made a difference."

"Would it?" I said. "I didn't know it myself until now!"

She made an odd little, half-despairing gesture, as if she would reach out for me, and then seemed to think better of it and shrugged in the gloaming and stepped below.

When she was gone I locked my hands behind me and glowered out across the moonlit prairie toward the low, sprawling bulk of Fort Gibraltar. It was ironical, I thought, that now that it was too late all of the things that I had hoped and sought for should be all at once within my grasp; for I would not delude myself, my whole hope and reason for being here was Jean. Until this moment she had left me uncertain. But now, when I had only to open my arms for her to come into them, I could not! Why was that, I wondered. Why shouldn't I just give it all up and go down the river with them, as she had suggested they would? Why should I stay here, on the field of the dead, so to speak, and try to be the one and only one to hold?

On the face of it it seemed a stupid gallant gesture. In a matter of weeks we could be at York Factory, where Alec could marry us. After that it would be merely a case of waiting for the ships from Scotland to carry us back to the Old World and shake the dust of Canada from our heels forever. Perhaps, indeed, the ships would still be there in Hudson's Bay when we arrived, and we'd not even have to wait a winter for them!

Yet somehow, only the thought alone was repugnant to me, and I felt instinctively that it would be so to her. I turned and stared down toward the dark line of trees that marked the Parsonage Creek, and the place where my own schoolhouse and cabin had been only the day before. Within me I felt the fury rise as I did so. What right had they to destroy it? To tear down and smash and defile the only real home I had ever known? They had set torch to it, and I was sure they had laughed as they had watched it burn. But, damn them, I told myself, there would be another school and another house in the place of the one they had destroyed—an even better one, that would help bring people into this land that would know how best to make use of it. They would be folk who would not just get red men drunk and debauch the Indian women merely to barter for furs and kill the buffalo! Their children would come here to grow up free men and women. They would till the soil and build their homes and own their lands and would not knuckle under to any lord or combination of them, be they real or commercial.

But where would my students come from? The one thought led me logically to the next. If our own folk left would they be the ones to come back? Apart from Jean and her father, I found, it did not greatly seem to matter. If it were not they then it would be others. There would be no halting the tide I envisioned, and clearly there must be someone here to hold the land for them! So far as Jean and Alec were concerned, it was wisdom that they should go out with the rest. Someone, and Alec was the logical man, must keep their faith and their spirits up on the outward journey; and as for Jean she was safer away than here! When Magnus Isbister relieved me at midnight I knew what I must do.

I climbed down to the main assembly room and there found a half dozen or so of our stoutest men yet huddled in argument about the fire. As I joined them Alec MacLean looked up. There was an almost beaten air about him, which I could understand. He had as much of himself in his kirk and his parsonage as I had had in my school, I realized.

"What d'ye think, Malcolm?" he asked. "We've about come t' th' notion that there's nae stayin' here."

I accepted the cup of rum that James MacIntosh thrust into my hand without looking at it.

"Aye!" I said. "In the circumstances there's not much else you can do, if you can make it. There are the women and the bairns to be considered, and they're not safe here. Go—and come back later, if you're able, when all this is settled! But go now!"

He looked at me.

"Ye sound as if ye'd no be comin' wi' us," he said.

"I shan't," I replied and glanced around the ring of interested faces. "Mister MacIntosh?"

The factor grinned.

"I'm a Company man," he said. "They'll no be botherin' me. I'm stayin'."

I looked at Archibald Currie.

"What about you?" I asked.

"Och, I'm in th' same canoe!" he replied.

"And Isbister?"

"He'll stay," James MacIntosh said.

"That's four of us then," I told him. "I've no ties, and as Lord Selkirk's agent here I think I'd better stay on hand!"

"I ought to stay," Alec MacLean put in.

"Nonsense, man!" I retorted. "You've Jean to think about!"

I could feel myself flush as I said that, and I hastily turned the subject.

"We've some canoes, but not enough for all," I said, "and you should have an escort!"

That problem was solved for us the next morning when a light canoe swung in to our landing and two Indians stepped out of it. They came directly up the path—that same path by which we had first climbed to the Red River plain—and I, who was back again on duty in the tower, studied them as they came. One was barrel-bodied, bandy-legged, the color of weathered mahogany. I did not know him. But the other, who was tall and dignified and carried himself with ineffable pride, was Aceguamanche. I quickly called my relief and went down to greet them.

"*Bo' jou',*" said Aceguamanche. "This Katawabetay, of Sand Lake Sau'too—strong chief with his people."

I could see that the Cree did not think much of the Saulteurs and was a little impatient. It seemed to me that we had more pressing problems at the moment, but it was wise not to antagonize them.

"*Bo' jou',*" I said. "You come in, eat breakfast, have rum, then MacIntosh Bourgeois make trade."

"Not come for trade," Aceguamanche said. "Come for talk with you. You nearest big chief now MacDonnell Bourgeois gone away."

"You flatter me!" I said. "But come in. What's worrying you?"

I think I feared some sort of Indian ultimatum, backing up the stand the Northwesters had taken, despite what Aceguamanche had said to us some time before. After all if strong pressure were brought to bear upon the Indians they would have little more choice than ourselves, I reasoned.

But there, apparently, I was wrong. After we had gone through the ceremony of the pipe and eaten breakfast and brought out a cask of high wine for them to take back to their camp, it appeared that pressure had been brought but they had resisted.

"Excuse me," said the barrel-bellied Katawabetay, in English far more refined than my own rough Scots. "If you will allow me, I will tell our story. Some time ago a number of agents of the North West Company came to me and urged me to send my young men on the warpath against the settlers at Red River, this place. I said that I wished to know if this was the desire of the government before I did so, and that when I learned that I would act as they wished. The government has evaded my question, and so I think this is a private fight in which I do not wish my people to take part. I have consulted with my friends, the Crees, through Aceguamanche, and they confirm what I have thought. Two days ago we came down to Fort Gibraltar to say let us have peace. Red men should not fight red men, unless they are savages—as some are, and white men should not fight white —though it is not long since they did. Neither should the red men fight the whites."

"That is true," I told him. "We wish only peace, but we have not been allowed to have it."

"We understand," he nodded. "Since we came to Fort Gibraltar we have been offered much rum and asked to fight against the people at Fort Douglas. This we do not understand, for we have watched the settlers at Fort Douglas and we like what you do. We have asked MacDonnell Bourgeois, who is in charge at Fort Gibraltar while Cameron Bourgeois is away, not to fight with you. But he is much influenced by *Boisbrûlés,* who are bad people, and he will not listen. Yesterday there was war. Today, who can tell? They have evil plans."

"Would you fight beside us against the Northwestmen?" I demanded.

He shook his head.

"We do not want war," he replied. "But even if we did we would not be able to fight against them. They are very strong, with many guns that they have taken from you, and it is useless to fight against cannon."

"I understand you, Katawabetay," I said. "We have already planned to leave, all but a few men who will look after the fort and carry on business for the Hudson's Bay Company. But we have not enough canoes, and we are afraid of our enemies—that they will not let us go."

The two Indians looked grave. Katawabetay sucked at the pipe again and passed it to Aceguamanche.

"I understand," he said again. "This MacDonnell Bourgeois is not a reasonable man. We have asked him to make peace, but all he wants is war, white man against white man. We have forty warriors camped at the mouth of Rivière la Sale, and many canoes. If you will accept these, for the sake of peace, our warriors will escort your people to Lake Winnipeg and beyond the reach of this evil man. My daughter,

Qua-na-Shee-tits, asks this and she has reason. For her I would make this offer even if I did not wish peace!"

It was news to me that Qua-na-Shee-tits was his daughter, and I must admit that I did not quite see how she came into the picture. But I was certainly not one to go about examining the mouths of gift horses!

"We will be happy to accept, Katawabetay," I said. And so at last it was arranged.

A sudden thought occurred to me. These two might know.

"Tell me," I said, "has the Northwest brigade from Alexandria come down yet?"

Katawabetay glanced at Aceguamanche.

"Your people will know more of that than mine," he said.

Aceguamanche shook his head.

"*En haut* it is bad this year," he said. "Because of deep snow is no game. Many people die of cold and starving and windigo has walked. Then, when spring comes there is fire—bad fire over all prairie—which drives away the buffalo because there is no feed. The red one —he who is called Ross—at Fort Alexandria, he has stay to see that meat is found for his people. He has not come down yet."

"They'll be down soon?" I said blandly.

He shrugged.

"Soon I think, if the buffalo return," he replied. "If they do not come soon I think the Fort Gibraltar Brigades will go on to Fort William and leave him to follow."

That was an answer to something that had puzzled us. I thought Jean would be glad to have that piece of news, although I was strangely reluctant to pass it on to her.

Our Indians departed after the interview and came back, with all the men and canoes that they had promised, toward noon. Together with the craft that we could provide from our canoe sheds there was ample room, even for a double load of belongings for those settlers who wished to take it.

I will not say it was a cheerful moment. I walked down to the landing with Jean and her father and saw their gear stowed, realizing then that I should have taken her in my arms the night before on the lonely, deserted, moonlit platform of the lookout tower. All the things that were inside me now, battering at my teeth, crying to be said, could not be uttered in that milling group. When it came time for parting I could only take her hand in mine and beam down at her fatuously.

"Jean," I said.

"What is it, Malcolm?" she asked.

"You—you're going to York."

"I suppose so." She seemed surprised, as if she had not thought very much about anything except that they were going.

"If—if you should go beyond—I mean if you should decide to go back to Scotland with the supply ship," I stammered, "will you write to me? Let me know what the trip was like, that you're safe and—and all?"

"I will, Malcolm," she promised.

"Au canot!" the bourgeois of the fleet bellowed, and there was no time then to do much more than hand her down into the craft.

"You will write, Jean?" I reminded her.

"I will truly, Malcolm," she repeated.

"Send it through York," I told her. "It may take a little while, but it will find me."

"And you will write me the news of—of how things are here, Malcolm," she said.

I nodded. They were already shoving off, swinging into the stream.

"By the way!" I cupped my hands about my mouth and called after her. "Aceguamanche tells me that the Alexandria brigade has not yet come down, so Andy Ross is not involved in this business!"

I don't know why I said it. I hadn't meant to, hadn't even thought of it in fact. But there is no doubt that she heard me. From midstream she turned about and stared at me with an expression that was a mixture of panic and surprise and pleasure all at once. Then she shouted something back, but the canoe was too far away and I could not hear it. I waved, but she sat like a figure turned to stone and did not wave again, though I could see that she was looking back at me.

As long as the canoes remained in sight I stayed on the landing. When the last of them had gone, sweeping off swiftly, down around the bend, I turned and went back heavily, up the path to the little fort and the cluster of log buildings at the top. James MacIntosh and Magnus Isbister were in the little smithy, cutting up bits of chain to use for shot.

"Weel, laddie me buck," MacIntosh grinned, "maybe we'll have tae stand off a siege just th' four o' us. Can ye manage one o' they?"

He nodded toward the swivels, which he had fetched back to the shadows where they would be hidden, so that any sudden, stealthy raiders that might take us by surprise would have difficulty finding them.

"Those? Oh, aye!" I said listlessly. "I daresay I can do it as well as the next."

" 'Tis amazin' th' things a man can learn when he must," Magnus Isbister remarked dourly.

Facetious as the words were meant to be, they, more than anything that had happened, I think, brought home to me, suddenly and forcefully, the complete, the utter, the overwhelming isolation of our situation.

4. THE *VOYAGEURS*

IT DID NOT TAKE THE ENEMY LONG TO DISCOVER THE DEPARTURE OF our people. They may have learned it from some of the not so friendly Indians of the neighborhood. Or it is even possible that some of their own number set to keep watch on us, from the safety of their cover, had witnessed the exodus. But the very next morning a score of mounted *Boisbrûlés* rode boldly to within hail of our little fort and summoned those of us who remained to surrender. MacIntosh, Currie and Isbister they promised transportation to Norway House, since they were merely *engagés* of the Hudson's Bay Company, with whom they felt they had no real quarrel. But my own case was different, for I was an employee of Lord Selkirk, and the only one of all the hated settlers who had dared to remain in what they arrogantly termed "their lands." They promised me only a variety of subtle but terrible tortures that would culminate in the most painful death they could devise as a punishment for my alleged misdemeanors!

I will say for James MacIntosh that he was a staunch defender of the Bay Company's property. I don't think he actually cared a groat what became of me. But the fort was Hudson's Bay property, and while he lived to fight for it no hostile warrior, be he red, white or Brûlé, would set foot inside. He made that abundantly plain to them, in language that would have made the sinners in hell blush—standing prudently below the level of the wall as he spoke, for he was not so magnificently foolhardy as to be out in full sight of the villains.

Angered at his words, the *Boisbrûlés* attempted a ragged sort of rush for us. But we let them have a couple of rounds of our homemade grapeshot from the swivels and then poured a steady fire of musketry at them, and the swiftness with which they broke and fled for the safety of their own fort told us plainly that they had already had a bellyful of that.

That afternoon another contingent of them rode out from Fort Gibraltar, and giving our own post a wide berth, they circled and rode far down toward the end of the colony, to the empty and silent houses and untended fields at the Frog Plain. There they entered upon a systematic program of destruction and devastation.

One after another, beginning at the most distant and working up toward us, they put the cabins to the torch, broke down the fences we had so laboriously built, galloped their horses this way and that, crisscross, over the fields we had wet with our sweat and had ploughed and then planted so carefully. From the beginning we could hear their yells and howls of drunken revelry, faint at first, but growing gradually louder as they drew nearer; they filled me with almost violent nausea at my stomach and a clutch of pain, like a fist, at my throat. It was not that I was afraid, but rather that I was hurt and sick to see all that we had done so ruthlessly destroyed.

Yet there was nothing we could do save sit in the watchtower, with the swivels handy and loaded, and watch the licking flames climb higher and higher. Four men against forty in open fight, with the scant cover that the prairies below afforded, had slim chance of winning. The flames marched closer as they fired each cabin: Frog Plain first and then Kildonan Parish and Seven Oaks and then the lower end of Colony Gardens. When I could bear it no longer I went below where the sheltering walls of the post would shut out the sight, leaving word with my fellows to call me if they needed my help. There I stuffed buffalo wool in my ears so that I would not hear the savage, taunting yells of the *Boisbrûlés* as they went about their wanton work, and seriously eyed the rum cask, thinking that drunkenness would be a mercy at this moment. But I decided against that at length, not from any feeling of prudishness, but rather because before we were done a steady hand and a sure eye might be needed!

But the *Boisbrûlés* did not attack us again. I think they had had enough of our tiny swivels and our rusty nails and ragged links of chain. I had been on my feet for almost seventy-two hours by then, and the emotional strain had been enormous. I did not intend to go to sleep when I sat down for a strong cup of tea, but it must have overtaken me. The next thing I knew Archibald Currie was shaking me by the shoulder. The tea was cold and the savage yells could no longer be heard beyond the walls. The gray light of day showed under the door and through the cracks of the chinking.

"Come, lad," he was saying, " 'tis all over now. Tha've gone back t'Gibraltar, an' we've na more t' fear from 'em for th' present. Come, come! Yon table's na comfortable for sleepin'!"

He was right. If you've ever gone to sleep with your back crooked over a table and your head on your arms, you'll remember the cold shudders that gripped you when you woke. Somehow cold drafts find their way into your blood and blow their breath on your vitals. Like anyone else in such a situation I was startled and stupefied; unable to collect my wits or even think coherently until I had something hot in my stomach, in this case tea laced liberally with rum. The few hours of sleep that I had had were enough for the moment, at least, and I did not want to take to my blankets. I had a gnawing fear lest the Northwesters go in pursuit of our people, and the only way to know about that was to sit in the watchtower where the river could be watched and any passersby noted.

I went up and relieved Magnus Isbister and sent him down to breakfast and bed. I cocked my musket and laid it on the rail of the tower, where it would be handy, and then went round and round, from corner to corner. But all I could see, or all I did see, through that long, tense day was the smoke of our burning cabins to the north, the empty, open prairie on the west, the silent bulk of Fort Gibraltar to the south, and only the placid flowing river, with never a canoe or any other craft to mar its surface, on the east.

I do not know why they did not follow the fleeing colonists. Perhaps they felt that there was no possibility of further danger from them. Perhaps they were too deeply involved in a grand *boisson,* celebrating their "victory." Perhaps the Northwesters at Fort Gibraltar felt somewhat like the Bay people at Fort Douglas: that there was no real quarrel between them as fur traders other than mild competition, and that the real fight lay between, in this case, the colonists sent out by Lord Selkirk and the *Boisbrûlés.* Once the colonists were gone the Northwesters lost interest, and the *Boisbrûlés* wanted no more of our swivels.

At any rate there was neither pursuit nor further attack on the post. The cabins were burned and the fields trampled; the colonists were gone and the Northwesters were satisfied to let it go at that. We sat for a time in the post, and when it became clear that, for the moment at least, no further violence was intended, we walked out—James MacIntosh and I—and surveyed the extent of the destruction.

It was a sickening sight, to me, at any rate. Scarcely a cabin remained, and those that still stood did so because they were built of green timber and had not thoroughly burned. The foundations were there but hardly much more. Fences were laid flat, and the fields that we had so carefully planted looked as if they had been used for a racecourse. No one came near us, though we carried our muskets and were prepared to fight or run as the occasion demanded. I returned to the fort sick at heart and stomach at what I had seen, and even James MacIntosh was grim. Though the smoke and the flames and the derisive yells of the maddened *Boisbrûlés* had scarcely troubled him. He had known these folk, and liked most of them. Now when he saw what had actually been done he was furious.

For three days we clung close to the fort, ready to dash for its safety while, I suspect, the Northwesters celebrated their triumph. We looked over all that we could salvage. The saw pits, of course had not been touched, and the piles of lumber that had been turned out of them and stacked on the point at the bend of the river—and so were within musket range—had been left alone. So were the frame and foundations of the larger, stronger Fort Douglas and the proposed, new, two-story governor's residence nearby. Two or three of the cabins—notably within gunshot—had been spared, as had such fields that had been seeded with wheat and potatoes that were within range.

On the second day Katawabetay and his Indians returned with a supply of fish.

"Your people are safe now," he said in his meticulous English. "We went with them to the mouth of the river and some distance up the west side of the lake. When we reached the Narrows and none of your enemies came in sight we left your people with instructions to keep on along the eastern shore after they had passed through. This will bring them to Norway House, where they will find friends who will send them on to York Factory. There has not been pursuit?"

"None!" I shook my head.

"Then they have nothing to fear now," he assured me. He looked out at the desolation done by the *Boisbrûlés* and shook his head. "It is too bad that white men and half-white should fight with each other when each has so much else to fight!"

"That is true, Katawabetay," I said. "There is room here for us all."

He gave me a curious glance, and then suddenly smiled as if he had remembered something.

"A small squaw, not bigger than a girl but old enough a woman," he said, "the daughter of Wind-in-the-Mouth said I must say to you 'take care.' And she also asked about the brigade from Alexandria."

I looked at him sharply.

"They haven't come down yet," I told him. "At least I haven't heard about it."

"I understand, Little Bourgeois," he replied. His face was wooden, almost without expression, yet with a hint of a smile about his mouth. "I will let you know when they come."

We waited two days after the Indians went on up to their camp at the mouth of the Rivière la Sale, above the Assiniboine, we scarcely knew for what. Then, one morning, a long string of canoes appeared from the direction of Fort Gibraltar and, one by one swung down past our landing, rounded the bend and passed on down the river. As they went by some of those aboard shook their fists toward us and shouted words that, at that distance, we could not understand. A few hotheads even ventured pot shots at our stockade, which of course had no effect, though I think that if we had fetched up our swivels to the watchtower we might easily have done some damage to their frail bark craft.

But we did not bother. From the fort it was hard to be sure, but I thought I recognized Bostonnais Pangman and Cuthbert Grant, François Boucher and Antoine Hoole, of Fort Qu'Appelle, and Alexander Fraser and Michael Bourassault, of Fort Gibraltar, though I did not anywhere see anyone resembling the cadaverous Alexander MacDonnell. This led me to believe that this was the brigade from these latter posts for Fort William. Later that same day an Indian came down from Katawabetay's camp with a message confirming this.

"The brigades with the furs for Fort William go out this morning," he said through James MacIntosh, who acted as interpreter. "They tire of waiting for the upriver brigades from Fort Alexandria and places even farther away, and they begin to fear that if they wait too long they will miss the rendezvous and all of the grand *boisson*. MacDonnell bourgeois will not go down to Fort William this year but will stay at Fort Gibraltar. Until the people come down from Fort Alexandria he has only a few men. We think you will have peace until then."

We gave him a cask of high wine for Katawabetay and a flask of the same for himself, warning him strictly that he must not open it until he had delivered our thanks to his chief. When he was gone I had some qualms lest the vengeful brigade overtake our fleeing settlers until I remembered that Katawabetay had said that the latter had gone up the west side of the lake as far as the Narrows and realized that our people were well out of the Northwesters' reach by now. After that I breathed more easily.

The next morning I took my musket and went out and, keeping well down along the bank, at least until I was hidden from Fort Gibraltar by the line of trees along Parsonage Creek, went down all the way to the Frog Plain. My tears were salt in my mouth as I looked on the charred ruins of the schoolhouse and the church and the residency where the MacLeans had lived. But though these emphasized my sorrow and made it more poignant, yet my fury was not for them alone. All along the way, from Colony Gardens to the bottom of the settlement, those half-bred devils had not left one stick standing upon another.

Clearly there was not a thing that I alone could do about them. At Frog Plain I turned and walked out to the limit of the long fields. All the way and even at the ends, everywhere I looked, the fences had been laid flat. But though the cross pieces and split rails had been tossed willy-nilly, many of the uprights remained, and some order might be brought of the chaos.

But to what end, I wondered helplessly. Disconsolately I started back toward the Parsonage Creek, cutting across diagonally, over the fields pockmarked with the tracks of galloping horses. I had not slogged discouragedly all the way over the second field when my tear-blurred eye focussed on something that made me stop and shake my head and look again, more closely, to make sure that I was not dreaming.

I was not. It was there, in the very hollow of a deep hoofprint—a tiny spear of green that showed sharp and clear against the red-brown of the mauled earth.

I ran over to it and dropped to my knees, flinging down my musket carelessly, not even bothering to see where it fell. I bent over the tiny plant. It was a sturdy little shaft, bent but not broken, and of course it could have been grass. But this field, like most, had been sown to oats, and I believed—I hoped—God knew how I hoped!

Tenderly, carefully, I straightened it—even as it would have straightened itself in time—scratching down a little earth around it, from the walls of the hoofmark, to help it stand upright. As I did so I uncovered four other seeds that were fertile and had burst and were sending out tiny shoots. Excitedly I grabbed up my musket and stood up and looked around carefully. From where I stood I could see hundreds— even thousands—of just such tiny green spears thrusting up out of the soft, trampled earth. I stared at them and scratched my head in wonder, and then it came to me, the thing that could account for it. There were millions of these tiny seedlings, not yet even burst from the ground. Had they been higher—even half grown—the trampling hoofs, racing to and fro across them would have broken them and laid them flat. As it was a few may have been crushed. But there were far too many. To the millions that remained the churning of the ground was only a form of cultivation, speeding them in their growth, even strengthening some in their struggle toward the sunlight.

I turned and raced back to the corner of the lower field, where I had started, and from there began to crisscross the ground, studying, examining the multitude of seedlings, pausing now and again to straighten one that was more bent than the others, mounding a little hillock of earth about those that seemed to need it, covering the living seed where it had been uncovered.

In my excitement and delight I lost all track of time. I daresay I did as much damage as a horse with my plodding back and forth. I even forgot where I was, though instinctively I kept my musket near me. Midday came and went and I doubt if I had even reached Seven Oaks. It was only when the sun dropped and the evening shadows lengthened across the prairies that I realized the day was gone and they would be wondering about me at the fort.

All of this, it came to me then, would be better done with a hoe than with fingers that by now were beginning to become a little bit raw. I picked up my gun and cut across to the road—as we had now come to call it—that ran up along the row of charred ruins, and without even seeing them, lighthearted now that I discovered something that might be salvaged, set my face toward the post.

But my lightheartedness did not last long. I had not come to Parsonage Creek when I saw the shadowy figure step out of the trees and stand hesitant, as if looking around in bewilderment. I remembered abruptly and uneasily that, to all intents and purposes, this was a country at war. I shifted my gun up into the crook of my left arm, so that my right hand was on the lock and my fingers curled around the trigger guard. But since I must reach the fort and there was no cover where I stood I went forward.

It was too dusky, and I was still too far distant to see who he was. But when I moved he caught sight of me and came straight toward me. I shifted my gun nervously and glanced down at the priming, which looked all right although I would have preferred to give it a new one. As he drew near, to my amazement, I recognized Andrew Ross, and the expression on his face was grim and violent. I swung the muzzle of my gun toward him when he was no more than thirty feet distant.

"Stop where you are!" I commanded.

He couldn't have halted more sharply if I had hit him with a rock. A look of astonishment spread over his face.

"MacAllister!" he cried. "What in th' name o' God—"

"When did you get here?" I demanded fatuously.

"Th' brigade came down this afternoon," he told me. "I came straight over."

"What do you want?" I said coldly.

"For th' love o' Christ!" he cried. "I came straight over t' see ye all, but I find—this!" He waved his hand around without taking his eyes from my own face. "What's happened?"

"Didn't they tell you at Gibraltar?" I replied.

"I didna even go t' Gibraltar," he told me. "I left th' canoes at Catfish Creek an' sent them on. I cut straight across country myself. As for what's happened here, we've heard naught upriver. I daresay we're th' first through. Tell me! What's happened?"

The route he described was quite possible. In fact it would be the fastest available for a man in a hurry to see us, for it cut out a number of loops and bends in the river. And his surprise seemed genuine enough. I lowered my musket from my shoulder but kept the muzzle of it pointed at his breast warningly, and having done that I took a certain grim pleasure in telling him.

He did not move, nor did he speak, but listened as if spellbound until I came to the place where I told of the others leaving. He interrupted me then.

"An' ye let 'em go?" he cried, almost in a voice of anguish.

"What would you have them do?" I demanded. "We were outnumbered, and there were women and children among them. Would you want them to stay here and be murdered? Or at best to see their homes burned and their fields laid waste?"

He flung me an impatient, almost savage look.

"There's been one killed among us already," I reminded him.

He hardly seemed to hear me.

"Ye say Katawabetay's at Rivière la Sale?" he demanded.

"Aye, but what's that to do with it?" I replied.

He half turned away, and then swung back with just a hint of a smile.

"Ye'd best clean out th' muzzle o' yer gun," he said. " 'Tis all stopped up with earth an' 'twould burst in yer face if ye tried t' shoot it!"

Then abruptly he turned about and started running swiftly up the track, through the dusk.

"Wait! What?" I called after him.

But he did not seem to hear me. Or if he did he paid not the least attention.

Half automatically I turned up the muzzle of my musket and

glanced at it. It was perfectly true. The bore held a solid mass of red earth and weeds and little pebbles. They must have jammed into it when I dropped the gun aside in the excitement of my first discovery of the seedlings, and all day long I had carried a worthless weapon!

Swearing feverishly I jerked out the ramrod and cleaned the mess out. By the time I looked up again he was just disappearing in the gloom amid the trees along Parsonage Creek, still running steadily. Half sheepishly I realized that if he had meant me harm he could easily have attacked me while my attention was on the gun. I looked to a fresh load and priming and went cautiously forward. But I met no one in the trees and came safe to the fort, where the boisterous relief of their welcome—for they were wondering what had become of me— quite drove the incident from my mind until later; at the time, for some reason I thought it best to say nothing about it, although I was full of the fact of my discovery that the crops were far from destroyed.

How he managed to cross the Assiniboine, above Fort Gibraltar it never occurred to me to find out. No doubt he swam. But at that moment it did not even occur to me that he would try. We ate an early supper, and I for one was glad enough to tumble into my blankets for a few hours of sleep, for my turn at the watch began at midnight and lasted until dawn. When I was finally aroused and climbed up into the little stockaded tower James MacIntosh came up with me to suck on his pipe and talk with me. He was wakeful, he said, and there were things we should discuss.

"What'll we do now?" he said finally.

My mind was still full of the oats I had found to be not beyond salvage.

"Get out with hoes and save what we can, I suppose," I said.

"For what?" The glowing bowl of his pipe swung in an impatient arc. "Th' grain'll graw wi'out th' help we can gi'e it if it's t' graw at all. We're a thin lot now, considerin' th' odds against us, an' we'll be thinner yet if we spread oursel's out yon."

He hit on the very problem that troubled me there, but I was loath to give up the idea.

"Then what do you suggest?" I demanded.

"D'ye ken," he pulled at his pipe, "will there be a fresh lot o' yer folk out frae Scotland th' summer?"

"I don't know. I suppose so," I told him. The same thought had come to me, but isolated as we were there was no way of knowing what was going on so far away.

"I heard that Laird Selkirk himsel' was comin' out," he said questioningly.

I stared at him.

" 'Tis news to me!" I said.

"MacDonnell dropped a hint o' it before he was ta'en," he nodded. The old devil, I thought. He wouldn't tell me about it if he knew.

"In any case," MacIntosh went on, " 'tis like there'll be more o' ye, an' there'll surely be reinforcements frae York when they hear o' what's happened here. At th' verra least there'll be th' brigade wi' trade stuff an' provisions. We maun do what we can t' mak' th' place ready for 'em."

"But how?" I asked.

"We've lumber in plenty," he said, "an' some's stout enough for a real stockade. There's th' frame o' a new an' bigger fort an' th' frame o' a real, twa storey house for the new governor, if he comes. If he doesna 'twill be inside th' walls an' will be a safe place for th' women an' weans. 'Tis a' handy by t' th' fort we've got now—wi'in easy range, which is why 't hasna been destroyed before now. I say let us be finishin' that, an' if th' de'ils come at us again we can run t' th' protection o' what guns we've got. We canna be doin' that out yon!"

I had to admit, even to myself, that there was truth in what he said.

"Think it o'er, lad!" he said, and dropped down the trap that led to the fort below.

I thought it over all through the long night as I paced from one corner to another and scanned the prairies, the woods and the swirling river in the darkness, trying to catch the least sign of movement. But nothing stirred, it seemed to me, until the last hours before dawn, when the mists began to rise from the water. Then I thought I saw a shape slip down upon the current, only swifter than the current, along the farther shore. I thought it was a light canoe, though it might have been a combination of mist and my imagination. I watched it as long as it was in sight, ready to give the alarm. But when no attack came I forgot it and turned my mind again to what James MacIntosh had said.

I was still asleep next morning when Alexander MacDonnell, lean and sour, came riding over from Fort Gibraltar. But I was wakened by the alarm bell that rang as soon as he emerged from his own gate. Sleepy-eyed I bounced from my blankets and snatched up my musket and ran for the smithy, where Isbister and I were assigned to work the swivel guns. MacIntosh and Currie were in the watchtower, and they called down to us that a handful of horsemen were on their way from the Northwesters' fort and that there was no sign of any approach from the side toward the river, so that we set up the guns quickly, according to plan, where they would cover every inch of the approach over the plain. If they tried to come that way, I thought, they would pay dearly for it.

But when they came in sight there were only a half a dozen of them, and all but MacDonnell halted. He rode forth with a white rag tied to a stick; clearly angry and just as clearly half frightened to death. He halted his nag when he came within shouting distance and held up his hand, pointing to the rag.

" 'Tis a flag o' truce!" he bawled. "We mean ye no harm. I want t' parley wi' ye!"

"Parley from there, Man!" I heard MacIntosh retort. "I can hear ye."

MacDonnell fussed and fumed and pleaded. But MacIntosh was inflexible.

"If ye come one step nearer, MacDonnell," he called, "we'll blast th' guts out o' ye, if ye have any. What d'ye want?"

Alexander MacDonnell was convinced at last that it was no use to argue.

"We want th' man, Ross, that ye took prisoner yesterday," he bellowed.

I stiffened. What was this? But MacIntosh was speaking again.

"Ross?" he bawled. "Who th' hell is Ross?"

"Th' bourgeois o' th' Alexandria brigade," MacDonnell retorted. "He left th' canoes at Catfish Creek, an' was last seen by our folk comin' across th' plain toward ye. Gi'e him up an' we'll gi'e ye no more trouble!"

There was a moment of puzzled silence from the tower above, and in that moment I had time to remember. I remembered how Andy Ross had turned and run when he could easily have shot me where I stood, fiddling with my own gun. I remembered that wraith that looked like a canoe, passing down the river in the misty dark of the morning. But for some reason I thought it best to say nothing, then or later. Above me the bull voice of James MacIntosh was bellowing again.

"We know naught o' yer man Ross, MacDonnell. An' we don't want prisoners. We're none here but good Hudson's Bay men an' that's all we want. Now get out o' here, an' remember that if ye come back we're ready for ye an' we'll be happy t' blast ye t' hell!"

MacDonnell and his followers did not stand on the order of their going, but clearly grumbled among themselves as they rode away. Nevertheless, they did not come back. I wondered, but still something kept me from speaking, although, of course, in the circumstances it seemed wise to follow MacIntosh's suggestion.

After that there was only one other alarm. But it was not a serious one. It came when the Alexandria brigade appeared on the river, bound down to Fort William. Our bell rang and we tumbled out and took up our stations. But the canoes ignored us and kept well to the far side of the river, out of gunshot range. When they were gone we saw nothing of the people at Fort Gibraltar for several weeks, and they saw nothing of us, although I daresay their lookouts watched our gates as alertly as we watched theirs for anything that might indicate a sally.

On our part, we were much too busy to attempt anything of the sort, even if we had been strong enough. Mister MacIntosh, I discovered, was a driver. Three of us worked at hauling and carpentering, while one of us stood watch, and I often wonder now, when I look back upon it, when any of us slept.

Since the frames of the big, new fort and store and the governor's fine house—as grand a building as any I had seen since leaving Scotland— were already standing as the men working upon them had left them when the colonists fled, we started with them. The walls of both were of thick planks, lapped against the weather, and as we built we cut out the openings for doors and windows, leaving them for framing when we had time later. The roofs were of seasoned boards overlaid with hand-riven shakes, and I can remember hitching my loaded musket along with me as I nailed each one in place.

With the outline already there before us that part of the work went swiftly, despite our small number. By the end of the first week in July the shells of the buildings, at least, were done, giving the appearance from the outside almost of completion. When we had finished that much we turned our attention to the work of palisading, for we felt that we could not turn to work indoors until we were protected by some sort of a stockade. For this we used stout, squared timbers laid flat, since we found that this way we went faster, and secured to double uprights at intervals of eight feet. It was hardly a fence that would withstand the battering of heavy artillery. But we felt it was likely to repel any such attack as we were likely to meet.

By the beginning of August we had been five weeks at work and had finished a wall that ran from the end of the old, quite serviceable palisade all the way around the front and sides of the new buildings. We built a stout gate, of course, that led out on the side toward the plain, and within there was a reasonably large compound. This left only the steep bank on the river side unguarded, and since we feared that it would take too long to build a wall there too, we solved the problem of defense by cutting willow and aspen and poplar saplings from the bank itself, sharpening the stubby ends of the branches, and laying them in a sort of spiked *cheveux-de-frise* all around the top of the bank from fence to fence, leaving only a gate at the path from the landing. No man, we felt, without the covering fire of prepared attack, could slip through that without being seen by our lookouts!

But at least when that was done we felt more secure. We were able to lay the floors and raise the main partitions and frame the doors and windows of the new fort and governor's house without feeling that in the event of an alarm we would not have time to tumble out to our posts. In the meantime I watched the fields that we could see from the fort turn green and grow waist-high and then begin to yellow. From time to time, when a Sabbath halted work on the buildings I would take a hoe and slip out and do what little I could. But it seemed to me that the time for harvest was approaching, and it was clear that even the four of us could never harvest all that was there.

At the same time, I believe, another thought came to each one of us, though we never mentioned it to one another: this was that the time was approaching when the brigades would begin to return. None of us said anything, but each of us knew that our own fate depended upon whether the first of the canoes belonged to the Northwesters or the Hudson's Bay Company. Our fort and our fence were strong. But they would only be as strong as the numbers behind them. If the Northwesters came first they could overwhelm us. What could four men and two small swivels do against a hundred, or more likely two hundred? None of us had any doubt that the North West Company meant to eliminate this troublesome post at the Forks. More and more the eyes of the lookout in the watchtower swung from the somber bulk of Fort Gibraltar toward the bend downstream in the river.

It chanced to be my turn at the afternoon watch when it came. The sun was well over in the west, reddening for his plunge below the prairie horizon, when the sound came up to me faintly; the sound of many throats, thundering out the song. It was distant at first, and so elusive that I was not sure I heard it. And then it crept closer and seemed to swell in volume, and I knew it was not my imagination:

En roulant ma boule, roulant—

Voyageurs! Only voyageurs sang that song in this country. What was more, it was a Northwesters' song—one that had been brought from eastern Canada, not one that our own men from York knew. I rang the alarm bell. Our men tumbled out of doors and windows in the new governor's house and scurried for their posts. It had been agreed that whoever was lookout would remain and fight where he was, relieved by his alternate below. I stayed there, listening. James MacIntosh came up and took his post beside me.

"What is it?" he demanded.

I held up my hand.

"Listen!"

The voices came swelling, much nearer now, just around the bend:

> Derrièr' chez nous, y a-t-un étang!
> En roulant ma boule!
> Derrièr' chez nous, y a-t-un étang!
> En roulant ma boule!
> Trois beaux canards s'en vont baignant,
> Rouli, roulant, ma boule roulant,
> En roulant ma boule!

In that moment James MacIntosh's expression was one of grim defeat and despair that was only an echo of my own.

"So they got here first!" he whispered.

Archibald Currie was staring up at us anxiously from the new post to which we had moved the swivel. MacIntosh looked over at him.

" 'Tis th' brigade," he called. "Th' Northwest brigade!"

Currie swung his gun down toward the river, just as the first canoe came in sight around the bend.

"Dinna fire unless they attack!" MacIntosh called down to him.

Archibald Currie looked disappointed.

> Rouli, roulant, ma boule roulant,
> En roulant ma boule!

Sang the oncoming paddlers.

We watched them in silence as they came around the bend and straightened down toward us, counting—one, two, three—five—ten—fifteen—twenty! Would they never stop appearing? I thought I knew then what those settlers must have felt who had first seen us approach —those same men and women who came out on the bank and watched us with, I had no doubt, this very same fear and despair in their hearts. But I did not. All at once MacIntosh caught at my arm.

"Haud on!" he cried. "Look yon, in th' number one craft, at th' black-browed laddie. 'Tis Colin Robertson! He's been wi' us e'er since he quarrelled wi' 'Crooked Armed' MacDonald!"

In the same breath I gasped and caught hold of him.

"Aye, and look yonder, in the second canoe," I cried. " 'Tis Andy Ross!"

"Ross?" He flung me a curious look. "I seem t' ha' heard th' name."

I think I turned brick-red.

"Aye, aye!" I cried. "I'll tell you about it after a bit. But look, man, at the canoes that follow if you've any doubt!"

He turned and looked down along the line of high-prowed boats that were just now coming into focus.

"Yon's th' dominie, Mister MacLean, an' his lassie!" he shouted. "An' yon's th' widow Sutherlan' an' her weans!"

"And Pat Corcoran and Mister MacKay!" I added.

"They've come back!" he cried.

"Praise God!" I retorted. I knew then really what those first settlers had felt when they burst from stolid watching into waving cheers.

But I don't think he heard me. He leaned over the parapet of the watchtower and called down to Archibald Currie.

"Dinna shoot, man! Mak' sure ye dinna shoot!" he bawled. "They're na' Nor'westers! They're our ain!"

We boiled out of the river gate, through the *cheveux-de-frise*—if you can say that four men boiled—and went pelting down the patch to meet them. The lead canoe slid in to the landing just as we burst on to it, and Colin Robertson, big and expansive and black-browed as ever, leapt out to meet us with widespread arms and a grin that was all over his face.

"Colin! Colin!" cried MacIntosh. "I ne'er thought I'd live t' see th' day I'd bless yer comin'."

"We wondered if ye would," retorted Robertson. "But some o' us were sure ye'd be waitin'!"

"Mister Robertson," I put in, "it *is* a pleasure to see you!"

He grinned at me, and then bowed with mock ceremony.

"Mister MacAllister!" he laughed. "Ye've a gift o' understatement, if 'tis a gift. I'll confess t' ye that I'm damned glad t' see ye again. I wasna at all sure that I would!"

Before I could ask what he meant by that I felt myself seized by a huge hand and spun halfway around. I found myself face to face with the huge, red-topped Andy Ross.

"Mac! Mac!" he cried. "So ye're all right? I was afraid, I hated t' go off so, but—"

"Andy!" I exclaimed.

It seemed to me an awkward silence fell on the little group.

"Friend o' yers?" said Robertson.

I glanced around at him and at the others and spoke instinctively. "Certainly!" I replied. "He brought you up, didn't he?"

"Not exactly," said Robertson dryly.

But even as we talked the third canoe was landing, and before I could reply there was a rustle of skirts and two arms about my neck; two sweet lips upon my own. I swear I thought I would swoon, and I am sure I turned red as the wattles on a bubblyjock.

"Malcolm! Oh, Malcolm!" she cried. "Ye're all right?"

"Aye!" I laughed gaily, and gave her back as braw a hug and a kiss as she had given me. "Aye, sound and safe and better than ever, now that you're back!"

Oddly she seemed even more confused than I at that, and she drew away from me a little shyly, although I would have preferred to hold her close beside me with my arm about her shoulders. It seemed to me, too, that Andy Ross gave me a startled, almost astonished look. But there was no time then to ask questions. Over Jean's shoulder I saw Alec MacLean loom up, and in the next instant he was pumping my hand happily and thumping me upon the back.

"Lad, lad!" he beamed, smiling, I think for almost the first time since I had known him. "But 'tis good t' see ye!"

I looked at him sheepishly, and then glanced bewildered from them to Colin Robertson.

"And 'tis good to see you, too, believe me!" I assured him earnestly, and then glanced at the obviously hand-picked canoemen. "But what, how? Where did you come from, and these men? We were all confused here, almost fired on you, in fact!"

Colin Robertson laughed uproariously.

"An' well ye might be," he admitted. " 'Tis a long tale. We met yer friends at Jack River, waitin' transport t' York. Came out wi' these lads meself from Montreal—first time a Bay Company brigade's come out over th' Northwesters' own road! I'll tell ye 'twas a picnic! Pick o' th' lot they are, all fighters! But 'tis long tellin'. Let's get up t' th' fort an' let these folk go on t' their homes. There's another brigade comin' up from York—be here in a few days—a hundred an' fifty settlers an' a new governor."

I broke in.

"That's good news, Mister Robertson," I said. "We can use all the settlers we can get. But I'm afraid there aren't any homes. There's a good deal of grain, but no homes. The Northwesters burned them all. We'll have to start from scratch."

"No—no homes?" Colin Robertson looked from me to Ross. "Northwesters? Did ye know aught o' this, Ross?"

The big, red-headed man shook his head, and I think it was the first time I had ever seen him look abashed.

"Not until I came down from Alexandria," he said, "and he told me. I've told ye o' that. I'm sure he'll confirm it."

Robertson glanced at me and then at Ross. Jean and her father had been swallowed up in the crowd that was now filling the narrow landing, though I would have liked to have had her beside me.

"Well, it's a long story," said Robertson again. "Let's go up an' get straight for th' night, anyway. Then, maybe, we can get t' th' bottom o' it all."

He picked up his *sac* and tossed it over his shoulder and turned and strode off up the path. The rest of us followed, strung out in a long line, not a little perplexed, some of us, by the way things seemed to have turned out.

5. FORT GIBRALTAR

It was a long story, all around, even as Colin Robertson had said. When the fires were lit and supper done; when the two hundred or more voyageurs who had come out from Montreal were encamped upon the plain near the saw pits and the returned colonists had been spread about and accommodated as best they might be inside the new compound; when the baggage and all the cargoes of all the canoes had been toted up the short path to the stockade, and even the canoes themselves were tucked away in the canoe sheds—for we dared leave nothing to the mercy of the Northwesters—then there was time to hear it.

Robertson, brashly of course, as he would, settled himself at once in the new governor's house and invited as many of us as possible to be his guests at a sumptuous supper.

"Might as well break it in!" he said, and I recall at the time I thought here is a match for Duncan Cameron.

They called upon me first—I suppose because I was more articulate in the face of strangers than MacIntosh or Currie or Isbister—for the story of all that had happened at the Forks from the beginning, and I told it much as I have told it here, though, to be sure, not nearly at so much length, and necessarily on that account leaving out some details which might, perhaps, have been better mentioned. Jean Mac-Lean and her father and the others bore witness to the truth of all that I said of what happened up to the time the colonists fled, though of course only my three companions could support me in my account of the events that followed, and not all of that.

Colin Robertson was black wrath itself when I told of the destruction of the settlement, systematically house by house, by the *Boisbrûlés*. But he was all smiles, and there was a general roar of delight, when I reported that the grain our enemies had tried to trample had sprouted despite their efforts and was now up and near ready for harvest. I told,

then, of how I had met Andy Ross on the trail that day, and how he
might have cut my throat if he wished, but he did not; how he had
turned and run, and how the next dawning I had thought I had seen a
light canoe hurrying down the river. Colin Robertson glanced over at
the huge, red-haired Northwestman.

"Yer story confirms what Mister Ross has told me," he growled half
doubtfully.

"It should," I told him, "if Mister Ross is an honest man, and I think
he is for all he has been on the wrong side of the fence. You were
yourself once, Mister Robertson, if you recall!"

That rocked him back a bit on his heels, as I thought it might, and
he had no answer. It was James MacIntosh who looked a bit angry
and spoke.

"Ye didn't tell me o' this when Alec MacDonnell came o'er," he
said.

"I didn't think it necessary," I told him blandly. "Our meeting in
the fields came to naught, and I was not sure that I had seen a canoe.
If I had told it might have set a hive of hornets on Mister Ross's trail.
It might have stirred up a nest of hornets about our own ears. It seemed
best to say nothing."

Andy Ross gave me a surprised, almost grateful glance, and Colin
Robertson uttered a burst of guffawing laughter that made the rafters
ring and brought smiles to every face.

"Mister Ross!" he cried. "Ye're vouched for! 'Twould seem ye've
seen th' light!"

"I hope ye'll believe me now, Mister Robertson," Ross said.

Apparently I had done him a greater favor than I realized.

When I sat down Colin Robertson told his tale, and an epic one it
was. Only the bare bones of it can be repeated here.

He had come out the winter before, sailing in advance of Selkirk
himself, who meant to visit the colony in the coming year. He had
a scheme that was not merely grand. It was daring, and Lord Selkirk
had backed him up. For years the Hudson's Bay Company had received
all its supplies through York Factory and Hudson's Bay itself. The
North West Fur Company, of Montreal, had monopolized the route
west by way of the Ottawa and the Great Lakes and the rivers above
and beyond them. If the Bay Company could send out supplies by that
same route, Robertson argued, it would be quicker and cheaper—and
it would carry the fight to their rivals! What was more, he said, he was
the man who could do it. He had countless friends among the voyageurs and the fur hunters, and each one of them knew one or more

others. In Montreal his optimism had been justified. He had had more applicants for service than he could accept. More than a thousand had flocked to him in response to his public appeal. But he had only sixty north canoes—which he preferred to the larger *canots du maître,* usually used on the voyage between Montreal and Fort William—and so he had been forced to select only as many hands as he could use. Four hundred and eighty had been chosen, and with these—their birch bark craft laden with supplies for Red River and for the Hudson's Bay posts in the Athabasca—they had come up from the Ottawa and over through Nipissing, into the Lakes. From Superior they turned up into the Nipigon and crossed, through Lac Seul and English River into Lake Winnipeg, and at Jack River, near Norway House, they had come upon the remnants of the Red River colony fleeing northward.

Colin Robertson had been beside himself. He had threatened. He had cajoled. The colonists hesitated, seeing such a force, and began to feel renewed hope. Then, while they hesitated, debating, word came from York that the new governor and some hundred and fifty new colonists had landed and would presently be on their way to the Forks.

That word was the deciding factor. Robertson doubled the loads and cut down the crews of the Athabasca brigade and took the dispossessed people under his wing. He sent the Athabascans off in a score of canoes, under a man he could trust; and with all the rest, and the fleeing colonists, he turned south toward the Forks.

Nearly four hundred of them! That posed a problem, for though they brought supplies with them, those that they brought added to what we had—even counting the grain that we would be able to harvest— would not do for all, let alone keep the added settlers who were expected daily. We met to consider the problem, and after we had worried about it for some time Colin Robertson solved a part of it for us. He glanced at Andy Ross.

"Ye, Mister Ross," he said, "here's yer chance t' prove yer interest in our cause. We've more than a hundred good hunters among us. Take yer pick o' 'em an' go on, upriver t' Fort Daer, at th' mouth o' th' Pembina. Th' buffalo're thick thereabout this year I'm told. We'll set up a supply post there an' hunt from it from morn till night. Ye should kill far more than ye'll need yerselves, an' all that ye kill an' can't eat ye'll send down t' us. We'll take it in relays through th' winter, an' that way there should be some fresh meat all o' th' time. Fair enough?"

It seemed to me that Andy Ross looked somewhat crestfallen. But his answer was prompt.

"As ye say!"

He picked forty of the best guns from among the voyageurs who had accompanied Robertson and went on upriver with them, an event which I think was fortuitous in view of later happenings. As a matter of fact they were hardly out of sight, beyond the mouth of the Assiniboine, when the first canoes of the North West Company's brigade hove in sight around the downstream bend. I doubt if they knew then, or for a long time, that Andy Ross was one of us. Indeed I wonder if it was not a part of Colin Robertson's purpose in sending him upstream to keep it a secret. But, of course, I could never be sure of that.

Nor had I time to think about it then. The Northwesters came, singing as had our own people, around the lower bend, not more than a week after Robertson's arrival, and as each canoe rounded into the stream the paddlers fell silent. They had expected, naturally, to see a spot of desolation: a place where once cabins had stood, and a fort, but where now nothing but charred stumps and crumbling foundations remained. Instead they saw new and even larger buildings, more strongly walled, and many people.

They looked. They rubbed their eyes. They glowered, and we watched them pass in silence from the watchtower, marking down familiar figures among them: Cuthbert Grant, Bostonnais Pangman, Alexander Fraser, Antoine Hoole, François Boucher, Duncan Cameron and many more that we could not name, although I thought I recognized Seraphim Lamar. Each, as his canoe passed around our bend, glared up at us as if he could not believe his eyes, and Cameron —still in his dirt-streaked, scarlet uniform coat—looked almost as if he would leap overboard and swim ashore and attack us singlehanded.

Yet it is a fact that he did no more than fling around his great blond mop of hair in surprise and stare up at us; then shake his fist at us in vengeful fury. But Robertson glanced first at me and then at MacIntosh.

"We'll have t' do somethin' about that," he said.

When the last of the Northwest canoes had gone by he turned to us again.

"Ye see their attitude?" he demanded. "There'll be no peace here until one or th' other o' us is gone, an' I mean t' see 'tis not ourselves. Ye'll mind, Governor MacDonnell told 'em t' get out over a year ago, but yon tawny old goat chose t' ignore it. In fact he turned about an' destroyed th' colony! Well, gentlemen, we'll carry th' war to 'em an' see how they like it! Cameron'll be on our necks if we don't!"

"Haven't we had enough of quarreling?" I said.

He gave me a blank, almost contemptuous stare.

"Ye'll have more if ye dinna do as I say," he retorted. "Mister Mac-Intosh, gather up th' Bay men—"

"There's no but three o' us," MacIntosh interrupted dryly.

"—an' th' voyageurs." Robertson ignored him. "Mister MacAllister, ye'll call up th' men o' th' colonists, both o' ye, every mother's son that can carry a gun. Have 'em meet in th' compound. We'll give these bastards a dose o' their own!"

His manner made it clear that his orders were not to be disputed. When we had dropped down the ladder and he had gone to get ready himself MacIntosh rubbed his hands.

"We've a man t' lead us at last!" he grinned.

"I still don't like it," I retorted.

There was reason for my gloom, but it was nothing that I could foresee then. More than two hundred of us answered the summons. Colin Robertson grinned as he came out, musket under his arm.

"We'll settle things tonight, lads!" he said.

A score of voyageurs, all stout men, were given canoes laden with pemmican packs and told to come up to the river gate at Fort Gibraltar and cry for entry. They were to say that they were belated North-westers, who had been forced to stop and gum their canoes. When I ventured to protest that by such subterfuge we might lose precious supplies Robertson laughed.

"We won't lose 'em, MacAllister," he said, "if it gets us in, an' it will!"

And it did! The canoes went up and forty voyageurs slipped along the bank beside them, and when the river gates were opened to the canoemen, all pushed through and fought their way to the far side, where they opened the main gate to the rest of us—and Fort Gibraltar was ours. The Northmen were clearly in no condition for a serious fight. Duncan Cameron was magnificent and indignant. With his blazing yellow head and his spotted scarlet coat and white breeches he stood up and gave us defiance—except that he was more than a little drunk.

"Gen'lemen!" he cried. "What've I ever offered ye bu' hos—hos-padilidy. What—why—?"

"Per'aps ye'd like t' see?" retorted Robertson, who was not far behind him.

"Yer servant, sir!" retorted Cameron with a bow that all but set him on his nose.

"Since ye're interested," said Robertson, "I'll be mickle pleasured t'
show ye. Meantime will ye gi'e me yer parole, an' be m' guest?"

" 'Twill be 'n hon'r" Cameron hiccupped, and they went forth, arm
in arm, though I noticed that Robertson winked at MacIntosh as he
went. After that the guns, the powder, the ammunition, the furs and
rum and supplies that had been taken from Fort Douglas in the spring
were all fetched back in carts—though not by Northwestmen, as I
thought might be appropriate since we were going so far.

It was a peculiar triumph. I remember Cuthbert Grant standing by
the gate of the fort and watching the carts pass out, glowering and
refusing to speak. On the whole the *Boisbrûlés* seemed more distressed
than the Northwesters. The reason, I daresay, was a matter of subtlety.
As I had said, we must expect some defeats and learn to accept them.
But at heart the *Boisbrûlés* were children. They could not bear to be
crossed.

But that was not an obstacle that seemed insurmountable at the
time. I recall that all of us felt that Duncan Cameron was the key to
the situation. In the morning, when the guns and all that had been
taken from Fort Douglas were back within our walls, Colin Robertson
and his prisoner and several of us, including Alec MacLean and James
MacIntosh and myself, walked out to show him exactly what had been
done by his allies.

We showed them the burned-out ruins of the cabins, and he smiled.
Alec MacLean pointed out the charred shell of the church.

"Ye used t' come t'kirk yon, Mister Cameron," he said.

"So I did, Mister MacLean," the Northwester retorted. "But 'twas
a matter o' policy, ye may be sure. Yer sermons were verra dull!"

I looked across the way where settlers and voyageurs were busy
reaping the harvest of grain that had grown despite him.

"There's one thing you could not destroy, Mister Cameron," I said.
He scowled.

"We'll do better next time!" he retorted.

"There'll be no next time, Cameron," Robertson assured him.

But no one should assume the power of second sight!

We were not more than an hour returned to Fort Douglas, and were
debating what should be done with our prisoner when the alarm bell
in the watchtower rang. We piled out to our posts instinctively to see
a fresh mass of canoes rounding the bend and heading for our landing.

These were Company folk obviously, and Robertson and MacIntosh
and I went down to meet them. The first out at the landing was a tall,
moon-faced man, a little paunchy, and, I thought, rather soft until

I saw his hard blue eyes. He wore a tail coat of latest fashion, giving nothing to the wilderness through which he had been traveling, tight-fitting breeches and Hessian boots with tassels and a tall, beaver top hat. To my astonishment Colin Robertson cried out in recognition.

"Bob Semple!"

The chubby man turned toward him.

"Colin!" he exclaimed. "I didn't think to see you here."

Robertson grinned.

"But ye do!" he said, and introduced us round.

The newcomer was Robert Semple, the new governor, sent out long before there had been any inkling of Miles MacDonnell's seizure, to replace him, and with him were close to two hundred new colonists.

I have described a landing, and the joy of it, more than once already, and I have no mind to go into it again about this one except to say that this was more sedate and somber. It seemed to me that the new governor was a little pompous; a little overimpressed with his own importance. Certainly he knew nothing of the ways of the country and seemed little inclined to learn. He was to serve as governor for both the colony and the Hudson's Bay Company, in which capacity he would act as a voyaging winterer—an occupation of which he had no slightest conception—and would supersede James MacIntosh, who was to return to York with the furs that had been collected at Fort Douglas. And, of course, at table he sat above Colin Robertson.

It was a fine enough welcome that we were able to offer him, but I could not help thinking that it was a sorry business for the colonists that came with him. He had a fine house, a finer house than the former governor. They, expecting a flourishing settlement, found only the blackened cellar holes of our former cabins awaiting them. Yet I will say that they accepted it with fortitude and courage, after all, what else could they do?

Perhaps he was tired from his long journey. Perhaps he was as arrogant and stupid as I thought him. I doubt if I am the man to say. I know only that he ignored most of us who would have made him royally welcome. He attached himself to Colin Robertson, and walked up with him from the landing. He accepted our grand, new governor's house as a matter of course; as something that had grown naturally by the side of the river, like a tree, without recognition of our human sweat and pride. He was a dainty gentleman who had Colin Robertson to dine—and Duncan Cameron, when he found that the latter was a prisoner among us. The rest of us he ignored as if we were cattle, necessary to the domain but hardly recognizable. I am afraid I did not much care for Robert Semple, though, God knows, I hope his ashes rest in peace—the reason for which will presently appear!

His first act, on finding that Duncan Cameron was a prisoner, was to release him on his promise not to foment trouble for the colony. In council Colin Robertson argued in vain against the move. He tried to convince the governor that this was a raw country, peopled by savages, and that the least trustworthy of them all were Duncan Cameron and his kind, who for their own ends would incite the decent, honest red men and the *Boisbrûlés* against us. Robert Semple would not listen. Duncan Cameron, as I believe I have shown, was what our Yankee neighbors called a "smooth article." He had talked himself around most of us during that first winter we had been there. He talked himself around Robert Semple now, and Governor Semple let him go back to Fort Gibraltar, where he could plot and plan ways to be a thorn in our side, if he could not for the time being destroy us.

Governor Semple's arguments were reasonable enough. Governor MacDonnell, he said, had been heavy-handed in his enforcement of the pemmican edict, and no one could argue against that. But having said as much, a few of us noticed, he did not repeal the ban. At the same time he argued that if we seized Fort Gibraltar and shut off the Northwesters' supplies we would have a starving multitude on our hands. And that was so true that none of us, even Colin Robertson, could dispute it. But he made no such move toward coalition with the North West Company as was to follow so long after, when both companies combined. His policy appeared to be a static one of "wait and see what happens." I noticed that after that first dinner together, and after Duncan Cameron was paroled, and after our first council meeting there began to be a definite coolness between Governor Semple and Colin Robertson which I deplored, for whatever his faults might be Robertson was acquainted with the country, in and out, and Semple was not.

Yet Robert Semple was a popular governor. I daresay he had displayed certain qualities of leadership on the way out, and these had endeared him to the folk that came with him. Since they outnumbered those of us who had lived at the Fork before by more than three to one—even as we had those who were there when we arrived—I think most of our people fell into the same habit.

But this was a matter of local politics and actually not terribly important save in a crisis, which certainly none of us foresaw. There was much to be done. The harvest came first, of course, for our very lives depended on that. To our astonishment the yield of oats per acre was almost what we had estimated it would be in undisturbed times, although about half of it must be saved for seed, as it would have in any case. The rest ground down to a supply that would allow each family a small ration of oatmeal daily. Another year we hoped for more, and there was no corn, of course, but the Indian women showed our own how to harvest the wild rice that grew so prolifically about the mouth of the river. The potatoes we had planted apparently had been destroyed by the pounding hoofs.

But food was only part of our problem. Every cabin had to be rebuilt, and even a few more added for we numbered more families now than ever before. We were handicapped a little by the lack of sawn lumber, since the saw pits had been idle for so long, and we had used all the ready stock in building the fort and the governor's house and the stockade. But there was plenty of wood available across the river, and we built our first houses of logs, with roofs of sod, and the only riven timbers we used were the puncheons for the floors and the frames for the doors and windows. Twenty or thirty men worked on each cabin, often raising it in a day, and then moved on to the next so that each family would be housed before snow fell. Some, oldtimers of a year or more, like myself, carried our muskets, and kept them primed and close at hand. But Duncan Cameron had apparently warned the *Boisbrûlés* to hold themselves in check until he gave them the word, for not once did we see one of them—not even Cuthbert Grant, though we were several times invited to soirees at Fort Gibraltar. None of us went, of course.

But apart from grain foods and housing our two greatest problems were how to get enough meat and how to preserve it. The latter we who had lived in the country left to the womenfolk. Once the grain was in and the cabins raised we hunted and fished close by. Ducks and geese, flying south, for a time gave us an abundance of fowl; there were prairie chickens on the plains and grouse in the woods across the river. In the river itself a line stretched across from one side to the other; baited hooks at intervals of two or three feet, left overnight, would fetch up a dozen or more catfish or sturgeon, ranging from ten to seventy pounds. All of these could be smoked or pickled, and there were bear and *biche* across the river, but hardly in sufficient quantities, those of us who had been out for some time knew well, to take care of all our people for the entire winter.

I daresay I was something of a thorn in our governor's side in this respect, for I knew what starvation could be, even though I had been lucky enough not to experience it myself. I plagued him. I argued.

"Our hunters are sending down meat from Fort Daer every week, but we must have more for so many," I said. "Mister Ross must be told our needs, and he must have help!"

Governor Semple turned to me finally, in desperation, and said:

"Very well! Mister MacAllister. Take what hunters you think you will need and go to Fort Daer and stay there for the rest of the winter and send down all the meat you can!"

I must have looked startled or angry, or perhaps the order gave him an idea, for he turned sharply to Colin Robertson.

"And you'd best go along, Mister Robertson," he said, "to take charge and see that the hunters are working as they should."

He said nothing of the relief of any who were there already. Robertson gave me a half grin, and so it happened that I was banished to the same spot as Andy Ross. Before I left Jean MacLean came to me, and I realized all of a sudden that I had been so busy I had seen very little of her.

"Good—good huntin', Malcolm," she said. "Ye'll be seein' Andy Ross?"

"Surely," I told her.

The way she looked at me you'd have thought she was angry.

"Remember me to him," she said.

"I will," I replied, "but I doubt he'll need reminding."

"Why, Malcolm!" she cried. "That's the nicest thing ye've e'er said t' me!"

It didn't make sense to me!

The river was not yet frozen so we went up in canoes, several days' journey above the forks. The fort at the mouth of the Pembina was little more than a log stockade, built about a hewn cabin, and apparently our coming was such an unusual occasion that it called for a mighty *boisson*—a general carouse of all the hunters and the Indians in the neighborhood; a form of entertainment that I did not much enjoy myself.

Colin Robertson and Andy Ross, however, seemed to savor it. Katawabetay was there—very drunk—and his daughter, Qua-na-Shee-tits, somewhat the worse for wear since Cuthbert Grant had pushed her over the fire. Yet she seemed to have an eye for me. I had difficulty evading her.

I managed, however. After a little I caught Ross's eye and signaled him over to a corner where I gave him Jeannie MacLean's message of remembrance. He stared at me.

"Ye're in love with th' girl, aren't ye?" he demanded.

"Certainly!" I retorted. "Aren't you?"

He blinked.

"Aye, I daresay," he replied. "I wouldn't feel the way I do if I weren't!"

"Then she'll make her own choice between us," I said. "She's an intelligent girl."

He goggled at me.

"I'll be god-damned!" was all he could say. "I'll be b'Jesus-Christly-god-damned!"

You might think we would be deadly, bitter enemies after that. But you'd be wrong. I came to know Andy Ross that winter as a friend. We ate and hunted together, and slept in the same great barn of a fort with all the rest of the men assigned to this task of finding meat for the settlement downriver. But while I liked the others, and got along with them as well as could be expected, I felt a special bond with this great, hulking Scots-Canadian. Perhaps it was our joint interest in Jean MacLean. But I don't think so. If any woman had been our only common interest we would have been at one another's throats before Christmas. As it was we both got roaring drunk at both Christmas and New Year's—since there wasn't much else to do in that God-forsaken spot—and both made love to Qua-na-Shee-tits, who enjoyed it thoroughly.

He was just a good comrade, that was all; a man who, whether he could say so or not, saw eye to eye with me in many things, and quite by mutual consent, to avoid argument, we did not mention Jean Mac-Lean again after that first night.

Our hunting was spotty. There were buffalo in the dells, in small bands, and now and again we would manage to knock over enough to send a dozen carcasses down, over the river ice, to the colony at the Forks. But we could not do much more. An occasional *biche,* or red deer, came our way. The bears, of course, had gone to ground for the winter. We heard that the folk at the Forks were having a difficult time of it; that their food was strictly rationed; that they had killed some of their horses to eat. We heard that they said we were not working at Fort Daer; that when the snow got deep we sat indoors and played cards and kept what we shot for ourselves!

It wasn't true, of course. The game just wasn't there. Day after day we went out across the snow, spreading fanwise from the fort. And when one of us found a little bunch of buffalo he did not shoot at once, but signaled the others to come up, so that as many as possible would be killed.

But one morning, toward spring, a little before dawn, I woke to feel the whole building, the ground under me, the very stockade itself, shaking and trembling and there was a steady roar like thunder muttering in the distance, except that it never stopped. It was not my imagination. Others, too, heard it and felt it. Someone sat up and picked a coal from the fire and lit a candle.

"The herds!" someone else said.

At the words there was a concerted rush for the ladder leading to the watchtower, and as I climbed up I wondered if it would hold us all.

But it was stoutly built and showed no sign of collapse. As I came up and looked over the parapet I saw a sight that was beyond everything that I had ever imagined. There had been prairie out there the night before. Now it was a sea of tossing horns and heaving backs—shaggy, humped backs, and curved horns—with hardly an island of land to be seen. Eastward lay the Red River. Too wide to be crossed. But south and west and north, flowing across the Pembina as if it were no more than a brook, the great mass passed.

That day we killed as much as all our canoes would hold, and by that I mean only the choicest parts. The tongues, the testicles, the hearts, the humps, the steaks we took, and left the lesser delicacies for the Indians and the crows. We had as much as our people could eat, and since the ice was already out and the water high we all went down at once.

We were none too soon, as it turned out. We landed our cargo and learned that Governor Semple had gone off on a circuit tour of inspection to Swan River and Brandon House, and was not expected back for several days. That, of course, left Colin Robertson in charge, and the very afternoon that we arrived from Pembina a half-canoe came struggling around the river bend, fighting to make its best speed against the swirling waters. Colin Robertson watched it for a moment, until it became clear that it was not for us.

"That bugger's carryin' despatches for Gibraltar!" he exclaimed. "I'm goin' t' stop 'im."

"You can't interfere with the King's mail!" I cried, aghast.

"King's mail, my arse!" he retorted. "There's no mail out here but what's carried by either the North West Company or the Hudson's Bay Company—an' either one o' them's fair game, specially if it might concern yerself. Who's with me?"

Half a dozen men stepped forward, and almost before I could offer any further protest—which I was scarcely inclined to do—they had intercepted the Northwester and brought him on shore. Colin Robertson himself brought up the despatch case and summoned the men of the council into the governor's room. As we sought seats and made ourselves comfortable he broke open the case and began to read.

I have not the space nor the time, here, to give copies of those letters. Nor do I think I should say to whom they were addressed, for some of those men are with the Company now! It is enough to say that each and every one of the letters contained instructions for an attack upon the colony, and came from people in Montreal—some of them very important people indeed—connected with the North West Company.

As Mister Robertson read and we listened, one after another, to the names that were signed to the letters, and he passed them around for each to see for himself, we stared at one another in incredulous amazement.

"Well, gentlemen," said Robertson when he was done, "does that convince ye? 'Tis them or us!"

"You don't need to convince me," I said impulsively. "My school was burned once."

"Manfully said, Mister MacAllister!" He gave me a look of approval. "What o' th' rest o' ye?"

Several spoke up, much as I had. I noticed that only a few kept silent. He nodded, glaring at us all.

"Verra well," he said. "I tried t' do somethin' about this last autumn, but it went for naught. This time we ha' th' evidence o' their intentions, an' I don't think it wise t' delay matters for th' governor's return. How many o' ye are wi' me?"

By a show of hands it was unanimous.

There is no need to dwell on it. In fact the thing was done exactly as we had done it before, except that this time a single canoe swept up to their landing, pretending to bear despatches. When they opened the gates to the canoemen a flood of our own armed men swept through and secured the inner compound. These then opened the main gates to our forces advancing overland, and the thing was done.

It was early spring and none of the brigades had yet arrived. They had only such people as ordinarily manned a post, and they did not expect us. Duncan Cameron was snatched from the bed he shared with his pretty Indian mistress and allowed only time to slip on a shirt and a pair of pants and step into some moccasins before he was hurried across to our own fort and imprisoned. But there seemed to be none of the others there that we had hoped to find.

This time, however, we did not content ourselves simply with seizing the place and its commander. On the contrary, every man in the fort was given an equal share of what transportable goods there were and was sent on his way, with the clear intimation that he could go to Fort William if he pleased—or hell if he preferred that. After that we removed whatever we could to our own fort: anvils, tools, cannon, powder, shot, even the very timbers of the post itself we tore down and carried back to replace, as we said, those they had burned! What we could not carry we burned or dumped in the river.

When we were done there was only a hummock left where Fort Gibraltar once stood.

When we were done, too, Colin Robertson called another meeting of the council.

"I mean t' take no chances o' our bird escapin' us this time," he told us when we were assembled. "We've enough evidence o' his crimes t' tuck him away for a long time. But we'll get no fair trial here. I'll take him out myself t' York wi' th' brigade an' set him aboard ship for England t' stand trial. That way, at th' least, we'll know that if we don't get fair treatment frae th' courts we'll anyway be shut o' him for a while!"

We all applauded and I suppose it would have been almost indecent for us to do so if we had not known the man to be such a scoundrel!

The next day a number of us made depositions against Duncan Cameron, to which we swore and which were properly witnessed so that the court might act, and after that we baled the winter's furs. On the third day Governor Semple had not yet returned. Accordingly we set out the canoes at the landing and loaded them with furs and provisions. At the last minute the bedraggled blond man, whimpering like a child, was dragged out and manacled to a bale of furs, so that I wondered what would become of him if the canoe he was in capsized. No one else, however, seemed worried about it. In time I was to find that it was almost a standard procedure, and now, even though I felt sorry for him, I held my tongue.

A moment later the canoes shoved off and swung into the stream. The current swirled and eddied and hurried them down toward the bend, while the red paddles flashed in the sun. When they turned and swept out of sight, around the bare, brown point of leafless trees, it was the last any of us ever saw of the big yellow-haired man—or of Colin Robertson, for that matter. But our troubles were far from over.

6. SEVEN OAKS

WHEN THE TWO GASCONS WERE GONE AT LAST, OUR LITTLE COLONY at the Forks settled back with a sigh of thanks to enjoy the blessed peace that was all the more welcome after our recent "alarms and excursions." That it might be but an interlude did not occur to most of us. I noticed that both Andy Ross and Archibald Currie seemed preoccupied, but the rest of us were far too busy to have time to give much thought to the consequences of our action. What mattered most to us was that Fort Gibraltar was gone at last, wiped away completely, and now there was no Northwester nearer than Fort Qu'Appelle to bother us.

Having thus wiped our consciences clean upon the seats of our breeches, like a pair of muddied hands, we turned our attention to the needs of the season: to the preparation and planting of the fields and the incorporation of those building materials that we had salvaged from the demolished fort into our own fort and into our cabins. In fact we were even able to raise a small new storehouse from the timber, hard by the wall, outside our fort for the winter storage of our crops and pemmican, and to put up an archway over the gate, facetiously dubbed our "Triumphal Arch." We built a sentry box beside it so that we could keep some of our number on guard there at all times, as well as maintaining the usual lookout in the tower.

It was more than two weeks before Governor Semple returned from his tour of inspection in the west. By that time we had completed our ploughing and had begun to sow our seed—seed salvaged from the very crops that our enemies had tried so hard to destroy the year before. As soon as he arrived a number of us hurried him up into the watchtower proudly to show him our handiwork.

"Come, come, gentlemen!" he snapped pettishly as we stepped on to the platform. "I just had a long journey. I'm very tired. What is it you want me to see?"

I took the liberty of pointing off, up the plain along the river, toward the point where the low, grim bulk of Fort Gibraltar had until so recently loomed.

He turned and looked, casually at first and with only mild interest, as if he were humoring a flock of children. And then he gaped. He stared and all but rubbed his eyes.

"Why, why, 'tis gone!" he squeaked. "What?"

We told him then, all that had happened; how Colin Robertson had intercepted the Northwesters' express and found on board the damning letters from Montreal and Fort William calling for our destruction and suggesting ways of accomplishing it; how we had then taken matters into our own hands and seized Duncan Cameron and sent the rest of the garrison packing, and then had systematically set about leveling Fort Gibraltar completely, so that it could never again be a threat to us.

"Where's Mister Cameron now?" he demanded sharply.

"Mister Robertson took him to York Factory under arrest," I told him. "From there he'll send him over to England for trial. We feared he would be acquitted in the Canadian courts. The Northmen have tremendous power in the east."

"Nonsense!" Governor Semple snapped testily. "A court of law is a court of law and is not influenced by private interests. I regard Mister Robertson's action as impulsive but legal enough, and I daresay it's what the man deserved. Probably of a piece with what he would have done himself! At least he won't give us any further trouble for a while."

He turned and glanced again toward the place where the other fort had been.

"Nor will that!" he added, and made a little dusting gesture with his hands, brushing one palm against the other as if to say that that was all there was to it.

"We hope!" growled Archibald Currie dourly.

The governor blinked at him in surprise.

"What's that?" he demanded.

"I mean we hope it won't, Yer Excellency," Currie repeated.

"Why the devil?" The governor reddened at the man's temerity. He did not like to be disputed, and he felt that he was being doubted now, and by a mere clerk at that. "How the devil can it? It's gone, isn't it?"

"All th' same, Yer Excellency—" Currie began stubbornly and then hesitated, groping for words to express his thoughts.

"I think what Mister Currie means t' say, Your Excellency," Andy Ross broke in, "is that it may well be th' cause o' worse trouble gone than it would ha' been if we'd left it."

Governor Semple glowered at him.

"What do you mean, Mister Ross?" he demanded caustically. "I think 'twas a good riddance. What do you think, eh?"

I think that in Andy's boots I would have been quaking, for the governor was clearly impatient with all of this and anxious only to get down to his own quarters where he might have a tub and a glass of toddy in peace. But Andy was unruffled.

"I'd say Mister Currie was right, sir," he replied.

"Indeed?" the governor snorted.

"Aye, sir!" Andy said. "I know th' temper o' th' Northwesters, an' somethin' o' their bounden determination t' throw us out. They've no love for th' Hudson's Bay Company, an' less for th' colony. The letters in th' express that we stopped should prove that t' ye, even if I were not here t' assure ye o' it. Now, when they find that we've halted one o' their canoes an' tampered with their despatches, especially such letters as some o' them'll have on their conscience, th' partners will be in a fury. An' when they find we've dared t' seize one o' their forts an' tear it down, t' arrest one o' their partners an' send him off t' England t' be tried—"

"They were trespassers in the territory that we hold under charter from the king!" the governor interrupted him hotly. "They were warned. As my deputy, in my absence, Mister Robertson was entirely within his legal rights."

"I am not speakin' o' that, Your Excellency!" In his turn Andy broke in upon the governor. "It has little t' do with th' matter! What I am sayin' is that when th' Northwesters hear what's been done they'll clamor for vengeance. They're not th' men t' take an insult lyin' down. Mark me well, they'll strike back, an' strike back hard. 'Twould not surprise me a bit t' know that they're gatherin' themselves for just such a blow this minute."

Archibald Currie nodded, and I felt as if a chill finger had touched my heart. Of course, I thought! Why hadn't I realized that. I remembered the lengths to which they had gone the year before, and I recalled that one of the letters we had intercepted had been addressed to Cuthbert Grant. There had been others for Bostonnais Pangman and Alexander MacDonnell, and the things they had suggested were not pretty. Rouse the half-breeds, the partners had urged. Let the métis carry the war to the colonists in defense of their hunting grounds. Give them guns and whiskey and then look discreetly in the other direction. In that way the North West Company cannot be called responsible for what the aroused *Boisbrûlés* might do!

We had stopped those letters, of course. But I could not help thinking that others, of which we were unaware may have slipped through!

"He's right, Yer Excellency," Currie said soberly. " 'Tis what I've been thinkin'. 'Tis a serious sit-uation."

"They'd never dare!" cried Governor Semple pompously.

"They dared once," Andy Ross retorted darkly, "and they damned near succeeded. D'ye think they'll let it rest at that?"

"But—the law, man!" Semple protested.

"Beggin' Yer Excellency's pardon," Archibald Currie put in, "there's damned little law west o' th' Lakes!"

"Oh, nonsense!" the governor snorted as much as to say that now that he was here matters would be very different. Nevertheless he rounded upon Andy with a somewhat less critical air. "I understand you were a Northwester once yourself, Mister Ross?"

"Aye!" Andy nodded, abruptly stiff and on his guard.

"What made you change?" Governor Semple asked it softly as a cat purring.

The suggestion was clearly there that perhaps Andy's tongue was in his cheek, but Andy, in his honesty, never saw it. He scratched his head, and I smiled a little. Andy saw me and flushed crimson. But I think his answer surprised us all.

"Well, now," he said, "it's a little hard to express, but I'll try. Ye see, sir, I've been out in this country since I was a young lad. My folks weren't rich, an' as soon as I'd got a bit o' schoolin', back in Cape Breton where we lived, they apprenticed me t' th' North West Company, an' I came right out t' Grand Portage first, an' when that was given over t' th' Americans, to Fort William. After a while they made me a winterin' bourgeois, an' I've had posts just about all over this country. I mind I was fourteen when I came out, an' I grew up with lads like—well, say, Colin Robertson, an' Cuthbert Grant an' Bostonnais Pangman an' even Duncan Cameron, though he was older than myself. O' course we all worked for th' North West Company. We were *hommes du nord*. We liked t' show off how good we were, especially when there were men from one o' the other companies about: Bay men, say, or Mackinaws or some o' th' free traders—XYZ Company men—'Potties' we used t' call 'em before they went out o' business and were swallowed up by th' Northwesters. O' course we were all in th' same work—furs; gettin' th' red devils drunk enough so they'd sell us their furs for less than th' other fellow; gettin' 'em t' owin' us so much that come spring they couldn't take their furs anywhere else. O' course, if we met up with some Indians that wanted t' see what they could get from the Hudson's Bay people, for instance, we'd do whatever we had t' t' get the furs away from 'em. That's natural. That's just th' trade!"

"What's all this?" Semple began.

"I'm comin' t' that," Andy cut him short, in the effort of his own self-examination not realizing how curt it was. "But before I left home, I mind, there were a lot of folk that came over from Scotland an' settled on Prince Edward's Island—ye know? 'Tis just off th' tip o' Nova Scotia. They were good folk: hard workin', sober, happy, kind! I used t' see quite a bit o' 'em where we lived. They were sent out by Lord Selkirk."

"You never told us this!" I said.

He grinned at me.

"Never thought much about it 'til just now," he replied. "Well, Your Excellency, ye can bet I didn't think much about 'em when I was a kid, an' especially after I got out here. I remembered 'em, surely. But they were something I'd known long ago an' had no reason t' think about later. I never stopped t' think what that settlement on Prince Edward's Island might mean t' 'em—not until these folks came out an' I remembered that Lord Selkirk had sent out those others, too. I guess it was that made me stop an' think about it more than once."

He paused.

"Go on," said Semple.

"Ye know, Your Excellency," Andy obeyed, "when ye spend a winter at a post like Alexandria ye have plenty o' time t' think—an' think—an' think. Sometimes that's about all there is t' do! So I did a good deal o' thinkin' about this. An' th' more I thought about it th' more it seemed t' me that th' Northwesters an' th' *Boisbrûlés* weren't giving ye a fair shake. This is a big country, an' it seems t' me there's plenty o' room in it for us all. There're buffalo down on th' Pembina an' over on th' Qu'Appelle, just t' name a couple. They've been hunted for years by th' métis, an' they ha'nt gone away. Just because some settlers came into one small patch o' country, I judged—that's not goin' t' drive 'em out. There's beaver in plenty over by Swan Lake an' down in th' Hair Hills. Yer people an' th' Northwesters've been tradin' with th' Indians for their pelts for a long, long time. But they ha'nt been all trapped out by a long shot!"

"And so?" the governor prompted him.

"An' so I judged that somebody was givin' us a lot o' false talk, just so they could hold t' th' whole roost," Andy went on. "Come to think of it, I wondered a little about one thing: Who needed th' land more —th' *Boisbrûlés,* who could hunt over in another part o' their territory and find just as many buffalo, or th' Northwesters, who could go anywhere from Fort William up t' Athabasca an' beyond an' get all th' beaver they could trade. Or was it th' folk that needed a place t' live an' had nowhere else t' go?"

"You decided in favor of the colony, I gather?" said the governor.

"Would I be here else?" Andy demanded, and I gathered that he was becoming irked at this cross examination for he did not even bother to add "sir."

Semple shrugged.

"Do your former comrades know that you've come over to us?" he demanded.

For an instant I thought that Andy was going to hit him, and it seemed to me that the others caught their breath. Then Andy seemed to realize that it was only the man's ingrained arrogance that made him put it in that way. He shook his head.

"I don't think so," he replied, and this time his omission of any form of address was apparent to all. "As soon as we came back from Jack River, Mister Robertson sent me up to th' Pembina with th' hunters. I've been there since, that is until we all came down. I don't think they know it, yet."

"Hmmmmm! Rather subtle in many ways, Mister Robertson," the governor mused, and all at once it came to me that things might have been ordered that way for some special purpose that we had not guessed, but that Colin Robertson and Robert Semple had already discussed.

"Do you suppose," Robert Semple went on, "that you could pass among them now and be accepted? That you might be able to find out what they plan to do?"

Andy scowled.

"I'm no spy!" he protested.

I smiled a little then, well aware that there was a very different reason for his reluctance. Like myself he had been a caller nearly every evening since our return, at the MacLean cabin, and to my unaccountable annoyance Jean had not seemed to object.

"Spy, no! Scout, yes!" Governor Semple said quickly, seeing his hesitation. " 'Tis for the good of all!"

"Well-ll-ll-l!" Andy flung a quick glance at me. What the governor had said was perfectly true, of course. The rest of us were well known to be connected with the colony, and if we tried to find an Indian to do the job, how would we know that he would not just turn about and sell information about our activities and plans to the North-westers for a cask of high wine? Andy Ross, experienced as he was and thoroughly familiar with the country, was ideal for such a job.

"All right," he said at length, "if that's what ye think I ought t' do!"

He slipped out the next morning, and I think there were few beside myself that were aware of it. Jean was there, and the way she kissed him and wished him luck and held on to both his hands, for a moment, almost made me jealous. But then, I thought, what if I were leaving and he were staying? Obviously, it seemed to me, the advantage was all on my side!

Yet he still managed to put me at a disadvantage. He beckoned to me just as he was about to step down into his light canoe.

"Have a care for her will ye, MacAllister?" he said sentimentally. "She's verra dear t' me!"

"Oh, aye!" I replied. "Since you ask it. Of course she means no more to me than an old shoe!"

He grinned.

"Ye hear, Jean?" he said, and then he was away before I could quarrel with him.

His way lay up the Red to the mouth of the Pembina, where he planned to join some Indian friends, who would accompany him up and over to the headwaters of the Souris, which they would follow down to Brandon House and its mouth at the Assiniboine, thus making a circuit which would give him a clear picture of all that was going on in that most threatening direction.

"What if they ask where you've been?" Governor Semple demanded. Andy Ross laughed.

"I'll tell 'em I'd a friend among th' Sioux or th' Mandans or th' Dakotas, a handsome wench, an' they'll not question me further! There's many a one does th' same!"

We heard nothing from him for more than three weeks. Then a Saulteur came down the Assiniboine with word that things looked serious in the west. The *Boisbrûlés*, he said, had been gathering at Fort Qu'Appelle, swearing vengeance for the destruction of Fort Gibraltar, but at first making no move other than to drink all the high wine available.

When there was nothing more to drink at Fort Qu'Appelle, Alexander MacDonnell, who commanded there, and who was the prime instigator of the whole business, had slyly suggested that a further supply—as well as other items of value—might be found at Brandon House, the Hudson's Bay Company post that stood at the junction of the Assiniboine and the Souris. His hint was all that was needed, and accordingly the whole drunken, quarrelsome mob surged that way—which happened to be in our direction!

On their way down the Assiniboine they overtook and captured five flatboats belonging to the Bay Company and laden with furs and pemmican en route to the Forks. These they sent back to Rivière Qu'Appelle, and after that they fell upon and sacked the post at Brandon House, which they burned after first removing a large quantity of rum and high wine, the season's fur catch and a valuable stock of trade goods and provisions.

Many of the *Boisbrûlés,* he reported, came from as far away as Cumberland House and the Saskatchewan—a clear indication that they had been especially roused for the purpose. Just at the moment, he said, they were all too dead drunk to stir, but he warned that as soon as they had swilled all this supply away they would probably move again in our direction. Besides MacDonnell, he said, they were being led by Cuthbert Grant, Bostonnais Pangman and Seraphim Lamar.

After that one message we heard nothing more from Andy Ross, and I think, in the tense days that followed—days that actually seemed to shiver with uncertainty—even the governor, despite his attitude of expressed scorn, began to grow somewhat apprehensive, for he doubled the watch in the tower and the guard at the gates. Work in the fields and down the village street came virtually to a standstill, for our people preferred to remain nervously near their loaded weapons. One of our horses was killed when he ventured to walk at night from one side of his pasture to the other. An apprehensive settler, hearing the thud of his hoofs in the dark, was certain that the half-breeds were at hand and did not stop to investigate before beginning to shoot. And Alec MacLean had a narrow escape when he stepped out to the necessary one evening and a skittish neighbor fired at him mistaking him for a prowling enemy. Not I, fortunately! I was taking my turn on guard at the fort that night.

Even Jean was affected by the general tension, or at least I attributed it to that. Never before had I seen her so distraught. She would eat next to nothing, and I guessed that she slept poorly, for there were hollows in her cheeks and dark shadows beneath her eyes. Five or six times a day she would come to the fort and ask if there was any further news from up the Assiniboine, not that she was alone in that, for it seemed to me that everyone in the settlement was moved by the same urge to judge from the number of times we had to answer the question. But my heart always went out to Jean, and I tried to reassure her as much as possible, telling her not to worry so, that we were all alerted and ready for whatever might come; that no one was likely to be hurt if they hurried straight to the fort as soon as an alarm sounded. But these protestations only appeared to irritate her, and somehow it never occurred to me that she might be more distressed about something else other than the one great fear that seemed to pervade our entire community.

But all of this tension and waiting ended as abruptly as a summer thunderstorm breaks upon the mountains. Under pressure of the apparent emergency we had organized a colony militia, composed of all the younger men between the ages of sixteen and thirty, and the bachelors of whatever age without families. This force was to stand duty at the fort at all times, so that there was a permanent bivouac in the center of the compound. The other men of the colony—those that for one reason or another could not take constant duty—were divided into eight hour shifts, so that beside our regular force we had always an emergency group standing by. By this system we could be sure that there would be forty or fifty men on call at the fort at all times.

As a bachelor, of course, I was included in the more or less permanent group, and I recall that I was one of the guards at the main gate that morning, late in June. Young Rob Matheson, no more than a boy, was stationed in the watchtower; his eyes were sharp—sharper than mine would have been in the same circumstances. That I am sure. We at the gate were startled suddenly by his high-pitched, squeaking yelp:

"Hi-yi! Here they come. Jesus Christ God-damn!" I am sure that in the midst of his arm flapping excitement he had no idea what he was saying. "Ho dammit, ye lads down yon. Somebody come up here! I tell ye they're comin'!"

I was the nearest officer, and I dashed toward the ladder and was halfway up before Archibald Currie and Governor Semple came to it. When I reached the platform Rob Matheson was dancing up and down and pointing, his finger wobbling over half the horizon in his excitement. But the general direction was toward the trail from Catfish Creek. I glanced that way and saw what he meant. The horsemen were bold and clear outlined against the bright sky and were following a course that would bring them to the Red River about at Frog Plain. They were still too far away to identify, man for man. But I judged there must be about seventy or eighty of them, and I had little doubt as to who they were.

I had not much more than looked that way before the governor came on to the platform behind me and snapped a long telescope out from under his arm and focused it on the riders. Currie was close behind him, and although I was seething inside for a look through the telescope, neither of them paid the least attention to me. Instead the governor, after a moment, passed the glass over his shoulder to Currie.

"D'you recognize any of them?" he asked.

Currie swung the telescope this way and that, and then picked them up. He growled a curse under his breath.

"Oh, aye!" he said then. "They're *Boisbrûlés* right enough! An' lads I recall ha' been some time wi' th' North West Company. That one, yon, in th' lead is François Boucher, an' ye can see Alec Fraser an' Rafael Lacerte none so far behind, an' yon's Antoine Hoole an' Tommy MacKay an' Michael Bourassa! Aye, yer Honor, there's a score o' 'em I could name."

"Remember them!" The governor reached out and took the telescope and snapped it shut, and I realized then that he was not going to offer it to me. "We may need a witness! Come along!"

He turned and started down the ladder. Currie followed, and I was next, wondering what in the world I had done. As we reached the ground the alarm bell in the tower began to toll, and we found that the men already on duty had crowded out into the compound. Through the open gate, now, we could make out the horsemen moving at a course diagonal to the fort, but one which would bring them to the village near its end, though of course they were yet too far away to recognize.

Whatever else I might have thought of Robert Semple, I had to admit then, as I did later, that he was no coward. He turned abruptly to face the men who were pressing forward curiously, looking more than a little incongruous in his shiny top hat and his bottle-green tail coat with its bright brass buttons, his tight buff breeches and his fine Hessian boots. The lace at his cuffs and stock was as immaculate and starched as if he were merely contemplating a stroll through a London park. For a moment it was easy to forget his pompous air and admire only the courage of the man.

"Very well, lads!" he said, not raising his voice, yet speaking in such a way that all of us there could hear him. "We must go out to meet these people and find out what they want. I want twenty volunteers to follow me."

"Your Excellency!" I cried. "May I?"

He turned about and raked me from head to foot with his eyes in a way that I think no man has ever done before or since.

"You are a friend of Mister Ross, Mister MacAllister?" he demanded.

"Of course, sir," I replied. "But—"

"I would suggest that you stay here, at the fort," he said coldly. "We will need some to guard and hold the place in the event we meet with trouble!"

Clearly he resented the fact that he had not heard from Andy recently, although any fool could reason that Andy Ross might not have been able to get a message through. At the same time, it was equally plain that his mind was made up and there was no point in argument.

But I was not alone. I think every man in the compound offered to go, but he had set the figure at twenty and he would take no more. Nor would he listen when someone suggested that it might be wise to take a fieldpiece along.

"Let us see first what it is they want," he said. "The sight of artillery might only precipitate a fight."

It occurred to me that the sight of artillery might also prevent a fight. But he was in no mood to listen to any suggestions that I might make. More than half of those who volunteered were rejected, yet in the space of a few minutes he had made his selection. He picked Mister Rogers, his assistant; Mister Wilkinson, his personal secretary; Mister White, the surgeon; and Lieutenant Holt, of the Swedish Navy, who had come out only to see how our experiment was working. He took John Bourke, the storekeeper; Michael Heden, the cadaverous interpreter; and Daniel MacKay and Michael Kilkenny, a laborer; George Sutherland, Anthony MacDonnell and John Pritchard, another interpreter and some eight or nine others.

When he had made his selection he turned to the crestfallen remainder.

"Your place here," he announced, "is important. If all of us go there will be none left to hold the fort if anything should go wrong with us!"

That was sensible and was at least solace.

"The settlers will be arriving soon in response to the alarm," he went on. "I want you men to hold the gates and admit all who have a right to enter. If aught happens to us you will close the gates and man the guns and make the best defense you can. Sheriff Allen MacDonnell will command in my absence. If we need help I will send back for a fieldpiece, and only as many as you can possibly spare from the defense of the fort will bring it up. Am I understood?"

He did not wait for an answer, but turned about to his volunteers. "Very well, gentlemen," he barked. "Shall we go?"

His rejection of my services, I daresay, saved my life. But it was hardly a moment when I considered that. I was resentful as I watched them march out and turn northward along the track that we called a road, in the direction that would intercept the riders. The horsemen themselves were now just about abreast of the main gate, about a mile distant, across the plain and following a trail that would bring them into the general track beyond the screening trees of Parsonage Creek, between Seven Oaks and Kildonan Parish. But if they noticed the governor's move they paid no attention.

Our warriors had hardly marched out before the first of the settlers from the village below began to arrive at the fort, those living nearest, of course, coming in first.

"The half-breeds! The half-breeds are coming," each group of them told us, as if it were news to us. Clearly they were badly frightened.

Archibald Currie and I stationed ourselves at the main gate and passed them through, offering a few words of cheer and encouragement to each lot as they came.

"Don't worry!" I told them. "We're ready for them this time!"

"We stood 'em off once with less'n we've got now," I heard Currie saying. "If it's a fight they want we can gi'e it to 'em."

Alec MacLean and Jean came in fairly early in the crowd, since the Parsonage Lot was one of those nearest the fort. Jean looked as ill as if she were on a ship at sea in a bad storm, although I don't recall that she was seasick once during our actual crossing. I had never before noticed what great freckles she had. They stood out like blotches against her pale skin—not that I thought the less of her for that! At sight of me by the gate she turned aside from the inflowing crowd and came over.

"Have ye heard aught o' Andy Ross?" she demanded.

The fact that she should speak of Andy at this time, just as the governor had, startled me.

"No," I said, "but don't worry, Jean. He probably couldn't get word through to us."

She hardly appeared to hear me.

"He—he's not one o' them?" She nodded toward where the riders had disappeared behind the trees of upper Parsonage Creek.

"Good God!" I cried, astonished. "Of course not! Whatever makes you ask that?"

"He—he was a Northwester, ye mind," she told me.

"Well, for God's sake!" I cried. "That doesn't mean he's one now. Forget such nonsense, Jean! He's an honest man, and he'd be here today if he could. I've got to tell you that, even if—even if—"

My voice trailed off miserably, for I found myself quite unable to say what was in my heart in the middle of all that crowd.

I was pleased to see, though, that somehow what I had said seemed to relieve her. She put her hand on my arm, and a little pleasurable excitement shot through my whole body at her touch.

"Ye're a sweet lamb, Malcolm," she said. "Sometimes I wish—I wish—"

She never told me what it was that she wished, but she did raise up suddenly on her tiptoes and brushed my cheek with her lips. Then she turned and fled after her father, in through the gate, and I stood gaping after her until I became aware that at the opposite side of the gate Archibald Currie was staring at me with a quizzical grin on his lips.

"Come on!" I said gruffly. "Let's hustle these folk through!"

He laughed outright at that, but I never had a chance to ask him what he was laughing about, for at that moment John Bourke, the storekeeper, who had gone off with Governor Semple, came panting up at a run.

"Th' guv'nor thinks we'd best have a fieldpiece," he puffed.

Archibald Currie sobered and looked at him.

"What's up?" he demanded. "They hostile?"

"They ain't friendly!" Bourke panted. "He don't like th' look o' things."

Our two wheeled cannon had been placed at embrasures on either side of the gate, where they would be handy for just such an emergency as this, and now half a score of amateur warriors came forward to help us kick out the chocks and catch up the drag ropes and haul the gun out through the gate in a grand rush. As we worked John Bourke kept up a running fire of talk, reporting what he had seen.

"We got beyond th' trees at Parsonage Crick afore we got a sight o' 'em anywheres near close to," he said. "Then they was still a good ways off, but we could see 'em plain. They're painted like savages. Aye! *Boisbrûlés* right enough—I reco'nized that fellow, Grant—but got up like a lot o' Injuns, with streaks o' white across their faces under their eyes an' on their cheeks an' foreheads. They mean business, that's clear, an' th' way they turned showed they was comin' down through th' glade into Seven Oaks. That's when th' guv'nor called me an' told me t' run back an' fetch up a gun!"

We were a dozen rods from the fort by then and moving swiftly when Sheriff MacDonnell came panting up behind us with a couple of men from the garrison.

"Hey!" he bawled. "Where'n hell d'ye think ye're goin' with that?"

Sweating John Bourke looked over his shoulder.

"Th' guv'nor wants a gun!" he retorted.

"Well, hell now! Wait a minute!" The bulky sheriff skidded around in front of us and halted. We stopped perforce. "You can't take all them men with ye. Remember, I'm in charge here!"

"Chrissakes, man!" wailed Bourke. "We ain't got time t' argue! Get out o' th' way!"

"Out o' th' way, hell!" retorted the sheriff, nettled, glaring first at Bourke and then at the gun. "All ye're goin' t' do is lose it. Where'n hell's yer ammunition? That thing ain't no good 'thout ammunition!"

We all gaped at one another for an instant in silence, all of a sudden realizing that in our haste we had forgotten the most essential ingredient.

"I'll get it!" One man started to turn back.

But just at that moment came an abrupt ripple of far-away shots and a chorus of yells, not a whit less hideous and blood-chilling because of their distance. John Bourke went ghastly white.

"That's it!" he gasped. "That's it! They've attacked!"

I must give paunchy Allen MacDonnell credit for quickness of wit in spite of his size. He jerked his head toward the gun.

"That goddam thing's no goddam good now!" he bawled, and pointed at the two youngest of our party. "Here, ye Murray, an' ye Bethune, get th' damned thing back inside th' fort an' tell 'em t' shut th' gates an' don't open t' anyone that don't identify 'emselves. Get, now! Th' rest o' ye, come on with me!"

We turned and were off, racing along the road, toward the sound of the distant shots and yells, and I doubt if any of us looked back to see how the two youngsters were managing with the heavy fieldpiece.

We leapt the Parsonage Creek at a single step and went racing across the level flat beyond toward the fringe of trees where the road dipped down and crossed the glade by Seven Oaks at an angle. Like the untrained militiamen that we were we stayed bunched together, eleven of us, each one finding a measure of courage and comfort in the company of the others. When we should have spread out and filterèd down through the trees—as I only realized later—we went charging ahead in a compact crowd, rushing down the road and out into the open glade, as if the scant dozen of us, by our very ferocity, could hope to scatter the seventy or more savage *Boisbrûlés* that we found milling around there.

I daresay the suddenness of our appearance surprised them almost as much as the sight of them did us for an instant—a fact that probably accounted for some of our lives! Governor Semple had gone out with twenty men. But as we looked, all at once, upon that scene of carnage it seemed to us that all of them must have been slain in that first sharp flurry. I learned later that six had survived: four, in the midst of the melee, making their way to the river and escaping across it, and the other two, by sheer luck, chancing to meet men whom they had befriended at one time, being protected and made prisoners.

But at that point there was no way for us to know that. Nor would it have made any difference if we had. The bodies of our friends lay huddled in little, grotesque heaps, all horribly mutilated, the bright red of their life's blood standing out sharp against the fresh green of the new, spring grass. Robert Semple—that man whom I had thought pompous, but whom I never wished any such fate as this—lay in the middle of the field, shot through breast and hip, clearly at close range, and with his belly ripped open by some savage knife and his bowels lying scattered all about him. Mister Rogers lay a little further away, with his head blown off and his body treated in a similar fashion.

There were others, of course, but there was no time to take note of them then. The half-breeds were still at their gory work, robbing and stripping and then ripping open the bodies of their victims. But on the instant that we appeared fifty muskets were aimed at us from the whole semicircle of the field, and I can remember hearing Cuthbert Grant's voice ringing out, loud and clear:

"Lay down your arms!"

I remember being momentarily surprised, for I had not realized that he was one of them. Then, I think, the same thought came to each one of us at the same instant. The sight of those mutilated bodies was enough to warn us that surrender was no guarantee of our lives! As one man we flung our guns aside and turned, each one his own way, scattering like a covey of frightened birds, and ran, jouking, dodging, weaving and bending over as low to the ground as we could get so as to offer as small a mark as possible.

Call it craven if you like. What were a scant dozen men to do against seventy or more who already had them in the open and in their sights?

Behind us the ragged volley crashed, and something like a great bee went humming past my ear. But it was my luck that I was not touched. Just ahead of me and crossing my path diagonally, I saw John Bourke fling his arms across his face and stumble and then fall.

Perhaps it was instinctive. I have been told it was foolhardy. But I can vaguely remember thinking that the *Boisbrûlés* must reload before they could fire again, and in any case the man was directly in my path. As I came to him I reached down and jerked him to his feet. The red blood bubbled from a hole in his back, but he was not dead, nor was he unconscious. He could not speak, but his eyes gave me thanks enough. I thrust my shoulder under his armpit and, half carrying him, half dragging him, half aided by his fumbling run, scurried for the cover of the fringe of trees along the river.

We reached it, the Lord alone knows how! Perhaps the savage devils behind us were too busy with their work of carnage to notice us. Once in the leafy shelter of the trees I did not stop, but plunged with him directly over the bank and then turned upstream, remembering fortunately that James MacNaughton kept a light canoe cached in the brush by the riverside, behind his cabin, which was not so very far above. MacNaughton would not be needing the craft again, I thought grimly, for he was one of those poor, disemboweled devils that lay dead on the field behind us.

The canoe was just where I remembered it, and good MacNaughton had even had the foresight to keep the paddles under it! Hastily I slid the frail craft into the water and eased the wounded man aboard. In the next moment I was kneeling against the stern thwart myself, paddling for dear life, shooting out across the river and then turning up along the farther shore, hoping to reach the fort, if I could do so unseen. Otherwise I would drive ashore on the other side and take to the woods.

Apparently, however, we were not noticed. I daresay the half-breeds were too busy now to look for us, for they had evidently turned their attention to pillage and a black column of smoke was beginning to rise from among the cabins. Once we were around the bend I felt safer, but not until we were directly opposite the landing did I dare swing back across. Once on the landing stage I hailed the fort, knowing that from there they could easily see who was calling, and at my shout two of the men at the rear gate came down and helped me lift poor John Bourke out of the canoe and carry him back up the path to the fort. I will admit, however, that it was not until we were inside that I was finally able to breathe freely once again!

It is no part of my intention here to go into all the grim details of the rest of that siege—I suppose that is what it should be called. I was the first to return, apparently, so that what account I could give of the tragedy of Seven Oaks was news to them all, and I was called upon to tell it over and over and over, so that—it is the only reason I can think of—the widow might find some shred of hope; the skeptic might find some flaw. But there was always poor, half-dead John Bourke to bear me out, even if he could not speak coherently; and James White, our surgeon, was not there. He had gone out with Governor Semple, and he did not return.

But if some inside the fort were skeptical at first, I had support for my story in the course of the day. Michael Heden and Daniel MacKay and Michael Kilkenny and George Sutherland—who had all been with Governor Semple's party, and had escaped across the river—came in and confirmed a part of what I had told. Then several of our later group crept back, including Sheriff Allen MacDonnell; and, of course, when he appeared I dissolved gratefully into the background. I had seen enough widows turn away into the arms of their friends; felt enough of the frustrated anger of men who had not been there and thought they might had done better if they had, to let someone else taste the bitterness for a while.

But we were not done yet. Toward sundown there came a thunder at the gate. It proved to be John Pritchard, prisoner on parole, sent to discuss peace terms. He had an offer, dictated of course by Cuthbert Grant, who was in command of the enemy. We were to surrender the fort and the post and all our claims to the land to the *Boisbrûlés*, in return for which we would be guaranteed safe passage to York Factory with all our personal baggage, which would not be molested.

I think that a good half of our people were inclined to accept the terms. They were listless, like Jean MacLean, whom I tried to cheer up without success, and did not care. They had had enough of strife and war and bloodshed, and they wanted only to get out and go home. But Sheriff MacDonnell and I both remembered that bloody field at Seven Oaks, and we were not inclined to put much faith in the promises of the half-breeds.

"Are there no Northwesters in the camp at Frog Plain?" I asked, for that was where the *Boisbrûlés* had established themselves.

Pritchard shook his head.

"There're no whites there but me an' th' Sutherlands an' Alec Murray an' his wife an' a couple o' th' Bannerman youngsters—all prisoners," he said. "They picked th' others up before th' fight—so, ye see, they've hostages."

"That's awkward," I admitted.

"Nayth'less," Sheriff MacDonnell said—and I could have kissed him for it, "ye go back an' tell 'em that we'll not treat with Grant, or any other *Boisbrûlé,* but with th' Northwesters only!"

So Pritchard went. He returned about midnight with word that the half-breeds were insulted and sent threats of retaliation upon their hostages unless we accepted their terms. That made it more difficult, but we sent back word that we must have time—twenty-four hours at least—in which to consider.

Again Pritchard went away, and since he did not return at once we guessed that so much, at least, of our terms were to be granted. But our own people were growing restless now. Get it over and done and let us begone, was their attitude. Tempers within the fort rose hourly, and we were near blows among ourselves when, late the following afternoon Pritchard presented himself once more at the gate. We let him in and I thought he seemed somewhat crestfallen. I noticed that he glanced first at me and then at Jean MacLean, who was standing off to one side, and only after that around at the rest.

" 'Tis not twenty-four hours yet!" Sheriff MacDonnell said.

"I know," Pritchard shrugged, "but some o' th' Northmen have come down from th' Assiniboine, an' they say ye must surrender t' Grant an' his comrades, but they will guarantee yer terms. Ye'll be carried out t' Fort William—"

"Fort William?" I cried. "But we specified York!"

"I can only repeat t' ye what they say," he replied.

"Take it! Take it, an' ha' done!" growled a number of voices at the back of the crowd.

I glanced at Jean. She looked angry.

"Oh, take it," she said, "and let's have an end of all this bickering!"

I looked at Sheriff MacDonnell and shrugged.

"Very well!" he said grimly to Pritchard. "We'll accept. But they that wish t' go back t' Scotland must be sent at th' expense o' th' North West Company."

Pritchard nodded and backed out. An hour later he was reported from the watchtower at the head of a small army, coming up from the Frog Plain.

"Come on up an' look 'em over," the sheriff invited me.

"To hell with 'em!" I replied. "I don't want to see them."

When he was gone I turned to Jean MacLean.

"Do you really want to call it all quits and go home, Jean?" I asked.

"What difference does it make?" she retorted listlessly.

Sheriff MacDonnell was back before I could think of a convincing answer to that, and it seemed to me that he gave Jean and myself the same sort of quizzical glance that John Pritchard had earlier in the day.

"They're here," he said. "It looks like this is th' end!"

We drifted down into the compound and watched the great gates that we had built so carefully swing open. Cuthbert Grant and Bostonnais Pangman were the first through. After them swarmed a conglomerate mass of *Boisbrûlés* and Northwesters. Alexander MacDonnell was one, Seraphim Lamar another, Antoine Hoole yet a third, and there were a host of others. But one made me rub my eyes and look again, and at my side I heard Jean MacLean gasp and cry out in protest, for he was taller than the rest and had red hair and blue eyes and a strong jaw. There was no doubt about it, much as we wished it were otherwise. There was Andy Ross!

7. ANDY ROSS

I DID NOT BLAME MYSELF FOR NOT HAVING FORESEEN THAT THE BIG, handsome, open-handed devil, in whom we had all put so much trust, would be among those triumphant conquerors who would come swaggering in through our gate. No mortal could have foretold that. But I did rap myself over the knuckles for not realizing that Cuthbert Grant would surely be among the first to enter, or that the place where we were standing made Jean one of the first upon whom his dark eyes would fall. It was almost as if we were a committee of welcome, and I cursed myself for not having gone up into the tower to watch their approach. If I had done so, much might have been avoided. Somehow or other I could have kept her in the background, perhaps even have turned her away altogether, so that she would not learn the bitter truth about Andy Ross until later, when I could break it to her more easily.

But it was too late now for any such speculation. As they came strutting in through that arched gateway of which I had been so proud, Cuthbert Grant immediately caught sight of her, and his eyes widened. He licked his thin lips, and his leer before he hid it under the pretext of wiping his mouth showed clearly the evil thought that was in his mind. He turned and came straight toward us, walking with quick, short steps and an air of exaggerated bravado, like a cock partridge drumming on a log. The distance was not great, and he was beside us before we could think what he was about.

With assured arrogance he shouldered in between us, with a sweep of one arm carelessly knocking me off balance and thrusting me aside. At the same time, with his other arm, he reached for Jeannie's supple waist, grinning and mouthing something in the local French-Indian patois, the words of which I could not understand—and I am sure Jean did not—but which we both sensed was indecent.

But Jean was quicker witted than I and had braced herself. As he reached for her, her hand flashed up with all the speed and strength of her small but wiry body and slapped him across the face so hard that he was rocked back on his heels.

In his surprise the confident grin he had worn seemed knocked askew and twisted into a flaming snarl of anger. He lurched forward toward her furiously, reaching for her this time with both hands clutching, and it was at that moment that I recovered my balance and hit him.

He was moving so swiftly, however, that I fear my aim was poor. My fist bounced off his cheekbone and skinned along the side of his head, raking my knuckles harshly, though I am afraid it did him little damage. The unexpected attack did have the effect, though, of throwing him a little aside, so that Jean could twist away and elude his hungering clutch.

But the man was quick as a cat and as light, I believe, on his feet. Without even seeming to falter he spun and smashed a savage fist into my belly, just over the groin. I stumbled and half fell, while my legs went weak and wobbly as a new calf's. I could hear the wind go out through my teeth with a racking grunt, and it seemed as if all of my guts at once were trying to push their way together into the constricted space of my gullet. Hideous pain shot through me, so sharp and so violent that it seemed as though I could taste it. I do not know if I cried out, but I know I must have turned gray. I braced myself for the next blow that would blot out the light and send me tumbling into the chasm of unconsciousness.

But it did not come. I was too dazed to see exactly what was happening, but my ear caught the sound of thudding feet, and it seemed as though the air all around me was filled with flying fists. Then I heard the sharp smack of flesh on bone and a sort of surprised sighing grunt, after which everything grew strangely quiet—and then Jean was at my elbow, shaking it lightly but urgently, sliding an arm about my waist as if to support me. From a long way off I heard her voice speaking to me.

"Mac! Malcolm! Are ye all right?"

I shook my head to clear it, and heard my own voice answer.

"I'm all right!"

Then all at once, as if by saying it I had made it so, the whirling, wavering mass of faces and bodies before me steadied and returned to focus, and I found that I could breathe again. To my astonishment, Cuthbert Grant lay stretched upon the ground, as limp and unconscious as a wet rag, and for an instant I stared at him, wondering if I could have done that—although I was quite sure that I had not. Then my eyes turned a little to the left and I saw—or rather guessed—what had happened, for Andy Ross stood there with his feet braced wide and a curious, wolfish grin upon his lips as he blew lightly upon the knuckles of a mighty fist and stared down at the fallen man. As I glanced toward him he looked around at us, then turned and came in our direction, his eyes lighting and the savagery of his grin turning to a friendly smile.

But there was no responding light in Jean's eyes. She dropped her arm from about my waist, having reassured herself about me, and turned to meet him. He stopped in front of her and started to speak, but as quickly as she had lashed at Cuthbert Grant she struck at him.

It was a full-armed swinging slap, and it had behind it all the force of her anger. It crashed full against the side of his face, and it must have hurt, for it rocked his head back. Yet his surprise was apparently sharper than any physical sting, for an expression of intense astonishment spread over his features, and whatever it was that he had been about to say tumbled back into his throat.

"Don't speak t' me!" Jean flared at him. "Don't ye dare, ye—ye—ye Judas!"

She turned to me and took me by the elbow with her small, strong hand, drawing me away.

"Come, Mac!" she commanded. "They've got a' they've wanted these three years past, an' they've tossed th' friendship we'd ha' been glad t' gi'e 'em on th' dunghill! I see no need t' haver an' blether. I know we canna go far yet, but I'll ask ye t' take me where I've no need t' see their ugly faces, at least until 'tis time t' go!"

At the sound of her voice; at our movement away, Andy seemed to awake.

"Wait!" he called out. "Jean, Mac—MacAllister!"

I faced about.

"Thank you, Mister Ross," I said stiffly, "for coming to Mistress MacLean's assistance. That was decent of you, and we give you credit for your impulse. But, after all, it was no more than is called for by the terms of our surrender—that our people would not be further harmed. Wasn't that the agreement? I think there is no more to be said between us!"

For an instant I thought he would come at me, for he flushed furiously red and the veins of his neck swelled and throbbed. His eyes clouded, and his great fists clenched. But I turned my back upon him and offered my arm to Jean. The little cluster of folk about us opened

to let us pass through, and I led her across the compound to the steps
of the Company store where Magnus Isbister and Alec MacLean and
Sheriff MacDonnell and three or four others of the council were
standing—all that were left of us now that the governor and the rest
were dead.

That seemed to me to be about as far away from the Northwesters
as I could take her, now that they were inside the fort. In a few
moments, I knew, they would overrun the place and no one would be
out of their sight or their reach if they meant to extend it. But here,
at least for the moment, was a certain solidarity. As we climbed the
steps I noticed that her hand on my arm trembled, and I thought it was
reaction to the tension of the moment we had just passed. I turned
her over to her father and patted her hand as I lifted it from my arm.

" 'Tis all right now, Jean," I assured. " 'Tis all over!"

To my bewilderment she snatched her hand away and gave me an
angry glare, but she said nothing. Sheriff MacDonnell caught my eye
and gave me a brief nod of approval, but none of the rest so much as
hinted by their expression that they had seen what had happened. I
felt I could understand that, for it was a bitter moment. When I turned
and looked back to where we had been Andy Ross was nowhere to
be seen, and Cuthbert Grant was being helped to his feet by several
of his companions, but for the moment he seemed still too groggy to
be fully aware of what had happened. The man would be in an ugly
mood, I thought, when he did realize it. We would be wise to keep
ourselves on guard.

I could not say, of course, whether or not this little episode had anything to do with the fact that for the rest of the time we spent at Fort
Douglas not one of the settlers was again personally molested. But
knowing the temper of Cuthbert Grant and his ilk, and encountering his
surly, smoldering stare a dozen times a day, I suspect that it did. At
least, I think, it may have reminded the Northwesters of their pledge
and their humanity, which I truly believe they almost sought to forget
at moments! At any rate we were herded off into a corner of the
compound and given two empty warehouses for our use. For rations
we were allowed a pound of pemmican, a cup of beans and a cup of
cracked corn and a tablespoonful of tea per person per day—all items
seized from our own stores, and aside from the daily issue of these we
were left strictly to our own devices, although we were allowed to
leave the fort only for the purpose of bringing up river water, which
was all that we were allowed.

So far as our personal baggage was concerned, however, or the contents of our homes—items that had also been a part of the surrender agreement—they were not so meticulous. Our homes were broken open and ransacked and, often as not, burned to the ground; such boxes and packages as some had been able to bring away were systematically looted and anything that caught our foes' fancy was carried off and put to their own use.

For two days we remained, waiting, in our corner, as utterly segregated as if a wall had been built around us. During that time the *Boisbrûlés* and the Northwesters equally roistered and caroused on the rum and stores that they had looted from our warehouses. I gathered that they were most disappointed to find that Colin Robertson, toward whom they appeared to have a particular grudge, was gone from among us.

"If the murdering swine were here," I can remember Cuthbert Grant howling, "damn me, I'd cut out his liver with my own hands and fry it and feed it to my dogs!"

Some of them, I gathered by inference, for we were told nothing, rode up to Portage la Prairie and brought down the skeleton crews of voyageurs and all the canoes from Fort Qu'Appelle and Souris and Brandon House which they had gathered there, apparently for this very purpose. But Andy Ross was not one of these, for I saw him several times among the roisterers, though he never appeared to see me and we exchanged no words.

Neither was Jean communicative. She retired behind a wall of brooding, miserable silence, and I thought that she locked up inside herself a grief for all that had happened to our little settlement that was all out of proportion to reality. In vain I tried to cheer her; tried to point out that everything had not come to an end. Lord Selkirk would try again, and even if he did not we ourselves were yet alive and still had our best years before us if only we were willing to make them so. For answer she only told me to hush and to mind my own business. Indeed, I do not think she spoke to me three times in those two days in which we waited.

The canoes from Portage la Prairie reached our landing late in the second day, and that night, in the large hall that had been our main Company store, there was a wild, crashing *boisson,* at which apparently every man among them tried to drink as much of the captured rum and high wine as he could hold, for when they returned there would certainly be none left. In our own dark corner of the compound we captives listened to the brawling and the revelry in grim, tight-lipped silence. More than half fearful lest the revelers come at us and our women when they grew drunk enough, we armed ourselves as best we could with staves torn from the walls and floors of our warehouses. But though we waited in the dark they seemed to have forgotten about us for the moment and never appeared.

In the morning, long before dawn, surly, thick-tongued voyageurs, far from colorful now after their long night's spree, routed us out with cries of *"Au canot!"* We gulped a hasty breakfast of raw pemmican and cold bean porridge—hardly fare, I thought, for a delicate stomach—and then were herded all together down the path to the landing, where we found that such canoes as we ourselves had held in storage had been brought out of their sheds and launched.

All of the craft had already been loaded with the furs and assorted loot of the fort, and now we prisoners were told off in lots of four or five and assigned, willy-nilly, to canoes as they were brought up. The men and boys were given paddles and told they must work for their passage, but the women, at least, were allowed to travel as passengers.

Such a haphazard arrangement, it seemed to me, had serious elements of danger, for the crews were a mixture of French-Canadian voyageurs, who might or might not be trusted, and savage *Boisbrûlés,* many of whom I recognized as men who had taken part in the fight at Seven Oaks. But as a prisoner it was hardly for me to protest. Some of the canoes had no prisoners at all on board. In others nearly half the complement was made up of our people. I was pleased to see, at least, that Jean MacLean and her father, with two of the Sutherland girls and one of the boys, went into a canoe that was otherwise manned entirely by French-Canadians and commanded by a Canadian clerk named Cadotte who seemed a decent and reasonable fellow. At least he had taken no part in the fighting at the Forks, but had come down later from upriver.

Andy Ross, I noticed, commanded a canoe about the middle of the brigade, which carried none of our people, though whether that was ordered that way by design or not I do not know. Both Bostonnais Pangman and Cuthbert Grant, I saw, were going with us, though for what purpose I could not imagine. At that point I was only glad that I was not assigned to either of their craft. The commander of the canoe in which I found myself was a middle-aged Scot named Craig, who seemed gloomy and morose and unhappy about the whole business. I never did learn which of the posts on the upper Assiniboine had been his station. At the last minute poor, stricken John Bourke, whom I had not seen since our return to the fort, was brought down and dumped roughly in amid a pile of baggage, despite the fact that he was in obvious pain from his wound. In the next moment the signal was given and we thrust off, sweeping out into the slow swirling current on the first leg of that long and dreadful voyage.

This, haphazardly, as I have described it, was approximately the order of our going—if indeed it could be called an order at all— throughout the journey, and I see no reason to describe each single hardship, each weary mile, each chute and portage as we reached and passed it. Under the best of circumstances there is a monotony about canoe travel that grows deadly after the first two or three hundred miles. Under such conditions as ours it was almost murderous.

But there were certain occurrences that must be told. On that first day, with the current at our heels, we went rapidly. The water was high, and it was not necessary to portage over the one long, swift chute between us and the Lake. By night we were able to camp at the mouth of the river. As prisoners, of course, we were segregated; given our own camp and ringed about with guards to see that we did not make general trouble. But in such a wilderness there was not much that we could have done. We were allowed to gather our own firewood, cook our own rations, and later to wash at the lakeside so long as we did not make any move toward the main encampment.

It was dark when I went down to the lake myself, and I did not see him come up behind me until he spoke.

"I want to talk to you," he said.

I started up and spun, ready for the attack I half feared. But in the gloom I saw it was Andy Ross, not Grant, and my growled reply was half relief.

"I'm not interested," I said and returned to my washing.

"Ye damned fool!" he whispered harshly through the dark. "I've been tryin' t' reach ye with this for three days, but there's been never a chance. Ye're goin' t' hear me now, whether ye want to or not!"

"Go ahead," I growled over my shoulder. "Talk as long as you like. It will make no difference to me!"

"Won't it?" he retorted. "Listen! Ye think me a traitor—ye an'— an' all th' rest o' ye! Ye're wrong!"

He paused, but I made no reply.

"I came down th' Souris an' found Brandon House yet smokin'," he went on eagerly, almost pleading. "I sent ye a message. Did ye get that?"

"We got it," I replied.

"All right," he said, "what would ye have done in my case? I could cut around 'em while they were still too drunk t' notice an' come on down t' ye at th' Forks. Or I could lie back in th' hills an' wait t' see what they'd do next. What good would it do ye for me t' cut an' run? I lay back!"

"What good did that do?" I demanded bitterly.

"Aye, I know!" he retorted. "I misjudged th' speed they'd use. By th' time I reached th' Assiniboine they'd already reached Portage la Prairie. I thought they'd have another *boisson* there, but they must have used up all their rum at Brandon House. I meant t' join their spree an' find out their plan an' then come on t' tell ye. But by th' time I got there th' breeds had already gone on, an' I knew there wasn't a chance in the world o' reachin' ye first. So I stayed there an' pretended t' be one o' 'em—that was the only way I could be any help t' ye if it came down t' things as they are. One man inside—"

"Who are you pretending to be one of now?" I asked him insultingly.

"God damn ye, MacAllister!" he cried, and for a moment I thought he would leap at me then and there. But he dropped his fists at his side in a gesture of resignation. "Listen, ye fool! I can't blame ye for what ye believe or how ye feel. But I tell ye, ye're wrong! I'm not what ye think, an' I've not been idle. I've had t' eat an' drink with 'em an' listen t' 'em boast, though it's turned my stomach. But I've learned somethin' important t' ye!"

"Have you?" I said dryly.

"Aye!" he whispered excitedly. "Listen, MacAllister, Lord Selkirk is on his way out. He's—"

He broke off abruptly and stood for an instant, listening. Steps ground on the gravel of the beach, coming toward us.

"I'll tell you another time!" he breathed hurriedly and then faded back in the darkness and was gone.

The French-Canadian guard who found me, an instant later, still dawdling over my washing when all the others had finished cursed me for a lazy dog and ordered me peremptorily back to my own camp, but I think he had no suspicion that anyone else had been there.

I must admit that for a few moments I found the information exciting. My first impulse was to go straight to Jean and tell her that we had misjudged him. Then caution suggested it might be wiser to mention this to Alec first. But even as that occurred to me skepticism came onto the field and I asked myself what possible difference it could make to any of us now if Lord Selkirk were on his way out? We were already prisoners of the Northwesters and on our way back!

I decided to say nothing yet, but to wait and see if this was really a sincere effort to help, or if Andy Ross, for some obscure reason, was merely trying to win back our confidence with a wild cock-and-bull yarn. After all, we had been burned once—or, at least, we had reason to believe we had!

We went on the next day, across the traverse, to the Grand Marais. But I had no opportunity at any time for any words with him. The next morning we were just setting out again when a strong brigade came sweeping around from Isle à la Biche, bound for the Forks. They were Northwesters, of course, and I noticed that each man was armed and that a *batteau* that was with them carried two small fieldpieces.

Obviously these were not intended to be used for shooting beaver! And nearly a hundred men, armed to the teeth, were not on a peaceful trading venture. Since they had come from Fort William, to which we were bound, some hundreds of miles to the eastward on Lake Superior, clearly they could not have heard of the fall of Fort Douglas and the Red River settlement—although, as it turned out, they had heard of the destruction of Fort Gibraltar. They were blandly innocent and astounded at our meeting. But when Roderick Mackenzie, who was in general command of our brigade, identified us and told them what had happened they could not suppress an Indian whoop of triumph; Mister Archibald MacLeod who was in command of them, and who was a partner in the Company—and no doubt by virtue of that a magistrate for the Indian Territories—ordered us all back ashore for examination and questioning, so that he might as he put it come at the justice of the thing.

But the nature of his "justice" was not long left in doubt. He was a short man, very heavy set and square-built, but red in the face and apoplectic in appearance. His first question as he stepped onto the beach was "whether that demmed rascal, Robertson," was with us. When he found that the best bird had gone from the covey, I think even his own men thought he would have a stroke on the spot.

But he did not. He recovered sufficiently to have all our scanty baggage searched, as if this had not been done already! He studied our books of account and all our papers so that we wondered if, should he find an error of addition or spelling among them, he would charge us for it! When he could find nothing wrong with them he ordered several of us, John Pritchard, Michael Heden, Pat Corcoran and Daniel MacKay, to write out their versions of what had occurred at the Forks. Thank the Lord he did not call upon me, too, as he might have done since I was schoolmaster, and therefore sure to be able to write! But apparently I was considered already prejudiced and so ruled out. What the others wrote clearly did not please him either.

"All lies! All lies!" he stormed. "D'ye men want t' be charged wi' perjury, dammit?"

He solved the whole problem so far as he was concerned—though how he came to the conclusion I never did understand—by formally charging poor, helpless, agonized John Bourke with felony and ordering him ironed and manacled at once. At the same time he subpoenaed the four I have named to appear as witnesses for the crown against Bourke; just to make sure that they would appear at the time and place designated—Montreal, on the first day of September—he ordered them manacled also, and only after that allowed us to proceed upon our way.

But the meeting was not exactly unproductive for us, either. These hearings, these depositions that proved to be unacceptable to Mister MacLeod, and finally the drawing of the charges and the subpoenas, consumed the entire day and part of the evening as well; while it was all going on there was little for the rest of us to do but to set up our camp again and make up our minds to stay where we were until it was done. For the prisoners—we were actually that although our captors never used the term—the interval was particularly irksome. We might wander a hundred yards or so in search of firewood or to gather reeds or boughs for bedding or attend to other, more personal necessities. We might go down to the lakeside to wash our mess kits. But we could not go hunting or fishing. We could not go for a walk. Most of us solved the problem by sleeping, and I was no exception.

The fire that I shared with a half a dozen other bachelors was on the outer circle; we thought it best to put the women alone at the very center, then the family groups, and last the unmarried men on the outside of the circle, so that in a sense we, too, were guards, keeping the Northwesters out as they hemmed us in! They had a guard station close by, and as I dozed and drowsed on the sunlit sand a number of Archibald MacLeod's men came over to pass the time of day with their comrades from the Red River. Their yells and their laughter awakened me, but I was sleepy and I was stubborn, and I was hanged if I was going to let them see that they had disturbed me. I pretended to be still asleep, keeping my eyes tight shut, but at the same time hearing all that they said—not because I wanted to eavesdrop, but because I could not help it without plugging my finger in my ear.

Their talk at first, like most of their conversation, concerned the virtues and frailties of the women of various tribes with which they had or hoped to come in contact. This was so usual that it was soporific and I almost dozed off again. Then one of the Red River men began to boast of the way they had gotten the best of us, and my blood began to bubble and boil and I came sharp awake and almost leapt to my feet and called him a liar, for he made it seem that the right was all with the Northwesters and that even our dead had played the part of poltroons.

But by luck I did not stir, for even as I was considering what I should do their talk switched; led from one topic to another.

"Ho! It was a good thing," said my Red River man, laughing as if it were a huge joke on us, "that they did not get the letters that were sent out to them in the spring from Montreal, for if they had they might have fought harder against us and made real trouble, hoping Lord Selkirk would protect them when he arrived."

They spoke in French, of course, but by this time I had learned enough of the patois to be able to understand. I opened my ears at the mention of Lord Selkirk, though I stayed very still so that I would not distract them.

Apparently the Red River man had touched upon something that was a deep secret at Fort William, known to only a few partners. Such secrets are harder to keep in the back country, for the men who carry them out often boast in their cups—especially if they are convinced that retribution is unlikely.

The voyageur from Fort William scratched his head.

"What is this?" he demanded. "I have not heard. There has been some talk of Lord Selkirk at the Lake, but of a messenger I have heard nothing."

"*Sacré!* You have not heard?" These voyageurs, I thought, were like old crones. If they knew something they must gossip! "This Lord Selkirk, he has been for more than a year in the east and he wishes to visit the colony that he has sent out to the Forks. Our bourgeois are very clever. I do not know how they discover this, but they do and they send out word to MacDonnell Bourgeois that he must do something about it."

"About what, then?" demanded the man from Fort William impatiently. "And what did he do?"

"I will tell you," replied the Red River man, recognizing his advantage and making the most of it. "This Selkirk writes many letters, to his governor, to the priest"—I almost laughed aloud, wondering how Alec MacLean would like that!—"to the schoolmaster, to all his friends, that he will be coming out soon. And then to carry these letters out through Fond du Lac he hires Laguimonière. You remember Bateese Laguimonière?"

"Laguimonière—but, yes," the man from Fort William sounded surprised. "But you say, 'remember.' "

"Even so!" replied the Red River man emphatically. "MacDonnell Bourgeois has orders that something must be done about this, so we talk with Katewabetay, of the Saulteurs. But Katewabetay will not do it, so we find some Ottawas who will kill him just as dead, and afterward the letters are carried to MacDonnell Bourgeois, at Rivière Qu'Appelle, but now I think they have gone back to Fort William for the big Bourgeois to see."

"Ho! This is a fine joke," cried the man from Fort William. "Here are these letters right under our very noses, but we know nothing about it, though I wondered where was Bateese Laguimonière. I have not seen him for so long a time."

The Red River man nodded soberly full of importance.

"But this is not all!" he said.

"There is more?" cried the Fort William man.

"But certainly!" the man from Red River assured him. "This Lord Selkirk will come out this way soon—in a few weeks—to visit the settlement that is no longer there at the Forks. He will follow the same route, this he wrote in the letters, through the Fond du Lac and the Rivière Saint Louis to Red Lake, and so to the Red River. But somewhere along that way Bostonnais Pangman and Cuthbert Grant and some of their people will be waiting, it has been arranged. This, I think, will be the last we will hear of Lord Selkirk, and afterwards we will have no more of this sort of trouble!"

"Let us hope not!" the man from Fort William agreed earnestly, and after that they fell to discussing matters of no interest to me, so that I actually did fall asleep. When I woke the guard had been changed and it was falling dusk. All along the beach the rekindled fires glowed. Supper kettles had been put on, and the air was redolent with wood smoke and savory with the aroma of cooking stew. I suddenly realized that I was very hungry, and this was the first thing that must be attended.

I went down to the lakeside and washed the sleep from my eyes first, which gave me a few moments to consider what I ought to do. Obviously some steps had to be taken. Some way must be found to warn Lord Selkirk—if it were actually true that he was already on his way—not merely of the fate of the colony, but also of the fact that if he tried to pass by way of Fond du Lac he would be walking straight into a trap. Curiously, as I saw it now, the problem had completely reversed itself. It was no longer a case of what could Lord Selkirk do to help us, but rather it was one of what we might do to save him.

I remembered my interrupted conversation with Andy Ross, and it seemed to me that if he were honestly sincere in his sympathies he should be able to find some way to get such a warning out. Certainly he had a far better chance of doing so than any of the rest of us. Yet I hesitated. I felt that I must discuss the problem first with someone whose judgment I could trust.

I returned to the fire and filled a mess kit with the savory rubbaboo that was simmering on the coals, and with this in hand crossed over to the MacLeans' fire. I was in luck I saw as I approached, for all of their messmates had either eaten their supper or gone visiting, and only Jean and her father were there. That at least would make it easier to talk, I felt. As I approached their fire they glanced up and greeted me; Jean a little listlessly, giving me hardly more than a mirthless smile and a slight nod, though her father was more than usually cordial for such a dour man. He rose and shook hands and waved me to a seat on their log beside the fire.

"We've na seen much o' ye lately, Malcolm," he said.

"I've not been sure I'd be welcome," I replied, glancing at Jean. "But tonight I think I've some news that may make a difference."

"Any news that's not a' bad would be a fine thing for us th' now," he said. "What is it, lad?"

I hesitated and looked around to make sure that we were not overheard.

"Lord Selkirk's on his way out," I said.

"Lord Selkirk?" Both their heads lifted as they stared at me with sudden interest.

"Ssshhh!" I warned them. "What I've to tell you must not be bruited about. Alec, I know a word is sufficient for you. But, Jean, I must warn you especially—"

She flushed angrily.

"Have I ever been one t' gossip?" she demanded.

"No, Jean," I smiled at her, trying to smooth her ruffled feelings, "you've never. But I've heard this now from two sources, and when I tell you one of them I think you may find it a difficult thing to keep locked up inside you. You'll feel that you must speak of it to someone. That's the only reason why I warn you particularly—because the slightest hint or word, dropped lightly in the wrong place, might have terrible consequences."

She stared at me with lips parted slightly and some of the old animation that I loved so well creeping back into her eyes. I think, I'm sure, that she already guessed one of the sources I mentioned, but she dared not let herself hope or believe it until she had heard it surely from me.

"We will say naught, Malcolm," she promised in a voice so different that even I was startled.

"Why d'ye come t' us, though?" Alec asked, and I could not help but smile for it was clear that the whole thing was still a mystery to him.

"I come to you for two reasons," I told him. "One, because I think that you, Jean, will be especially interested. And, second, because I want your advice, Alec, before I attempt any move."

"Aye, then, what is it?" he asked. " 'Tis plain there's more t' it than ye've said yet."

"There is!"

I nodded emphatically, and then I told them, first of that swift, whispered conversation with Andy Ross at the mouth of the river, and then of the talk I had overheard among the canoemen that afternoon. I left nothing out, and neither of them interrupted me, though I noticed that Jeannie's eyes widened and brightened and her lips curved upward once more in a smile of delight when I told of what Andy had said. I cannot say that I took any particular pleasure from that for myself. But at least she had smiled again, and that was something.

When I had reported all I had heard the lank dominie could contain himself no longer.

"But if a' this is true," he cried, "surely we maun warn his lordship!"

"Aye, 'twas my own thought," I told him. "But how? There's the problem!"

"Aye, how!" he agreed morosely.

I watched them both closely. This would be the time, if they felt he could be trusted. I wanted it to come from them, for I felt it would be a surer indication of their real opinion if it did. Jean hesitated an instant, and then looked over at me.

"Andy could do it," she said.

I looked at her father.

"What do you think, Alec?" I asked.

He studied the fire for a long moment, seriously, considering. Then at length he nodded.

"Aye!" he said. "Aye, I believe th' lad's honest."

He glanced at me.

"In any case," he added, "we've sma' choice!"

I rose, for some reason feeling all at once very much better.

"Very well then," I said. "I will try to speak to him about it. But leave this to me; remember, please, both of you, not a whisper to anyone! Not even to Andy, Jean, until I give you the word!"

Neither of them spoke, but they both nodded, and I could tell by the light in their eyes that I had their promise.

But finding an opportunity to speak to Andy was easier to promise than to do. The brigade moved on, of course, the next morning, and in the course of the next few days we rounded Traverse Point and ascended Traverse Bay, passed Fort Bas de la Rivière Winipic, where we paused to replenish our supplies, and then plunged into the long, tortuous, portage plagued ascent of the Winnipeg River.

Until we reached that point it seemed to me that every time we came near one another either I was under the watchful eye of a guard, or there were too many other people around who would have been quick to note that we did not preserve quite the right attitude of hostile indifference and who would have been quick to take exception to it. Yet he must have noticed the eagerness in my eye when we occasionally did meet and pass, for when we were embarking at Bas de la Rivière for the journey upstream he found an opportunity to brush against me in the melee. In the hubbub and the shouting, words spoken in an ordinary tone could scarcely be heard more than a foot from the speaker's mouth. Now he glowered at me and curled his lip in a snarl, as if he were cursing me. But what he really said was:

"Wait for the portages! We'll have a chance to talk then."

He swung past me then and pushed on toward his own canoe, and I am afraid I came very near to betraying the whole thing at that moment, for I caught myself staring after him in what must have been quite evidently pleased surprise, not at all with the expression of a man who had just been given a brief but biting tongue lashing.

The River Winnipeg I found to be a great, turgid stream, widening every now and again, throughout its course from the Lac des Bois, into numberless wooded and island-studded lakes. Between the lakes it plunged; sometimes foaming and roaring and churning and seething; sometimes in long, slick chutes, down through the cool, green forests. It was here that I learned what he had meant, for all the way up, often five or six times a day, we found it necessary to land and carry our canoes and their loads up around the snarling rapids. To my vast disappointment, most of these portages were short—too short for any real chance to talk. Most of them were not above three or four hundred yards, and some were as little as fifty. But the confusion of coming and going that reigned during them made the hurly-burly at Bas de la Rivière seem like a dress parade. Each man had his allotted load to carry across—sometimes two loads, if the going was very steep or rough; no one had either the time or the energy to worry much about what his neighbor was doing. I could see that on a long carry there might be plenty of opportunity to talk. But here, on these short crossings, where the stream of men passing back and forth was almost constant, it did not seem to me that we would be able to say much.

Andy, however, contrived it more effectively than I had thought possible, and sooner than I had dared hope. On the first day after leaving Bas de la Rivière we went no more than a dozen or so miles, for we had five short portages to get over, and at each one, of course, no matter what the distance, we had to unload the canoes at one end and reload them again at the other. On the second day our first carry was a short one, but the second, the Portage du Bonnet, was nearly two miles long, over a bald, rocky ridge. As each man prepared his pack for the crossing, Andy, who could certainly have led us all off if he wished, dallied until I had set off up the trail. Then he swung in behind me.

At the start we were all close together in single file. But presently the faster walkers drew ahead, while the slower ones fell behind, so that we were scattered at irregular intervals all along the way. Andy waited until a distance of several rods separated us from those ahead and those behind. Then he spoke.

"What's in your mind?" he asked in a low tone. "I've watched ye tryin' t' slip a word t' me this week past."

"I want to talk to you," I said. "Somewhere where we'll have a better chance than we do here."

"What about?" he demanded, and I could tell by his tone that the way I had spoken the other night still rankled.

"Lord Selkirk," I told him.

"I told ye he was comin' out!" There was a ring of triumph in his voice. Apparently he had assumed that I had confirmed it.

"Aye!" I replied. "But what do you know of the plan to waylay him?"

"What?" The way he barked the word told me how startled he was. He said nothing for a moment. Then spoke in a lower tone. "I know naught o' it. I told ye they'd talked, but they said nothin' o' that."

"I think it may be something they've planned since then," I told him.

"Aye! But ye're right. We can't talk o' this here," he said. " 'Tis too dangerous."

There was a long silence, and I ventured a backward glance. He seemed to be thinking carefully.

"Th' Portage des Rochers will be a long one," he said at length.

" 'Tis on Rainy River, well above Lac des Bois, a good two weeks travel from here, but still 'tis th' best for our purpose. Halfway over there's a steep climb over a brushy hill. Th' trail's narrow, an' winds between big boulders, an' there's a place where we can duck aside behind th' rocks an' talk as long as we like without anyone th' wiser. When we come t' th' carry I'll tip ye th' sign, then go on ahead an' wait for ye at th' spot."

"That's what we want," I told him. Then something prompted me to add, "If you don't mind I'd like to bring Jean MacLean along. She's— well, I think she'll be interested."

"Mac!" he cried. I dared not look back at him for we were on a straightaway now where we could easily be seen, but by the lift of his voice I could sense his excitement. "Mac, d'ye mean it?"

"Of course I mean it!" I growled, and we said no more after that.

I think those two weeks of voyaging, before we came to the eight mile Portage des Rochers, were among the longest I have ever known. We wormed our way slowly up the Winnipeg, through the Dalles and over the Rat Portage, into the broad, island studded Lac des Bois. Not until we reached the Rainy River, at the upper end of that lake, did I take Jean into my confidence. When I did tell her what we had planned, the unconcealed delight with which she greeted the news cast a chill over my spirits and left me with a hollow feeling in my heart. Was I a fool, I wondered, to be doing this? But I avoided the answer.

We were three days on the Rainy River before we came to the Portage des Rochers. There, at the place where we landed, Andy Ross adjusted his pack and gave me an almost imperceptible nod and went swinging off up the trail. I sought out Jean and picked up my own *sac* and a few minutes later we followed—Jean leading so that I could adjust my pace to hers. Alec had elected to keep out of sight.

"Th' fewer are in it," he said, "th' less danger ye'll be discovered!"

That seemed sensible to me. Indeed, I wondered that I had drawn Jean into it. Yet somehow I could not help myself.

We must have walked three miles or so before we began to climb steeply up the hill that Andy had described, through rocky, scrub-covered, brûlée studded with great massive boulders. Near the top, where the trail made a twisting, snakelike wiggle, we came upon him, leaning, as if resting, against the rock. At sight of us he smiled and motioned us off quickly to the left between two huge boulders, down a winding deer track that in less than twenty feet rounded the face of the rock and took us out of sight of the trail.

Andy continued on another dozen rods until we came to a tiny glade, no more than a wide spot in the track actually, about forty feet long and twenty across, with brush screening both ends. A sheer rock wall rose upon one hand, while on the other the hill rose steeply, strewn with stony rubble, charred stumps and fireweed and brambles. Had he spirited us fifty miles away, I think, we could not have been more isolated, at least for the moment.

As we came into the place Andy dropped his pack and turned about soberly, as if he had something he must say.

"Jean," he said.

"Oh, Andy!" she cried, and then there they were in each other's arms and I might have been a thousand miles away.

I looked at them, and swallowed, and looked away, and then looked back again. And then, abruptly, I turned away with a clutch at my throat as if a great hand were fastened there and it hurt. I went over to a nearby clutter of rocks and dropped my pack and sat down and wiped the back of my hand across my eyes and forehead so that it would look as if I were wiping away the sweat of our climb. Inside me two separate voices seemed to be arguing.

"Well, you damned fool," one of them said, "what did you expect?"

But the other answered, "Listen to me! If she's in love with anyone else she'd never be happy with you. You might as well face it!"

But it was Andy's voice that drowned out those others.

"Great God, Mac!" he was saying. "What's wrong? Ye're green as moss. Are ye ill?"

I looked up at them and saw the glow in their eyes.

"Me?" I pushed up a laugh that was like the cawing of crows in my own ears. "I'm all right. Just a little bilious, I'm afraid, too much pemmican!"

But somehow that did not fetch up the grin that I expected in reply. Instead he turned suddenly very serious.

"Now, what's this about Lord Selkirk ye were tellin' me?" he demanded.

I explained what had happened and how I had come to overhear the talk, and then told him what had been said.

"Cuthbert Grant and Bostonnais Pangman will be the leaders," I said. "I daresay they'll take the rest of the crew with them to Fond du Lac."

"Grant and Pangman!" He slapped the rock beside him. "So that's why they're here! I should've guessed 'twould be some such!"

"Can you get a warning to Lord Selkirk?" I demanded.

"I can try!" He glanced at me sharply, then looked at Jean. "Aye, I can try!"

He began to walk up and down the little glade, pondering, worrying the problem, scratching his head, fingering his jaw. We watched him for a moment. Then it was Jean who cried out.

"Andy!"

He turned toward her with the old grin that we both remembered but had not seen for a long time.

"O' course I'll try!" he exclaimed, and then abruptly grew deadly serious. "Now hark t' me, both o' ye! I said I'd try, an' I will. But, mark me, if aught happens t' me—or if ye think aught's happened t' me, mind—I don't want a word o' this told t' a soul. D'ye understand? Not a solitary, livin' soul! I'll not try it unless ye promise me that!"

I nodded.

"You can count on me," I said.

Jean hesitated an instant.

"All right, Andy," she said then.

He turned to pick up his pack.

"Good, then!" he smiled. " 'Tis all settled! Now let's get out o' here before we're missed."

Jean looked across at him in a way that would have made my own head swim.

"Wait a minute, please, Andy," she said.

I snatched up my pack and slung it over my shoulders, fixing the tump line.

"I'll go first," I said.

I did not hear either of them object.

It was only when we were back on the river, driving upward toward Lac la Pluie, that I remembered we knew nothing of his plans. But he had made it clear, it seemed to me, that he wanted to keep them to himself, so I did not mention them to him. I did not even ask Jean if she knew what they were.

We went on up across Lac la Pluie and carried past the Chaudiere Rapid and then crossed lakes Namayacan and Vermillion, where the Ojibway gather their pipe clay, and beyond that we came into a mass of islands and water called Lac à la Croix. Here the old route that used to run down to Grande Portage turned off through the Bottle Rapids and Lake Saginaga. But the new road to Fort William, by way of the Kaministiquia, also branched off here, to follow up the Rivière Maligne to the Lake of the Thousand Lakes and from there across to the Dog

River and Dog Lake and so, down past Kakabeka Falls to Lake Superior.

We paused for a moment at Pointe Maligne, where the new and old ways divided, and Andy Ross seemed quite delighted to find an encampment of Ojibways there. To the rest of us they seemed a rather disgusting nuisance, for though they made fine canoes to replace those smashed in the brawling waters above, they insisted upon payment in rum, and once paid they refused to make more canoes until the rum was all gone. But they were old friends, Andy insisted, and their chief, Charlo, was entitled to a present.

I thought the present—two casks of rum—rather extravagant considering the fact that they were no more than casual acquaintances. But it was no business of mine and of course I said nothing.

From there we went on up the Rivière Maligne, toward Sturgeon Lake, and it was upon this stretch that we experienced one of those inexplicable tragedies that occasionally happen to the most expert canoemen.

There were only two short portages on the Maligne, neither of them around truly desperate rapids. Had we been coming downstream, I believe, we would have been inclined to try the chute—that is, to run them—so as to save the labor of the carry. But since we were going upstream we had no choice. We picked our way around the first Maligne rapid, which was a brawling, tumultuous thing, and by far the worst, without any mishap, and a dozen miles beyond we came to the second falls, which looked much worse than they were.

All the rest of our canoes carried over here, a distance of a hundred yards or so. But Andy appeared to be in a recalcitrant mood. These rapids could be tracked, he declared; that is, with a steersman to guide the craft and hold it just offshore, the crew, hauling on a line made fast to the bow, could drag the canoe upstream against the current and thus save a tedious carry.

The crew were reluctant. Indeed, the steersman said he would not attempt it. Andy sneered. Very well then, he said, let the others do the work! If they would handle the lines and haul the canoe up he would undertake the most dangerous part, which was that of steersman.

I felt that he literally goaded them, finally, into attempting the thing. Certainly none would have undertaken it if he had not challenged them with his taunts, and I wondered if he had not dipped a little deeply into the rum cask with his Indian friends, although it seemed to me that if he had it should surely have worn off by now. At first the thing seemed to go well. Andy was an expert with the paddle, and as the men hauled on the lines the lightened canoe followed up through the swirls and eddies and pockets that clung close to the shore, though the current in midstream thundered and crashed.

At the upper end of the rapid more than a few of us gathered to watch and see how the thing would come out, and I must say that for a moment it seemed to me that Andy's argument would be proved true. They came around the bend with the canoe in perfect position to take full advantage of the little inshore eddies and currents that run opposite to the main stream. The crew doing the tracking were clearly expert, and Andy's steersmanship was a delight to watch. They came up, hugging the north shore, which was the side the trackers were on, and it seemed to me that they were almost in the clear, at the top of the rapids, when something went wrong. Without warning the canoe swerved out into the current, and the suddenness of it apparently jerked the lines from the hands of most of the crew. A few held for a moment, but clearly their small efforts only served to hold the craft momentarily broadside to the stream, and put it in danger of capsizing.

Andy half rose against the stern thwart, his paddle pressed close in against the side of the canoe.

"Lachez! Lachez la corde!" His voice rose above the roar of the rapids. "Let go!"

The crewmen obeyed the command at once, but it was too late. The big canoe, caught now by the offshore eddy, moved out toward the whitewater, the main current. It moved slowly at first, sweeping down, broadside to the stream, and Andy first seemed to lie back on his paddle in an effort to backwater. Then, apparently, he came to the conclusion that only by going forward and gaining steerage way could he bring the runaway craft under control, and he began to paddle furiously.

But a laden north canoe does not answer well to a single paddle, especially in the grip of the stream. They gathered speed, but it was the speed of a racing current; inert speed so far as Andy was concerned, for it gave him nothing against which to use the pressure of his paddle. Yet somehow he seemed to win a measure of control, for the ponderous canoe, though it plunged toward the dancing, white-capped water at the bend below, was at least headed downstream when we caught our last sight of it.

"Andy! Andy!" I heard Jean cry out behind me in an agony of helplessness.

" *'Cré nom!*" muttered one of the men nearby. "Never will 'e mak' this run alone in such a *canot*. 'E will be capsize an' drown! *Au 'voir*, M'sieu Ross! *C'était un bon bourgeois!"*

Nevertheless, despite that pessimistic prediction, two unloaded canoes were hastily manned and pushed off, to run the rapids behind him, and all the rest of that day we waited for the return of those men and their boats, hoping against hope that by some miracle he would be with them.

But it was dusk when they arrived, bringing with them the sodden bales of furs and bags of provisions and even the battered canoe that they had found floating, bottom side up, in the quiet eddy below the chute.

Of Andy, however, they had found no trace.

8. RED RIVER HARVEST

It is true that a little more than a week of travel still lay ahead, before we would be able to traverse the last steep portages on the lower reaches of the Kaministiquia and come out at Fort William, on Lake Superior. Yet it seems to me that there is little more that need be told of that heartbreaking journey.

On the morning after the tragic accident the brigade got under way once more, wearily, reluctantly, since Andy had become a general favorite among us all and was especially loved by the French-Canadian voyageurs who had idolized him. There was one of us, of course, who was even more reluctant than the rest. Jean would have had us wait and search the river even as far back as Lac à la Croix. She pleaded with the partners who were in charge of the brigade to allow us just one day for that purpose. But they said it could not be done. She even appealed to the men in the name of the friendship they had borne for him. But they dared not defy the partners. When, at last, she was practically forced to leave, she allowed herself to be seated in the canoe, but she was listless and dull and would talk to no one.

I must admit that I watched this display of her great grief with some concern, for as we pushed on it did not seem to diminish. Nor did she make any effort to hide it, and I began to fear that she would destroy her own health and her mind if she persisted in it. Finally I decided that it could do no harm if I had a word with her. Who could tell? It might even do some good. When we came to camp at the upper end of the Lake of the Thousand Lakes I waited until supper was finished. Then I strolled casually over to their campfire and sat down near her. Alec looked at me gloomily and shook his head slowly.

"I'd like a word with Jean, if I may, Alec," I said.

He glanced from me to her and back again, then nodded and rose, understanding.

"I'll leave ye two t'gether, then a bit," he said. "I maun gather some more firewood anyway."

He rested his hand for an instant affectionately on her shoulder, and then turned away.

"Jean!" I said. "Jeannie, lass! You can't go on being like this, you know. Andy would never approve of it."

At the sound of his name she looked at me, but she made no reply.

"Jean!" I went on persistently. "Do you mind that day on the Portage des Rochers. What was it that he said to us? Remember he said: 'No matter what happens to me—no matter what you may think has happened to me' and he put a good deal of emphasis on the word 'think.' "

She looked up at me again with that same strained, haunted look in her eyes. But this time, it seemed to me, there was just a faint spark of interest about them. Of course those hadn't been his words exactly, but they were the gist of them.

"Mac—Malcolm!" she whispered, and I felt a surge of elation. That was the first time since we had left the portage that anyone had heard her speak! "Malcolm, ye don't believe?"

Her voice trailed off, but I nodded emphatically.

"I do!" I told her. "I am sure that the reason he said that was because he had just some such plan as this in mind—a trick to make them think he was dead so that he would have a chance to get away without making them suspicious. He didn't want us to think so, though. That's why he said what he did."

The strained eyes grew bright for a moment with hope, then turned dull again. She shook her head.

"No, Malcolm," she said. "No, 'twas an accident. Mind, we watched it happen, with our own eyes! We saw it. He—he's dead!"

She buried her face in her hands, but I reached out and caught her wrists and pulled them away.

"Nonsense!" I said sharply. "In the first place Andy was far too good a canoeman to let his craft get out of control at such a spot while the men were tracking it upstream! Didn't it occur to you that it was strange that the canoe should swing out into the stream just there—at the very head of the chute—when he must have known that all the rest had finished the carry and there were none below? In the second place, remember, Jean, you didn't see the canoe turn over! I didn't see it! Nobody saw it! He could have taken it through safely, into the pool below. He was good enough with a canoe to have done that. Then, when he had reached the still water, he could deliberately

have turned it over and swam ashore, long before any of the others
got there!"

She was staring at me now with a definite glow of excitement in
her face, and the hope that had come back into her eyes was not the
kind that would die.

"Mac!" she cried, and even her voice I noticed was more vibrant
now and alive again. "Mac, d'ye really think?"

I nodded emphatically.

"I don't just think so," I replied. "I'm sure of it! Mind, now, they
found everything but Andy. And if nothing else was carried away
downstream, why should he have been? No, Jeannie! I'd be willing
to make a small wager with you that all the time they were searching
the pool and the stretch of river below, Andy was lying hid in the
brush on the far side, watching them!"

I stood up and patted her shoulder.

"You think about that now," I said, "and see if you don't come to
the same conclusion. Good night, Jean!"

I left her sitting there, gazing into the fire, puzzling over the things
I had said, studying them from every angle to see if there was a flaw
in it. Looking back at her, as I left, I prayed silently that my guess
was right. It might be doubly hard for her if it turned out that I was
wrong. But now, at least, I noticed, the listlessness was gone.

The next morning, when we were just starting over the long meadow
carry, Alec MacLean came over to me.

"I dinna ken what it was ye said t' her, lad," he said, "but whate'er
it was it's made a different lass out o' her already."

"Has it?" I said. "It must be I've a way with women!"

"Then ye've a rare fine gift, Malcolm!" he replied.

Only one other thing happened during the rest of that voyage, and
that, too, concerned Jean. But the promptness and efficiency with
which she settled it showed more eloquently than anything else how
thoroughly she had recovered.

After we crossed the height of land, and entered the waters that
flow east and south into Lake Superior, we came one evening to Dog
Lake, which is the main feeder for the Kaministiquia. This lake, we
found was teeming with fish, and since we were growing weary of
our diet of pemmican, nearly all the men belonging to the settlers'
party went down and scattered along the shore to catch as many as
we could. Alec MacLean and I, of course, went with them, and we
left Jean tending the fire and making ready for a good fish supper.

Now, ever since Andy's restraining influence had been gone Cuthbert Grant had grown more and more intolerable. He was insolent and arrogant, and what was particularly infuriating was his attitude toward our girls. He seemed to think them all fair game, but apparently he had a particular letch for our Jean, and at this moment he seemed to think that at last his chance had come. She was bending over the fire, putting on the porridge, when he came up behind her and tried to catch her in his arms and throw her to the ground. But she was quick and she had a sharp wit. Even as she turned she caught up a burning brand from the fire and so belabored him about the head and face and neck with it that his long, greasy black hair and his shirt took fire, and he was forced to run down to the lake and plunge in, clothes and all, in order to extinguish it. When he returned to camp he was the butt of so much ridicule from his companions that he very nearly turned about and went home.

Alec and I, of course, knew nothing about this until we came back with our fish. When she told him about it then, in a calm, completely self-assured voice, Alec's only comment was dry.

"Ye'd think th' girt gowk'd learn t' stay awa' from ye when ye're nigh a fire!" he said.

Apparently the same thought occurred to Cuthbert Grant, for he did not molest her again during the journey, and before we could have any more such trouble from any of the other young bucks who might be anxious to prove themselves smarter men than he, we arrived at Fort William.

I must say that in spite of myself I was impressed when I saw the place. It was far more extensive than I had expected. Indeed, to our eyes, after the years we had spent at the Forks, it had the appearance of a thriving and very busy little city. Actually it was as big as a small town. There was a large fort, with a palisade that enclosed several acres. Inside there were a score of buildings, ranging in size from three immense, slate-roofed structures in the middle, each three stories high, down to tiny smithies, armorer's shops, cooperages, gunsmiths, a tailor, a saddler and a shoemaker, carpenter's shops, and even a small forge.

This, I learned later, was the very heart and life center of all the North West Fur Company's operations in the west, and the three central buildings inside the palisade were its core. The building at the left, as one entered the gate, was the depot for all of both incoming and outgoing goods. Furs from the up country were sorted, graded and baled here; on another floor the trade and Indian goods and all supplies that could not be drawn from the country itself were carefully checked and apportioned to one or another distant post. The central building housed the meeting rooms, the kitchens, the vast dining room, in which the partners held fabulous feasts, and the luxurious apartments assigned to the more important partners when they came out from Montreal each summer or down from the forests and the lakes for the annual meeting. The third building housed the permanent staff of the post: the apprentices, clerks, minor partners and the like; it also contained quarters for winterers—as those men who spent the winters at the posts in the hinterland were called—of the same ilk.

Outside the fort, especially on the northern side, and along the river, there were a number of other large, barnlike buildings; storehouses of various sorts, canoe sheds, granaries. There were even a few small but neat houses assigned to those who worked the fort's gardens. Behind the fort and to the south of the wall there were three separate and distinct camps. One was for the *mangeurs du lard*—the pork eaters, the men from the north contemptuously called them—the voyageurs who brought the big canoes out from Montreal in immense brigades but who rarely went beyond this point. Another was for the swaggering, boasting voyageurs of the north—*les hommes du nord*. The third camp —actually no more than cleared ground on which they were permitted to pitch their tepees—was for the Indians who flocked each year to the rendezvous, to dance and drink themselves into a brawling stupor, and incidentally to trade and get their supplies for the winter's hunt.

But, although it seemed to us a very hive of activity, the bustle and rush that was so impressive was but a shadow of what the post had seen that year, for the great summer meeting was over. The Montreal Brigade had left and the brigades for the more distant posts in the *pays d'en haut* were already on their way. There were, however, some partners still there, both winterers and men from Montreal—very important men.

Indeed, one of them was probably the most important of all the partners at that time, the leader of the strongest political faction among them, and the man who stood opposed, tooth and nail, to anything that was done or attempted by Lord Selkirk and the Hudson's Bay Company. This was William McGillivray, a man of moderate height and moderate girth. In fact he was shaped rather like a pear. But he had a great, leonine head, a powerful voice and a very arrogant expression.

I found out about him, and discovered he was there, when along with the rest of our refugees I was herded up to the fort. For a moment I wondered if they were going to take us in and put us under lock and key in one of that multitude of buildings. But apparently they had no intention of doing that. They halted us at the gate, and it was then that I saw the great man, for he came out and surveyed us with evident distaste for several minutes, after which he harangued us.

We had, he said, shown ourselves to be very stupid people. We had begun by allowing ourselves to be duped by a charlatan who had no interest in our welfare, but wished only to advance the Hudson's Bay Company at the Northwesters' expense. For some reason that infuriated me.

"That's a lie!" I shouted.

He glared at me.

"What the devil do you know about it?" he bellowed.

"A damn sight more than you do or ever will!" I retorted.

He pointed a finger, trembling with rage, at me.

"Put that man in irons!" he bawled. "Throw him in the jail with the other prisoners."

There was no sense in resistance. There was a stout Northwester at each elbow as soon as he began to speak, and almost before he was done the manacles were on my wrists. I expected to be trundled away immediately. But apparently my guards wanted to hear him, so though we moved back out of the line of his vision we did not leave. Mister McGillivray paid no further attention to me, and began:

"Ye've shown yourselves to be poltroons by clinging so stubbornly and stupidly to the notion that any permanent settlement, fit for white men to live in, could be made at such a Godforsaken place as the Forks of the Red River. And ye have shown yourselves in the bargain to be thieves and dishonest people, first by trying to steal and expropriate to your own purposes, the lands of our blood brothers, the métis, and second by seizing feloniously and willfully a fort, the property of the North West Company, and everything in it!

"In view of all this I think ye should be grateful to the North West Company for its forbearance in not permitting the understandably angry métis to murder you all. And ye should be grateful to us for the kindness we do ye in bringing ye out again to a decent, Godfearing, white man's country!"

He paused and glared down at them.

"When I go down to Montreal," he said finally, "I shall take ye all with me, that will be in a very few days. Once ye are in Montreal we will allow ye a choice: Those that wish to may return to Scotland; those that elect to stay will be settled on land of our own choosing, at our terms, of course! Now, while ye're waiting to start the journey ye may pitch your camp over there."

He pointed over their heads toward a flat, cleared space between the north wall and the first of the large, barnlike warehouses.

"Th' men in irons, of course," he added, "will lodge in the jail. That's all!"

He turned about and strutted back through the gate. For an instant I caught Jean's eye, and at the expression of misery and distress I saw on her face my heart sank. Oh God, I thought, is everything to be undone now? Is this the end of everything? Why can't we have a little share of peace and quiet and happiness and stability? Why must we always be shunted around just because we happen to interfere with some pompous fool's profits?

But, of course, I had no answer for such questions, and it was foolish even to think of them, for in the next instant I was thrust forward and herded with the other men in irons—Pritchard and Heden, Corcoran, MacKay and the tough, wiry John Bourke, who had amazed us all by surviving his wound and his treatment!—into the fort and led to the jail, the only stone building in the place. Apparently the others had been brought up from the landing belatedly and so they had not heard the start of the harangue. They were surprised to see me in irons.

"What'd you do?" John Pritchard demanded.

"Talked back to the master," I replied grimly.

"Haw! Haw!" Pat Corcoran guffawed.

"Shut up!" one of our jailors snarled.

The other slapped him across the mouth.

They then opened the thick oak slab that was the door and motioned us into a tiny, windowless cubbyhole, whose floor was strewn with verminous straw and which was furnished only with a wooden bench.

"Get in!" they commanded, and when the last of us had entered they slammed and locked the door.

We discovered then that our only light and air came through a crack under the door and through a tiny opening, half covered with bars of strap iron. It was almost pitch dark in there.

"So this is civylization?" I guessed it was Pat Corcoran who said that, and thanked God that we could still laugh!

No one wanted to lie down on the verminous straw, so we groped our ways across the cell and ranged ourselves upon the bench—and there we sat for almost a week. They gave us food and water, of course—if you could call it food—and provided a bucket for necessary functions. But apart from that they ignored us.

Sitting there in the dark, like a row of owls, we almost lost track of time. And a man does not get much sleep sitting up shivering on a bench against a dank stone wall. We got very tired. Then, all at once, without any warning, on the fifth day—or it might have been the sixth—our cell door was flung open and one of our jailors asked us, oh so politely, to come out. We did not waste any time about it!

But the bright sunlight hurt our eyes and made them water, so that it was a few moments before we could see what was going on. When I finally could make him out I saw that there was a very straight standing young man in a bright red uniform coat and white trousers about ten feet in front of us. He wore a sword at his side and a tall shako on his head, and he was looking first at us in astonishment and then at the jailor in surprise.

"I thought these men were not prisoners?" he demanded.

The jailor shrugged.

"Don't blame me!" he whined. "I only do what I'm told."

"Very well!" The young man looked at a paper he held in his hand. "Malcolm MacAllister?"

"Here!" I stepped forward, and he reached out and shook my still manacled hand, and gave a jerky little bow and clicked his heels together.

"Charmed to make your acquaintance, Mister MacAllister!" he said. I noticed that he spoke with a curious little accent, but I was too bewildered to ask him his name or what was happening.

He turned to the jailor.

"Strike off his irons!" he commanded, and the turnkey obeyed.

He repeated the performance with every name on his list, which included us all. And in each case the jailor obeyed until he came to Bourke and Pritchard. These he refused to release.

"Why?" demanded the officer.

" 'Cause these men is criminals," the turnkey said. "They got warrants out fer them. They're charged with felony."

"We shall see!" replied the young man, which led me to believe that he was acting under orders from someone else, though I could not guess who. He looked at the two disappointed men.

"I regret, gentlemen!" he said, with that same jerky bow. "A little longer delay, but not too long I think, eh?"

He saluted the two ragged scarecrows smartly and then turned to us.

"Will you come with me please, gentlemen?" he asked.

We were only too happy to do as he asked, though we could not guess what it was all about. He led us out through the gate where two more smartly uniformed men fell in beside us and escorted us down the slight hill to the landing. As we walked I studied them curiously. They didn't look like officers, but they were obviously soldiers.

At the landing we found a trio of large *canots du maître* awaiting us. We also found ten or a dozen of our people, including, to my great delight, Jean and Alec MacLean. At sight of me Jean ran over to me and kissed me on the cheek and made sympathetic noises over my unshaven face and my dirty hands. But she was clearly bubbling over with excitement about something else.

Before I could ask her what it was, however, the officer was ordering us aboard the canoes, still in the same courteously curt way with which he had done everything else so far. I managed to find a place just behind the MacLeans, and as soon as we had pushed off and were on our way I leaned over and tapped her on the shoulder.

"Now," I said, "will you please tell me what this is all about?"

She glanced back at me, over her shoulder, smiling gayly.

"Lord Selkirk," she said.

"Selkirk?" I blinked, even more bewildered than ever.

"Yes, he's come!" she replied. "Oh, Mac, isn't it grand?"

I agreed that it was soberly, for I was still mystified by the soldiers. But neither of them could enlighten me there. They knew only that they had appeared suddenly as if from nowhere and announced that they were acting for the Earl of Selkirk. They had then produced a paper with a list of names and demanded that these people be released to return with them to Lord Selkirk's camp on an island across the bay. Wily old McGillivray had warily declared that we had always been free to come and go as we pleased, though it was quite obvious to the soldiers that he was lying. But that hadn't mattered, for now here we were, in the canoes and on our way.

Jean looked around at me seriously, almost fearfully this time.

"Mac!" she said. "Do you—do you think—?"

I smiled at her gently. I knew what she was excited about now, and it was not Lord Selkirk.

"We'll soon see!" I replied.

We did see, even sooner than I expected. We were skirting an island shore then, and as I spoke we rounded a headland and shot into a sheltered cove. At the head of the cove we could see the smart tents of the camp, marching in exact rows up into the trees. There was a sandy shingle for beaching the canoes, while a flat ledge of rock that projected at one end of the curved strip of beach made an ideal landing place for passengers. Everywhere I looked there seemed to be soldiers, some in the same red coats of the men who had come for us, others in green.

But what really caught our eye were the two figures standing waiting on the flat rock, watching our approach. Both of them were red-haired, though that of the man in front was less flaming, more coppery. Both were tall, but the man behind was slightly the taller and broader of the two. The man in front stood quietly, only smiling, but nonetheless even in that letting us see the warmth of his welcome. That was Lord Selkirk, of course. The other man was restless and kept moving from one side to the other, trying to see who was in each canoe before it was anywhere near within range. When, finally, we were close enough for him to see he began to wave violently with a grin that split his face from ear to ear and showed all his fine teeth. In front of me Jean began to wave back and call out:

"Andy! Andy! Andy!"

As we drew alongside the rock she leapt out and flew straight into his arms. The rest of us were less precipitate. We stepped out and one by one shook Selkirk's hand. Most of us couldn't find words to say how glad we were to see him, but I think we showed it. When I had greeted him I turned to Andy, who was by now able to disengage one huge hand and nearly crush my own.

"Andy!" I said. "I see you found him."

"Aye! But there was a moment there, in that chute, when I wasn't sure I'd make it!"

I looked at Jean.

"You see?" I said. Then to Andy, "She thought you were dead."

"I've fallen overboard in too many rivers to drown!" he laughed.

I was glad when Lord Selkirk, finished with his welcomes, came and took me by the elbow and led the way up the path with me.

"Quite a lad, your Mister Ross," he smiled.

I nodded and was just going to ask about the soldiers when he interrupted me.

"You look as if you'd had a rough time yourself," he said.

"Not as rough as some," I replied.

He glanced at me quizzically.

"No?" he said, and something in his voice told me that he had immediately guessed how I felt about Jean. But he did not wait for me to answer. "Well, we've a good deal to talk about. I want you close by, for I'll be wanting your help from time to time. I'm going to put you in with Ross—that is, if you don't mind?"

"Not at all!" I assured him. "In fact I couldn't ask a better tent-mate."

"Good!" he chuckled. "I thought you'd say that. You'll want to shave and wash, I imagine. I'll send over my man with a razor and towels and things. Take your time, and when you're ready come over to my tent. I'll want you all at my table for supper tonight. Here you are! Until later, then!"

He paused in front of one of the row of tents, and now he started to turn away to the group behind.

"Just one thing!" I said.

He turned back, I think a little surprised.

"What's that?" he said.

"I've been trying to ask you," I said. "Who are all these soldiers, and what are they doing here?"

He laughed.

"Those?" he said. "They're Swiss mostly, though there are some Scots from the old Glengarry Fencibles. Those in the red coats used to be with the de Meuron Regiment. Those in the green were de Watte-villes. They were brought over to fight the Americans, but the war ended almost at once and they were mustered out at Quebec. About two hundred of them wanted to stay in Canada, so I thought I'd kill two birds with one stone. They're mercenaries, you know, so I hired them to serve as my personal guard on the way out, and promised to give them grants of land at the Forks on the same terms as the rest of the settlers! So—we have both new settlers and soldiers, both of which I understand we need rather badly!"

As he turned away once more I could not help thinking that I wished we had had them in June!

I find it impossible to describe the peculiar luxury of getting clean again, so I will not try. As promised, his lordship's man—a very sober, disapproving gentleman's gentleman—appeared bearing not only a razor and towels, but also soap and hot water. After he was gone I was busy for nearly two hours, but when I was done I was shaved and bathed, my clothes were brushed up a bit and I had combed my hair so that I felt fit to live with once again. But I was tired—so very tired. And the tent I was to share with Andy Ross had real cots and warm blankets in it! I was sorely tempted—but I put the temptation behind me, and crossed to his lordship's tent.

That was a most excellent supper that we had that night; actually, I think, a more delicious meal than any of us had ever tasted before. After it the talk was equally fine. But I could not tell you exactly to this

day what either was composed of. I believe that Andy and Alec Mac-
Lean carried most of the conversation for our side of the table, giving
Lord Selkirk a pretty full account of the massacre at Seven Oaks and
everything that had happened since. When they were done his lordship told of the difficulties he had met in getting colonists and of the
obstacles that had been put in his way at every turn by the Northwesters. I found myself continually dropping off halfway to sleep,
and then coming back with a start. One thing I remember, however,
was Lord Selkirk's announcement to us that he had gotten himself
appointed magistrate and Justice of the Peace for Upper Canada and
the Indian Territories, so that now he held a power that was at least
equal to that of some of the Northwesters—such as Archibald Mac-
Leod. This power enabled him to issue warrants, make arrests, issue
subpoenas to witnesses and even to try cases in his jurisdictions or to
seize property if necessary. It was a power, he said ominously, that
he intended to use—and Fort William seemed as good a place as any
to start.

The supper party broke up shortly after that, and high time I
thought, too. It was nearly midnight, and I believe that I was asleep
even before I crept into my blankets.

It is an indication of my exhaustion, I think, that it seemed hardly
a moment before someone was shaking me awake. I opened my eyes
and saw that it was broad day and Andy was standing over me. But
what surprised me most was that to judge from the angle at which
the sun struck the canvas of the tent, it must be late in the afternoon.

"Time t' get up!" Andy grinned.

"Good Lord! What time is it?" I asked, sitting up.

"Past mid-afternoon o' th' day after tomorrow," he laughed.

"What the devil are you talking about?" I demanded.

"How else would ye say it?" he retorted. " 'Twas night before last
when ye got into those blankets. That's all o' forty hours ago, an' ye
ha'nt stirred since."

"Do you think I believe that?" I snorted. "Go play your jokes on
somebody else."

"It's true, Mac!" he assured me. "I wouldn't rouse ye now but we're
movin' an' th' tent's comin' down."

"Moving?" I stared at him. "Where? Why? What's happened?"

"A lot o' things have happened around here since ye went t' sleep,"
he laughed. "Ye've missed some fun. First Lord Selkirk heard th'
complaints o' some o' th' settlers, an' after he'd heard what they had
t' tell he sent up a warrant for th' arrest o' William McGillivray an'

a couple o' th' other partners. They didn't give us any trouble, but after Lord Selkirk had talked t' old McGillivray for a while he decided that he had good grounds t' arrest th' lot o' 'em."

"And I slept through it all!" I groaned.

"Ye did, indeed!" He nodded. "That an' more! Lord Selkirk sent a force over to bring down th' rest o' th' partners—six o' 'em. But some weren't inclined t' be so peaceable about it. There was a scuffle, an' our lads had t' seize th' fort t' keep 'em from barricadin' 'emselves in. After he'd finished examinin' 'em last night, Lord Selkirk let 'em all go back t' their quarters at th' fort, after takin' their parole t' behave. But this mornin' when we got over we found th' dogs had been burnin' up their papers in th' fireplace all night long, so's we'd not be able t' use th' stuff for evidence against 'em. What's more, we found where they'd hid about fifty stand o' arms in one o' th' barns, an' another place where they hid eight barrels o' gunpowder an' a supply o' shot."

"That looks as if they were up to their old tricks," I said.

"That's what Lord Selkirk thought," he replied. "So he's decided t' occupy th' fort himself an' turn th' Northwesters out—an' damned good I call that! Give th' devils a taste o' their own! Anyway, that's where we're movin' to, an' why. Now get up an' get dressed, an' I'll show ye how!"

It was past dark before we got the entire camp moved over and the tents up on the level ground near the wall. In the meantime all of the *Boisbrûlés* and the voyageurs and the other people belonging to the North West Company were set over across the river and their canoes taken away, so that if they wished to indulge in any more such tricks they'd have to swim first. Of them all, only the nine partners remained at the fort, and they were under lock and key.

Call me vindictive if you like, I must nevertheless admit that I got a great deal of satisfaction out of sitting in the North West partners' biggest and most comfortable chairs; out of eating in their vast dining hall on the best of their food; out of drinking their wines and warming myself before their great fireplace.

We had a comfortable supper that night, and I was not too tired or sleepy to enjoy it. When it was done we sat for a time at the great table, idly chatting about inconsequential matters, until presently— since there was nothing formal about the gathering—our members began drifting out by ones and twos or in groups, until after a bit there was no one left in that great hall but Lord Selkirk and myself.

"Well, Milord," I said. "What now?"

He looked at me and smiled.

"Frankly," he replied, "I think we'll just stay right here for now. It's too late in the season to go on and try to re-establish the colony at the Forks this year. Oh, yes, we could get there, but we'd be in a rather awkward position without houses or supplies. In the spring we can go on up early and throw the Northwesters out of our fort. Then we'll rebuild and establish ourselves there firmly! How does that sound to you, Mister MacAllister?"

"It sounds sensible," I told him.

"Good!" He rose. " 'Tis a fine night. Would you care to go for a stroll along the lake for a breath of air before we turn in?"

"I'm flattered that you'd ask me, your Lordship," I replied. "I'd like to."

"Excellent!" he said. "I am particularly pleased because I have something in my mind that I want to talk to you about."

He led the way, and we passed out through the gates of the fort and turned down so that we would follow the curve of the shore, not down right at the water's edge, but part way up the slope, so that even by moonlight we could get the full sweep and glory of the view. It was a fine night, soft and bright with a great silver moon that left a shimmering track across the water. We were not the only ones, apparently, who were taking advantage of it. Below us, but some distance along the shore I could see the figures of a man and woman, strolling hand in hand. I had not need to look twice to know who it was.

I became suddenly aware that Lord Selkirk had said something to me and I had not even heard him.

"Forgive me, my Lord," I said. "I'm afraid my mind was wandering. You were saying?"

"I was saying, Mister MacAllister," he replied, "that I have been very favorably impressed with the way you have worked out here; with the way you have understood the problem and tried to help; with your loyalty. I think you see what I have been trying to do and you leave nothing undone that can be done to help me do it."

"Thank you, sir!" I said.

"I am sincere in that," he said. "But I think, Mister MacAllister, that a very large portion of your talents are wasted at the Forks."

He startled me with that. Did this mean that I was about to be dismissed—advised to go somewhere where my talents could be used to better advantage—by somebody else?

"I don't understand, sir," I said.

He laughed.

"Don't be alarmed!" he told me. "What I mean is simply this: I shall stay here this winter. In the spring I shall go on out to the Forks and help re-establish the colony. Then I hope to return to Scotland where I will seek out more and more and more settlers to send out."

He paused. My eyes wandered down toward the shore and I saw Andy and Jean down there, standing very close.

"However," Lord Selkirk went on, "I must have help with it. I need a man who is sympathetic with the work; a man who sees human beings as people—not just as cattle to be moved around at will. I need a man who can see people such as these settlers are, coming into a land like this and working with it and in it and for it, making it a home that is sturdy and strong and productive and that, above all, is theirs. In short, Mister MacAllister, I need a man like yourself to help me with it. Would you like the job?"

I glanced down again toward Jean and Andy. They were even closer now, and her face was lifted toward his. I thought then that if Lord Selkirk did overestimate my abilities and think more highly of my qualities than they deserved, yet there was one point upon which he was quite right. The Red River Colony would not be the place for me now! I turned to him abruptly, with my mind made up all at once.

"Why, yes, your Lordship," I said. "Yes I would, if you'll have me. Thank you very much!"

Postscript

I AM AWARE THAT THE ENTIRE STORY OF THE RED RIVER COLONY HAS not been given here. What I have been able to tell is actually little more than the beginning. After the resettlement at the Forks there were new clashes with the *Boisbrûlés* and with the Northwesters. Colin Robertson was captured—and he escaped. There was an intermittent trickle of newcomers to the land. But there were also continued defections and desertions and removals. To cap it all there were the tedious, long-drawn-out and somewhat malodorous bouts of law at Montreal between Lord Selkirk and the North West Fur Company. I know that these in particular led ultimately to Selkirk's departure from Canada, a broken and discouraged man, who thought of his great undertaking as a failure. Lord Selkirk died in France in 1820, before he was fifty, almost certainly a victim of the persecution of his enemies. Yet it is interesting to speculate that perhaps even in death this warmhearted man exerted his influence on the new land, for within a year of his passing the Hudson's Bay Company and the North West Fur Company recognized the suicidal nature of their quarrel and joined forces. Thereafter the little settlement at the Forks became more secure; its growth slow but steady.

I realize, too, that there are those to this day who look upon Lord Selkirk's motives with doubt and suspicion, and who maintain that because of its insecurity and impermanence the Red River Settlement was not actually the beginning of the civilization that grew up at that place. With these I prefer to take issue. Lord Selkirk undoubtedly made a number of mistakes, the greatest of which was his seizure of Fort William and his unauthorized use of the North West Company's supplies stored there, for this gave his enemies the legal weapon they needed to attack him. Armed with that they were able to carry the fight into the courts of Canada where, unquestionably, they held a distinct advantage. Yet in spite of highhandedness, and in spite of the fact that he charged a price for the land—obviously insufficient to afford a profit—I find nothing in the record to indicate that Selkirk's motives were not fundamentally humanitarian.

Neither do I agree that the settlement was impermanent. It is true that it was established several times and the colonists forced, by one means or another, either to flee or accept other grants. Yet each time this happened some of the former settlers returned to build up their homes again in the same place, and always there were new ones with them. By the same token there was always one or more representative of Lord Selkirk and the Hudson's Bay Company who remained on the grounds. Thus, from the very beginning of the undertaking there was a vestige of human habitation at the Forks—and if this is not permanent settlement, what is it? The seed was planted. It struggled against drought and frost and flood and the snows of winter. It withered and almost died. Yet in the end it flourished, and it is still my contention that it was from this one seed that the present city of Winnipeg truly sprang.

But in these days of soaring costs it would be impossible to put all of this into a single novel. It would also be confusing and structurally impractical. An historical novelist must instruct as well as entertain, to be sure, but he can never lose sight of the fact that if his story is not interesting and easy to follow no one will bother to read it. If that happens both purposes go unfulfilled. I think we have all read novels in which the thread of the story was swamped in the sea of history—or at least begun them. It has been my feeling that to attempt to tell everything about the Selkirk venture here would be simply to bring this book to that end. As a result I preferred to stick to the comparatively simple story of three peoples' part in the undertaking and leave the ramifications and details and ultimate outcome to better qualified, academic historians, who have only facts to relate.

Still there may be some who have read this story with a prickle of curiosity, and who would like to look further into the facts behind it. To such I recommend *The Honorable Company,* by Douglas MacKay; *The Great Company,* by Beckles Willson; *The Hudson's Bay Company,* by George Bryce. These give the general background of the fur trade in the area, the story of the clash between the two great fur trading companies, and take up in considerable detail the story of the colony itself. *The Red River Colony,* by Louis Aubrey Wood— Volume 21 of the Chronicles of Canada—published at Toronto, by Glasgow, Brook & Co., 1915, I think provides the most complete and concise account of Selkirk and the undertaking. Grace Lee Nute's *The Voyageur* gives an insight into the character and way of life of the fur hunters of that time and place, and the *Henry Thompson Journals; New Light on the Early History of the Greater Northwest*, in 3 volumes, edited by Elliott Coues, is even more detailed, citing specific journeys and events and is crammed with notes giving specific information as to a number of characters that I have been able to find nowhere else.

All of these, of course, are secondary—with the possible exception of the last. But I have cited them because they are the most readily available to the casual student. Should anyone be impelled to delve more deeply into the subject he will find in these volumes extensive bibliographies and notes which will direct him to more primary sources.

JOHN JENNINGS